ENDORSEMENTS

We're Going Down makes me think that *The High and the Mighty* was comic fiction. This work is flooded with the life and blood, the sweat and suffering of real people, flying real airplanes in the real world. An exceptionally vivid look into the human dimensions of the life, work and community of pilots and crews flying today. Exceptional book.

    –Dr. William McCreary, psychologist

As a platinum-level air traveler, I often wonder what happens in the front of the plane, on the flight deck. Samson positions the reader between the captain and copilot for a virtual cockpit experience. It is fiction infused with facts that make it real and compelling.

    –Fred Roth, international computer consultant

Samson's foundational knowledge and rich storytelling skills immediately seduce the reader with a "behind-the-scenes view" of the airline cockpit and workplace challenges within the airline industry.

    –Tracy Budge, corporate trainer and flight attendant

Few pilot training methods outside the flight simulator are as effective as a compelling story; it's an ancient art form that still works beautifully today. From my perspective as a pilot training manager and aviation safety consultant, *We're Going Down*'s gripping narrative propels us along like a jet. At the same time, it instructs us about the role of *human factors* in safe airline operations. The book is good science and a good read – a difficult combination to achieve. I highly recommend this novel for aviation professionals and armchair enthusiasts alike.

    –Chris Hallman, aviation safety consultant

We're Going Down

Enjoy the ride !!

Your neighbor

Art Samson

10995 Desert Sky Loop

A NOVEL BY
CAPTAIN ART SAMSON

Incubation Press Bend, OR

CaptainArtSamson.com
© 2012, 2015, 2021 by Art Samson

First edition 2012
Second edition 2015
Third edition 2021

ISBN: 978-0-9998584-5-5 (paperback)
ISBN: 978-0-9998584-6-2 (e-book)

Printed in the United States of America

Dedicated
to my dear friend
Jim "Buzz" Blohm

ACKNOWLEDGMENTS

I am forever grateful to the team. My writing coach, Ms. Linden Gross, led the way—pushing, refining and shaping the text at every juncture. Captain Tony Borra provided invaluable technical critique. Reader Elizabeth Crane provided a global perspective, and copy editor Cory Jubitz applied an incisive scalpel. Website developer Scott Burns created the book's link to the cyber-world. And Lieve Maas pulled it all together with her professional book design.

Along the way, friends and family weighed in. I am particularly grateful to Ruthie Douglass for her comments and encouragement. Marcia Stevenson, Karen Shepard, Susan King, Chris Hallman, former Blue Angel, Captain Kevin Lauver, and flight attendant instructor Tracy Budge also provided significant insights.

My biggest fan and platinum level flyer, Fred Roth, has cheered from the beginning, while psychologist and dear friend Bill McCreary added a note of gravitas to the conversation.

Thank you all.

PREFACE

Does the title *We're Going Down* trigger a memory or nightmarish fear? Perhaps you're recalling horrific events such as the Korean 777 that slammed into the seawall in San Francisco or another 777 disappearing into thin air over Malaysia. Then there was an Indonesian Airbus that inexplicably fell out of the sky, and a suicidal copilot who dove an airliner into the French Alps. Of course, there were others.

Most recently, two state-of-the-art 737 MAX aircraft went down under nearly identical circumstances in far-reaching parts of the world. The starkly similar chains of events in those accidents have prompted me to re-title and re-release the original book *The Captains' Airline: Pushing Back From the Brink*. The original book foretells Boeing's painfully reminiscent denial during a similar flight control failure in the early '90s. In this edition, you will find a vivid epilogue in which the protagonist, now a senior executive at his airline, dives into the current swirl of controversy as hundreds of the premier 737 MAXs sit idle on the tarmac.

Back in the '60s and '70s, U.S. airlines experienced catastrophes such as these on a regular basis. Following a 1978 accident in Portland, Oregon, in which the aircraft simply ran out of fuel, a mandate from the National Transportation Safety Board (NTSB) changed the focus of flight crew training in America forever. The new training program, known as crew resource management (CRM), focused on creating new protocols and a team culture that would prove to be an essential ingredient in air travel safety. The program, however, required an unmitigated shift in crew procedures and focus that challenged big egos, macho bluster, and entrenched rigidity among cocksure pilots.

This is the story of that transformation and the unparalleled results fostered by such training. As of this writing, at the end of 2020, the flawless safety record among major U.S. airlines remains nearly unbroken since 2001; a single fatality occurred when a broken turbine blade punctured the fuselage of a Southwest aircraft in 2018. The extraordinary outcome of CRM training is both simple and profound. Today, the resulting well-honed communication skills and team interaction undergird the entire operating philosophy within our airlines in the U.S.

Still, an important question lingers: Could this training regimen be the missing link in other countries' aviation practices? For that matter, is this the missing link in a host of other organizations and corporations around the world that have seen far too many breakdowns in team performance? Unfortunately, and often unfathomably, the practices and skills that turned around the U.S.'s airline safety record are still not embraced by many countries' aviation programs. Most other industries have also overlooked CRM. From medicine to manufacturing, adopting its principles could certainly prevent personal injury and death, to say nothing of financial loss, in numerous instances.

As this story shows, getting there can be a hair-raising task. It is a tale of resounding success, one that with all of its ups and downs now all but ensures that you never hear the fatal exclamation *We're going down*.

Prologue

HUBRIS

"It is only hubris if I fail."
—William Shakespeare's *Julius Caesar*

Ever-increasing hubris propelled the *Titanic* toward disaster on that April night in 1912. Described as unsinkable, the largest, most marvelous ship afloat set sail with only half the necessary life rafts to accommodate the 2,229 souls on board. Additional rafts were *a wretched eyesore*, her managers reasoned. Compounding the vanity, with little regard for an icy colossus, Captain Edward J. Smith altered course just slightly and proceeded confidently through the treacherous North Atlantic toward the awaiting gala in New York City.

Nearby, on the SS *California*, a more cautious Captain Stanley Lord chose to lie to for the night. Before retiring, he signaled the *Titanic* about the numerous ice formations in a wireless message that was met with "Shut up, shut up, I'm busy . . . " Radio operators Phillips and Bride discounted numerous iceberg-warning reports to accommodate perfunctory personal messages from passengers the likes of Astor, Guggenheim, and Lady Duff-Gordon. Holiday spirits resounded across their future grave.

At midnight, raveling incompetence continued as the *Titanic* listed badly to starboard while officers aboard the SS *California* observed her distress flares flickering in the distance and failed to respond. Captain Lord was awakened and advised. He instructed the second officer to attempt contact with the unknown vessel using the Morse light, then returned to sleep. No one considered waking the *California's* radio operator, and the *Titanic's* radio distress calls went unheard by the one vessel in position to save lives. Failure by any account.

Sixty-five years later, elegant transoceanic travel had become defined by leisure suits and jumbo jets crossing comfortably in eight hours rather than the eight days required by ship. On March 27, 1977, a terrorist bombing closed the airport at Las Palmas, and numerous aircraft were diverted to the adjacent small island of Tenerife off the coast of Morocco. The tarmac was jammed while fueling and provisioning took place. After an extended delay, the first aircraft ready for departure were Pan American Flight 1736 and KLM Flight 4805, two enormous Boeing 747s. Due to taxiway congestion, both were directed to taxi down the active runway. KLM preceded Pan Am as they crept through the dense afternoon fog toward the departure end. They could not see each other, nor could the tower see either of them.

Like a ghost from the North Atlantic, hubris propelled the KLM 747 toward her fate as Captain Jacob Van Zanten maneuvered his craft into position, disregarded the expressed concerns of his second officer, and, in a moment of confusion, initiated the takeoff without authorization from the tower. The Pan Am aircraft continued to roll blindly along the murky runway toward the oncoming behemoth. The ensuing collision took the lives of 583 passengers and crew. "From the people who made punctuality possible"—the KLM slogan vanished forever in the smoldering wreckage.

Today, airlines in the United States are experiencing a relative calm. Why is the safety record so remarkable? Because now, the basic principles of effective human interaction and team dynamics—known in the industry as crew resource management (CRM)—are critical ingredients in maneuvering our technological marvels safely through the skies. Effective problem solving occurs when leaders elicit information and expertise from every team member. Greater success does not result from a new technological gadget, a more detailed operating manual, or an arbitrary government mandate, as previously imagined. It is all about the team.

Two starkly contrasting examples of these principles played out just miles and days apart in 2009. On January 15, US Airways Flight 1549 lost all thrust and glided safely to touchdown on the Hudson River in Manhattan. In the three and a half minutes from the time the jet sucked geese into both engines to the moment it gracefully touched down on the river, Captain Chesley "Sully" Sullenberger and First Officer Jeffrey Skiles intuitively crafted a perfect outcome from the ingredients of disaster. Unlike the *Titanic* and Tenerife teams, the US Airways team relied effectively on more than fifty years of collective experience. The pilots worked seamlessly together to execute checklists, maneuver the aircraft, and communicate with air traffic controllers as they flew toward the river and notified the passengers to brace for touchdown in the icy water. It is essential to note that these are the highly experienced and well-trained professionals of a major United States air carrier.

In contrast, less than a month later, an inept, inexperienced and poorly trained cockpit crew of Colgan Air Flight 3407 created its own fatal circumstance by failing to recognize the impending stall that resulted from an intentional power and speed reduction. When the stall warning occurred, the young captain responded like a frightened third grader in the class play. He completely forgot his lines and pulled back on the controls—rather than pushing forward, as nearly every other pilot on earth would have done—thereby causing the death of all forty-nine on board.

As poignantly portrayed in testimony before Congress in February 2010, the feeder airlines have a long way to go to achieve the same safe operating environment enjoyed by major carriers.

Yet it is important to note that for the major U.S. carriers, the past forty years have been a bumpy and convoluted journey on which many perished. During that time, airline managers, academicians, the government, and the rank and file worked tirelessly to develop the interactive methodologies now in place to save lives. In this book, I pay tribute to all those lost souls and the lessons they taught us along the way as I combine the historically accurate accounts of many accidents and hair-raising incidents with a tale of transformation within one fictional airline.

Ladies and gentlemen, I invite you to sit back now, relax, and enjoy your flight.

Chapter 1

FAIRBANKS, FEBRUARY 1988

A single white beam flashed across the tundra in a ninety-degree arc, then stopped between the distant rows of blue lights. A voice crackled over the radio, and the captain's raspy baritone responded, "Roger, Omega 409 cleared for takeoff." Alex Freeman, the copilot, smoothly moved the throttles forward moments before releasing the brakes. The jet lurched slightly and began a slow roll down the snow-covered Alaskan runway.

It wasn't the instant zero-to-two hundred zinging adrenaline rush Brad Morehouse, the second officer, had relished in past-life cat shots from the deck of the *Enterprise*. Nothing at all like the F-14 Tomcat, but a much more predictable outcome in this workhorse Boeing 727. From his side-facing seat behind the captain and first officer, he scanned the wide array of gauges on the flight engineer panel as the speed increased steadily. Engine instruments stabilized. "Power set; green light," he reported.

By swiveling his seat ninety degrees to the left and inching forward in the shoulder harness, he positioned himself directly behind the center console separating the two pilots. The position enabled him to monitor the performance of the three Pratt & Whitney JT8-15B engines.

"Eighty knots; engine instruments checked," reported the captain, Dick Hamlin, as the copilot calmly maneuvered the controls.

Clatter from the nose wheel pounding the snow-packed runway crescendoed into Dick's call, "Vee one, vee are, vee two." When the speed reached VR^1, Alex responded with imperceptible back pressure on the control column and the nose rose, by the book, at three degrees per second toward the eighteen-degree nose-up climb attitude.

"Positive rate; gear up," Alex recited as the captain reached across the center console and jerked the landing-gear handle up.

Relative quiet in the cockpit outpaced the roar of combusting gasses scorching from the three tail-mounted engines as the jet climbed rapidly in the Arctic night air. A thousand feet into the climb, Alex continued the litany of commands with "Flaps five." The airspeed increased, and he called, "Flaps two . . . flaps up, climb power, after-takeoff checklist."

The captain positioned the flap handle as requested, and Brad reached forward to adjust the power levers to a predetermined setting. Then he grabbed the folded checklist and scanned the forward and overhead instrument panels. Any missed item could trigger a cascade of errors. He silently completed the checklist, noting that the landing gear and flaps were, in fact, retracted; the pressurization system was maintaining a slow climb in the cabin altitude. Engine anti-ice and ignition switches were off. Swiveling his seat to face the side-mounted engineer's panel, he ensured that the temperatures and pressures were normal, fuel evenly distributed, hydraulic quantity stable, and cabin temperature within the prescribed range. He positioned one switch off, then pivoted his seat to face forward again. Finally, he readjusted the power levers, consulted the checklist one last time, and reported, "Climb power set, after-takeoff checklist complete."

Following the tightly scripted crew maneuver, the 727 was safely airborne and climbing toward 35,000 feet. It was thorough and predictable. Only three minutes elapsed from brake release to stable climb, and Brad took comfort in knowing precisely what the others would do throughout the takeoff and initial ascent.

"Omega 409, contact departure on one-one-eight-decimal-five. Have a great flight, gentlemen." The woman in the tower at the Fairbanks airport relinquished control to the radar facility responsible for air traffic within twenty-five miles of the airport.

Dick responded, "Roger, departure on one-one-eight-decimal-five. Good day, now." He scribbled the numbers on the scratchpad mounted on the sill of his side window, then reached down and spun the radio dials to the new frequency. "Hello, departure. Omega 409 climbing through eight for one-zero-thousand."

"Good morning, Omega 409. Radar contact," the controller responded. "Turn left to one-seven-zero, climb, and maintain one-five-thousand."

Dick reached to the HSI[2], slewed the heading cursor to 170 degrees, and set 15,000 in the altitude alert window. "Roger,

··· ━ ━ ━··· ━ ━ ━ ━ ━··· ━ ━ ━··· ━ ━ ━ ━ ━ ━··· ━ ━ ━··· ━ ━ ━···

409 turning to one-seven-zero and climbing to one-five-thousand," he replied.

Meanwhile, Alex rolled the jet to twenty degrees of left bank and also set the orange cursor at the 170-degree position on his primary compass. He continued to scan the instruments, confirming airspeed of 250 knots and the needle on the vertical speed indicator (VSI) hovering near a 2,000-feet-per-minute rate of climb. After verifying the nose attitude at approximately five degrees up, he returned his gaze to the compass as the aircraft continued to turn in the direction of the assigned heading. The compass rotated toward the point at which 170 degrees appeared under the white lubber line. He reduced the bank angle gradually until the wings were level, and the aircraft headed essentially south. Raising the nose by a degree by referring to the pipper under the cursor on the large, round horizontal situation indicator (HSI) in the center of the instrument panel directly in front of him, Alex countered the air-craft's tendency to accelerate once the wings were level.

Even with the wings level, Alex noted that the nose of this aircraft tended to drift to the right. He reached down and turned the round rudder-trim knob slightly left, then reduced the forward pressure on the control column by toggling back on the elevator trim switch on the top right knob of the yoke. Finally, he validated his professional acumen by removing both hands from the yoke. Nothing changed. The aircraft was perfectly trimmed and stable, climbing on heading and airspeed toward the assigned altitude. Satisfied, he reached up and engaged the autopilot.

At 1:00 a.m. in central Alaska, they were the only game in town. The three pilots settled into the relative quiet, mesmerized by the pulsing band of northern lights and unimpeded dazzle of the stars. They flew on course toward Juneau, while air traffic controllers monitored the plane's progress on radar and passed them from one sector to another. "Omega 409, Anchorage now on one-two-six-decimal-niner." Climbing through 18,000 feet, they completed the climb checklist, reset the barometric pressure window in their altimeters to 29.92 inches of mercury, and turned the seat belt sign off.

On cue, the flight attendant call chime sounded, followed by two solid knocks on the cockpit door. Brad reached over, turned the knob, and gave it a gentle shove. Sarah's tousled red head popped through the door. She was a feisty one, for sure; perfectly shaped, freckle-faced, about five-foot-two and supremely self-confident. "Coffee, guys?" she asked as she stepped into the cockpit. The unspoken protocol required that the captain respond first.

"Yup, cream with two sugars," she replied. "You, Alex?"

"Like my women, Babe: strong 'n' hot."

"Lots o' luck, King Kong," she fired back. "And how about you, Hotshot?"

"Black, please, Sarah," Brad responded, wondering if every flight engineer was her "hotshot" or if carrying her bag through the snow to the hotel van had earned him extra points.

"Back in a flash," she said, slamming the door.

Alex whistled. "Whoa! That one sounds like a handful."

"Maybe a little high maintenance," Brad observed. But for some lucky guy, she was most certainly worth the trouble, he imagined. A vivid contrast to the perfectly coifed news anchor he called wife.

"Youngster, if she doesn't look like she's worth a couple of thousand a month to you, just look straight ahead and diddle those knobs in front of your face."

Moments later, two knocks followed, and Brad reached for the door. "Room service!" Sarah elbowed the door open and stepped in, balancing the three Styrofoam coffee cups. "Hotshot, grab that center one. It's yours." She paused for him to reach up, then stepped around his seat in the darkened space toward the center console, her perfect slender physique stretched out in front of him.

"Cream and sugar, Dick, and weak and lukewarm for you, Kong."

Alex sipped the tepid brew and grunted.

She stepped back, gently touching Brad's shoulder with her left hand. He couldn't deny the tremor he felt as he looked up into her mischievous blue eyes. *There is still some life in these bones.*

"We have the governor and several of his staff on board, and they're making a big deal about the aviation subsidy bill they're pushing in the Alaska legislature later today. It sounds like millions in subsidies, and even the fate of our company all rest on you guys," she joked. "What's our ETA for Juneau, Brad?"

"Oh, we're about thirty-five out," Brad replied as Sarah stepped out of the cockpit. He tweaked one of the cabin temperature knobs and wrestled with the flutter in his stomach. *Not what I need right now. She's no different than the hundreds of other flight attendants I've flown with during the last three years,* he lied to himself, then reached over and grabbed the list of crew names. Los Angeles based, he noted. Sarah Marconi, employee number 194625. From the number, he could tell that she had been hired several years earlier than he had been. He sipped the strong black coffee from the cup labeled HOTSHOT in red block letters.

He scanned the engineer's panel. Flying this bucket was like eating sawdust, he painfully acknowledged to himself. In light of the Blue Angels accident, these mind-numbing routines were a welcome salve, an escape from the self-incrimination—the guilt over not speaking up, over not having made the call that would have saved Matt.

For the thousandth time, the accident flashed through his mind in vivid Technicolor. There he was, with the steady gaze and sensitive touch of a neurosurgeon, sitting motionless in the seat of his Skyhawk, hurtling just a few feet above the water at 400 knots toward the runway. Only inches separated their wingtips as he manipulated the controls minutely to remain fixed in position to the left of Blue Angel 1. The intense focus masked all other sensations; no sense of speed and position, no fear, no doubt or hesitation, no hunger, thirst, heat, or cold, only his place in the perfect synchrony of six thirty-ton speeding projectiles. In the back of his mind, he knew the waters of Pensacola Bay were menacingly close, but he failed to speak. The splash to his right went unnoticed.

The senseless reality of the years-ago accident haunted him still. He had failed, and the team had failed. A simple word of caution from Brad or any of the others would have jolted the boss back to reality. Instead, on their triumphant Pensacola homecoming, they had flown lower than ever before, stirred up a blinding watery vortex, and Matt Percible paid the ultimate price as he plunged into the bay at warp speed.

It was tragically ironic. The accident occurred while flying straight and level, the first thing fledgling aviators learn to do. After a perfect season of hair-raising gyrations, nose-to-nose passes at 500 knots, formation rolls with only three feet of wingtip separation, and the punishing g-forces of impossibly tight turns and pull-ups, it all ended with a failure to communicate. The emergency transmission, "Angels—knock it off," would have prompted all six to take evasive action. But no one spoke.

As a result of the accident, the team disbanded. Following Matt's funeral, Brad was discharged and returned to the Northwest. There his friend and now-colleague Gradin Jones and Brad's bride Audrey Spears kept him sane with the frenzy of new life adventure following the glitzy wedding. A wife, an island cottage, the airline job, and the world's greatest Saint Bernard consumed him.

Times were relatively good. He was an honorary uncle to Gradin's kids and an eager bridegroom restoring the old house on Bainbridge Island. It was nonstop play. Yet the torpor persisted even now. Brad shook his head to banish the relentless sense of remorse that coalesced with his growing marital malaise. *Will I ever learn to assert myself?* he wondered vacantly. *How shallow can a person be?* Was it Audrey's dazzling blue dress that had blinded him like the new paint on a Blue Angels Skyhawk? There she was, Seafair Queen, regal, self-assured, even a bit aloof. Not the typical air show groupie. *I was easy pickings. She marched me straight to the altar, then set out to vault up every step of the KSEA News ladder, further and further from our island retreat. I didn't resist. I never seem to. It has always been easier not to lead.*

He saw himself as merely the vapid stud on her arm, ol' nice-smile Morehouse. Since the ignominious end to his Navy career, he had become an aviation bit-part player. A Boeing 727 flight engineer. A checklist-reading, fuel-balancing, number-crunching, no-opinion lackey. Easy.

✈

So there he was, en route to Juneau on the midnight rocket. The radiofrequency change came at precisely the moment Dick noted the altitude they were climbing through and reported to Alex, "Thirty-four for thirty-five," a reminder that 35,000 feet was the assigned cruise altitude.

Alex responded, "Roger, a thousand to go," as the autopilot maintained the nose attitude of the 727 for a relatively slow 500-foot-per-minute climb at eighty percent the speed of sound; point-eight-oh (.80 Mach).

Dick hurriedly jotted down the new frequency, then dialed it in to the radio control head on his side of the center console. "Good morning, Anchorage. Omega 409, out of thirty-four for thirty-five." Several seconds passed, and there was no response. Dick waited. "Anchorage Center, Omega 409 checking on. Thirty-four for thirty-five." He repeated. No response. He paused and noted the absence of radio chatter on the assigned frequency. The aircraft continued to climb toward 35,000 feet. He consulted his notes on the scratchpad and selected the previous frequency. "Anchorage. Omega 409, no joy on one-two-two-six. Say the frequency again, please."

After a brief pause, the controller responded. "Uh, Omega 409, Anchorage on one-two-two-decimal-*seven*."

Dick chuckled, "Well, we were close. One-two-two *seven*. Thanks. Good day.

"What's one digit among friends?" he groused, dialing in the correct frequency.

"Anchorage, Omega 409, checking on, three-four for three-five."

"Omega 409, roger. Just a heads-up, a Northwest 747 reported a couple of moderate jolts in your vicinity approximately ten minutes ago. If you like, I can clear you direct down the line a ways."

"Turbulence ahead? Sure, we'll take a little shortcut. Go ahead." Dick watched the long white needle on the round altimeter gauge move past the six toward the seven, indicating a steady climb from 34,600 to 34,700. Alex, hands resting gently on the yoke, stared straight ahead.

"Omega 409, fly heading one-three-zero, direct Yakutat, direct Juneau."

"Roger, heading one-three-zero, direct Yakutat, then Juneau."

Dick reached up, turned the HIS selector knob, and dialed in 130 degrees on the gauge. The needle on the altimeter pointed at 35,000 and continued to rotate slowly upward. No one on the flight deck seemed to notice. He reached for his chart to confirm the frequency of the Yakutat (new fix) VOR navigation facility.

At that moment, the entire airplane lurched and shuddered from a burst of wake turbulence. The nose pitched up slightly as the autopilot electrical servos holding the flight control surfaces in the climb attitude were released by the pressure of the jolt. The autopilot automatically disengaged as a warning horn began to wail incessantly, all at precisely the moment Dick looked down at the chart.

Brad's head snapped forward to scan the instruments. "Altitude!" he yelped, noting the altimeter needle passing beyond 35,400.

Jarred from his quiet reverie, Alex grasped the yoke firmly and stabilized the rolling and pitching motion induced by the turbulence. He shoved the control column forward, and the nose abruptly dipped while the altimeter registered the reversal, moving rapidly down toward the 35,000-foot target.

"Cancel that damned horn!" Dick yelled as his hand dropped to the radio panel and selected the off position on the transponder. The tiny block of information depicting the altitude of the aircraft on the controller's radar scope disappeared. A warning horn on the controller's console sounded. "Omega 409, say altitude," the controller demanded.

"Uh, 409 is level three-five-zero. We just encountered a pretty good jolt here at three-five. Any other turbulence reports down the road?" Dick stammered, hoping to divert the controller's attention.

"No, sir. Nothing reported. Your present position is right where Northwest reported the bumps a few minutes ago. Uh, 409, please check your transponder, sir. I seem to have lost your squawk."

Again Dick reached for the transponder, but before flipping the switch, he confirmed the altimeter was steady at 35,000. He placed the transponder back on, then reached for the autopilot toggle. "Autopilot?" he asked, frowning at Alex.

"Yeah, thanks," Alex said. "Sorry about that, boss." He bit his lip and shook his head, acknowledging that he had flown through the assigned altitude.

Dick turned back toward Brad and said, "Better give 'em a call in back and see if everything is okay. Then make a PA— say something eloquent about minor turbulence, smooth ride ahead, and maybe the weather and ETA for Juneau."

Just as he reached for the interphone handset, the flight attendant call chime sounded. Brad brought the phone to his ear, and consciously adopted a more relaxed manner than he really felt. "Engine room," he intoned.

"God damn it! What was that all about?" Sarah demanded. "Jesus. We've got shit all over the place back here, Hotshot. What the hell is going on up there?"

"Whoa, whoa, whoa. Calm down, Short Stuff. Come up here for a sec."

"NO! I have a huge mess back here to clean up, and I don't think the governor is enjoying the champagne in his lap. What I need to know is whether or not we're going to get any more of that turbulence. The damned seat belt sign isn't even on. Will you please make a PA, Brad?" she implored. "People are pretty frantic right now." And she was gone.

Brad grimaced, reached up and flipped the switch to illuminate the seat belt sign, and summoned a theatrical tone. "Ladies and gentlemen, this is the second officer speaking," he said with a deep baritone emanating right out of Hollywood casting. "I apologize for those bumps. We apparently passed through the wake turbulence of a Northwest 747 that is twenty or thirty miles ahead of us."

He paused for a moment, then continued his attempted cover-up in a calming tone. "To avoid any additional turbulence, we've taken up a slightly diverging course at 35,000 feet. We are estimating Juneau in approximately twenty-five minutes, and we can expect light snow showers on our arrival." Another pause. "Again, we apologize for the bumps. Please just sit back, relax, and get a little sleep if you can."

Silence filled the cockpit until Alex finally spoke. "Well, that was fun. Wonder if Anchorage noticed our altitude?"

Brad knew that the controller had seen them climb above 35,000 feet. For the controller, the question was whether the deviation resulted from wake turbulence or crew error.

"For Christ's sake, of `course they did! We set off the alarm. Why do you think he asked?" Dick bellowed. "I got the transponder off as quick as I could, but they obviously saw it. Thank God for the turbulence. Maybe they'll think *that* was the cause of our deviation," he fumed. They all knew the facts. The protocol was clear: Even when the copilot is flying, the captain is responsible.

"Damn it, guys, we better pay attention to what we're doing here. Brad, give the company a call and see about the latest Juneau weather," Dick requested curtly.

"Can do," Brad answered as he reached down and dialed the ARINC[3] frequency in to the number three VHF radio. "ARINC, Omega 409, over." No answer. "ARINC, Omega 409 on one-three-zero-decimal-niner, how copy?" Still nothing.

"Omega 409 on one-three-zero-decimal-niner, how copy?" Still nothing.

"Try 'em on twenty-nine-nine," Dick suggested.

"Okay." Brad rolled the knobs to uncover 129.9 in the window.

"ARINC, Omega 409 on one-twenty-nine-nine, you copy?"

"Good morning, Omega 409. Go ahead," the female voice responded.

"Omega 409 requesting a phone patch with Omega dispatch, over."

... — — —... — — — —...— — — — —... — — — — —...— — — —...

"Stand by," she said. Thirty seconds passed as the ARINC operator established contact with the dispatcher located at the Omega Air Lines headquarters in Memphis. Dispatchers share responsibility with the captain for the safe conduct of the flight. *But none of those guys ever go down with the ship*, Brad, like all pilots, was quick to note.

"Omega 409, this is dispatcher Jones. Go ahead."

"Dick, dispatch is up twenty-nine-nine. You wanna listen?" Brad asked.

"Yeah, thanks."

Putting the dispatcher on speaker, Brad continued. "Good morning, Jones; 409, was off Fairbanks at one-zero-zero-zero Zulu, estimating Juneau at one-one-zero-zero, requesting the current Juneau weather and forecast for Seattle, over."[4]

"Okay, 409, I was just looking at that. Juneau is currently forecasting 3,000 [overcast] and five [miles visibility] with light snow. Temperature minus five [centigrade] and wind out of the north at ten. Altimeter three-zero-one-two. No recent braking action reports. Last arrival was an Alaska 727 at 9:00 last evening. They reported braking action 'fair' with patchy snow and ice. Good news is that the frontal system passed several hours ago so we can anticipate continued clearing. How copy?"

"Thank you, sir. We got that. How about Seattle?" Brad asked.

"Well, let me take a look. Yeah, that high-pressure system is hanging over the Northwest coastal area. Seattle is showing sky obscured, one-quarter-mile visibility. Ceiling is only 500 feet, but that cloud cover extends beyond Olympia and McChord all the way down to Portland. The east side of the mountains is clear, so I'm still planning Spokane as your alternate. Over."

████ ██ ████ ████ ████ ████ ████ ████ ███

"Dispatch, 409, we copy all that. Thanks for the info. Be advised that we encountered significant wake-air turbulence about twenty-five north of here. We'll talk to you in Juneau." He concluded the conversation with the dispatcher and ended by saying, "ARINC, Omega 409, terminate phone patch. Thanks for the help." Then he replaced the mike in its bracket and reset the radio to the Omega operations frequency in Juneau.

The conversation in the cockpit was sparse. "How's the temp, boss?" Brad asked, knowing that the front sidewalls of the 727 quickly became cold-soaked in the night Alaska air.

"Another log on the fire would help."

Brad looked up and toggled the temperature switch farther toward the "hot" position. "There you go. Let me know how that works. Lots more hot air where that came from."

"Omega 409, contact Anchorage on one-two-eight-decimal-five. Have a nice day."

Silence. Dick and Alex sat sullenly, staring into the dark sky.

"Omega 409, Anchorage."

Still no response. Brad leaned forward and tapped Dick on the shoulder. "Dick, that's for us!"

"Oh, okay. Uh, Seattle, Omega 409, go ahead." Brad knew Dick was flustered.

"Omega 409, this is Anchorage Center. Contact center on frequency one-two-eight-decimal-five. Over."

"Roger. Anchorage one-two-eight-five. Thanks for the help."

Dick immediately switched radio frequencies to 128.5, checked in with Anchorage Center, and received instructions to descend to 25,000 feet. Alex squirmed, adjusted his seat farther upright, placed his left hand on the autopilot panel on the center console, and rolled the altitude knob down to establish a constant rate of descent. "Going down," he muttered, reaching for the throttles to reduce power.

"Anchorage, Omega 409 departing three-five-zero for two-five-zero. Over."

"Omega 409, roger."

Brad reached to the pedestal console between the two pilots and selected the radio frequency on the second VHF radio for the Automatic Terminal (weather) Information Service (ATIS) at the Juneau airport. Then he faced back toward the flight engineer panel, reached to the audio select panel, toggled the VHF2 switch up, and prepared to copy the info he was hearing. "This is Juneau information Charlie at one-zero-two-zero Zulu. Skies are one-two-thousand broken, 8,000 broken, 3,000 overcast. Winds, one-two-zero at one-eight. Temperature minus six degrees Celsius. Altimeter, two-niner-eight-niner. Landing runway zero-eight. Braking action reported 'fair' by ops vehicle; patchy ice and snow on the runway. Taxiway Bravo closed. Expect to roll full length. LDA-1 approach to runway zero-eight in use. Advise approach control you have received information, Charlie."

He copied the ATIS in shorthand known only to pilots, then reached for the aircraft performance binder the size of a New York City phone book. He quickly thumbed to the Juneau pages and computed the critical speeds, flap settings, and landing distance based on the aircraft weight and the forecast braking conditions. That complete, he tapped Alex on the shoulder and handed him the formatted card with the information scribbled in bold black felt-tip pen.

Alex took the landing data card, digested the info, then reached forward and placed several small white triangles and

··· — — —···— — —···— — —····— — —···— — —···

orange cursor on the airspeed indicator at points corresponding to the critical approach speeds Brad had computed. He
made note of the runway in use, handed the card across to
Dick, then extracted a binder containing all of the instrument
approach and runway diagrams for major airports in the U.S.
from the large black flight bag next to his seat on the right.
He removed page 12-1, the Juneau LDA-1 (localizer-type di-
rectional aid) Runway 8 approach diagram, and also pulled
out page 10-1, the Juneau airport diagram. All the while, he
continued to monitor the instrument panel as the aircraft
descended through 31,000 feet, at 1,000 feet per minute,
310 knots, heading 180 degrees. He attached the approach
diagram to the small clipboard in the center of the control
column, reached down and selected the localizer radio frequency, and placed the required inbound course in the small
window of the course deviation indicator (CDI).

Alex gazed back at the instrument panel and noted a
slight lateral out-of-trim condition. Automatically dropping
his left hand to the rudder trim knob, he rotated it slightly to
bring the rudder trim index perfectly back to center. His hand
moved up to the throttles. As he squeezed back on the three
levers, he noted a corresponding reduction on the three engine pressure ratio (EPR) gauges on the center console. With
the reduction in power, the nose of the aircraft pitched down
slightly, and Alex rolled the elevator trim knob up to reestablish the 1,000-foot-per-minute rate of descent he desired. The
airspeed slowly decreased.

Dick checked the data, set his airspeed indicators, and
arranged the necessary charts as he continued to monitor
the track of the aircraft through the darkness off the coast
of Alaska. Brad gazed intently at the flight engineer panel.

He checked the cabin temperature and pressurization gauges, ensured that the fuel was balanced among all three tanks
and that the engine-driven generators were providing a constant output. Satisfied that all was in order, he tapped Dick
on the shoulder and pointed to the seat belt sign switch. Dick
nodded, reached up, and flipped the switch forward as Brad
grabbed the PA microphone and began the sonorous dialogue known to every frequent flyer. "Ladies and gentlemen,
we have commenced our gradual descent into Juneau. The
weather there includes overcast skies, temperature approximately twenty degrees Fahrenheit, wind out of the east at
eighteen knots. We will be landing to the east and should be
touching down in fifteen minutes or so. You will notice that
the captain has illuminated the seat belt sign, and we request
that you return to your seats and remain seated with your
seat belts fastened for the remainder of the flight. If you are
leaving us here in Juneau, we certainly hope that you have
a pleasant day. For those of you continuing on to Seattle, we
will be on the ground for about forty minutes. Thanks for
joining us this morning on Omega Air."

"You silver-tongued devil," Dick muttered.

"Just like you taught me to do, captain, oh my captain,"
Brad said, smiling to himself at the thought that his oral theatrics had reached a particular audience.

"Twenty-six for twenty-five," Dick said.

"Roger, a thousand to go," Alex responded as he rolled the
elevator trim farther back and reduced the rate of descent to
500 feet per minute. He pushed the throttles slightly forward.
The increased thrust caused the nose of the aircraft to pitch
up very slightly and consequently reduce the rate of descent
even further.

The continuous flow of minor adjustments was all part of the effort to provide the fewest number of uncomfortable sensations for the passengers. Done properly, the series of altitude and power changes during their arrival would be almost imperceptible in the back of the aircraft. And in light of their recent gaffe, each of them paid particular attention to every detail.

"Omega 409, Anchorage. Turn right to two-one-zero, descend to one-seven-thousand, and contact Anchorage now on one-one-eight-decimal-five. Talk to you on the way out."

"Roger, right to two-one-zero, descend to one-seven, and approach on eighteen-five. See ya in a bit," Dick replied, acknowledging that the same radar controller would likely be on duty as they departed Juneau for Seattle.

Alex spun the heading knob to the 210-degree position on his compass, set 17,000 feet in the altitude alert window, and rolled the elevator knob down to reestablish a more rapid rate of descent.

Dick set the new radio frequency and immediately said, "Anchorage, Omega 409, out of two-five-zero for one-seven-en-thousand, turning to two-one-zero, and we have, uh, information Charlie."

"Good morning, 409," the new controller responded. "Turn further right to two-three-zero, descend to one-two-thousand. Expect LDA-1, runway 8. Juneau altimeter two-niner-eight-seven. Tower reports patchy fog at the approach end and blowing snow on the runway. Over."

"Roger, right to two-three-zero, descend to one-two; 12,000. We'll expect the LDA-1. Altimeter two-niner-eight . . . what'd he say it was?"

··· — — —··· — — —··· — — —··· — — —··· — — —···

"Eight-seven," Brad said, knowing that the hard part was just taking shape. Whether going aboard ship or finding the dark, snow-covered Alaskan runway, it takes all the skill you can muster.

"Altimeter two-niner-eight-seven," Dick said, completing the scripted response and verifying the critical bits of information exchanged between the crew and the controller.

Alex made the necessary adjustments to the autopilot and dialed 12,000 in to the altitude alert window, then asked for the descent checklist.

Brad reached for the checklist slipped into the left slot of the engineer panel. He folded it from the after takeoff and climb side to the approach and landing side, swiveled his seat facing forward, and scanned the overhead panel. Then he read each item on the checklist as they all responded in the prescribed manner.

"Seat belt sign is on," Brad began. Then, "Altimeter?"

"Two-niner-eight-seven," Dick responded.

"I thought it was eight-niner," Alex said.

"No, eight-seven, from Anchorage," Dick said, as they both leaned forward and dialed 29.87 in to the barometric altimeters.

"Okay, two-niner-eight-seven set," Alex said.

"Approach briefing," Brad continued, content in the familiar routine.

"I'm looking at plate 11-5 for Juneau, November 16, 1978. It'll be the LDA-1 to runway 8. Localizer frequency is 109.9, identifier Juliet Delta Lima." Alex continued with the laundry list of minutiae as Dick followed along on the five-by-eight-inch page. Both had clipped to the control column in front of them.

Brad completed the checklist and listened intently as Alex finished the approach briefing. "Speed bugs," and they both verified that the four small white triangles and orange cursor were set at the same points on the circumference of the airspeed indicators, targets for minimum maneuvering speeds associated with the wing-flap position during the approach.

"Checklist complete," Brad concluded when all eight items were verified. The ironclad methodology filled him with quiet confidence. *This is such a beautifully orchestrated routine.*

The aircraft continued to descend gradually, and at 13,000 feet, a discordant chime sounded from the altitude alert system. "Thirteen for twelve," Dick inserted quickly.

"Roger. Thirteen for twelve," Alex responded. He rolled the nose of the aircraft up slightly and reduced the power very gradually, causing both the rate of descent and airspeed to decrease simultaneously.

"Omega 409, further left to one-seven-zero, descend to six thousand one hundred. You're twenty miles outside DIBOL. Cleared LDA-1 approach to runway eight. Contact Juneau tower on one-one-eight-decimal-seven at DIBOL."

"Roger. Left to one-seven-zero, down to sixty-one hundred, cleared approach, tower at DIBOL," Dick said.

"Damn. I can't handle more than three things at once," Alex muttered in jest as he reduced power to idle, turned to 170 degrees, set 6,100 feet in the altitude alert window, trimmed the nose up, and pushed the LOC button on the autopilot panel. The aircraft slowed through 210 knots, and he called, "Flaps two."

Dick set the flap handle at the two-degree position. "Flaps two," he verified.

Brad double-checked that the seat belt sign was illuminated, then picked up the PA mike. "Folks, we have been cleared for approach in Juneau, where it is snowing lightly. We expect to be touching down in approximately seven minutes. Flight attendants, please complete your cabin responsibilities and also be seated for landing."

"Seventy-one for sixty-one," Dick said.

"Roger, flaps five," Alex responded as he maneuvered the aircraft twenty degrees closer to the inbound course.

"Localizer's alive," Dick said as Alex turned farther left to center the vertical cursor in the HSI.

"Flaps fifteen, leveling at sixty-one," Alex said while turning the airspeed knob to 180 knots and setting the next prescribed altitude in the altitude window. The aircraft continued to slow.

"Here comes DIBOL," Dick said.

"Landing gear down," Alex commanded as they crossed DIBOL. He had configured the aircraft to track the inbound course. Then he adjusted the power to descend to the mandatory crossing altitudes.

Dick reached across the center console and placed the landing gear lever down. Three red lights flashed in the panel above the gear handle. After four or five seconds, the lights turned green, indicating that the hydraulic system had unlocked, extended, and relocked all three of the wheel assemblies in the down position.

Alex adjusted the airspeed to 137 knots and said, "Flaps thirty. Landing checklist."

Checklist in hand, Brad began, "Landing gear?" "Down and three green," both pilots responded. "Flaps?"

"Thirty, thirty, green."

"Speed brake?"

"Armed."

"Landing checklist complete," Brad concluded, as he placed the checklist back in the slot and shifted his gaze between captain and copilot instrument panels. Everything matched.

"Good morning, tower. Omega 409 is at DIBOL, inbound for zero-eight."

"Good morning, 409, Juneau tower. You're cleared to land runway eight. Wind is light and variable. Braking action reported 'fair' by an Alaska 727. Temperature is two-two, dew point two-two. Be advised that a fog bank has formed off the approach end. It appears to be moving very slowly toward the runway. Over."

"Roger, we copy. Cleared to land. Omega 409," Dick said. Then, anticipating that the fog might prevent their landing, he commented to the crew, "Shit, that's all we need. Governor on board and we miss the damned approach to the state capital! How's our fuel, Brad?"

"It's good. Seattle's the alternate. Bingo fuel is twenty-seven and we have twenty-eight-five right now. Seattle weather was 500 overcast."

"Great. Okay, Alex, any questions on the missed-approach procedure?"

"No, let's just not do it," he said in feigned humor.

"We have no control over that, big guy. 'Bout a thousand to go, nothing in sight."

Alex's hands rested lightly on the controls with his right thumb placed strategically on the disconnect button of the autopilot as it continued to track toward the runway.

"Five hundred. Nothing in sight," Dick said as clouds continued to engulf the descending 727.

"Two hundred above. "One hundred.

"Missed-approach point. Nothing in sight, GO AROUND!" Still in the clouds, the only choice was to execute the missed-approach procedure.

"Roger!" Alex belted as he pushed the power levers forward. "Flaps fifteen, positive rate, landing gear up! Turning right, climbing to fifty-two. Give me heading two-eight-zero," Alex said excitedly.

"Airspeed, Alex," Brad cautioned, his adrenaline surging as he noted the decreasing speed. "Shoot for one-eighty."

"Rog . . . " Alex grimaced and lowered the nose very slightly to allow the airspeed to increase.

"Okay, you got flaps fifteen, gear's comin' up, turn looks good, you've got heading bug at two-eighty, climbing to fifty-two. I've got that in the window." Then Dick keyed the mike. "Juneau tower, Omega 409 missed approach, climbing to fifty-two, direct SISTERS, over."

"Omega 409, Juneau tower, roger. Climb to 6,000, heading two-five-zero, and say your intentions. Uh, just for your info, we began to see your landing lights before you missed, but that fog bank appears to be drifting our way. Why don't you go back to Anchorage center on one-two-five-seven?"

"Roger, Anchorage twenty-five-seven. Thanks for the help." Hurriedly Dick switched frequency and checked in. "Hello, Anchorage, Omega 409 is back with you heading two-five-zero, climbing to 6,000."

"Well, hello there, 409, didn't expect to see you guys so soon. You want vectors around for another try?"

"Stand by, please," Dick responded. "Brad, what's our fuel state?"

"A thousand above bingo, boss. Give it another try?"

"Ahhh, damn it, damn it, damn it," Dick spat. "No. If we do that and miss again, then we cut ourselves really short on fuel for Seattle. We gotta go, guys. Sorry, Governor.

"Anchorage, 409. We're gonna call it a day. Will you get us a clearance to Seattle, please?" Dick requested.

"Roger, stand by, 409."

"You'd better make a PA, David Brinkley. Soothe them into believing that through all that skill and cunning, we narrowly avoided certain death."

"Oookay, sir." Brad turned back to face the engineer panel, glad that Dick had made the tough call. He did a hasty computation of flight time to Seattle, then gathered his wits for a few more seconds and unleashed the motor mouth. "Well, folks, as you are certainly aware, it was necessary for us to discontinue the approach due to fog at the approach end of the runway. Tower reports that that fog bank is continuing to move toward the runway, and for that reason, Captain Hamlin has determined that the prudent thing to do is continue on to Seattle. We are painfully aware that many of you have important commitments in Juneau this morning. However, our first priority is your safety, and for that reason, we'll go on down to Seattle, where our ground personnel will make arrangements for your passage back to Juneau when the weather is a little more hospitable."

For an hour, the only sound was the 300-mile-an-hour wind and the hum of several dozen gauges. Finally, the cockpit chime punctuated the silence. Brad reached for the interphone handset, a device much like the old black phone in his parents' home in Bellingham. He pitched his voice low and purred, "Speak to me," hoping that Sarah's would be the voice on the other end.

"Bingo," she said. "You all just won omelets with Alaskan king crab. Any takers? And what to drink?"

"Thanks. Hang on." Brad turned toward the two pilots. "Omelets, guys? What to drink?"

"OJ and a black," Dick said. "Nothing for me," Alex mumbled. "Really? Nothing at all?" Brad asked. "Nah, I'm okay."

Brad passed the info on to Sarah and added his own request for orange juice and coffee.

Thirty seconds and two rapid knocks later, Brad reached down and released the latch to the cockpit door. Sarah stepped into the darkness, balancing one tray and reaching back for another. She slid the second tray onto the small desk at the base of the flight engineer panel, pulled the door closed behind her, and stepped forward to hand the tray to Dick. Without a word, Sarah stepped back, leaned casually on the back of Brad's chair, and took a deep, relaxing breath. "Say, Dick," she finally said, "the governor was very complimentary about our service and the way we recovered from the big bounce. But then he asked if I knew anything more about what happened. Said that it felt like the nose really pitched over abruptly. Asked me to ask you for some more info. What should I tell him?"

"Hmmm," Dick said, stalling. He sat in silence for a few seconds. "Give me a few minutes to think about that. He just happens to be good friends with the secretary of transportation. I need to be very clear about what I say."

Sarah shrugged, turned, and patted Brad on the head as she unlatched the cockpit door. "Call if you need me," she said, stepping back into the cabin.

"Shit!" Dick blurted. "Wouldn't you know that the one time in my life I bust altitude, the governor of fucking Alaska is sitting right behind me."

Alex slipped farther down in his seat. No one would contest that it was really he who had screwed the pooch.

Chapter 2

OMEGA HISTORY

Lost in thought, Brad winced at the sobering truth as they flew toward Seattle. *Our screw up is so indicative of what Omega crews have been doing lately, he realized. In less than a year since the Omega-Pacific merger, we've had the near miss over the Atlantic, a landing at the wrong airport, the unintentional double-engine shutdown out of L.A., the MD-88 hitting the sea wall at LaGuardia, the Dallas accident, and who knows what else? That awful summer of '87. Jesus! This company really will go down the tubes if we don't get a grip.*

From his perspective, the arrogance was breathtaking. The Omega pilots imagined they could do no wrong. Hadn't Tom Wolfe debunked the idea of pilot infallibility in *The Right Stuff?* The attitude that great pilots can handle anything thrown their way was still profoundly entrenched at Omega; only the weak sisters screw up, never those with the right stuff.

••• — — —••• — — — — —••• — — — — — — — —••• — — — —••• — —•••

Brad watched quietly. Alex was undoubtedly beating himself up with that old expectation. Never mind that the wake turbulence occurred precisely at the moment he should have engaged the "altitude hold" lever. And never mind that two other aircraft he was qualified to fly had automatic "altitude capture" and "altitude hold" functions built into the autopilot. He was flying, and it was his job to maneuver the aircraft as prescribed.

To a degree, Dick was using the same cudgel. As the designated pilot in command, the captain is responsible for everything that occurs on the flight deck regardless of who is at the controls. At an FAA[5] hearing, the captain will never be exonerated while the copilot is held solely responsible for an error. All crew members share responsibility for the safe operation of the aircraft.

Brad gloomily reflected on the recent phone call from Andy Caldwell, Omega's VP of flight operations. He was so damned passionate. "The board of directors has gone ballistic, Brad. They're convinced that if we don't get our pilots on the right track, Omega is headed for extinction. My job is to put together the best crew resource management program in the industry, and to do that, I need a team of our best performers. You interested?"

The compliment stunned him, and even though it wasn't clear precisely what he was being asked to do, Brad enthusiastically signed on.

"This is really a complex issue, Brad," Andy attempted to explain. "The company has a history of very hierarchical cockpit management. In truth, I think we have gotten by because the junior guys are so smart and adaptable." Andy let the little stroke to Brad's ego hang in the air for a moment.

"At any rate, the law of averages is catching up with us—two decades of incidents packed into one God-awful year. It has to stop!"

Brad winced at the thought of his own culpability moments earlier. *Why wasn't I watching more carefully? It is so easy to drop the ball,* he realized.

Andy went on to cite the LaGuardia example to make his point. "It was classic, Brad. These guys were on the first leg of a four-day trip, exactly when the data says an incident is most likely to happen. They didn't know one another, didn't know what to expect or what the other guy'd do under pressure. They hadn't developed the dance yet.

"So when the captain began to decelerate and go below the glideslope, all the copilot could do was say, 'sink rate, sink rate,' and BAM, they hit the sea wall.

"Simple as it may seem at first blush, there was a whole range of mitigating factors. We've gotta 'fess up and attend to them all."

A little confused, Brad went along. "Yeah, I totally agree, Andy."

Two days later, an envelope had arrived at Brad's house with the report of an accident from thirteen years prior involving a Northwest 727 in upper New York state enclosed. The aircraft had departed JFK on a December night in 1974. Their departure and initial climb proceeded without incident.

Brad looked around the cockpit now and realized that everything had looked, felt, and smelled exactly the same for those Northwest guys. The same worn, gray seat covers, glowing circuit breaker panel, and humming backlit instruments. The dangling oxygen masks, gray knobs and levers, and even the same short-sleeved white shirts, black epaulets, and gold stripes on their shoulders.

Probably one of them had a new baby. Maybe another was an alcoholic, toughing it out 'til the next drink. And one may have been the local Cub Scout leader. All weary professionals who had set out to do a good job.

So how did the subtle visceral warnings register with them? It was known that at approximately 16,000 feet, while still climbing, the crew began to experience a collective uneasiness. Then the aircraft started to climb more rapidly and accelerate inexplicably. *That must have felt otherworldly; airplanes don't do that.* One crew member commented that the plane they were repositioning to Buffalo was climbing rapidly "because we're so light." Yet the airspeed was nearly 100 knots faster than normal, the rate of climb more than double the standard rate, and the nose attitude six times higher than expected. They were virtually standing on end.

God, were they just so sleepy that the facts didn't register?

Moments later, climbing through 23,000 feet, a warning horn sounded, suggesting that the maximum allowable airspeed was being exceeded. Panicked confusion followed.

Someone said, "Would you believe that shit?"

And another, "I believe it; I just can't do anything about it."

The first voice again, "No, just pull her back, let her climb."

As the story played through his mind, Brad couldn't resist the urge to look at the forward overhead panel to ensure that the pitot heat switches were in the on position. They were.

A similar uneasiness in any one of the Northwest guys would have led to the discovery that their pitot heat switches were off. The tubes were freezing over and causing false airspeed indications on their gauges. Instead, the crew attempted to slow down by reducing power and raising the nose.

"Pull it up!" the captain demanded.

Two seconds later, the landing gear warning horn sounded, indicating that the power levers had been retarded to idle. Examination of the flight data recorder, one of the "black boxes," indicated that the next sequence of events resulted from the aircraft entering a "low-speed stall," rolling into a seventy-degree bank to the right and commencing a rapid (15,000-foot-per-minute) vertical descent.

The confusion and disorientation must have been intense. The upper half of the attitude indicators, which are ordinarily blue, completely disappeared from sight. The aircraft had rolled into a seventy-degree right bank in an extreme nose-down attitude. The investigation went on to describe the array of conflicting data and sensations the crew was reacting to.

They were plummeting toward the ground in a tight right spiral. The NTSB concluded that had they taken appropriate corrective action within the first thirty to forty seconds of the stall, it is likely that they could have recovered. However, they were experiencing gut-wrenching g-forces, a high rate of descent, and lower than normal indicated airspeed—conditions to which there is no intuitively correct response.

In fact, their actual responses compounded the problem. By pulling back on the control column and remaining in the tight right turn, they were unable to reestablish normal airflow over the critical airfoils. There was no hope. All three perished.[6]

Pilot error. But why?

The answers weren't obvious to Brad as he revisited the images in his head, all the while aware of the gauges on the panel in front of him. Then a chime sounded overhead, and he was jolted back to the present.

"Get that, will you, Brad?" Dick requested.

"Roger, roger," he responded, casually reaching for the microphone and selecting the number three radio.

"ARINC, Omega 409 responding to SELCAL, go ahead," he intoned.[7]

"Omega 409, San Francisco, stand by for phone patch with Omega dispatch, over."

"Roger, standing by."

Thirty seconds passed until Brad heard a microphone click as the company dispatcher in Memphis checked in. "Omega 409, dispatcher Jones, how do you read? Over."

"Mornin', Jones. 409 reads you loud and clear. Go ahead," Brad responded.

"409, I have a weather update for Seattle when you're ready."

"Go ahead."

The seasoned Southern drawl came back with, "Seattle is currently reporting sky obscured and one-quarter mile. Runway visual range is 600, 400, and 600. Temperature three-five, dew point three-five. Altimeter three-zero-one-five. Wind is light and variable. How copy?"

"Stand by," Brad responded, tapping Dick on the shoulder. "You might want to hear this, Dick." The captain reached down and flipped the toggle for the number three radio.

"Dispatch, 409 copies Seattle with sky obscured and a quarter, RVR 600, 400, 600, temp three-five, dew point three-five, altimeter three-zero-one-five, light, and variable, go ahead," Brad said.

"That's all correct, 409. I'm expecting a breeze to develop out of the east, but for the moment, I'd like to change your alternate to Paine. They are reporting clear and greater than ten and forecast to remain the same. Would like you to hold over Paine at altitude until Seattle clears. I calculate that will give you about forty-five minutes of holding fuel. And this way, you can duck into Paine for fuel if necessary. How copy?"

Dick held up a hand to Brad, reached down, and switched his transmit selector to the number three radio, then spoke to the dispatcher. "Dispatch, 409, this is Captain Hamlin. We copy the change in alternate to Paine. Just wondering what the chances are that fog will move in there, too. Over."

"Uh, 409, dispatch, the trend all week has been for this fog to dissipate just before sunrise. Currently, Paine has a two-degree temperature/dew-point spread and talking with the tower up there, they say there is an intermittent light breeze out of the northeast. My guess is that we'll see the same dissipation throughout the area again this morning. Over."

"He guesses? Shit! We place our lives in these guys' hands?" Dick muttered.

"Okay, dispatch, 409 copies. We're about 300 north of Paine. We'll check in with you when we enter holding down there. Please keep us advised of any changes in the weather. Over." Dick replaced his mike in the bracket and said, "You've got it, Hotshot."

Brad continued the cadence on the radio, "Dispatch, 409. Expect to hear from us at about one-four-zero-zero Zulu. ARINC, Omega 409, terminate phone patch. Thanks for the help. Over."

"Omega 409, ARINC, roger. Phone patch terminated at one-two-four-eight. ARINC, out."

"Brad, calculate our fuel for holding down there. For the time being, I want to have enough to get over the hills to Spokane if it isn't looking really good at Paine. That was our original alternate, wasn't it?" Dick asked.

"Yeah. They had us programmed for thirty-five minutes en route; burn of four grand."

"Okay. That'll give us a bingo of twelve. How much hold time will that allow us there?"

"Stand by a sec," Brad said as he scratched a few numbers on a pad. "Looks like we'll have about thirty minutes' hold time if they let us stay at altitude. Glad we pulled the plug in Juneau when we did."

"Yeah, that's why I earn the big bucks, Hotshot." Dick smiled ruefully.

An occasional glimpse of village lights along the Canadian coast punctuated the early-morning darkness. Breaks in the clouds foretold further breakup, but it was too early to know if that trend would continue to Puget Sound.

Brad busied himself opening and closing fuel valves and depowering a pump to balance fuel among the three tanks of the 727. He held a light bulb cover in his hand as a reminder that the valve and switch position would need to be returned to normal within a short time. The theory was that by constantly holding the cover in one's hand, the mild irritant would be a reminder that the fuel-balancing task was incomplete. *Not rocket science, but hey, it works,* he reminded himself. Reaching back, he lifted a heavy black manual containing performance data for the aircraft. He placed it on the small work table below the flight engineer panel, and from among the 853 pages, he found the chart corresponding to the weight and altitude of the aircraft. A grid of data boxes filled the page. Consulting the one containing a number corresponding to the outside air temperature, he determined the prescribed speeds and power settings for a variety of circumstances. He jotted down the Mach number and power setting corresponding to the maximum endurance attainable.

After passing the note forward, he placed his hand on the power levers while Dick digested the info and acknowledged Brad's intent to reduce the power to achieve the max endurance setting. The unspoken exchange occurred, and he retarded the power to achieve the prescribed EPR.

Alex continued to maneuver the aircraft along the airway toward Seattle. Brad knew he was acutely aware of the need to be error-free. Neither the governor nor the FAA would let this one pass.

The flight attendant call chime sounded, prompting Brad to think, *Oops, I'd better get back there and kiss up to the governor.* He picked up the handset. "Engine room," he answered.

"Ha," Sarah responded. "You'd better get your best damned mechanic back here right now. The natives are very restless. One of them has been on the air phone almost constantly since we left Juneau. Lots of hushed chatter about how to reschedule the aviation subsidy hearing." Following deregulation in 1978, millions in subsidies were allocated to continue air service to small communities. For some of those communities—many of them in Alaska—economic prosperity hinged on the subsidies.

"Okay. I don't have any good news, but I'll give it a shot. Be right there," Brad said, replacing the handset in the bracket.

"Restless natives, Sarah says. I'd better get back there and charm the gov." He stood and reached for his jacket. "Any final words of wisdom, my liege?" he asked Dick.

"You're on your own, Hotshot. You know as much as I do, but I don't think I'd tell him the part about a possible fuel stop someplace. Let's save that little nugget for our encore," Dick deadpanned.

Brad grabbed his hat, scanned the instrument panel one last time as he replaced the light bulb cover, and flipped the adjacent switch. "Essential's on three," he said, stepping into the cabin.

Sarah stuck her head out of the galley and whispered, "He's sitting right there in 1C."

Brad squared his shoulders, adjusted his hat, and stepped forward confidently. *You always have the advantage standing over someone, looking down.* He removed his hat.

"Excuse me, Governor," he said as he extended his hand. "I'm Brad Morehouse, the second officer. Captain Hamlin asked me to come back and express his apology for the inconvenience we've caused you today. That fog bank slipped in just as we reached minimums in Juneau. As you know, that area east of the runway is a box canyon, so you have to break it off pretty early, or you're committed to land. The fog just wouldn't allow us to do that."

The governor was a Clark Gable look-alike, complete with a slightly hooded right eye. He looked up, extended his hand to Brad, and said nothing.

Before Brad could speak again, the fastidious-looking guy next to the governor leaned forward and said, "But how come I could see that Alaska jet on the taxiway right after you made your turn? They must have gotten in. Are they better? Do they have lower minimums? What's the deal?"

Brad's jaw tightened as he choked back his instant dislike for the arrogant young aide. "Well, obviously they got in, but that was probably last night before the fog developed. And now that you mention it, I haven't heard an Alaska flight on frequency. They're probably still sitting there waiting for the fog to lift. At any rate, it's the captain's job to make those tough calls, and Captain Hamlin is one of the best."

The governor finally spoke. "Say, I recognize you. You're Joe Spears' son-in-law, aren't you? Former Blue Angel, naval aviator extraordinaire?"

"Uh, yes, sir," Brad said, sorry that he'd been identified. "I married Audrey Spears four years ago during Seafair. The team made a fly-by at the end of the ceremony."

"Just like Joe Spears. Nothing small about that guy," the governor said. "He still on the Omega board?" "Yes, sir, he is. Chairman of the finance committee, if I remember correctly."

"Okay, I get it," the young guy cut in. "Audrey More-house, evening news anchor at KSEA, is your wife and Joe Spears' daughter, right?"

"That's right," he responded uncomfortably. The kid behaved like a Chihuahua teasing a black Lab. "And you are?" Brad asked, leaning forward to shake the young guy's hand.

"Bill Archer, Brad, the governor's chief of staff," he said, extending his hand. "Grew up in Seattle. Yew Dub and Stanford Law. I remember when Audrey Spears was Seafair queen. What a great couple. Former queen and her Blue Angel."

"Well, it may look glamorous from the outside, but we're both just grindin' it out. Which reminds me, I'd better get back up there and go to work.

"Governor, the last weather report showed fog in Seattle, too. Our dispatcher has suggested that we hold over Paine Field in Everett until it lifts. Hope we'll only need to make a couple of turns before we can get in to SeaTac. I know the folks on the ground in Seattle are making arrangements to get you back to Juneau just as soon as possible. Really sorry for the inconvenience, sir."

"Well, thanks, Brad. I've been meaning to give Joe a call. I'll tell him we met," the governor replied without looking up. *Ominous*, Brad thought as he turned toward the cockpit. "Ooooh, former Blue Angel and a news anchor wife.

Ooooh," Sarah taunted as she stepped confidently out of the galley to confront him.

"Hey, Short Stuff, beam me up, will you, please?" he said as he reached for the cockpit door handle with feigned nonchalance. Sarah pushed the cockpit chime button twice. Brad knocked twice, listened for the lock mechanism to disengage, pulled the door open, and stepped into the cockpit without further comment. He failed to see her look after him with a mix of desire and disdain.

He stowed his coat and hat, swung into his seat, took a deep breath, and exhaled loudly. "Charming guy, the governor. Seems that he knows my father-in-law. Says he's going to give him a call, will say that he met me. That can't be good, boss. He is *not* a happy camper."

"Your father-in-law, who's he?" Alex asked.

"Joseph Spears, Seattle attorney and Omega Board of Directors. He's pretty well-connected. He advises the governor on North Slope oil issues."

"Damn. What did you tell him about the Seattle weather?" Dick asked.

"Just said that they have fog, too, and that we will probably make a few turns in the pattern over Paine. The gov seems to think that the Alaska guys have bigger *cojones* than we do. His snot-nosed chief of staff is sitting in 1A and saw an Alaska airplane holding short when we turned out on the go-around. Figures those guys got in when we couldn't. I told him that they're probably still sitting there at the hold-short line waiting for the fog to clear. Not sure that I got through to him," Brad concluded.

"Well, right now, we've got bigger fish to fry. Puget Sound is barely visible up there. Looks like the clouds are hanging over the water, not moving onshore.

"Brad, get the latest Seattle weather and compute our holding fuel. I have the Paine VOR on my side. It shows us about 120 out."

"Okay, Dick, stand by," Brad said, as he turned toward the engineer panel and donned his headset. He proceeded through the familiar script of conversation and computation and four minutes later turned back toward Dick.

"Seattle's still WOXOF.[8] Paine is severe clear. Wind calm. Temperature/dew point three-eight. It looks like we'll have about 3,500 pounds to spare when we enter the hold. The charts say that'll give us forty minutes of hold time if we can stay at or above flight level two-five-oh."

"Thanks. I'd better let Seattle know what we're planning," Dick said. "Seattle, Omega 409, over."

"Omega 409, Seattle Center, go ahead."

"Seattle, 409, weather at Sea-Tac is below our minimums. Requesting holding at Paine. We have about forty minutes of holding fuel. Requesting right turns and twenty-mile legs, over."

"Omega 409, Seattle. You are cleared to hold north of the Paine VOR, right turns, twenty-mile legs. Expect further clearance time is one-four-one-five Zulu."

"Roger. Omega 409 is cleared to hold north of Paine, right turns, twenty-mile legs, EFC⁹ one-four-one-five. We'll give you a call entering the hold, over."

"That's correct, 409. Descend now and maintain flight level two-eight-zero. Speed at your discretion, over."

Dick reached up and dialed 280 in to the altitude alert window of the autopilot, then responded, "409 is leaving three-five for two-eight, and speed at our discretion."

"Roger," the controller responded.

Alex clicked off the "altitude hold" function of the auto-pilot, placed his left hand on the three power levers, and walked them back slowly as he allowed the nose of the aircraft to drop very slightly below the artificial horizon on the attitude indicator. With his right thumb, he toggled another switch on the control column to position the horizontal stabilizer in the tail section of the aircraft, countering the tendency of the nose to drop in response to the power reduction. "Figure a holding speed, Brad," he demanded.

"Two-thirty should do it," Brad answered. "I can set that fuel flow if you want, Alex."

"No. Never mind, I'll do it." Alex's tone had become harsh. "Dick, can you put Paine in my side, too? I guess we're cleared direct, right?" Alex asked.

"Yeah, you've got it. Go direct," Dick said as he spun the knobs on Alex's navigation radio.

✈

Brad sat patiently and observed, occasionally tweaking the temperature or checking fuel, but mostly just watching. Plenty of time for stray thoughts as images of icicle Audrey and firecracker Sarah competed for position in his mind's eye. There was a solid winner and a corresponding wave of guilt.

The weather at Paine Field was as advertised, and Omega 409 proceeded with a lazy racetrack pattern 28,000 feet over the field. The runway lights were clearly in sight while a white shroud hung motionless along the shoreline.

Alex casually maneuvered the aircraft with the control knob on the autopilot panel, and all three pilots monitored radio traffic for information about any changes in the Sea-Tac weather. Other aircraft were holding at various fixes throughout the area, and as time wore on, flights began requesting clearance to alternate airports on the east side of the Cascades.

The plan for 409 was pretty well fixed in Dick's mind. Hold here until they needed fuel, then duck into Paine, fuel up, and wait for Sea-Tac to open up.

"Fuel for about one more turn in the pattern, Dick. We gonna bingo to Spokane?" Brad finally asked with a tinge of concern.

"Oh, sorry, guys. I had it all mapped out in my head but forgot to tell you. Paine looks good to me. Let's stay here for fifteen minutes more, then drop in for fuel. Sea-Tac will certainly be open by then. That sound okay?"

"Fine by me," Alex responded.

"I'm right behind you guys," Brad said, reluctant to voice the concern he had about the limited options once they committed to Paine. "You want me to give dispatch a call with the plan? He should be able to get us set up for fuel down there."

"Yeah, do that, and I'll check in with the Paine tower and give them a heads-up," Dick replied.

Fifteen minutes later, they executed their last remaining option. "Seattle Center, Omega 409, request, over."

"Omega 409, Seattle, go ahead."

The conversation with Seattle Center continued as 409 received clearance to descend for landing at Paine. Dick took control of the aircraft since Alex had been flying all the way from Fairbanks. In turn, Alex assumed responsibility for radio communications and the backup duties of the pilot not flying (PNF).

Right behind them, on the entryway jump seat, Sarah looked up from where she sat counting the drink money. The flight attendant call light illuminated halfway back in the cabin, and the chime sounded. As she stood to get a better look, passenger heads bobbed up, people stood, and a general commotion erupted. Someone waved an arm for her to come. Clearly, this was not just a request for another drink.

Before heading down the aisle, she grabbed the inter-phone and rang the back. "Hi, sweetie, what's up?" her friend and flying partner responded.

"Hey, Rhonda, something's happening about half-way back. Meet me there!" Sarah ran through first class and plunged into the crowd. "Excuse me, 'scuse me." She elbowed her way through the curious passengers.

An overweight giant of a man was flopped back against the window, wedged against the seat in front. Wide, glassy eyes bulged from his pallid blue face as saliva oozed over his lower lip.

"A heart attack, just like my husband's," a small woman gasped with a hand to her mouth.

"Rhonda, call for a doctor and let the cockpit know that we may have a heart attack here," Sarah commanded.

"Sir, can you hear me?" she began uncertainly.

"He's not breathing, miss," a passenger leaning over the seat insisted.

She looked up, said, "Help me get him into the aisle," and began tugging on his right arm. "Grab his other arm!"

Someone approached from the other seat and supported the man's head as they pulled him upright and inched his mass toward the aisle.

"Easy, easy," she strained as they lowered him on to the floor between the rows of seats. He barely fit. Sarah hop-scotched from seat to seat and landed nimbly on the floor be-hind the man. She knelt, tilted his head back, and stuck two fingers in his mouth, searching for an obstruction. *Nothing there.* Next, she slipped down the knot of his tie. It unraveled, and she pulled it out from under his collar, which she unbuttoned. Then she leaned forward, placed her mouth on his, and exhaled two full breaths into his lungs. Oblivious to the mayhem around her, she extended her arms, crossed her hands, and began the rhythmic compressions to his chest.

"Excuse me, I'm a doctor." A man jumped into the seat above the victim and looked at Sarah. "Have you checked his pulse?"

"No," she said breathlessly. "Would you do that, please?" The doctor grabbed a wrist and fixed a steely gaze on his watch. "Nothing." He looked up with deep concern. "But keep trying," he encouraged Sarah.

"Bring an oxygen bottle," someone suggested.

"Hi, I'm a doctor," a woman's voice sounded authoritatively behind Sarah. "What seems to be the problem, miss?"

"Tell her, Doc."

"Myocardial infarction," the first doctor responded. "Non-responsive. I think we've lost him."

Sarah persisted, furiously puffing air into the man's lungs and pounding on his chest.

Brad grabbed the interphone on the first ding. "Speak to me," he said casually, expecting to hear Sarah's tart response.

"Sir, this is Rhonda. We have a medical emergency. A man seems to be having a heart attack. Sarah is doing CPR, and we have requested a doctor."

"Uh-oh. Hold on, Rhonda." Brad held the interphone toward Dick. "Boss, we have an emergency in back. Sounds like a heart attack."

"Oh, fucking swell," Dick spat. "Too late for us to do anything. Tell 'em to handle it. We'll be landing in ten minutes. Can this trip get any worse?" He shook his head and gripped the yoke fiercely.

"Okay, Rhonda, listen. We're on our way into Paine Field; that's in Everett, north of Seattle. We'll be landing in about ten minutes, and we can have EMTs meet the flight. Can you guys handle it 'til then?" Brad asked.

"Yeah, but hurry. This looks pretty bad."

As they spiraled down through 5,000 feet, Brad could see fog obscuring the lights of houses perched along the sea cliffs off the approach end of the runway. "Looks like the fog may be drifting toward the runway, Dick. Wanna set up for the ILS?" he inquired.

"Oh, wonderful. Jesus, that's all we need," Dick fumed again. "Yeah, get your plates out, Alex, and set us up for the approach. I'll handle the radios."

Alex scrambled to retrieve the necessary charts from the flight bag directly below the right armrest. He selected the page depicting the pattern for the instrument landing system approach and attached it to the control column, then reenacted the script they followed in Juneau.

Level at 3,000 feet, the 727 turned toward the runway and intercepted the radio signal extending out from the centerline of the runway. Dick reduced power slightly and called for the extension of additional wing flaps. Moments later, the horizontal bar across the top of the HSI began to flicker and move down very slowly. Dick called, "Gear down, flaps thirty, landing checklist." He reduced power further to establish a descent rate of approximately 700 feet per minute. The horizontal and vertical indicators on the HIS were crossed and perfectly centered in the gauge. The trick was keeping them centered with imperceptibly small adjustments to the control column. It was like flying on a wire directly in to a shrinking cone; the closer the runway, the smaller the adjustment tolerance.

Brad's heart pounded furiously as he recited the items on the landing checklist, then settled in to a watchful position behind the center console. He knew that the upcoming maneuver was among the most demanding an airline pilot might ever encounter. They were over the water and above the fog bank, but the airport was entirely out of sight. Combine the demands of the approach with their low fuel state and a medical emergency, and you had pressure matching that of a surgeon's initial incision.

At 1,500 feet above ground level, the landing-light reflection off the clouds changed to an all-encompassing glow as the aircraft plunged into the clouds just 700 feet above the minimum allowable descent altitude. One minute to go.

Alex made the prescribed altitude calls in measured tones. "Five hundred, cleared to land." Seconds later, "Two hundred, nothing in sight. One hundred, nothing." Then, "Minimums!"

Chapter 3

HOMECOMING

Eight hours later, Brad stepped out of his trusty old Land Rover and strolled down the street in Pike Place Market. Sarah was an absolute hero, he marveled to himself. *The poor guy was dead, and she simply wouldn't let that be. By the time we'd landed, he looked like he could have walked off the airplane on his own. Amazing!*

He breathed deeply. It was Friday afternoon, and despite his "tough day at the office," he was looking forward to the Saturday morning ritual he and Audrey had once enjoyed so much. *How can I rekindle the fire?* he wondered.

Their favorite bakery was here on the waterfront. He ducked in, selected half a dozen fresh bagels, a baguette, some cream cheese, and marionberry jam. Then he wound his way through the snarled traffic and elbowed his way into the blocks-long fish market.

The sounds and aromas were soothing in spite of the intensity. He found a calm new cadence as he made his way past dozens of stalls, admiring the day's catch. "Ah, Bradley Blue Angel," a familiar voice rang out. "Where you been, boy? New York City? Honolulu? Mexico City, maybe, eh?"

"Hola, Pepe," Brad joked in response. "Cómo estás?" That unleashed a fusillade of unintelligible Spanish.

Raising both hands in surrender, he cut in, "Whoa, whoa, whoa, amigo. *Ich spreche nicht* Mexican." Then he jammed his hands into his coat pockets, rolled back on his heels, and smiled broadly. "How you doin', Carlos? Business good?" he asked.

"Never better, my friend."

The pleasant banter went back and forth for several minutes before Brad selected a salmon fillet and two halibut steaks. Carlos wrapped them carefully and handed them to Brad. "Tell that beautiful lady of yours she should find herself a real man," he quipped. "Tell her to come see me."

"Ha. Fat chance, amigo. Stop dreamin' and get back to work."

Brad paid Carlos and continued toward the flower booths, grabbed a bunch of daffodils, and returned to the Land Rover. *Just fifteen minutes to make the ferry.* He inched the truck into the traffic and down the slippery-looking hill, drove aboard the ferry, and wearily dragged himself to his favorite quiet corner in the cabin. The comforting Friday afternoon commuter chatter contributed to his easy slumber.

The dream rolled into view without any opening credits; he'd seen it so many times before. She was so damned perky and congenial.

> *"Oh, excuse me. I'm so sorry." The well-coifed blond stewardess raised her head off her un-*

known seatmate's shoulder, rubbed the sleep from her eyes, and yawned. "God, I hope no one saw me dozing. You're not supposed to sleep in uniform." Angela strained to look around the cabin, hoping not to catch the eye of any of the other thirty PSA employees on board. The young man next to her tried not to stare at her delicious, fully exposed legs peeking out of the hot-pink short-shorts uniform.

"You here on business?" she asked, peering into her little round mirror. She flicked an eyelash off her cheek, then closed the compact and smiled at him. "Nice-looking suit. You should be an airline pilot, maybe even a PSA pilot." She looked him up and down and winked.

"Is it that obvious?" He blushed and tugged awkwardly at the red paisley tie.

"We get a couple of you guys every flight. Bring 'em down and run 'em through the meat grinder. How's it going so far?" she asked, knowing that the handsome young hunk was another hopeful sky god.

"Really well, actually. Got past the interview last week, and we do the physical today. Any advice? Like should I tell them you prescreened me or anything?"

"Yeah, you wish. You'll fit right in; I can say that much." She raised an eyebrow and looked out to see the Coronado Bridge arching elegantly over the shimmering San Diego Bay. Brad would be waiting at the gate, and they'd have time for a *stroll in the marina before her trip. What a fairy-tale this is, she mused.*

The 727 shuddered as the landing gear extended out of the fuselage, down into position. Passengers straightened up and stowed items in the pockets or spaces beneath the seats in front. The flight attendant crew made a final sweep through the cabin and scurried for the jump seats as the young man suppressed the exhilaration he felt at joining The World's Friendliest Airline. His broad smile rivaled the one painted on the nose of the aircraft.

The casual banter in the cockpit reflected the beauty of the glorious Southern California fall day. As they descended through 3,500 feet, the flight engineer chuckled and continued a conversation with the off-duty pilot in the jump seat. "He really broke up laughing. I said, 'So I'm late . . . '"

"Are we clear of that Cessna?" the copilot asked with concern.

"Supposed to be," the engineer responded with a cursory look out the window.

"I hope," the jump-seat rider added blithely as he buckled up.

Does one's heart stop permanently just before a fatal impact? Brad hoped that hers had. He could imagine her clawing futilely at the window and staring in horror as torn metal and fire erupted from the right wing. The landscape rolled under them before rushing up toward the aircraft. A fearful stench would have filled the air as a cumulative deafening scream provided the final punctuation in the lives of 131 hapless souls.

"Tower, we're going down, this is PSA—" were the captain's final words.

"Okay, we'll call the equipment," the tower responded helplessly.

And at the last moment, from an unknown voice in the cockpit, "Ma, I love ya."[10]

Brad groaned as he woke. *The accident had happened nearly ten years ago. Why am I dreaming about her now?* His mind was quick to supply the answer. Sarah. *Sarah is the new Angela. And the pain is that never-ending sense of loss, the one that started when Mom died twenty years ago.*

He roused himself, swung to the third step of the ladder, and scrambled up just as he'd done so many times on the *Enterprise*. The welcome sea breeze jolted his senses and carried him far from Puget Sound; for a moment, he was in the Mediterranean, off the coast of Croatia. The fatigue was familiar. He was bone-tired from ten hours in the cockpit. But as reality returned, he knew that it wasn't a day of fighter-jock heroics but instead a series of airline-crew miscues that was dragging him down.

Not that it had been his responsibility. On the contrary, he may have saved the day when he saw the runway at Paine. They were able to land and get that guy to a hospital. Nevertheless, he was on the team, and today they had not exactly been poetry in motion.

In fact, he was struggling to find his footing. *You enter this industry from a pretty high perch in the military. All of a sudden you're nobody; nothing but a number on the seniority list, same as the guy with a thousand hours in a Cessna. A lot of these Seattle-based captains were hired with less flight time than that—a few hundred at best. And within three or four years, they were sitting in the left seat of a 727 with guys like me sitting sideways behind them on the engineer's panel.*

Goofy system, he mused. But hey, it's not just a job; it's a kick in the pants. Lots of time off, reasonable pay, and all the airline food you can eat.

The fog was forming early as he rolled down the ramp at the Bainbridge Island terminal. Halos swirled around the streetlights in the February dusk as Brad maneuvered along the familiar north shore. For many, the misty skies of the Pacific Northwest were a security blanket. Not so for Brad, but he did warm with the realization that *the big guy* was waiting just around the next corner.

He set the handbrake and opened the door to a crescendo of canine clatter behind the hedge. Their routine was well established. Brad grabbed his bag and Pike Place booty, crunched through the gravel to the gate, and swung it open. Admiral sat motionless on the lawn, his perfect military bearing only slightly diminished by his slobbery, twitchy, whiny jowls. He remained still, awaiting the signal. Brad set his bags down, came to attention, and saluted crisply. "Evenin', Admiral," he said, and the 200-pound Saint Bernard bounded into his arms. The quick falling hug preceded his hilarious puppy scamper around the yard, interspersed with joyful dog bellows.

- - - ▪ ▪ ▪ ▬ ▬ ▬ ▪ ▪ ▪ ▬ ▬ ▬ ▬ ▪ ▪ ▪ ▬ ▬ ▬ ▪ ▪ ▪ ▬ ▬ ▬ ▬ ▪ ▪ ▪ ▬ ▬ ▬ ▪ ▪ ▪

Nice to be loved, Brad thought with a grin as he unlocked the back door, gave way to his buddy, and headed for the bedroom. Their routine continued as Admiral sat in the doorway, waiting for his commander-in-chief to suit up for their evening jog.

It may not be my first choice of activities at the moment, but who has a choice? he asked himself. *Ad has been anticipating this moment for days.*

Thirty minutes later, they stepped back through the door just as the phone began ringing. Brad hung the leash on a hook and grabbed the wireless handset. "Suicide hotline, can you hold?" he drawled.

"Damn it, Brad. Is that you?" a serious male voice responded.

"Oops. Sorry, sir. Yeah, it's me. Ad and I just got back from a run. Haven't even had a chance to sit down," Brad said as he maneuvered to retrieve a beer from the refrigerator and open it without interrupting the conversation.

"Got a call from a very angry client today, Brad. Did say that you seemed to be a fine young man, but he wasn't at all happy with his trip on Omega. I said that I'd check in with you. What the hell happened?" Joseph Spears demanded.

"Hmm. This puts me in an awkward position, Joe. I just got home myself; haven't really had a chance to reflect on everything that went on. The good news is that we got the governor here safely." Brad stifled his irritation.

"Safe? Maybe. Right destination? No!" Joe retorted. "Joe, we don't control the weather."

"Well, for some reason, he thinks you guys weren't mindin' the store up there. Says you got one hell of a jolt even before you missed Juneau; people, food, and luggage all over the cabin. Doesn't sound real safe to me. He says the nose pitched over and almost sent everyone through the overhead."

········ ▬ ▬ ▬·····▬ ▬ ▬·····▬ ▬ ▬·····▬ ▬ ▬·····▬ ▬ ▬·····▬ ▬ ▬····

"Yeah, we were behind a Northwest 747. Center gave us a heads-up just before we caught their wake turbulence. That stuff happens," Brad responded, purposely avoiding the pitch-over issue.

"The governor has a guy on his staff who flew tankers at Elmendorf. Says it just didn't feel like the captain was handling the airplane very well. Thinks he lost his nerve on the approach to Juneau. For God's sake, they could see an Alaska airplane holding short of the runway as you started the go-around. Why didn't you just go ahead and land the damned thing?"

"This is where it gets tough, Joe," Brad answered calmly. "First of all, and you know this, I'm the third in command up there. There aren't any flight controls on the engineer's panel. And second, it really is the captain's sole responsibility to operate the aircraft *safely*. And he did that."

"But you could see the damned runway."

"No, we couldn't. It may have been visible on the go-around, but by then, you don't even look. That's why they call the missed-approach point the 'decision height.' Beyond that point, it's too late to transition to a landing, regardless of what you see." Then, deliberately changing the tenor of the conversation, he added, "Unless, of course, you're a Marine. You know the ol' Marine jet-jock credo, right?"

"Can't say that I do."

"A smokin' hole in the runway is a small price to pay for a shit-hot approach."

"Ha." Clearly, Joe was not amused.

"Anyway, the issues we may have with each other in the cockpit we handle in-house. The Air Line Pilots Association (ALPA) has a very responsive Professional Standards Committee, and that's where we go to raise any issue about pilot performance. If a guy needs an attitude check, he should get it from his peers first, not from management.

"So what I'm saying here is that even if I did see something that disturbed me, I would need to either go directly to the person involved or take it to Professional Standards. Not air it with anyone else." Brad shook his head, waiting for the conversation to end.

"Okay, I get it," Joe said, as the legal perspective overcame his personal chagrin. There really wasn't much he could report back to the governor except that safety trumps everything else. And Brad's description of decision height was persuasive, too.

"Hey, one more interesting note before I catch the Ken and Audrey show." Brad brightened. "Got a call from Andy Caldwell this week. He wants me to be a part of the committee developing a crew resource management program. Omega is really late getting involved in this, but Andy is determined to make our program the best in the industry. First meeting's in Memphis on Monday."

"Ah, very good," Joe said. "I'm really glad you're gonna be involved. Yeah, the idea for this came from the board. We have way too much to lose if we have any more fuck-ups out there. Obviously, I couldn't recommend you, so it's great to know that Andy wants your input. Keep me posted. And give my daughter a hug, too, will ya?"

"Sure will, Joe. Thanks for your understanding," Brad concluded with relief.

"You got it, pal. Take care."

Chapter 4

THE EVENING NEWS

Good evening, I'm Ken Shaver."

"And I'm Audrey Morehouse, and this is *Seattle This Evening*."

Brad settled into his recliner with a handful of carrot sticks and the remainder of his beer. She looked good, as always. More confident and mature than when she moved into the anchor chair two years ago.

Audrey covered the latest fog-related pile-up on Interstate 5. *A little too perky,* Brad thought, but by now it was routine, and the overall tenor of the show was upbeat and positive. Brad tripped over Admiral en route to the refrigerator during the commercial. They tumbled around together on the floor for a moment. Then he filled Ad's food and water bowls, grabbed another beer, and returned to the TV just as the dark image of a twisted Omega 737 filled the screen.

"This just in," Ken reported, reading very deliberately from the script in his hand. "Another near tragedy for Omega

Air Lines. Less than one hour ago, this Boeing 737 departing the Tri-Cities Airport in Pasco swerved violently off the runway and came to rest against an embankment bordering the airport. Initial reports indicate there were no fatalities and, miraculously, only minor injuries to those aboard the nearly full aircraft."

Nausea filled his gut as Brad flopped into his chair and stared.

"From what we have been told by the Pasco airport authorities, Omega Flight 848 originated in Salt Lake City and stopped in the Tri-Cities before intending to continue on to Seattle." Lowering the script to the desk, Ken looked earnestly at the camera. "I want to emphasize that there are no reported fatalities and apparently only minor injuries to the passengers aboard Omega Flight 848 bound for Seattle. We will have additional details for you as they become available throughout the evening."

Ken's image gave way to Audrey's, and Brad could see the distinct change in her demeanor. Though much of their life involved aviation, she ranked flying among her least enjoyable activities. "Let's move over to meteorologist Rob Elhardt, who can tell us about any weather-related factors in tonight's incident. Rob?" she said, nodding to her left.

"Well, Audrey, Ken, it seems to me that there were no significant meteorological factors involved here. At departure time in Pasco, the official weather report showed clear skies, temperature thirty-four degrees, and just a light breeze out of the north. Checking past reports, there hasn't been any precipitation east of the Cascades, and the temperature has remained above freezing throughout the week. That suggests to me that there is little likelihood that icing could have been a factor, Audrey. And as you know, that cold, dense air is perfect for flying. Who knows?" He shrugged. "Ken?"

"Thank you, Rob. After these commercial messages, an unhappy outlook for area firefighters as the record drought continues."

Brad bolted out of his chair as the phone rang. "Speak to me," he said, knowing who was calling.

"Oh, Brad, you're there," Audrey's breathless voice exhaled. "Did you see that piece? I knew it couldn't be you, but it really shook me to see the Omega livery on that crumpled airplane."

"No, I'm fine, but I'm shaken, too."

"Any way you can get more information about this?" she asked.

"No way. ALPA will sequester the crew, and we won't get any official information for weeks. And you know I can't be a source for the media. That's treasonous in this industry."

"Oh, I know. A minor brain cramp, sorry. Glad you're okay. Stay tuned," and she was gone.

Brad cradled the receiver, took a long, deep breath, and stretched. He had been fully engaged for twenty hours. Exhaustion dragged him back into the chair. A little downtime was in order. He settled uneasily into the recliner, his mind still churning through the day's events. Admiral curled beside the chair and offered his massive head with an affectionate nudge. Audrey's face reappeared on the screen, but Brad muted the sound, leaned back, and closed his eyes.

A phone was ringing someplace in the distance, and he struggled to tune it out. Then his eyes blinked, and the dreamy image of a kayak on the water gave way to reality. *Damn! Let it ring,* he thought. *No. Can't do that with everything that's happened today*, he realized and struggled out of the chair toward the kitchen.

"Brad? Gradin. God, I'm glad you're there. Can you talk?"

"Gradin, hey, great to hear your voice."

"Well, you won't think it's so great when you hear this. That was me in 848. Did you see the news?"

"No shit? Yeah, I saw it. Buddy, are you okay? You didn't get banged up, did you? And where the hell are you right now?"

"No, I'm fine. They put us in a hotel as far away from the airport as possible. The crew's fine. One of the girls has a twisted ankle. Nothin' else. But my head's a mess, man."

"All right, pal, now listen," Brad interrupted, knowing how stressed Gradin really was. "If you aren't already doing it, sit down, lie down, whatever. Take some long, deep breaths. You're gonna get through this, buddy. I know it looks really bleak right this minute, but it's gonna be okay. Trust me."

"Yeah, yeah, yeah, I know. But damn it, Brad, why me? I'm always careful to a fault. There we were, rolling down the runway, and in a heartbeat, we were bouncing through the weeds."

"Whose leg was it?" Brad asked in an effort to shift Gradin's attention from the trauma to the details.

"The captain's, a guy named Danny Purcell. He's a good stick. It was so weird. We had just passed the 80-knot check, when 'BAM,' the rudder kicked full right. Even when I'm not flyin', I ride with my feet on the rudders, old habit from the P-3, I guess. The pedals *locked* all the way to the right. No amount of pressure was going to bring 'em back.

"Danny did a great job. Instantly slammed the power levers back and got the reversers in. We hadn't gone a hundred yards before we hit a ditch and knocked the gear off. Then, in slow motion, we pivoted to the right and slid up against an embankment. Noisy as hell.

"The rest is a blur. I think we did it all by the book. Shut 'em down, did the 'EVACUATE, EVACUATE, EVACUATE.' Danny and I went out through the cabin. The only problem was that with the gear gone, we were sitting right on the ground. The slides just got in the way. The people who went out over the wing probably had a much easier time of it. I actually went all the way to the back. Helped a couple of people through the over-wing hatches. I made sure everyone was off, then went out the left aft exit. By then, the emergency equipment had arrived, so we had good light."

Brad responded empathetically to keep Gradin talking. "Danny's a great leader. He even grabbed his coat on the way out. There was no question about who was in charge. He and the flight attendants had herded everybody away from the airplane.

"A couple of fire guys went back on board to look for strays. The fire boss quizzed me about the condition of the aircraft. Amazingly, it seemed to be in pretty good shape. We couldn't smell any fuel. Everything was shut down, and it was kind of eerie.

"A couple of Omega trucks showed up. Our station manager was there, and he worked with Danny and the flight attendants to tend to the folks. It took quite a while to get everyone back to the terminal because they had only one ten-passenger van available."

"Did the fuzz show up?" Brad asked.

"No, the only FAA guy was the tower supervisor, and I think he was just trying to get an idea of how long they needed to keep the airport closed.

"The station manager was stellar, man. After all the passengers were out of the area, he got the crew together, thanked us for our professionalism, and they even allowed us to get our bags off the airplane. Then he loaded us on the van and had the driver take us all the way out to the Sheraton Riverfront. They had the rooms all set up and even brought the room keys out to the van, so we didn't have to troop through the lobby—we went in the back.

"They set aside a small conference room for the crew. We all went to our rooms and got to make one phone call, then went to the crew room to debrief with Danny."

"So, Alice knows, right?"

"Yeah. She's driving down here. She was sure that her parents could take care of the kids."

"Good. That'll help you to have her there."

"Well, yeah. But there's a story there, too," Gradin said morosely.

"Oh, ouch." Brad winced fearfully.

"Back to the crunched airplane. Danny was really good with the crew. He made sure that no one was over-traumatized—plenty of hugs, pats on the back, and strong assurance that everyone did a great job.

"Then he gave a brief summary of what happened in the cockpit. There wasn't much to it. Ops normal until the rudder went hard over. The flight attendant on the back jump seat said she heard a pretty loud 'bang' just before we swerved off the runway. Of course, that was news to us, and it may prove to be a big piece of the puzzle.

"We all went back to our rooms and wrote down exactly what we remembered. It was pretty simple, just weird. I guess that the ALPA team is coming over from Seattle right now.

We'll meet with them in the morning. End of story." Gradin exhaled deeply.

"Well, pal, that's an amazing story, and I can certainly understand how tripped out you are, but you know how much worse it could have been, right? If you'd gotten that hard-over rudder any time after you did, you would have been toast!" Brad consoled his friend. "It would have been a totally uncontrollable situation."

"Yeah, you're probably right," Gradin mused. "Any time later and we would have snap-rolled into the ground. Okay, I'll try to keep that one in mind."

"There's an odd twist to this, too," Brad continued. "I got a call from Andy Caldwell last week. I guess the company is under real pressure to take some action to counter the number of crew-related incidents we've been having. We're way behind the curve in taking a hard look at the human factors side of this issue. Anyway, he asked me to be a member of the CRM steering committee. First meeting is Monday in Memphis."

"Well, that's very cool. I'm glad you're doing that, but there wasn't a human factor in what happened tonight," Gradin insisted. "This was purely mechanical."

"Think a second," Brad cautioned. "What was the outcome? An aircraft accident in which everyone involved walked away unscathed. Sure, it was precipitated by a mechanical failure, but the human response to that failure was flawless. Why is that? Would a 737 crew from a developing country have been as successful? I'm not so sure.

"What I'm saying is that your training, your inherent skills, your teamwork, leadership, and everyone's personal discipline all contributed in a big way to a very favorable outcome. Classic CRM."

"Yeah, okay, I get it. We were great." He paused. "Other than that, Mrs. Lincoln, how was your flight?" Gradin was forced to grin. "To paraphrase Yogi, *we were real lucky we didn't make the wrong mistake.*"

"Ha! And you didn't! Now, call room service. Have a burger and a couple of beers. Alice will be there in a flash," Brad said, then remembered to ask, "What was that you were alluding to about Alice?"

"Ah, man, I can't. I'm fried. Let's do that one later." Gradin's voice trailed off.

"Right. Get some rest, pal." Then in his deepest baritone, Brad went on, "And your honor, let the record show that on the night in question First Officer Gradin Jones performed flawlessly. His consummate skill and enormous valor brought great credit to his family, his community, Omega Air Lines, and the United States of America. Amen."

"Stuff it, turkey."

"Call when you get work." Brad's gusto gave way to fatigue, and he was asleep in his chair.

Chapter 5

JUST A DREAM

The long, sleek kayak sliced through the water, gaining speed with each powerful stroke. Brad dug harder and faster until the craft lifted out of the water and continued to accelerate. A 727 roared inches over his head, then disappeared into the clouds just as an Omega 737 skidded across the water below and slammed into the shore.

Brad could see Dick Hamlin jump out of the cockpit window and disappear into the trees. Then the left aft door sprung open, and Gradin bounded out.

A heavy weight pressed into Brad's midsection while a soft, fragrant mask enveloped his face.

"Hey," a distant voice whispered, "you winning the war?" Brad's orientation returned before he opened his eyes. Audrey's hands were touching his face, and Admiral's head rested expectantly in his lap. "Maria Shriver? King Kong? What are you doing in my dream?" he said with a smile. Then, with eyes fully open, "Oh, no. That's you, Audrey and Admiral, my two leading characters."

"Well, from the twitching and moaning, I have my doubts about that," Audrey responded, stepping back and looking down at her husband.

"Yeah, it was pretty erotic if you get off on Boeing airplanes hurtling around out of control. Wow, that was a weird one." He righted himself and shook his head. "What time is it? Sorry I wasn't standing at attention when you came in. I guess the admiral let me doze off."

"Brad, that's okay. You had a really early get-up in Fairbanks, didn't you?"

"Yeah, we were airborne by 1:00 a.m., so my wake-up call came almost twenty-four hours ago. And the trip was a real disaster. So bad that I got a call from my favorite member of the Omega Board of Directors."

"Daddy called? He called specifically to talk about your flight?"

"He did indeed. Seems that his friend Ted Meacham called to complain about the Omega service today."

"The governor of Alaska? Why? What happened?" she asked with concern.

"Well, it really wasn't anything all that significant. If we'd gotten him to Juneau, I'm sure we never would have heard about it." Brad went on to explain the entire sequence of events. He was left doubting his own effectiveness in the decision-making process. It hadn't been one of aviation's finest moments.

Audrey sat listening patiently, but her eyes began glazing over, and her head nodded abruptly several times. He ushered her gently into the bedroom, and within moments they had both drifted off to sleep with Admiral sprawled comfortably at the foot of the bed.

Brad and Admiral slipped quietly out of the room and closed the door. Audrey lived for these lazy Saturday mornings, which meant that they wouldn't be seeing her for a couple of hours yet. He made coffee, and Ad wolfed down his morning ration, then they headed down the cul-de-sac, across the road, and along the path to the beach. *How ironic,* he thought. *Twenty-four hours ago, you couldn't see 100 yards across this water. Now it's severe clear. Timing is everything,* he reminded himself. Admiral bounded after a flock of gulls pecking in the foam of a receding wave while Brad found his favorite human nest, well sheltered, with a great log backrest, a cradle for the coffee, and perfect exposure to the sun. He unfolded the morning paper and reluctantly gazed at the dark photo of a 737 perched awkwardly in the Eastern Washington tundra.

The headline read OMEGA STRIKES AGAIN. Rather than open with a description of the accident, the writer began by recounting the well-known catalog of mishaps Omega had experienced recently; all those from the awful summer of '87 and quite recently a potential disaster in Memphis when a 727 mistakenly lined up to land on a taxiway filled with airplanes waiting to depart.

Finally, the article went on with a boilerplate description of the prior night's mishap in Pasco. It concluded by suggesting that though mechanical failure might have been a factor, the FAA would be paying particular attention to the possibility of pilot error as the causal factor.

Brad grimaced at the reality of Omega's recent record, and at how close he had come to being a player in another ugly incident. Poor Gradin. He was in the wrong place at the wrong time, plain and simple. Brad's flight could just as easily have made the headlines. If they hadn't made that ninety-two-seventy (a ninety-degree turn followed by a 270-degree turn) and landed safely, the only remaining option would have been to declare an emergency and, regardless of the visibility, fly an instrument approach all the way to touchdown. Especially with the Alaska governor on board, that would have triggered a media feeding frenzy.

But hey, like a thousand times before, he had cheated death, and he was forced to grin as his 200-pound wuss barked and lumbered away from every miniature wave that trickled along the sand.

He thumbed through the remainder of the paper, pleased to see that the Sonics had won. Cold coffee was his signal to head for home. Admiral insisted on bringing along the branch he had adopted and struggled to drag it through the blackberry vines that lined the trail. Once in the clear, he pranced along with his prize as though he had slain a grizzly.

A little Mercedes SL sped by, then braked, swung around, and pulled up alongside them. The head and broad shoulders of John Williams, his stockbroker, poked out of the window. "Hey, Bradley Blue, glad to see that it wasn't you," he chuckled. "What happened over in Pasco last night?"

"Top o' the mornin', John. Nah, I had the good sense to get home before that happened." Admiral lay down and began gnawing on his branch. "It looks to me like an uncommanded rudder," Brad went on.

"A what?"

"Yeah, look at this picture," Brad said, unfolding the paper to the front page. "See how the rudder is deflected way over to the right?" Then, incredulous, he looked again. The rudder was perfectly aligned with the vertical stabilizer. Gradin had explicitly noted that the rudder was still deflected when they left the scene.

Brad quickly folded the paper, stunned at the possibility of tampering. Then, lamely, he said, "Something fishy happened over there, John. I happen to know that the rudder deflected without pilot input. There was no way they could keep the aircraft on the runway."

"Well, damn, don't you guys train for that kind of thing?" John persisted.

"Hell, no. That isn't even supposed to be a possibility. I'm only guessing here, John," Brad waffled, knowing that he had already said far more than he had intended to. "Pilot error is always the easiest conclusion. A real thorough look at these things almost always uncovers some mitigating factors. It'll be interesting to see what they find."

"Omega stock sure will take a hit. And God, it's already in the toilet, down fifty percent since the merger."

"Yeah, by late next week, it should be a great buy. Check in with Audrey; she makes all those decisions." He shrugged.

"She'd have to have pretty big balls to do it, but I'll tell her I got a hot tip."

"Thanks, big guy. Drive safe," Brad said as he scratched Admiral's head and continued toward home, the shock of Omega's perilous circumstance pulsating in his head.

Chapter 6

BACKGROUND

Brad threw the newspaper on the table, poured another cup of coffee, and leaned against the counter. "Wanna hear the rest of the Pasco story?" he asked Audrey as she looked up from her research notes.

"Ah, so you do know more."

"Well, I didn't until Gradin called after you and I talked last night. He was the copilot."

She removed her glasses and sat stunned for a moment. "Jesus Christ! Is he okay?" She leaned forward. "Brad, what really happened over there?" she asked, her concern for Gradin apparently forgotten.

Omitting his suspicion about the rudder, he spilled the story in exquisite detail. Even though Audrey had more information about the Omega accident than any reporter in the state, he didn't even consider that she would use it. That, along with the inside view of the company's financial peril, which he knew she'd received from her dad, was off-limits.

··· — — —··· — — —··· — — —··· — — —··· — — —···

Brad rambled on about CRM. His description of the United DC-8 accident, intended to help Audrey understand the genesis of CRM, had gotten him started. The story was both simple and inexplicable.

Brad became more and more agitated as he described the bumbling of the crew, enough so that Audrey sat a little straighter and listened more attentively. Admiral even perked his ears and gazed expectantly at his hero.

"So there they were, running on fumes, and the captain instructed the engineer to call the United ground personnel in Portland and advise them that they would be landing in fifteen minutes with 4,000 pounds of fuel. That took up another three or four minutes. Then—goddamn, I just get so steamed at this—then he sent the engineer back to the cabin to ensure that everything was in order for landing. When he returned to the cockpit at 6:01, he reported that the cabin would be ready in *another two or three minutes*."

Audrey's interest waned, but Brad pressed on, unaware, recounting how first one, then the other engine ran out of fuel. Ten people died in the landing . . . a miracle that anyone on board survived.

The failure of the second officer to communicate had prompted the painful birth of CRM in commercial aviation.

CRM would be a hard sell at Omega for that exact reason. The company always had been, and many expected that it always would be, "The Captains' Airline." The culture at Pacific had been so different. It was much more egalitarian, with a great deal more mutual respect and camaraderie in the cockpit. And that led to better outcomes when things went wrong. In fact, as he thought about it, there was a great story about a Pacific 727 with a landing gear problem more serious than the United DC-8's.

Brad told Audrey the old Pacific legend. It had taken place in Minneapolis several winters before. The right main gear assembly actually did fail to extend. But the outcome was so different. They went through the emergency checklist and landed with only two of the three gear extended. It was a little rough, and for two weeks, the airplane was out of service for repairs, but by any measure, it was effective teamwork. CRM before its time.

He smiled in recalling another story, this one from Pan Am in the old days. When Audrey asked what there was to smile about, he said, "Seems that a captain had a heart attack and died on a transatlantic flight to Paris. The copilot took over and landed without incident. As crews congregated in the international lounge, the captains huddled together and marveled that the copilot was able to take over for the deceased captain. The copilots were equally surprised that the copilot even noticed the captain was dead."

"Gallows humor." She rolled her eyes.

As though he needed to make a point, Brad pressed on. "The Pan Am captains' perspective certainly reflects the attitude at Omega. When my friend Ray Snyder checked out as captain on the 737 in Dallas, he stopped by the chief pilot's office to introduce himself. In the course of the conversation, Ray commented that he was sure he would learn a great deal from the Dallas copilots. The chief pilot, ol' Buzzer Bradley, held up his hand to stop Ray. 'No copilot can ever teach an Omega captain anything,' he growled." End of conversation.

He shared the anecdotes with Audrey but could see her interest had tanked. She heaped the last fragment of bagel with cream cheese and somehow fit it in her mouth. Then she gathered up the dishes and headed for the sink, where she added them to the growing collection.

"Wanna help me in the garden for a while?" she asked on her way into the bedroom.

"Your secret garden, maybe," he said, as he ran and gently tackled her onto the bed. "This bush definitely needs some attention," he whispered, slipping a hand under the elastic band of her shorts.

"No, the bushes outside," she insisted as she struggled free and left the room.

Chapter 7

TO MEMPHIS

Brad settled into his seat on the Sunday nonstop to Memphis as his emotions swung between hope for Omega and gloom for Audrey and Brad. He was convinced that the formation of the CRM steering committee was a very positive sign. He also knew it would be a struggle to drag the company, kicking and screaming, into the twentieth century. Omega's staid old Southern perspectives made George Wallace look progressive. A facelift wouldn't do it; a revolution was required.

As he rummaged through his briefcase looking for the NTSB report he had been assigned, the flight attendant placed his drink on the armrest tray separating the two first-class seats. Employees were always upgraded to empty seats in front, and apparently, this was Brad's lucky day. The girl asked if there was anything else she could get him, holding his eye a moment too long. Then, in a deliberate display of her profile, she moved languidly back toward the galley.

... — — —... — — —... — — —... — — —... — — —...

Chance of a lifetime, he thought, rapidly shaking his head to dislodge the prurient image.

His right thumb bent and released the pages of the NTSB report one at a time until the heading ANALYSIS AND CON-CLUSIONS appeared. *Nothing surprising here.* The crew had failed to activate the heating elements in the pitot probes, the pencil-thin protrusions on the nose of the aircraft that measure the impact pressure of the air passing over the aircraft in motion. Without heat, the pitot probes gradually iced over and provided the crew with erroneous airspeed and rate-of-climb indications. Because the airplane was so unusually light—no passengers, cargo, or long-range-fuel load—greater speed and climb rate were not unexpected.

The familiar gentle jolt signaled the aircraft's movement away from the gate. Out of habit, Brad reached for the seat buckle and gave it another tug. Then, right on cue, the flight attendant began her breathy recitation of safety instructions that were so dutifully ignored by the jaded passengers in the first-class cabin. He felt some comfort knowing that the curtain was rising on another well-scripted performance in the cockpit.

His eyes returned to the accident report and the description of the moment of confusion that occurred as the crew completed the before-takeoff checklist. Though Northwest apparently had slightly different procedures than Omega's, Brad could imagine the sequence of events happening in the cockpit as they taxied out. The second officer read the checklist, and the two pilots responded.

The anomaly began when the second officer called out "bugs," the airspeed indicator cursors. Without waiting for the appropriate response from both pilots, he skipped "ice protection" and called "pitot heat" instead. Despite the omission, the first officer recited his lines correctly and said: "off and on." Then he interrupted the flow of the checklist to ask the captain whether or not they needed engine heat.

The cockpit voice recorder (CVR) didn't detect an oral response from the captain. However, the investigators surmise that he may have given a nod or hand signal because the CVR did detect the sound of five clicks, sounds consistent with the positioning of five switches. The conclusion was that the first officer positioned the three engine anti-ice switches on, and the two pitot heat switches off, a reversal of the normal sequence, then returned to the task of positioning the airspeed cursors. Brad realized that just two misplaced switches the size of household light switches had led to disaster that night.

The sensation of the power reduction as the jet leveled off was nearly imperceptible, but Brad urgently released his seat belt and headed for the front lav even before the seat belt sign went off. When he returned, another scotch and soda was waiting along with a glass full of peanuts. *Very special treatment*, he mused. As he lifted the glass, a winking smiley face drawn on the napkin grinned back at him.

"Dinner this evening, Mr. Morehouse?" the sweet Southern drawl inquired. "You have a choice of either chicken or steak."

Dallas. She has to be Dallas-based, he thought. Only in Texas could she have perfected the long red fingernails and perfectly coifed blond hair, layered makeup that obscured her youth, and the smock drawn tightly around her very slender waist.

"Uh, yes, please, uh, Danielle," he responded, after glancing at her name tag. "Chicken would be great, thanks."

"And to drink?"

··· — —···— — —···— — —···— — —···— — —···

"Water would be good. And a glass of white wine, too, please."

"Yes, sir!" she responded in mock deference. "Coming right up."

Brad shook his head to suppress the images of her in an amorous clinch. He held the accident report with both hands, forcing himself to concentrate. Thus far, it seemed clear. The first officer had simply placed the pitot heat switches in the wrong position. Pilot error, end of discussion.

However, he remembered vividly that the first captain he flew with at Pacific had jokingly made the comment, "Guys, it ain't a mistake until all three of us do it." *In other words, we back one another up, like the pitcher dropping back behind the plate to cover for an errant throw home.* Many of the instructor flight engineers coached the second officers to always look and verify the switch position as they read the checklist for the crew. It wasn't policy, just technique.

Several years prior, PBS' NOVA had done a special on the growing number of CRM training programs in the airline industry. The show took a pretty thorough look at the programs at United and Continental and several European carriers. Most striking, however, was the brief interview with the senior Omega captain, some management guy. There he was, all decked out in his perfect double-breasted uniform, speaking to the world. "We don't need CRM because we hire the best pilots in the world, and our captains can handle any difficult situation that may arise."

Well, the past year had proven what a myth that was. The FAA was crawling all over Omega, trying to find cracks in the levee. The Friday evening crunch in Pasco would certainly put more stress on the dam. Brad realized how much pressure the steering committee would likely feel to come up with some innovative solutions. *And God, poor Gradin,* he thought. *He's really going to be under the gun. I need to remember to give him a call.*

Back to the accident. Why was there all that confusion during the execution of the before takeoff checklist? That question raised other questions about the purpose of a checklist in general. Was it really a *check* list—a list read to check that everything for a particular maneuver or phase of flight was already complete? Or was it a *to-do* list, in which every necessary action was completed in response to the prompt in the checklist?

Hmm. Brad thumped his fingers on the tray table. What are the chances that by having pitot heat and engine heat next to each other on the checklist, there was an inherent risk that the crew would reach for one, hit the other, and end up with a switch in the wrong position? The Northwest copilot had responded to the checklist by combining the two and saying "off and on." Was he reaching up and positioning the switches in response to the checklist, or was he merely confirming that the switches were already properly positioned?

The fact that the accident investigators found the switches positioned opposite of the response given by the copilot raised more questions than anyone could answer after the fact. Obviously, there had been confusion. Without dissecting all of the possibilities, Brad wondered if there was simply a better way of constructing and conducting checklists to avoid that sort of mistake. Good stuff for the committee.

Enough already, he thought, closing the report. He sipped his wine, relaxed back in his seat, and recalled the poor performance of his own crew just days before. *What could I have done, acting effectively as the junior guy, that would have contributed to a better outcome?*

The answers weren't obvious. Brad closed his eyes and let the scene unfold again in his mind. But the most consistent image was that feisty L.A. flight attendant. What was her name? He didn't recall, but he had saved the crew name roster and left it in his flight bag. *Ah, to be single again,* he thought as he dozed off.

The cabin chime sounded. He awoke and looked up to see the seat belt sign illuminated. The nose of the airplane pitched down just slightly, and the noise level diminished a bit, indicating a power reduction. The descent into Memphis had begun, which ordinarily meant that about twenty minutes remained in the flight. His dinner tray and linen were gone, replaced by a glass of ice water and a fresh napkin.

"Enjoy your nap?" asked the now-familiar voice. "You were gone for quite a while."

"Oh, hi. Yeah, airplanes do that to me." He smiled, sitting upright and stretching his arms. "I miss anything important?"

"Only the ice cream sundae, but I saved one for you. Any interest?"

"Ah, what a way you have with men. And since you insist, it would be rude of me to decline."

"The works? Coffee?"

"Coffee, black, and no whipped cream on the sundae—that stuff is fattening," he said with mock seriousness.

"Back in a flash."

Easy pickings. Brad shook his head.

Thirty seconds later, the new tray arrived accompanied by two mini-bottles of Baileys.

- - -- — — —--- — — — —--- — — — —--- — — —--- — — —---

"I thought you might like a little extra treat," she teased. "It's good in the coffee, on the ice cream—lots of ways, really."

"Really? Hmm, I'll give it a try."

"Anything else?" she asked, still smiling.

Oh, I get it. Anything else, like maybe your phone number? "Uh, no thanks, Danielle. You have surpassed my wildest expectations. Why don't you take the rest of the day off?"

"I wish." She winked and glided back toward the galley. She was forced to grab a seatback to steady herself as the plane suddenly seemed to drop, followed by a much more rapid descent. An audible rumbling and buffeting caused by the speed brakes—wing panels that can be deployed from the upper wing surface to disturb the airflow and reduce lift— could be heard.

Brad grinned to himself, imagining the scene in the cockpit. For some reason, it had become necessary to descend faster. It was likely that either the controller or the pilot flying had miscalculated, and now the crew had to use the speed brakes to reach the assigned altitude at a specific point. Good pilots held themselves to a standard in which they planned and executed a descent so that it felt seamless to the passengers; no abrupt movements or changes. In their humorously competitive world, using the speed brakes to comply with an altitude restriction was a sign of failure too. Unlike the incident in which Alex had blown through an assigned altitude and risked causing an accident, this was a minor miscalculation. The sudden drop, however, had been a dead giveaway. Oh, well. You screw up, you buy the beer, Mr. Copilot.

Chapter 8

THE COMMITTEE

Memphis was an Omega beehive, particularly at the Airport Holiday Inn, where Brad was staying along with several hundred other Omega pilots. He smilingly acknowledged several familiar faces in the lobby, then dragged his bag and briefcase to the desk to check in.

"Bradley Blue. Hey, buddy," a big voice boomed from the archway leading to the cocktail lounge.

"Yo, Bronco. Give me a second." Brad signed the registration form and took the key to room 320. The clerk handed him a note marked *Urgent*. He stuffed it in his pocket and turned to his friend. "What's up, man? You take a bid?"

"Yeah, I'm going to the seven-three[11] in Dallas. Start school tomorrow."

"Dallas?" Brad asked. "You guys gonna move down there?"

"Yup. Sandy already has a job in an interior design firm downtown. She's really jazzed. I can do my reserve shtick at

... — — —... — — — —... — — —... — — — —... — — —... — — —...

Navy Dallas. It should be a good time for us. What're you doin' here?" Bronco asked.

"Oh, Andy Caldwell asked me to be on a committee to design a CRM program for the pilots."

"A what?" Bronco grimaced. "Oh, man, say it ain't so. You're not goin' over to the dark side, are you? CRM? What happened to the ol' 'kick the tires, light the fire' mentality? Where's that rugged individualism, that can-do spirit?"

"Well, that's just the point." Brad smiled. "It's those rugged individuals who are landing at the wrong airport, bustin' altitude, and shutting down good engines on takeoff."

"I'm not talkin' about those old-fart captains. I mean the hot-stick guys like us. We're invincible, right?"

"Ha! The FO[12] in Pasco certainly wasn't invincible, and he's one of the best sticks in the world."

"Oh, yeah? You know who that was?" Bronco asked soberly.

"I do. And you know him, too. I'm sworn to secrecy, but you'll hear pretty soon, I'm sure."

"Damn! What the hell happened? They blow a tire or something?"

"D'know. My understanding is that they just swerved off the runway for no apparent reason. It should be an interesting topic in your 737 school tomorrow. Of course, there will be 100 theories before the actual cause is known," Brad cautioned. "Well, it should be a pretty hot topic for a CRM committee, too," Bronco retorted. "I have to admit that you guys have your hands full after all that shit that's happened recently. Who else is on the committee? Anyone we know?"

"There are ten of us. I only recognized one name, Chester Bowles. You know him?"

"Name's familiar, but I can't place him."

"He's a zoomie, an F-16 guy. Played football at the academy—built low and strong like a fire hydrant."

"Uh-huh, I know who you mean. He does a lot of safety stuff for ALPA. Great speaker, dogged researcher. I think he's leading the effort to get a better rest facility on the DC-10. Wow, the company is really pullin' in guys from all sides on this issue, aren't they?"

"It sure looks like it. I'm the token squid and junior shit bird. I'll probably be the designated gopher. But it should be fun. Andy Caldwell seems like a stand-up guy. We even have a couple of eggheads, one from Harvard and another from UT."

"Okay, Your Excellency. Knock 'em dead," Bronco said as he turned and ambled toward the elevator. "Wish me luck."

"You'll do great. Just keep the shiny side down, and remember that the captain is always right."

Urgent, huh? He turned on the light and unfolded the note. "Call Joe Spears. 206-775-3456." *Uh-oh!*

He dialed the number. "Joe? Brad. What's up?"

"Trouble," Joe spat in disgust. "Looks like Audrey combined what you told her with things she knows from me and came up with an award-winning scoop about the imminent demise of Omega Air Lines. It ran on the KSEA Sunday evening news, and she delivered it herself."

"What? She wasn't scheduled to work tonight." Then the greater significance of the incident hit him. "Goddamn! I am really sorry, Joe. I told her all that stuff was off the record." He collapsed on the bed in disbelief.

"No, no, don't worry about that. If anyone is responsible for her loose lips, it's me. I raised the girl." Joe paused to think. "Listen, let me handle it. This is a father-daughter thing, and I can afford to be a lot more blunt than would be wise for you. I knew she was ambitious, but she's done this at family expense, not to mention the damage to a great but struggling company."

"Fuck!"

"Indeed."

They were both silent for a moment. "Brad, I'm sorry," Joe finally said. "This isn't the girl you married. She is a very good newscaster, but her career seems to be consuming her. I understand how disappointed you must be."

"Yeah," was all Brad could muster.

"Well, now that I've ruined your evening, try to get some sleep. And hey, how is your buddy the copilot doing? Is he okay?"

"Yeah, the crew came out of that pretty much unscathed—physically, anyway. But you can imagine what a heyday the FAA will have with those guys. It's always pilot error. He insists that it was an uncommanded rudder, but you know how hard that will be to prove."

"Shit! Boeing will fight this one to the death."

A gray and drizzly Monday morning enveloped Brad as he squeezed his way onto the 6:30 shuttle bus to the Omega training center. Flight bags were stacked high on the front seats, guys were standing in the aisle, and he was forced to perch near the door and grip the entry rail for support. *God, 4:30 a.m. Pacific time,* he realized. *This is brutal.*

The ride was only three or four minutes in rush-hour traffic along Airport Boulevard. Omega headquarters was located on a sprawling corporate campus of red brick buildings, and the training center occupied a brand-new structure across from the main entrance. The bus gingerly maneuvered to the front portico, where it disgorged thirty-five pilots and one maintenance technician.

"Executive seminar?" a voice asked as Brad waited for a chance to tip the driver. Alex Freeman, the copilot from the ill-fated Fairbanks trip, confronted him in a mocking tone.

"Hey, Alex, hi. Oh, this?" Brad asked, sheepishly holding up the black leather briefcase. Everyone else was lugging standard pilot gear, heavy macho flight bags crammed with charts and manuals. "Yeah, it looks like Omega is finally creeping into the twentieth century. They're creating a CRM program, and Andy Caldwell wants me to contribute my two cents."

"Hmmf, two cents might be about right," Alex said over his shoulder as he squeezed through the glass door into the foyer.

"Whoa, wait a second. What's that all about?" Brad insisted as he caught up. "You pissed?"

"Damn right I'm pissed. You really dropped the ball during the level-off Friday. Why the hell didn't you say something sooner?"

Brad stared at him in disbelief. "Alex, where does it say that the second officer will remind the copilot to level off at the assigned altitude? Jesus. Gimme a break!"

"A good SO[13] woulda caught it, or didn't they teach you that in Blue Angel school, Hotshot?"

"Ohhhh, I get it. This is one of those *trash-hauler* versus the *jet-jock* conflicts. A little ego thing, huh, Alex?"

"Yeah, you've got the fuckin' ego, that's for sure," Alex said, then disappeared into the crowd jamming the elevator.

Brad stood silently watching as the doors closed, then finally noticed the traffic moving toward the cafeteria and melted into the gaggle. He stowed his briefcase on the shelf inside the door, grabbed a tray, and took his place in line.

He took a calming breath and smiled. The view was spectacular. *Ah, another candy store, full of fresh, young talent,* he thought as he watched dozens of beautiful new-hire flight attendants bustling around with an air of importance. That explained why so many guys were lingering at the tables nursing cold coffee and glancing not too subtly over the tops of their newspapers.

As humorous as the scene was, there was an even more intriguing dynamic at work. These girls, and a few cute guys, refused to make eye contact with the pilots in the room. They steadfastly stayed in their own little worlds. *What a different culture,* he realized. *At Pacific, we were all buddies; everyone knew everyone, and there was an inherent desire to get along, to be a good team. After all, you flew together for three or four consecutive days sometimes. You worked together, played together, and, for the most part, enjoyed and respected one another.*

Not so at Omega. With a network of eleven flight attendant bases and eight pilot bases spread all over the country—18,000 and 10,000 bodies, respectively—crews often changed on every leg. A pilot could literally fly with a flight attendant once and never see that person again for his entire career. And the cockpit door was an impenetrable barricade for so many of them. It was amusing to speculate what they might imagine was going on up there.

Breakfast was brief, punctuated with competitive banter and incessant rumors. Today it was "747s by next March." Omega had had that airplane a decade ago and had gotten rid of it, Brad recalled. Not likely that it was coming back.

After all the greetings and salutations, he grabbed his coffee and muffin and set out to find the committee. Room 202 was a standard classroom with state-of-the-art audiovisual gear. A four-by-eight embedded screen lit up with "Crew Resource Management by OMEGA." Then, in small print in the lower-right-hand corner of the screen, "It's never too late." Brad nearly snorted out his coffee.

The room was arranged with three round tables and a dozen or so chairs. Several groups of people were clustered in various parts of the room, among them three women. Another good sign. He put his briefcase, coffee, and muffin on one of the tables and gravitated toward two guys engaged in a finger-wagging conversation up front. It looked to Brad like The Great Santini arguing with Howard Hughes.

"Brad Morehouse," he interrupted with an extended hand.

"Oh, Brad, welcome. Glad you could make it. I'm Jack Mumford, and this is Vinnie Pedoza," said the guy who looked like Santini. Pedoza was a burly rendition of a young Howard Hughes. Brad shook hands with both.

"Blue Angel, weren't you, Brad?" Jack asked. "Yeah, I was on the team in '83 and '84."

"Wasn't Max Cooper the leader during that time frame?"

"He sure was. In '82 and '83, so I got to fly with him one year. Great stick and a very funny man. I'm lucky to be alive," Brad spat with false machismo.

■■■ ■— — —■■■— — —■■— — —■■■— — —■■— — —■■■— — —■■■

"I know the rascal well," Jack retorted. "He was my room-mate one year at the academy, so I know what you mean about potential fatality. Where is he now? Any idea?"

"I think he became CAG[14] on the *Eisenhower*."

Vinnie stood with his arms folded over his chest, a wry grin on his face. "You candy-ass fighter jocks are such pussies. All hat 'n' no cattle."

"Oh, eat your heart out, sheriff. Vinnie was a spook," Jack explained enthusiastically. "DEA. Spent his youth shootin' up bad guys in Latin America. Personally, I think he's still with the CIA. The sad part is the guy has never flown a real air-plane unless you call the Studebaker[15] an airplane.

"But enough of this frivolity. We'd better get this show on the road." Jack patted Vinnie on the shoulder, winked, and moved to center stage. "Good morning, everyone, I'm Jack Mumford. Andy Caldwell couldn't be here this morning—some lame excuse about checking on a 737 in Pasco." A mur-mur rippled through the room.

"Why don't you all take a seat. If you would, please fill out and attach a name tag—first names only, block letters so we all can read it."

People shuffled around, finding seats at the various ta-bles. A few brief introductions took place, and Jack allowed the spontaneous chatter to proceed for several minutes. Brad found himself at a table with Vinnie Pedoza, Marsha Hilbert—the committee advisor from Harvard—and Chester Bowles. When the room finally settled down, Jack went on.

"Thanks, and welcome. So you're probably all wondering why Andy called you here this morning, and I have to confess that it was my fault. Well, partially my fault, at least.

"It's no secret that Omega has experienced a spate of very-high-visibility incidents in the last eighteen months. Some people say that it's simply the luck of the draw. Others think that we're all totally incompetent. Of course, the truth is somewhere in the middle, and somewhere in the middle is definitely not where we expect our pilots to be.

"I said that this was my fault because just before Christmas, I went to Andy Caldwell with a proposal to create a state-of-the-art CRM program for Omega. In my spare time," he said, rolling his eyes, "I've been working with Marsha Hilbert at Harvard on a PhD in psychology. I should graduate some-time early in the next century."

"Jack, don't you need to get a bachelor's degree first? They don't really count your time at Canoe U, do they?" Vinnie teased. "God, talk about 'equal opportunity,'" someone followed.

"Quiet, quiet. Anyway, here we are. They want us to roll it out by midyear and have allocated $11 million to accomplish our task."

"Heavyyyyyy," someone commented.

"Heavy indeed." Jack went on. "This is a vital job, and quite frankly, you folks are going to be guinea pigs. Some of what you will experience is scripted for the benefit of our line pilots. Your feedback will be enormously important in developing a high-impact program."

"Hey, yeah, what happened out in Pasco, Jack?"

"I have no idea, Bobby. Andy will probably have the scoop when he gets back, but we probably won't know for months. But thanks for the segue, Bobby.

"So. What exactly is CRM?" Jack asked the group. The room was silent.

"It's when yuh smile 'n' ack nice," Bobby Clark piped up.

"Ah, ya gotta love it, folks. That's why we brought you here, Bobby, a little comic relief."

"Very little," Vinnie frowned.

"Hey, Bobby, what do most pilots use as birth control?" Andrea, the self-confident, flight-attendant instructor quipped.

"I dunno, it never seems to come up for me."

"Ha! You make my point. It's personality, Bobby. Personality! So you just do without, right, Bobby?"

"Without what?" he shrugged and looked blank.

"Uh, well, without CRM, of course. Without CRM. Back to you, Jack." Hand outstretched, she smiled.

With mock gravity, Jack went on. "If either of our honored guests," nodding in their direction, "would like to leave, now might be the opportunity. No need to waste any more of your valuable time.

"Of course, that little vignette was staged to demonstrate just how inane, petty, shallow, and base some highly professional, exceptionally experienced crew members can act. Great job, you two.

"So let me tell you how this is going to shake out. For starters, we'll go around the room and have you all introduce yourselves. But this is how that's gonna work. You will pair up with another person at your table, preferably someone you don't already know. Introduce yourself to that person. The person listening will take notes so that he or she can introduce you to the entire group. After five minutes, you swap roles. As you describe yourselves, you are required to make one false claim—one and only one, Bobby—about yourself that is *not* true.

"Any questions?" No one responded. "The lavs are out the door to your left. Take the first left down the hall. The coffee bar is the last door on that cross hall; twenty-five cents a cup on the honor system. Okay, it's 8:52. Be back at 9:02," he concluded.

Over time they would come to appreciate those hourly breaks, which Jack adhered to almost obsessively and which contributed to important outside conversation and networking.

Brad slid his chair back and stretched. "Brad, why don't we work together after the break?" Marsha Hilbert said, extending her hand. He stood up to acknowledge her. *She is an interesting-looking woman*, he thought. About five-three, early forties, short salt-and-pepper hair. And she looked as fit as a reigning world gymnastics champion; she even carried herself with that energy and bounce. "I'd enjoy that, Marsha," Brad said, shaking her hand.

"Okay, everybody, back to work," Jack cajoled. People broke up various conversations and made their way back to the tables. Discussions continued as the participants reluctantly paired up for their initial assignments.

Jack began over the murmurs. "I'm reminded of the story about the old Omega captain who died and found himself hurtling through space. Not surprisingly, he flew right past the pearly gates and ended up at the entrance to an industrial-looking building. The devil appeared, welcomed the old guy to hell, and said that he'd been expecting him for quite some time. He went on to explain that since the old captain would be spending eternity there, he would be given a choice of how to spend that time. The devil gave him a tour of the entire facility. There was a room where people were hanging upside-down by their toes, another where everyone was anchored in place while water dripped on their heads, and others with a variety of atrocious options.

"Finally, they came to a room filled with eighteen inches of human waste and sewage. However, the people inside were standing around, drinking coffee, and having a relatively enjoyable time. The old pilot opted for that alternative. He grabbed a cup of coffee and joined the conversation with a group of guys. About the time he introduced himself, the devil poked his head back in the room and said, 'Okay, everybody, the coffee break is over. Back on your heads.'"

"Oh, that really stinks, Jack," someone moaned. "Shitty joke," whined another.

"Sorry, but it's time to get back on your heads and make those introductions. Is everyone paired up?" Jack asked, scanning the room. "Good. One of you introduce yourself, and I'll let you know when five minutes is up so you can swap. Have at it."

For a group of aviation specialists, there was remarkable diversity. Two college professors, one flight-attendant instructor, and a pilot instructor/Air Force pilot. Two PhDs among the pilots—one a psychologist and the other a systems management expert. Three younger pilots. And several old hands dominated by a sly old fox known to everyone as Bobby.

Several breaks and hours later, Jack glanced at the clock and moved to center stage. "So did we get to everyone?" No one responded. "I'll take that as a yes. The rude little interruption that called me away during the introductions was a call from the boss out in Pasco. He's happy to hear that you made it today, and again, he expressed his gratitude.

"Interesting stuff about the accident Friday." He paused and rolled his eyes toward the ceiling in thought. "And this gets a little touchy for all of us," he went on. "Essentially, there is a classified and a non-classified version of the story, and I'm going to give you both. But we really have to keep a lid on the classified stuff. It will inevitably have serious ramifications for the whole company.

"So here it is. The crew performed magnificently, and Andy really wanted to emphasize that. On the takeoff roll, just after the eighty-knot check, they got an uncommanded right rudder. They exited the runway instantly at almost a forty-five-degree angle. The captain, Danny Purcell, stayed with the airplane, got the reversers out, and reversed heavily on the left to counter the continuing swerve to the right. Then they hit a ditch that severed all three landing gear, and after that, they were just along for the ride. Both guys were attempting to get left rudder in, but the pedals were locked full right.

"The evacuation was flawless, and the crew deserves enormous credit for getting everyone out without any serious injuries. Every indication is that the scene was really calm, almost surreal. And our ground team in Pasco was stellar. Even though they had only two vans, they got everyone back to the terminal within thirty minutes. Then the manager was able to get the crew out of the area and sequestered before the FAA showed up.

"Now the classified stuff. The feds seem to believe that either the crew induced the problem or that it resulted from a maintenance screw up on our part. After all the problems we've had recently, they simply aren't going to cut us any slack. That has a couple of ramifications. First, they will probably be really hard on the crew. Those pilots are going to have to endure a thorough review of every page in their training records. It will all culminate in a really tough sim ride[16] where the fuzz hold all the cards.

"But here's the kicker. If that uncommanded rudder had occurred thirty seconds later, we would have lost the airplane and everyone on board. And, unless there were an immediate and very obvious discovery of a manufacturing flaw, Omega would be toast."

"Ouch!" someone breathed.

"On that happy note, why don't we go to lunch? Just remember, the crew did great, and the airplane will be back in service in a couple of months. See you back here at 1:00."

Everyone sat in stunned silence before somberly struggling out of their chairs and out the door.

Chapter 9

BREAKDOWN

When they reconvened an hour later, the mood had lightened. New friendships took shape, and conversations ranged from Andrea's recent African safari to the quail population on the Texas ranch belonging to Loren Hughes, an Omega captain, and systems management PhD.

"Back on your heads," Jack commanded, referring back to his opening joke. He strode into the room, and people reluctantly moved toward their chairs. Chester Bowles knelt down and raised his stocky frame into a perfect three-point headstand.

"How long do I have to hold this?" he strained.

"I'll let you know," Jack responded, pretending to ignore him.

"Now, the task at hand. I sent several of you accident reports to review so you could provide us with a synopsis. Andrea looked at the Air Canada DC-9 in Cincinnati. Tell us about that one, Andrea."

···—■——■···—————■···—————————■···——————■···

Chester maintained his headstand for almost a minute, then gave up and slipped back into his chair unacknowledged. "Okay, well, most of you probably remember when this happened, and very likely several of you know more about it than I do." She painted a vivid picture.

"Air Canada Flight 797, a DC-9, was en route from Dallas to Toronto on June 2, 1983. At approximately 18:51, while cruising at flight level 330, three circuit breakers associated with the aft lav flush motor popped in rapid succession. The captain immediately made one attempt to reset them; however, all three popped again. He assumed that the flush motor had seized and took no further action.

"At 19:00, he attempted a second reset with no success. At that same time, a passenger in the aft of the aircraft smelled smoke and suggested to a flight attendant that it might be coming from the lavatory. She discovered light smoke in the lav, closed the door, and notified the senior flight attendant."

Andrea went on to describe how the senior flight attendant had gone to the lav, encountered dark smoke seeping from a seam in the wall paneling, and discharged an entire fire extinguisher in that vicinity.

The copilot went to the back but couldn't reach the lav because of the smoke. He returned to the cockpit at 19:04 and suggested to the captain that they descend. Moments later, the senior flight attendant entered the cockpit and told the captain that he didn't have to worry. "I think it's gonna be easing up," the flight attendant assured him.

The captain delayed the decision to descend for several more minutes until a variety of electrical anomalies began to occur. At 19:08:12, he declared an emergency, and at 19:09:05, they executed a clearance to descend to 5,000 feet for vectors

to Cincinnati. Approximately ten minutes later, flight 797 landed, stopped, and evacuated. Midway through the evacuation,
fire erupted in the cabin, killing twenty-three passengers.[17]

"Ugly," someone whispered.

"Yup, pretty ugly indeed. So what caused that to happen?"

"Stupidity." Bobby sneered.

"Right, Captain Clark. You obviously would have handled that one very differently. What would you have done,
and why?"

"Gotten the damned airplane down on the ground about
twenty minutes earlier, for starters."

"Good. And what would have prompted you to do that?"

"Jesus, Jack. The goddamned airplane was on fire. It ain't
rocket science."

"I understand that, Bobby, but how would you have
known that the airplane was really on fire? The senior flight
attendant, who, of course, is most familiar with functions in
the cabin, said that they didn't have to worry. It didn't sound
like a major emergency."

"Well, it sure as hell was!"

"Yeah, but the captain didn't seem to know that. He
wasn't afforded the 20/20 hindsight we have. He was never
told—nor did he ask—exactly what the senior FA had seen
and done. You probably agree that 'I think it's gonna be easing
up' was not particularly specific."

"But what about the copilot's suggestion that they go
down?" Chester asked.

"Yeah, it was one of those times where the captain
didn't really *hear* the concern being expressed. It leads me
to believe that what we really need to zero in on are key
elements of communication." Jack walked over to one of the

flip charts hanging on the wall and in big block letters wrote
COMMUNICATION.

Vinnie described an incident in which a new captain
painted himself into a corner during his initial check ride.

"Wow! So 'flawed decision making,' huh, Vinnie?" And
Jack scribbled DECISION MAKING on the chart.

"There actually are a couple of other important skills embedded in what you described, but I think I'll leave one of
those for Doctor Hennessey, psychology professor and advisor to the CRM committee, to discuss."

"Thanks, Andrea. That was a good synopsis. I'm sure we
could pick it apart even more, but let's move on to the Northwest accident Brad reviewed. Brad?"

"This one happened way back in December of 1974, and
I don't remember it getting a lot of press," Brad began. The
group was quick to anticipate the tragic outcome as Brad described the confusing events leading the 727 to spin out of
control and plant itself in a cornfield. He pressed on. "So the
accident investigators were able to uncover *what* happened,
but except for relating the second officer's omission of an
item on the checklist to some confusion about the position of
the engine and pitot heat switches, they didn't even attempt
to ask why those errors occurred."

"Bad headwork again," Jack asserted.

"Yeah, exactly—fatally bad. I may be getting a little off
track here, but I've always wondered where that catch-all
came from. In our business, when someone screws up, we
simply call it 'bad headwork' and move on. How often do we
ask *why* a guy failed to think more clearly?

"Specifically, what I'm wondering about is the placement
of the pitot heat and engine heat right next to each other on

the checklist. We don't do that at Omega. Look at this checklist." He held up his own tattered copy of the checklist and passed it around for people to see. "I may be reaching here, but what I'm wondering is whether or not the layout of a checklist is a significant factor in crew performance."

"Brad, excuse me for interrupting." Loren Hughes, the lanky, raw-boned cowboy captain, raised his hand as if to stop traffic. His erudite manner contrasted with his appearance.

"Those are exactly the issues my ALPA committee looks at very carefully. I think you are absolutely right to question the potential impact not only of the construction but the implementation of our checklists. Look at this," he said, pulling a similar checklist out of his saddlebag briefcase. "This is an Omega DC-8 checklist, and it isn't remotely similar to your 727 checklist. Aren't we all doin' the same things out there? I mean, we all raise the landing gear, retract the flaps, set the heading bugs, engage the auto-throttles—dozens of things that are the same on every airplane in the fleet. But here we are doing it one way on the Boeings and another on the MDs[18]. What do we have, nine airplane types? And every damned one has a different operating philosophy, checklists, procedures, and even training requirements. In terms of common sense, it's ridiculous, and from a systems management perspective, it's prehistoric." Loren was almost frothing.

"Hold it, guys, I don't get it," Andrea chimed in. "Isn't a checklist just a recipe? Does it really matter how it is arranged? Help me out here."

"Okay, perfect," Jack said, jumping to his feet and holding up both hands. "Now we're getting someplace. Brad, I know you had more, but I want you to save it for later. Thanks."

Brad shrugged and sat down.

"You are all raising key questions, and I want to let Doctor Hennessey give us his take on the importance of corporate culture in this discussion. The time is 1:56; be back at 2:06." He dismissed the committee for a coffee break, rechecked his watch, then stepped into the A/V room and dialed the wall-mounted phone. Even though he was hidden from sight, those who remained in the classroom could hear parts of the heated conversation. "I told you never . . . well, I could . . . this isn't the time . . . I can't . . . " Finally, he closed the door, and only muffled tones seeped out of the room.

Ten minutes later, as people returned from the break, Jack was intently engaged in conversation with David Hennessey. The prescribed 2:06 return time came and went. Every-one sat patiently waiting. Finally, Pat Finch chided, "Anything you two would like to share with the group?"

"Oops, sorry about that, folks," Jack responded. "David, why don't you go ahead and give us some background on corporate culture."

David languidly moved to center stage as Jack slipped into a chair at David's table.

"Well, as one of you has so aptly stated, this ain't rocket science. It's quite simple, really," David began. "Every corporation has its own distinct personality, and those personality traits permeate the way people do things in the entire organization. The more hierarchical the management structure, the more the personality of the company reflects that of senior management. "Take your president, Ron Brown, for instance. When Ron speaks in public, whether it's to the Memphis Chamber of Commerce or a group of new-hire pilots, he is always attired in a dark suit, starched shirt, and tie. So guess what? When our good friend Jack Mumford began today's meeting, how was he attired? Right. Dark suit, starched shirt, and tie. There are quite a few layers of management between Ron and Jack, so it's safe to assume that there are lots of suits between here and there," he said, pointing in the direction of the executive offices.

"Now, why is that important, you ask? It is not important in and of itself. But it is formal and highly structured, and therefore an indicator of a whole range of predictable, formal behavioral norms at Omega. There are a lot more 'mister' and 'misses' and 'yes, sirs' and 'no, sirs' around here. It's like one of my colleagues observed about UT. 'We're not a bunch of yes-men around here. When the boss says no, we all say no.' Classic top-down management."

Most of the group nodded assent.

"To a very large extent, that management style exists in the Omega cockpit as well. You haven't gotten the reputation for being 'The Captains' Airline' because you're all so handsome. Was it one of you who said to the copilot, 'When I want your opinion, I'll give it to you'?"

There were a few smirks.

"Well, yeah, that may have been me, but if it was, I was misquoted," Bobby chimed in as he leaned forward on his elbows. "I often tell an uppity copilot that he can be my sexual advisor. When I want his fucking advice, I'll ask for it!"

"Ooooh, harsh!"

"Point well taken, Captain. You obviously run a tight ship."

"There's that birth control thing again, Bobby," Andrea offered with a false grimace.

"You know, in all seriousness, David has a valid point here," Chester Bowles spoke up for the first time. "Ten years ago, when I was a new-hire engineer on the DC-8—this is when we had the Houston base—I went out to fly my first trip. Literally, this was my first trip on the payroll at Omega. So   I got to the cockpit, set things up, did my walk-around, read the checklist, and everything else expected of me, and it wasn't until we had taken off and reached cruising altitude that the captain even acknowledged me. He turned around, looked me up and down, and the very first words he spoke to me were, 'Well, Omega sure made a mistake when they hired you.' Needless to say, it was a very long trip."

"What's your point?" Vinnie deadpanned.

"Well, at least now I understand." Chester grinned. "I know I will never be *totally* useless. I can always be used as a bad example."

Pat Finch jumped in. "Yeah, I was a copilot there in Houston during that time, and Chess makes a great point," he commented. "The captains down there were such mavericks that all the copilots carried little black books where they wrote the idiosyncrasies of every captain in order to remember what to do the next time they flew with him."

"Okay, I'm in the dark again, guys. Like what things are we talking about here?" Andrea asked. "Who buys the beer? Who talks on the PA? What things?"

"No, these were essential operational things, like when to extend the flaps or gear, how fast to fly to the outer marker, whether or not to use reversers on landing, that sort of thing. Let me see if I can remember a specific oddity. Oh, yeah, lots of guys wanted the circuit breaker for the voice recorder pulled from the time you stepped into the cockpit 'til the end of the trip."

▪▪▪ ▬ ▬ ▬▪▪▪ ▬ ▬ ▬ ▬▪▪▪ ▬ ▬ ▬ ▬▪▪▪ ▬ ▬ ▬ ▬ ▬▪▪▪ ▬ ▬ ▬▪▪▪

"Aren't those things spelled out in your manuals?" Andrea persisted, wrinkling her brow. "Don't you just do what it says in the book? We do. We'd get fired if we didn't."

"That is exactly the point," Pat went on. "A rugged, can-do individual doesn't need a damned book to tell him how to operate *his* airplane. It's kinda like his good ol' John Deere tractor. You drive her around a little, get to know her, figure out the idiosyncrasies, and then just let 'er rip. Only a wimp would look at the book written by some kid who couldn't tell a tractor from a trailer hitch. Same with his good ol' reliable diesel eight[19]."

Brad smiled knowingly as he listened to this exchange. "Well, those guys need a good dose of Esther Hempelshmidt. She is number one on our seniority list; been around since Orville and Wilbur. Apparently, she had Cassius Clay—or Muhammad Ali, I guess it is—on a flight one time. As she did her final walk-through, she noticed that he didn't have his seat belt fastened. She asked him politely to buckle up.

"He came back with, 'Superman don't need no seat belt.' Without missing a beat, she wagged a finger in his face and said, 'Superman don't need no airplane either, so fasten your damned seat belt.' And he did. Sounds like those crusty old captains might learn something from Esther," Andrea concluded.

"I have no doubt that they would," Pat continued. "But the moment she was gone, they'd be right back to their old tricks. That's why they want the cockpit voice recorder disabled. They destroy the evidence before it even exists."

"Yeah, I see it a lot when I give line checks," Vinnie said. "These guys are chameleons. As soon as someone shows up to evaluate them, everything is done exactly by the book. It does get a little funny when you see that they've forgotten what the book actually says. It's often the copilot or engineer who saves the captain's bacon."

"Ahem," Dr. Hennessey smilingly interrupted. "As I was saying, corporate culture has a powerful influence on how flight crews do their business out there. And the problem with this hierarchical structure is that it often marginalizes the subordinate crew members."

"Oh, Jesus. It does what?" Bobby groaned. "Single syllables, please, Doc."

"It cuts the other guys out of the pack, Bobby, like they're just along for the ride—just there to jerk the gear, as you guys say. The copilot and engineer are often bumps on a log."

Bobby rolled his eyes. "As they should be," he muttered.

"Who is going to discuss the United DC-8 in Portland?"[20] Hennessey asked. "That will make my point."

"I'm ready." Kent Harvey stood and passed around copies of the accident report.

"On the night of December 28, 1978, United Flight 173 circled over Portland, Oregon, attempting to solve a landing gear anomaly and preparing for a possible emergency landing. The problem began as the crew extended the landing gear in preparation for landing to the west on runway 28L. Gear extension was accompanied by several unusual sounds and a noticeable yaw to the right."

He explained how ordinarily a series of lights illuminate when the landing gear handle is moved from the up to the down position. "You would expect to see three red lights— left gear, nose gear, right gear—immediately after positioning the handle down. The red lights indicate that the actual positions of the wheel assemblies do not match the position of the handle. However, within a second or so, the lights turn amber to indicate that the wheels are in transit from the up to the down position. Several seconds later, when each gear is down and locked in position, green lights illuminate to indicate a safe and successful gear extension. The crew did not see either the red or amber lights during the gear extension process, and only the nose gear down-and-locked green light illuminated in the process.

"The weather in Portland that evening, at 5:12 p.m., was clear and cold, and the approach controller authorized United 173 to maintain 5,000 feet and to hold in visual conditions southeast of the airport while they attempted to resolve the problem.

"The report indicated the following:

> For the next twenty-three minutes, while Portland Approach was vectoring the aircraft in a holding pattern south and east of the airport, the flight crew discussed and accomplished all of the emergency and precautionary actions available to them to assure themselves that all landing gear was locked in the full down position. The second officer checked the visual indicators on top of both wings, which extend above the wing surface when the landing gear is down and locked.
>
> "All three landing gear assemblies seemed to be fully extended.
>
> At 5:38, the captain initiated contact with the United Airlines maintenance center and discussed the issue with them.

> He reported about 7,000 pounds of fuel on
> board and stated his intention to hold for another
> fifteen or twenty minutes. He stated that he was
> going to have the flight attendants prepare the
> passengers for emergency evacuation.

"At no time throughout the entire scenario did the captain express any concern or even an awareness of the rapidly diminishing fuel quantity. In the 727, a smaller and more efficient airplane, the unwritten objective was never to land with less than 8,000 pounds of fuel. In a DC-8, they should be squirming uncomfortably with 10,000 or 12,000 pounds remaining. The captain, in this case, never seemed to have the big picture; he was almost obsessed with providing the flight attendants ample time to prepare for landing and possible evacuation. And the other two pilots failed to figuratively shake him by the collar to get his attention.

> At 5:50, he asked the flight engineer to prepare
> landing weight and speed calculations for a touch-
> down fifteen minutes later.
> The first officer responded, "Fifteen minutes?"
> To which the captain replied, "Yeah, give us 3,000
> or 4,000 pounds on top of zero fuel weight." The
> flight engineer then said, "Not enough. Fifteen
> minutes is really gonna run us short on fuel."

"But the captain simply couldn't hear the flight engineer. They ran out of fuel and crashed."

"What do you mean, the captain 'couldn't hear'?" Andrea demanded. "The engineer is sitting one foot behind him."

"Think of it this way, Andrea," Kent continued. "You are driving down a busy street with the kids in their car seats in back. You've worked all day, picked up the kids, and are headed for the store to get the cake for the birthday party you're hosting in less than an hour.

"A fire truck, with lights flashing and horns blasting, is maneuvering through traffic going the opposite direction when the baby begins to cry. And just at that moment, the third car ahead swerves to the right, hits the car next to it, slides on the rain-soaked street, and blocks traffic in two of the three lanes. Your four-year-old says, 'Mom, little Billy's finger is stuck in the car seat.' And you respond, 'Okay, honey, I'll take care of it in a minute.'

"You are totally focused on the cars ahead, on the oncoming fire truck, the slippery road, and the people jumping out of their cars to help. At that moment, your overwhelming need is to get to the store and get back home in thirty minutes. Your daughter persists, 'Mom, Billy's finger is bleeding all over the seat.' The crying gets louder, but you can't even hear it because you are so intent on getting through the traffic safely. You know the kids are securely strapped in their seats in back, and you are comfortable with that.

"That is just what the captain in Portland was doing. He was preparing for the possibility that the landing gear might collapse and that an emergency evacuation would be necessary. And he knew that the flight engineer was strapped safely in his seat tending to the fuel. He couldn't hear—probably more accurately, couldn't register—that the fuel was below the amount he had designated.

"Now, obviously, there is an equally important question about the engineer failing to be more assertive, but does that make sense about not hearing?"

"Yes, yes, it does," she replied thoughtfully.

BAM! The door flew open and slammed into the wall. "You son of a bitch!" a twenty-five-year-old, raven-haired beauty screamed as she rushed into the room. Spotting her prey, she flung her purse at Jack and ran to the table where he was seated. "I did exactly what you asked me to do. I called the doctor, and I made an appointment for today—and now my husband knows. Now the whole goddamned world knows!"

She lunged with both fists at Jack's head. Reflexively he caught her arms as she tripped on his foot, lurched forward, and tumbled with him to the floor under the table.

Everyone scrambled up and moved toward the table. Andrea yelled, "Donna! Donna, stop!" just as a muscular bear of a man walked purposefully into the room and bellowed, "Knock it off! God damn it, woman, get your ass out of here before you get yourself arrested!" He strode to the table, grabbed one of her arms, and yanked her to her feet.

Flushed and rumpled, Jack righted himself. "Donna, I, uh, well, I . . . "

"Shut up, asshole! I'll be taking care of you later," the big man growled as he dragged the woman by one arm out the door. Jack staggered feebly after them. "Donna, wait," he pleaded.

"Well, well, well," Patrick Finch said as he moved to the center of the room and took charge. "Nothing like a little office romance to liven things up. Andrea, would you please pick up that stuff from her purse?"

"Sure." Andrea moved over, knelt by the outside table, and picked up a dozen or so items. "She works in my office; she's one of our instructors. Let me run this down there. Maybe I can help in some way." She scurried out as the rest of the team sat mute and embarrassed.

Patrick continued. "So here is what I think we should do," he said. "We'll call it a day. Don't get too excited about how early we're breaking. Before happy hour, I want all of you to sit down in a quiet place and write down exactly what you saw and heard from the time the woman burst into the room 'til now. Get every detail you can remember. And don't talk to each other about it, at least not until you have it all written down. One last thing. Let's take care of poor ol' Jack. No outside chatter about this. Maybe he will fill us in tomorrow. See you same place, same time in the morning."

Chapter 10

GRADIN JONES

The blinking red light on the telephone cast an ugly tint on the chintzy furnishings when Brad returned to his room at the Holiday Inn. He went to the window and wrestled the heavy plastic curtains to one side. His room looked down on the courtyard, where plastic deck chairs were toppled, and leaves and a tree branch clogged the shallow end of the murky pool. The roar of departing jets echoed through the horseshoe-shaped structure incessantly. *Ah, the glamour of it all.* He sighed.

He eased himself into a chair and reflected on the day's events. *Pretty good for the most part; an interesting group of people, but the wheels really came off at the end. Was that woman for real? What the hell had Jack gotten himself into? He seemed like such a straight arrow, really, just like Robert Duvall in* The Great Santini, *the firm and resolute Marine. Well, nothing to do but write it down and get the whole skinny tomorrow.*

He extracted a pad from his briefcase and began a bullet list of the specific recollections he had. Twenty minutes later, he threw the pad on the desk and noticed the blinking message light again. He dialed zero and inquired. "Gradin Jones in room 412. Please call," he was told.

He wanted to be light and upbeat. "Gradin, how's it hangin', m' man?" he chortled. "An all-expense-paid trip to Memphis, I assume?"

"Yeah, not my idea of a dream vacation," Gradin responded. "The whole crew debriefs with flight ops tomorrow—Andy Caldwell and the gang."

"You got time for a beer?" Brad asked.

"Sure. I'm buyin'. Ten minutes in the lounge?" "Give me fifteen. I need to call Aud."

Brad slammed the phone down in frustration. *Why can't I ever reach that damned woman?* Audrey had flown to New York earlier in the day and registered at the Waldorf as planned. *The network certainly takes care of its affiliate newscasters when they are in town for indoctrination,* he groused to himself. A couple of times each year, the network took the rising stars from major markets to the Big Apple for a combination of training and schmoozing, everything from makeup tips to story-scooping techniques. *Audrey already excels in both,* Brad assured himself.

The happy-hour crowd was elbow to elbow at the bar. There were not many airline guys there because most of the Omega pilots staying at the Holiday Inn were involved in training of some sort. That usually meant eight hours of class and study until midnight. The training regimen was more like drinking from a fire hose than from a longneck Budweiser. Gradin and Brad were the exceptions tonight. They found a booth in the far corner and ordered two drafts.

"So, did you get out of Pasco at all before coming down here?" Brad inquired.

"Oh, yeah. They let us go right away. Alice and I drove home early Saturday morning. Not much sleep that night, though. I've never been through this. You just keep playing it through your mind over and over, wishing you could do it all again."

"Isn't that how they define insanity? Doing the same thing over and over, expecting a different outcome?"

"Yeah, that's what it feels like. I just can't believe it's me, Brad. Damn!" He winced before relaxing into a wry smile. "But it does happen to good guys, I know that. Did I ever tell you about my buddy John Hoskins up at Whidbey?"

"Not that I recall. Lay it on me." Brad hoped that Gradin would stop beating himself up. Distractions work. Pilots love their stories, and Gradin was off and running.

"This guy was the best stick in the world, knew the airplane inside and out: every diode, beta-follow-up cams, flight control servos, everything. The funny thing was that he acted just like Dennis the Menace. He had a shock of blond hair and looked about twelve years old, or at least he did a couple of years ago.

"Well, anyway, he was out in the pattern one day demonstrating a two-engine-out approach to a new guy. It's a pretty tricky maneuver with all that asymmetrical thrust—you just pull both engines on one side back to idle—so you hold the gear until you are in close and have the landing assured. True to form, John flew it perfectly, got in close—really close, I guess—then added power on all four and went around. One of the guys in back called to say that he heard something unusual on the go-around, and by then, John realized that they had forgotten the gear."

"No gear warning horn on the P-3?" Brad asked.

"Nope. That electronic monstrosity doesn't have one, only a one-inch-long warning light that is easily obscured by sunlight on the instrument panel. Anyway, John decided to land and have the airplane checked. And oh, what a surprise it was to step out and see that four inches were ground off all four blades of the number two prop. Ruined his whole day."

"Well, better than ruining his whole life."

"Yeah, shit happens even to the best of 'em."

"True, remember the Thunderbirds a few years ago? On the back side of a loop, the lead had a control malfunction and flew the whole team into the ground."

"Ouch! Yeah, I remember. Well, okay, my little excursion could have been worse."

"Much worse, Gradin! Much worse," Brad insisted, sipping his beer. "You didn't do anything wrong, man, except maybe showing up for work. Think what would have happened if that rudder had gone nuts just after liftoff. You wouldn't be here right now, and, frankly, that's what worries me. Why did it do that, and when's it gonna happen again?"

"Remember the TWA 727 that fell out of the sky?"

"Vaguely, but that wasn't a rudder thing, was it?"

"No, but it very well may have been a Boeing thing, just like your deal may have been."

"Whoa, you've lost me, Brad."

"Okay, it's kind of a long story, but here it is. About two years after the incident, we had that TWA captain on the jump seat one day going from Las Vegas to Seattle, a guy named Hoot Gibson.

"Everyone from the media to the FAA speculated that the crew did something to induce a stall. They were at three-nine-oh[21], and that is max for the Studebaker; it flies like a wounded whale up there. In fact, now that I think of it, I've never been that high in the seven-two[22]. So people imagined that when they got up there, they were just wallowing along and that in order to get the nose down to accelerate, they might have decided to squeeze out just a tad of trailing-edge flap. But to prevent the slats from extending, too, they would have pulled the circuit breakers for all of the leading-edge device actuators.

"Now, Hoot insists that they did no such thing, but you can easily imagine the scenario. One guy leaves the cockpit while the other two are manipulating the flaps. He comes back and sees the circuit breakers out, resets them, the LEDs[23] pop out, that wing stalls, and the airplane rolls over and falls out of the sky."

"But the LEDs came out somehow, didn't they?" Gradin pressed.

"Yeah, apparently they did, but the crew insists, even to this day, that they didn't touch a thing, that the slats popped out on their own, that the latches failed spontaneously, that they hadn't touched either the flap handle or the LED circuit breakers," Brad went on. "And I found Hoot very convincing. I really do think that it was a mechanical fault."

"Hmmm." Gradin rolled his eyes and smiled.

"Part of the problem was Hoot's reputation. He's one of those guys who has no fear. He thumbs his nose at authority and convention, and everyone knows it. He regaled us with stories all the way to Seattle. The best one was a time on a night transcontinental flight he and the crew got out of their seats in the cockpit. The captain and engineer hid in the luggage bin, and the copilot wedged down behind his seat and the engineer's panel. They had turned off all the lights and dinged the new, young flight attendant to come up.

"When she opened the door and went in, the cockpit was dark and empty. She absolutely freaked out, ran through the cabin screaming. Great PR, huh?" Brad grinned.

"Then, of course, when the senior FA went up, everything was normal, and the crew denied the whole setup. Naturally, that didn't stop the story from adding to the Hoot Gibson legend.

"So when he fell out of the sky that day, it was easy to believe that it was just another of his high jinks gone wrong. And it *really* went wrong. It only took a couple of seconds for the airplane to accelerate into the transonic zone, where the shock wave blanked out all of the airfoils. So there they were, pointing straight down, yankin' the flight controls every which way," Brad said, mimicking the motion of someone frantically turning and pulling on the steering column. "And nothing worked."

"Can you imagine what was going on in back?" Gradin guffawed. "Ho-ly shit!"

"Not a pretty sight, I'm sure. Anyway, ol' Hoot finally had the presence of mind to throw the landing gear out, and that added enough drag to slow them enough that the airflow returned to the wings and tail. They were able to pull out at about 5,000 feet. They lost 34,000 feet. Damn near pulled the wings off the airplane. It was strike damage. That plane never flew again—it was overstressed so severely—but at least it flew long enough to let them land someplace."

"And they let that guy keep flyin'?" Gradin grimaced as he finished the last of his beer. "Most countries would have sent him to the gallows. Though now that I think of it, we had a guy do that in a P-3 one time."

"That sounds exciting," Brad said, signaling the waitress for two more beers.

"They were out on a pilot trainer with the outboard engine in the bag. The syllabus called for a slow-flight maneuver in that configuration, and they got the speed right back to the limit. Now here's the funny part. In all those years of flying the P-3, no one ever thought to compute the amount of lift created by the prop wash from the engines. It isn't much, but it's probably worth a couple of knots. So they must have turned into that dead engine, lost a little more lift, and all of a sudden, the whole wing stalled.

"The airplane just rolled over on its back and split-S[24]. They only lost a couple thousand feet. I had the duty that day and met the airplane when they taxied in. The crew's eyes were popping out of their heads. 'We just spun this damned airplane!' the first guy, one of the aft observers, blurted as he clambered down the ladder and kissed the tarmac. When the IP[25] explained the whole thing, it wasn't quite as dramatic, but from that day forward, he was always known as Spin Spencer, the only guy in the world to ever spin a P-3."

They both looked up to acknowledge the scrawny cocktail waitress. "Thanks," they said in unison, taking the beers. Brad reached for his wallet, extracted a Visa card, and handed it to her. "Y'better close us out. We know when we've had enough," he said with a smile.

"Oh, so soon? We haven't even gotten to know each other." She pouted, flung a hip, and turned toward the bar.

"Rots uh' ruck," Gradin muttered under his breath as he eyed her contemptuously. Then he went on, "Anyway, ol' Spin Spencer got all the way through the interview process with American Airlines when they called to tell him that because his father had died of a heart attack, he didn't meet their medical criteria. Any family history other than from old age and you were toast. I thought everybody knew that about the American selection process. He either didn't, or he forgot when he filled out the medical questionnaire. I heard that he got hired someplace else and ran into some problem there, too. Great a pilot as he was, he just had a cloud hanging over his head all the time."

"Yeah, some days you're the pigeon, other days you're the statue," Brad said through a sip of beer. "Sounds like he was solid bronze."

"So, where were you going with the Hoot Gibson stuff?"

"Oh, yeah. Well, there was one thing he told us that really stuck with me. He said that a day or so before the hearing, he got a call from the senior science correspondent at ABC. Somehow the guy knew that he was going to Seattle for the hearing, and he told Hoot to go, listen intently, but not to expect that anything he might say or do could affect the outcome of the hearing. Boeing would not be found culpable, period. There was far too much at stake if the world's number one producer of commercial airplanes was discovered to have a design flaw in the workhorse 727. The ramifications of something like that would be enormous.

"So Hoot was going up there with his eyes wide open, and as I recall, the final report did find the crew at fault. And that's my fear with your deal in Pasco. Will Boeing have the muscle to shift the focus away from the airplane on to the crew? "And now that I think of it, how was your rudder trim set in Pasco?" Brad asked with a note of concern.

"Zero," Gradin responded emphatically. "For some reason, I looked down and checked that just before I scrambled out of the cockpit."

"Cool. Well, anyway, Boeing is going to be a big player in this deal. What's on the agenda for tomorrow?"

"I don't really know. The whole crew will be there and ALPA has prepped us pretty well. Naturally, they will be there, and from what Danny Purcell says, they keep everybody honest. The moment the company steps over the line, ALPA just shuts the meeting down."

"Your dues all paid up?" Brad asked.

"Yeah, they are, and exactly for this circumstance, too. Think of all those Pacific guys who haven't paid since the merger. They're really hangin' it out. I know that ALPA would have to represent them in any case, but I sure wouldn't feel very warm and fuzzy if I was known as one of the bad guys."

They both sat silently nursing their beer. The lounge was completely packed now, and two guys in the next booth seemed determined to disappear in a Marlboro smoke screen. Finally, Brad waved a hand in front of his face, coughed, took one last sip, and said, "Let's blow this pop stand." Gradin led the way through the crowd to the door.

"Dinner?" he asked.

"Yeah. Why don't we wander down to the Hilton? I think the situation calls for a good meal. We'll have some privacy there, and somethin' tells me that there is a major subplot brewing in there," he said as he playfully cuffed the back of Gradin's head.

The mayhem on Airport Boulevard made conversation nearly impossible. They strode purposefully along, focused on the array of obstacles on the crumbling sidewalk. Brad laughed as he kicked a beer can into the adjacent lot. "I remember sneaking out of church early one Sunday when I was a little kid; needed to get home for the Packers-Colts game. I was running along and saw a coffee can sitting in the yard ahead of me. It became the perfectly placed ball awaiting my winning field goal kick. It almost broke my damned foot; it was full of ice."

"Ah, mama," Gradin winced.

"Gentlemen," the bellman nodded as he pulled the door open for them. "Welcome to the Hilton."

"Thank you, sir," Brad intoned as they turned right and headed for the small, well-appointed lounge off the main dining room. "They have the full menu in here, and it's usually real quiet."

Their drinks arrived quickly, and Brad held his up for a toast. The glasses clinked, and they sipped reverently. "Okay, ol' buddy, what else is brewing?" he ventured.

"Ahhh, shit, man, you won't believe this one." Gradin exhaled deeply and stared into his glass. "I couldn't bring myself to tell you this before. Your straight-arrow, God-fearin', family-lovin' asshole of a friend has met a woman." He grimaced in obvious pain.

"Uh, like *met* in every sense of the word, I guess." "Yeah." He sat silently.

"And Alice knows?"

"Right." His eyes brimmed with tears. "It hit me like a freight train, Brad, no warning. BOOM! Just giggling and smiling and stroking and adoring. I collapsed like a rag doll. Well, part of me did, at least," he said ruefully, with only a flicker of a smile.

"We just happened to fly a couple of trips together. Really unusual. It was kinda like the ol' Pacific days, bouncing around out west with the same flight attendants most of the time. The captain was a real Neanderthal, so I had to carry the ball; did all the crew briefings and basic PR. You know me. I thrive on that stuff. Every time I turned around, she was there, and it didn't take long to realize it was no mistake. It was a tremendous buzz."

"Yeah, I know," Brad said, aware that he had recently felt a similar excitement.

"So there we were in the bar sipping wine after the rest of the crew bailed. She had some excuse for inviting me to her room, and I was helpless to resist."

"Yup, that's when the little head starts callin' the shots."

Gradin sat, staring into the amber liquid as the images replayed in his head. Then, almost in a whisper, he said, "It was such an incredibly powerful, *powerful* attraction. I sort of resisted that first night, just a lot of kissy face and fevered groping, but she was so willing and warm and needy. God damn it!" He rested his head in his hands, inhaling and exhaling deliberately.

"Yeah."

Several minutes passed in silence.

"It went on for about three months, 'til just two weeks ago, in fact. We managed to meet maybe six or seven times, sometimes for a few minutes, others for the whole night. It was the most all-consuming experience in my life, Brad. I simply could not resist. The attraction took over completely. I could not get enough of that scalding-hot adrenaline."

"Probably a lot like heroin," Brad mused. "I remember hearing an LAPD narcotics inspector speak at my dad's University Club one time. He started out by saying, 'Drugs are good.' Then he went on to clarify, of course, but his point was that regardless of how ugly their lives may become, people do drugs because it feels so damned good. Pretty much the way you describe this attraction to—what's her name?"

"Peggy."

"And how is it that Alice knows?"

"A note in my uniform shirt."

Brad grimaced. Then the waiter approached, and they managed to order without consulting a menu.

"Look, Gradin, I don't need to know the gory details. That's entirely up to you. And I know this hurts. I can see that, and I'm sorry. But it strikes me that you are being way too hard on yourself. After thirty-five years of treading the straight and narrow, guess what? You *are* human, after all. You get to trash the Boy Scout uniform and be a real person, with all the awful bumps and blemishes everyone else has."

"I don't know, man, this is pretty harsh. Alice is tough, but she's also crushed. It might have been easier if she'd been fighting mad, but she just crumpled, sort of went into shock. I took the kids to her parents' for a couple of days. Al and I just hung out. Cried most of the time. Bleak, really bleak." His voice trailed off.

They sat silently. Finally, Gradin began again, determined to disgorge the demons. "The weird part was that I felt supercharged when I was with Peggy. Everything seemed brighter, funnier, smoother—harder, even—sweeter, softer, intensely more pleasing."

"Sounds like maybe you haven't been letting the 'brighter, smoother, sweeter' things into your life otherwise. Think about it. You've been on a treadmill since high school. Isn't that where you and Alice met? She was your queen, and you've been proving how worthy you are ever since? God, you were perfect, Gradin. Perfect student. Perfect athlete. Perfect naval aviator. Perfect bridegroom. Perfect dad. Perfect everything, for Christ's sake. Give yourself a fucking break." Brad breathed deeply and waited.

"Ha. Very funny."

"Well, okay, I didn't necessarily mean that in a literal sense, but you get the picture. You are always driving. You took that 737 bid, and aren't you the junior shit bird in L.A.?"

"Yeah."

"You're out there flyin' the worst schedule possible. When you get home, you simply suit up again and head for Whidbey. How many days a month do they expect of you?"

"Well, they'd like to have 'em all, but I'm usually over there at least four, sometimes as many as six, days every month. It's a grind. I've gotten, so I hate that airplane. Every time I climb aboard, there's sadness. Another day away from home.

"I gave up bein' an IP one Sunday afternoon when I was out over Mount Baker shuttin' down engines and failing systems, probably with some clueless jet-jock like you in the left seat," he said as his first smile in an hour appeared. "Anyway, I realized that all the guys sitting back in the bar were earning the same buck-ninety-eight I was, and their greatest concern was making the airlift on time to get home for dinner. I hung up my instructor spurs. But even with that, as a plane commander, I still have to train the crew. With twelve guys and all the individual quals they all need, it's a grind. And it's not like I can show up when it's convenient for *me*. I have to be there when the rest of the crew can, and that's almost always a weekend."

"Okay, buddy. It sounds like it's time for a reality check." Just then, the waiter appeared. "Gentlemen, steak and potatoes." He lowered the tray from his shoulder and expertly

placed the plates on the table. "Sour cream and chives?" Sure," they both responded. "And a glass of your house red, too, please," Brad requested.

"Oh, yeah, me, too," Gradin added.

"Coming right up. Anything else, gents?" the waiter asked.

"Nope, ya done good. Thanks, Ramon," Brad said.

They ate in appreciative silence for a few moments. Brad could sense the tension subside in Gradin. *Guys don't talk much about this kind of stuff*, he realized. *When they do, it's almost always empty bluster, envious speculation, or pointless competition. The airline life can be a very lonely existence.*

Chapter 11

NEAR DISASTER

Andy Caldwell unlocked his office door, hit the lights, and dumped his briefcase in the chair next to his desk. It was Tues-day morning, not yet 7:00, and he was back in the usual routine despite the late arrival of his flight from the West Coast. The senior flight ops guys would meet with the Pasco crew—Flight 848, or just 848, as it would always be known henceforth—and he knew that his boss John Haddington, senior VP of operations, would insist on a conversation before the crew debrief.

Boeing was resisting the possibility of a mechanical failure. The crew members, with the strong backing of ALPA, were firm in their assertion that the rudder had deflected spontaneously. Of course, the FAA would have its own perspective. Andy was in the awkward position of dancing to the tunes of the hypercritical media and the extremely sensitive Omega Board of Directors. Everyone had a dog in the fight, and Andy was the referee who could easily get bitten.

But first things first. He grabbed his Marine Corps mug and turned down the hall toward the flight operations command center. He filled his cup in the coffee alcove and stood watching the shift change taking place among dozens of dispatchers and meteorologists in the dimly lit room. Then he ducked into the glassed-in bay overlooking the massive sprawl of desks and tables.

The off-going ops manager was deep in conversation with his replacement. Andy grabbed a copy of the ops summary and listened in. "Two delays and one cancellation in NORAT[26] last night; 926 to Brussels turned back prior to departure with a hydraulic pump failure. It turned out that there were also two broken lines, and the spare aircraft had already filled in for 984 with a collapsed strut on the right main. So 984 was thirty minutes late off the blocks, and 919 took a fifteen-minute delay with an inertial alignment issue.[27]

"Out in the Pacific, 1212 from Seoul made an unplanned fuel stop in the Aleutians. Winds were way off, and Shemya gave us a thirty-minute advantage over an Anchorage stop. Misconnected the whole boat in Portland, but loads are light the rest of the day, so we expect to be caught up by tonight. One parts delay on 525 in Albuquerque. That is estimated as a two-hour hold, but we will reconnect everyone here later in the day."

The briefing continued as all the information was conveniently displayed on three formatted pages of data that Andy scanned quickly. He patted the oncoming manager on the shoulder and said, "I'll see you again at noon if nothing serious comes up. Give my beeper a check." The manager dialed two digits, and the long, thin device clipped to Andy's belt hummed intermittently. "Five by five," he said as he depressed the silence button and headed back toward his office.

The 2,500 scheduled departures every day, 536 airplanes, nearly 10,000 pilots, and 18,000 flight attendants all needing to be at exactly the right place at precisely the right time, virtually every minute of every day, was a massive undertaking. *And I manage this?* He grinned to himself. *God, if they only knew.* He shook his head as he walked back to his office.

At precisely that moment, another Omega drama culminated ten miles south of the airport. It had all begun the previous day in Los Angeles.

"Jake Allen speaking." The pilot set his coffee cup down and reached for a pen.

"Hey, Jake, this is Wilbur in Crew Scheduling. We have a trip for you, and we need you at the airport as quickly as possible."

"I'm ready. Whattaya got?"

The scheduler explained the trip sequence: a deadhead from Los Angeles, through Memphis to Montgomery, Alabama, with a short layover there, then a 6:00 a.m. departure from Montgomery back to Memphis the next morning, followed by Memphis back to L.A. "You depart from gate fifty-eight. Your paperwork will be waiting for you there with all the details. Flight 221 outbound."

Beats a fleabag motel, Jake muttered to himself as he stepped into the shower. Two hours later, seated as a passenger, he closed his eyes as Omega 221 lifted off. It would be a four-day grind, back and forth across the country twice with early departures from the East Coast both times. Combine that with the commute from Anchorage, and he'd be a hur-tin' scooter. He slept until touchdown in Memphis, where he changed planes for Montgomery. There he checked into the hotel and grabbed a few more hours of sleep.

Stumbling into the lobby at 4:30, he wiped the sleep from his eyes and found the crew. "Uh, Captain Crandall, I'm Jake Al-len, your new first officer."

Raymond Crandall shook his hand limply and motioned toward the hotel van waiting in the early-morning darkness. No one spoke during the ten-minute ride to the airport.

The warm electronic hums and whirs in the cockpit mixed with the shuffling of papers, the occasional warning horn test, and the quiet grunts and yawns of the three pilots as they prepared for departure. They were bleary, at best.

"Your leg, Jake," the captain commented casually, indi-cating that the newest member of the team would fly the segment from Montgomery to Memphis. *Knowing a little more about how the guy runs his ship would help.* Jake arranged his charts, consulted the flight plan, and finally called the tower for clearance.

The cockpit choreography unfolded flawlessly as it did hundreds of times each day. With little traffic in the ear-ly-morning skies, Omega 439 was given direct routing to the Memphis airport, which they approached from the southeast, contacted the approach controller for landing instructions, and prepared for a landing on runway 36C.

As the pilot not flying (PNF), the captain dialed in the ap-propriate radio frequencies and set up the autopilot panel and flight instruments as Jake maneuvered the aircraft toward the initial descent point. Once established on the final approach course, he slowed the aircraft and prepared to descend toward the still-dark runway.

"We need to get down!" Ray Crandall exclaimed a bit frantically as he reached across the center console, threw the gear out, and pulled all three power levers to idle.

Jake shook his head to clear the cobwebs, totally confused by Ray's actions. He struggled to comprehend the reason for going down prior to the initial descent point.

He squirmed and fought to maintain the designated airspeed and heading.

"Landing checklist." Again the captain hurried as though he were falling behind. The landing lights illuminated, and the white reflection from the clouds enveloped the aircraft. "Checklist complete, a thousand to go," he said in reference to the barometric altimeter. He squeezed the transmit button. "Approach, you want Omega 439 over to tower?" he queried the approach controller.

"Omega 439, say your alt . . . 439, approach, climb immediately, climb immediately!" the alarmed voice commanded.

"What the shit?"

The aircraft descended out of the clouds, and the lights illuminated a solid blanket of trees, just as the automated voice of the ground proximity warning system wailed "TERRAIN. TERRAIN."

Confused but certain of the necessary action, Jake slammed the power levers full-forward, raised the nose, and spat out, "Positive rate, gear up, flaps fifteen."

✈

▪▪▪ ▬ ▬ ▬▪▪▪ ▬ ▬ ▬▪▪▪ ▬ ▬ ▬▪▪▪ ▬ ▬ ▬▪▪▪ ▬ ▬ ▬▪▪▪

The phone was ringing as Andy stepped back into his office. "Caldwell," he answered. "Ahhh, top o' the mornin', John. Yeah, we were late getting in last night. Just briefed with the ops manager; all is well. Sure, I can be there in ten minutes." He frowned and replaced the receiver.

"Mornin', Andy." His secretary, Penny, stuck her head in the door. "I know that you have the Pasco 848 debrief at 10:00. Are you planning to drop in on the steering committee this morning? I got good notes yesterday, but we had a major blow-up right at the end of the day."

"Yeah, I heard," he responded, suppressing a smile. "I'm on my way over to talk 848 with John now. So go ahead and sit in for me and let them know that I intend to stop by sometime this morning."

"Will do. You may have seen it, but I made you a list of the calls you need to return today," Penny said, pointing to the credenza behind his desk. "Just a minute ago, Hank Maxwell called to say that a crew busted a PC[28] last night. Apparently, a new guy from the field office showed up unannounced and really rattled the captain. Hank wants to get the additional training right because it seemed like the guy was out to get the captain, and he certainly succeeded in intimidating him."

"Great," he sighed. "All we need is the feds breathin' down our necks on something else right now. They're already crawlin' all over the place. Okay, get back to Hank. Ask him to stop by with his recommendations before he leaves for the afternoon. Thanks, Penny."

The phone rang. She turned to her desk and, still standing, answered, "Good morning, Captain Caldwell's office."

···— — —···— — —···— — —···— — —···— — —···

"Good morning, Penny," the familiar but unusually serious voice of the local air traffic control chief greeted her. "Is
the boss in?" No pleasantries.

"Yes, sir. Hold for a moment, please." She pushed the hold
button, then the intercom. "Andy, Roger Murphy for you on
line one. Sounds serious."

Andy exhaled and grabbed the phone. "Mornin', Rog.
What'd we do now?"

"Almost put one in the trees off the approach end of
three-six, Andy."

The VP winced.

"Just happened that I was on the scope. I have to admit
that I had a mental lapse, too. The guy started down early, and I
didn't notice it. Broke out just as I saw the altitude readout and
called for a climb. Apparently, the crew caught it at exactly the
same time and started back up before we set off the alarms."

"Jesus. Thank God."

"Yeah, there would have been more than enough blame
to go around if they'd augered in," Roger confessed with nota-
ble remorse. "No one else saw it happen, so we're home free
this time, but Andy, what the hell is goin' on over there?"

"Hubris, big guy. Hubris. Our crews seem to feel invincible.
We have a CRM program in the works, but it'll be a couple of
months before it kicks in."

"We probably need that for our controllers, too. At least I
apparently do." Roger was contrite.

"Thanks for takin' care of us, pal."

"No problem."

Andy breathed deeply, then grabbed his briefcase and
headed for the elevator.

"Happy trails," Penny chirped.

✈

Andy spoke from the deep, upholstered chair in John Haddington's palatial office. First, he related the story of the most recent near disaster and promised to get more info. Then he turned to the Pasco accident. "So what we're left with is the significant likelihood that there is a design flaw in the 737 rudder actuators. But the evidence is so scant, and we are in such a precarious position with the feds, that I think it would be suicidal to go public with that theory right now.

"I have a couple of guys going back through our maintenance archives to see what they can uncover. Maybe we'll see a trend. And of course, we might also see something that points to us. In fact," he said, extracting a yellow pad from his briefcase, "I want to remind those guys to also note the *who* and *when* of any rudder actuator work that was done." He jotted down a reminder.

Haddington paced in front of the window overlooking the runway complex. In the window behind him, Andy saw the morning departures—referred to as the morning bank— lined up twenty deep on the taxiway under the low overcast. At regular intervals, a jet rolled down the runway to a spot opposite the window where the nose invariably lifted off the runway, then continued up at the prescribed three degrees per second. The lighter, smaller aircraft virtually jumped into the air and disappeared, whereas the heavy jets continued to roll, nose in the air, gaining speed and creating the lift necessary to carry them aloft. Some just crept into the air and were visible beyond the end of the runway, lumbering slowly upward.

He put both hands behind his head, elbows out, to stretch. "This is very delicate. On the one hand, we need to appear to be taking decisive action." He paused and walked to his desk. "You're always ahead of me on these things, but have you thought of getting some guys in the sim to wrestle with the same scenario?"

"Yeah, we have. It looks like we can pull four instructors tomorrow afternoon. Sim 203 is scheduled to be down for one six-hour period, just a minor software update, so we should be able to run a variety of scenarios with two separate crews."

"Better get ALPA involved," John suggested. "There is always a possibility that your guys will find that the event was 100 percent controllable or that some procedural screw up caused the damn thing. In that case, the crew would be in deep shit. We don't want this to look like we're setting up the crew. Might as well have their representatives there."

"Good point. I have both Allen Hughes and Chester Bowles here for that CRM development deal. I'm sure I can break them loose. They're probably itching to be involved anyway."

"That's okay, but don't let those two run away with this. Better balance your team with some equally strong company guys." John sat at his desk and scribbled a note.

"Another good point, Captain. You ever think of going into management?" Andy quipped while making a note.

"Hmph," John responded.

"Probably our strongest guy—most persuasive communicator, at least—is Hank Maxwell, the senior on the seven-three. He'll be there, and I could also tap Vinnie Pedoza from Dallas. He's a seven-two line check and my choice to take the L.A. chief pilot job when Hoxsworth is done."

"Okay, that'll be good exposure for Pedoza. He's the former spy, right?"

"Yeah, he plays the role perfectly—somehow leaves the impression that there's a lot going on that he simply can't talk about. Funny guy."

"I know. He's always jerkin' my chain about my ties. 'Oooooh, nice, *Haddington*,' he says when he sees me. I know that's a common greeting throughout the company, but I'm not the dandy he is, and my suits and ties sure aren't as expensive."

"So let's get our ducks in a row here. I need to be able to respond to Ron and the board with a coherent overview. We *know* the following," he said, ticking off the points on his fingers. "One, the crew was great. Two, no one was seriously injured. Three, the rudder actuation was uncommanded."

He continued, counting on the other hand. "We're *doing* the following: cooperating with the FAA. Thoroughly reviewing maintenance records. Three, consulting extensively with Boeing. And finally, reviewing crew training and operating procedures."

"All good but number four," Andy responded. "The typical protocol in a situation like this is that the FAA mandates a review of crew training and operating procedures. We have no choice in the matter. I would prefer not to mention that. If the question comes up, we can say that we are complying with FAA accident investigation requirements, reviewing all crew training, etcetera. But let's not give any hint of possible crew error. We certainly can't be faulted for *exceeding* the requirements, but let's keep the public statements as generic as possible."

"Okay, I agree. Three points each should be fine. I'm actually going to wait for Ron to ask. He always seems to embellish his public statements. If we give him that hint, he might inadvertently hang our guys. The board isn't scheduled to meet until next month, and we should know more by then."

" 'Nuff said." Andy rose and closed his notebook. "We debrief the crew at ten, and I want to look in on the CRM committee before that."

"Where are you debriefing?" John asked. "I think I'll stop by and pat a few backs. I really do want them to feel like they aren't under the microscope. Whether they know it or not, we all really dodged a bullet out there."

"Amen," Andy whispered, shaking his head. Then he grabbed his briefcase, stood, and smiled confidently at John. "We'll be in the conference room. Stop by anytime."

"Thanks," John concluded with a wave of his hand.

The committee gathered before eight and milled around nervously, most consulting notes containing their recollections of the previous day's confrontation. The only person missing was Jack, though someone had prepared the room for the day's activities. Twelve white two-by-four flip charts hung from a track encircling the room. Numerous colored felt markers were neatly arranged on the three tables.

Precisely at 8:00, Jack Mumford marched into the room and began speaking as if continuing an ongoing conversation.

"All right, now that you've had some time to record the facts, I want each of you to go to a flip chart and make a list of those facts, preferably in chronological order. I'll do the same. Take about ten minutes." He grabbed a black felt-tip pen and walked to a board at the right-front corner of the room. Everyone quietly followed suit.

"Two more minutes," Jack said. "If you can't remember it now, you never will.

"Good, that's it. Whatever you have is fine," Jack said, snapping the cap on the pen with his palm. "Everything else would be utter BS.

"Now, go on back to your seats and get comfortable. Andrea, why don't you stay put and give us your list of facts?"

Andrea strode purposefully to the easel. "Ahem. Your Honor, at exactly twelve minutes after three, on the seventh day of March 1988—"

"Whoa, whoa, whoa," Bobby groaned. "I happened to be looking at my watch just at the moment she so rudely interrupted our meeting. It was really 3:07," he insisted.

"Okay, okay." Andrea breathed deeply and wrote her bullet items on the chart.

- At 3:12 on March 7, Donna Albrecht entered room 110 in the Omega Air Lines training center.
- She screamed at Jack Mumford and threw her purse in his direction.
- She approached Jack, he grabbed her arms, and they fell on the floor.
- She yelled something about a doctor and the whole world knowing.
- Then Allen Kearney came in and took Donna away.
- Andrea picked up the stuff from Donna's purse and took it back to her desk.

"I rest my case, Your Honor."

"Very good," Jack responded. "Thanks, Andrea. I'm sure everyone else saw pretty much the same thing. Vinnie, you're next."

"Okay." He read from the board, "WOMAN ENTERS ROOM 202 BETWEEN 3:00 AND 3:10 AND YELLS AT JACK." He erased and corrected the first item on the facts list. "She wasn't just yelling; she was swearing at him," Vinnie said.

"No, she wasn't. Donna never swears!" Andrea responded with equal insistence.

"What'll it be?" Jack asked patiently. "Swore? Yelled? Bellowed? What?"

Andrea and Vinnie looked at each other.

"I certainly didn't hear any swearing," Andrea insisted. "How could you have missed the 'son of a bitch' she yelled just as she stepped into the room?"

Vinnie wailed. "It's etched in my memory. Nobody calls Jack Mumford an SOB. Nobody. And here comes this little twit yelling at him like that. It isn't something I can easily forget." He slumped back in his chair in disgust.

"But Donna simply does *not* swear. I know this woman. And she sure as hell didn't say anything about an abortion, Vinnie. Where the hell did you get that? Excuse *my* French."

David Hennessey winked at Marsha Hilbert and rolled back in his chair with his hands folded behind his head. Patrick Finch also watched with amusement while Chester intently sat stroking his stubble and looked quizzically at Jack.

The door opened, and Andy Caldwell strode confidently into the room. His stature as a Marine Corps reserve general was inescapable.

"Attention on deck!" someone barked. Several of the guys scrambled to their feet and stood awkwardly at attention.

Pencils and markers fell off the tables, and a chair tipped over as the spontaneous slapstick ensued.

"As you were," Andy responded, smiling and shaking his head. "Be seated, gentlemen; you too, ladies. Now, what's this about a woman yelling and screaming at you yesterday, Captain Mumford?"

"Well, sir, we are attempting to get to the bottom of that right this minute. So far, there isn't much agreement on the facts."

The casual banter continued as Andy made his way around to greet every member of the committee. He worked the room masterfully, expressing his sincere appreciation to each person, and making the personal contact they all would remember.

He had an especially warm conversation with Bobby Clark that resulted in side-splitting laughter for both.

Then Andy addressed the whole group. Without painting a picture of extreme doom and gloom, he managed to express to them how important their task was to the well-being of Omega Airlines. "The advantage of entering the CRM game so late is that there are plenty of known pitfalls to avoid," he said. "Marsha Hilbert and David Hennessey will be very valuable resources in that regard."

After concluding with a quick endorsement of the 848 crew, he excused himself to attend that debrief.

After seeing Andy out the door, Jack returned. "Great guy. He's given us carte blanche to create a great program. Let's not screw it up.

"Okay, back to yesterday's incident. Once again, what do we have?" Jack asked as he looked from Andrea to Vinnie. "Was there really anything about a doctor or an abortion?"

Vinnie stood his ground. "No, doctor."

"Nothing about an abortion," Andrea followed in despair.

"Okay, so no doctor, no abortion. Did she strike at me, or did I reach for her first?"

"She went after you like a crazed animal."

"Uh-uh," Andrea countered, shaking her head in disagreement. "You reached up and pulled her down."

"So no agreement there. But we did end up on the floor, right?"

"Right."

"Yeah."

JACK AND WOMAN TUSSLE AND FALL TO THE FLOOR, he wrote. "That okay?"

"Yup. What else?"

"Her big ol' husband drug her away."

"Vinnie, she isn't even married," Andrea almost shrieked. "That was her teaching partner, Allen Kearney."

"Well, what the hell was that ring doing on her left finger?"

"She didn't have a ring on her left finger!"

"Sure she did."

"No chance," she scoffed.

"Wait, wait. You *can* agree that a man—"

"A *big* man," Andrea interrupted.

"Okay, you can agree that a *big* man took her away."

"Yeah, and before he did, he threatened you, Jack."

"He did?" Jack responded, raising his eyebrows.

"Damned right he did. Called you an asshole and said that he'd take care of you later."

"Hmmm. I don't see that on your list, Vinnie. Is that what really happened?"

"Well, yeah, it is. I didn't know we were gonna be so liberal with the profanity, but that is what happened."

"But Andrea doesn't think so. So it's true in your memory but not something we can agree to as fact, right?"

"Okay."

A BIG MAN TOOK HER AWAY, Jack added to the list. "Moving right along here. How about, uh, you, Chester?" he said after looking over the room.

"Yes, sir!" Chester blurted. He stood, moved toward the flip chart, and pointed at his bullet list with mock urgency. "Crazy woman flight attendant ran into this room shouting at you. She threw her purse, attacked you, and knocked you to the floor. A big man came in and dragged her away. Andrea gathered up things from her purse and left the room."

"Ah, short 'n' sweet. Good," Jack said. "So, what made you think she was a flight attendant?"

"Well, I remember flying with her once."

"Oh, okay, so something you remembered from the past sort of merged with what you saw yesterday. It may or may not have been true, but it did influence very directly what you believe you saw yesterday. And if you look around the room, you'll notice that only you and Andrea said that the woman in question was a flight attendant, both influenced by past experience or knowledge rather than simple observation.

"I also notice that you didn't say anything about swearing, or a doctor, or a husband. How did you miss that?"

"Hmmm, well, those things are in my head back there someplace, but the implications were so unbelievable that they just didn't seem relevant, I guess."

"Ahhh, very interesting! So a previous mindset or prejudice can greatly influence what we remember seeing. Is that fair to say?" Heads nodded. "So it can influence what we expect to see in the future, too," Jack emphasized.

Brad found himself particularly interested in the discussion, knowing that Gradin and the 848 crew were engaged in a remarkably similar analysis at that very moment. *How comparable would their recollections of the event be?* he wondered.

Jack continued to cull through the individual lists and compile a surprisingly small master list of facts. After a couple of breaks and numerous disagreements among the eleven observers, he finally had a list they could all agree to:

- WOMAN ENTERED ROOM AT APPROXIMATELY 3:00 P.M.
- WOMAN SPOKE LOUDLY AND APPROACHED JACK
- WOMAN AND JACK FELL TO THE FLOOR WRESTLING
- BIG MAN ENTERED ROOM AND LED WOMAN AWAY

"Now, that hardly sounds like the scene of a crime. Of course, you haven't heard from the victim yet. But I can tell you what *really* happened.

"At precisely 3:02, Donna Albrecht entered this room— I know the time because we synchronized our watches beforehand. She threw her purse toward me, shouted that she had called the doctor as I requested, that now her husband knows and that probably the whole world knows. She approached me with both hands raised in fists. She leaned forward, I grabbed her wrists, and we both fell to the floor. Moments later, Allen Kearney entered the room and physically removed Donna.

"And yes, there was some swearing, and Allen did threaten me. However, a couple of things that were etched in some people's minds definitely did *not* happen. For instance, there was no mention of an abortion, and Allen Kearney was not identified as Donna's husband.

"Just for fun, do any of you remember what things fell out of Donna's purse?" Jack asked with a smile.

"Keys."

"Right."

"Pictures."

"Yup, and a folder of photos."

"I saw a gun, a small Derringer," Vinnie said confidently.

"No way," most of the others protested.

Jack looked at his watch to ensure that it was 11:10. "Tell you what," he said. "Let's take a look and see."

"Donna, are you there?" he said as he opened the door and looked into the hall. Then he swung the door open for Donna and Allen to enter. "Ladies and gentlemen, may I present, direct from an engagement off-off Broadway, the Omega Players."

"Otherwise known as The Duds." Donna blushed and gave Jack a quick embrace. Jack reached over and shook Allen's hand warmly. "Thanks, pal," he said.

"So yes, you've all been had, or more likely, I've simply made a fool of myself with the implausibility of this whole exercise." Jack grinned. "However, it all went better than I had imagined. Donna, you're good." He reached down to massage an apparently tender knee.

"Well, thanks, but I really should apologize. It wasn't in the script for me to knock you out of the chair. I actually tripped over your foot, Jack."

"Yeah, look at those damned things," Vinnie heckled. "Okay, we'll blame it on your feet." She smiled. "In that split second, I had to decide whether to try to catch myself or go for the attack. You were such an inviting target, Jack. You have no idea how good it felt to go after a captain like that."

"Oh, now that hurts, that really hurts," Jack said, bowing his head.

"Speaking of hurt, look at this." She pointed to the raw skin on her right elbow. "I think you won that round, Captain Mumford. Or you were winning until my hero saved me," she said, slipping her arm through Allen's.

"Aren't they cute? Julie Andrews meets Jesse Ventura," Andrea said with a sigh. Allen's bald head and muscular physique, along with Donna's glamorous smile and silky voice, provided an acceptable likeness.

"Best of all, you confused the hell out of everybody. After an hour of constant, heated debate, this is all they could agree that they remembered," he said, pointing to the list.

"Wow, what happened to all the colorful stuff?"

"People were too traumatized by Allen." Pat grinned.

"Yeah, imagine how he is with the belligerent passengers. We need one of these guys on every crew," she said, squeezing his ample biceps as she chuckled.

"Donna, set the record straight. Everyone thinks you were swearing at Jack as you ran across the room. I didn't hear you say one curse word," Andrea insisted.

"Oh, my," she demurred. "Was my foul mouth running off right here in front of God and everybody? I suppose it was. My gracious, I *do* apologize."

"But what came out of that was perfect," Jack interjected. "Andrea's prior experience with Donna made it difficult—well, *impossible* in this case—for her to even hear those words that seemed so out of character. And that is true for *all* of us," he emphasized. "Our prior experience colors everything we see. You are going to see that time and again as we develop this program."

"Indeed you will," Dr. Hennessey interrupted. "There are some very vivid examples of pilot error resulting from the mis-application of previous experience. Uh, let me see," he paused.

"Well, just look at the captain in Portland. It is likely that in all of his past experience, the flight engineer had ticked off the fuel remaining as it approached a predetermined limit, never when it was below that limit. So any mention of fuel remaining always preceded a bingo fuel alert. As long as the engineer was notifying him of the fuel remaining, he always knew they were okay. The terms '2,000 pounds, 1,000 pounds,' didn't even register. That isn't a perfect example, but you get the idea," he concluded.

"If I may," Marsha Hilbert said, raising a hand, "a great deal of what we see depends on what we expect to see—no, better yet, what we *prepare* to see. That being the case, for a flight crew, the key to arriving at the desired outcome is the mental picture all of the crew members have starting out. That very often is a function of the briefing done by the captain."

"Hold it. I'm hearing two opposing explanations for the same thing," Loren protested. "Help me out."

The academicians looked at each other, then Marsha went on. "The simplest explanation may be that crews need to expect the unexpected." She paused for that to sink in. "The crew in Portland didn't do that. Without ever articulating it, they relied entirely on different past experiences. The engineer had a picture of the captain taking decisive action in response to the engineer's *fuel remaining* calls. And the captain had a picture of the engineer getting the captain's undivided attention regarding the amount of *fuel remaining*. Two different mental pictures—expectations of the other person—of the same situation."

"How do we get around that?" someone asked.

"The briefing," Marsha responded emphatically. "If the captain had said to the engineer, 'Don't let us go below 4,000 pounds. When we get there, be sure that I know it. If necessary, tap me on the shoulder, hit me, something, but get my attention,' you can bet they would not have run the airplane out of fuel."

"Damn it, it's the engineer's responsibility to get my attention in situations like that," Bobby fumed.

"It is, Bobby," Marsha said firmly, holding her ground. "And it is up to you to ensure that he does that. I feel pretty certain that you won't find that spelled out in any of your manuals. I'd bet a day's pay that it says something to the effect that 'the engineer will *advise* the captain' of such and such. Not that the engineer will punch the captain in the shoulder to get his attention."

"Aw, shit," Bobby said as he threw his hands up in disgust.

"Bobby, try this," Marsha persisted. "Let's say it is the Lakers and the Pistons in the playoffs. Pat Riley doesn't go into the locker room before game three and say 'Okay, you know what to do, let's go.' He paints a mental picture for them, and they all get it. They not only expect the unexpected; they know that on that day, Kareem will move to the top of the key when Laimbeer collapses on Magic down low. When that happens, they feed Kareem, not Magic. They have that picture for that particular game. They'll create another picture for game four. Does that make any sense?"

"Yeah, yeah. You win, Doc. Now I have to be Pat Riley *and* God Almighty," Bobby muttered.

"Enough, enough," Jack interceded. "Thanks, Marsha. "I'm sorry, you guys. I didn't mean to have you standing at attention all this time," he said to Donna and Allen. "Can you join us for a few minutes?"

"Sure, I'm good 'til 1:00."

"Me, too."

Two additional chairs were rolled to the tables for them.

"Hey, Jack, may I follow up for a minute on what Marsha said?" Brad ventured.

"Sure, go ahead."

"Maybe I can help with this mental picture issue. I think I'm the junior guy here, so I can provide the flight engineer perspective. I also have some experience with those team dynamics Marsha was referring to. And please forgive me. I really try hard not to discuss the Blue Angels, but this is really relevant."

Brad went on to explain how the team developed each year, how they went to El Centro in California every winter and practiced nonstop for three months before they ever performed for the public, how they got to know precisely what every team member would be doing at every moment. The show never varied. And he emphasized that their behavior was much more like the Rockettes than the Hells Angels.

"But here is the key to the whole thing," he emphasized, sitting forward in his chair. "Before every show—and that's almost 100 shows a year—we spent one whole hour *briefing*. Now, we could have done what Marsha was saying—you know, the 'kick the tires and light the fire' routine. I mean, it was the same damned show every day. Same game. We all could have flown it in our sleep. But instead, we created a new mental picture every day.

"So there we were, the whole team sitting around one table, much like this," he said, pointing to the large round tables at which they were sitting. "And the boss took us through the entire show, maneuver by maneuver. We flew the whole show in our heads, in real time. And that included everything from turning out of the chocks to switching radio frequencies on takeoff.

"He made all the calls just as he would in the air. Like, over the top in the initial loop we would hear, 'pull . . . pull . . . ooover the top . . . easing power . . . easing power . . . smokes . . . now,' just as he would say in the show. So when we went out and strapped it on, every one of us had exactly the same mental picture and expectation."

"Perfect. Exactly," Marsha said excitedly.

Brad went on. "So now, from my perspective in the flight engineer seat, we have a similar opportunity. The captain can— and probably should—paint that mental picture for the crew. Go back to Portland for a minute. Imagine this. The nose gear warning illuminates during the approach. The captain says, 'Okay, guys, let me get clearance for a VFR hold, and we'll talk about this thing.' He does that. Then he says, 'Orville, I want you to keep flyin'. Maintain 3,500 feet; stay within about five miles of the airport, and you handle the radios, too. Wilbur and I will do the checklist. Got it?' Orville says, 'Yup, maintain thirty-five within five, and I got the radios.' Everybody's on the same page.

"So Wilbur and the captain go through the appropriate checklist, and they still have the warning light. Then the captain says, 'Wilbur, I'm going to notify the flight attendants and have them prepare for a possible emergency landing. It looks like we have about thirty minutes of holding fuel. That sound right?' The captain looks at the fuel panel and looks at Wilbur for confirmation. Then he goes on, 'I want you to monitor that fuel very carefully and keep me posted. When we get to 4,000 pounds, we'll set up to land regardless of the gear indication. Make sure that I know about the fuel, Wilbur. Got it?' And Wilbur says, 'Got it, boss: Even if I have to hit you with my clipboard, you'll know when we get to four grand.'

"If that conversation had taken place on December 28, 1978, we never would have heard of poor ol' Flight 173 in Portland," Brad concluded.

Jack jumped to his feet and hurried to the flip chart.

"Spot on, Bradley Blue!" With his black felt-tip marker, he vigorously underlined COMMUNICATION. "It will probably seem like we beat this one to death, but it cannot be overemphasized. Think about it. Nothing happens without communication—*nothing!*"

"Yeah, and you guys communicate in shorthand," Marsha insisted. "You take the average person, plop him down in the jump seat, and ask him to listen, he'd have no idea what you were saying. 'Five for four' or 'one to go.'"

"No, that's 'one taco,' Marsha," one of the pilots said, laughing, as the others joined in.

"Once again, you make my point," she said with an adamant gesture. "Who other than your weird peers could possibly guess that in longhand 'one taco' really means 'I'm reminding you that we have 1,000 feet remaining in our climb or descent until we reach our assigned altitude?' That is really serious stuff, and you guys say, 'one taco'?

"Okay, try this," she said, leaning forward. "Someone give me a hypothetical read-back of an initial ATC clearance."

"Thanks for volunteering, Pat," Jack said as he pointed to the Miami captain/psychologist. "Patrick specializes in concise communication," he joked.

"Uh, okay, hang on," Pat said as he jotted down some words and numbers. "We might say, 'Omega 325 cleared to Memphis as filed, Dade Four, Lake transition, 5,000, expect three-five-zero ten after, one-twenty-five-zero and seven-four-six-eight.'"

"And the controller replies, 'Readback correct, have a nice day,'" Marsha said. "Now, Captain Communicator, what was really shared in that clearance?"

"Well, air traffic control cleared—that is, gave authorization for Omega Flight 325 to fly from Miami to Memphis on a route depicted in the flight plan—a route requested by the company from the FAA. However, despite the brevity of the verbal exchange, the following is clearly understood: They are to fly the Dade Four departure procedure with a Lake transition—all depicted on the departure plate that both pilots and the controller have. And they are required to climb to and maintain 5,000 feet initially. They can expect to be cleared to 35,000 feet approximately ten minutes after they depart. They will communicate with the departure controller on frequency one-two-five-zero, and the code they will set in the transponder is seven-four-six-eight."

"Wow." Marsha continued with mock astonishment to make her point. "All of that communicated in about thirty words spoken in ten seconds. And, of course, there are dozens of additional agreements and expectations contained in that clearance. For instance, both the controller and pilots understand what airspeed 325 will fly. They all know what will occur if radio contact is lost and numerous similar details."

"Fabulous!" Jack exuded. "Now let's see if we can tie this communications tangent back to yesterday's outburst. How is it relevant?"

The room was quiet for a moment as people puzzled over the question. Finally, George Moffett spoke. "It seems to me that a lot of this has to do with context. For instance, when we receive an ATC clearance, we know it is coming, and we listen for specific key words. There is a known format, and we mentally fill in the blanks; we have a context to put things in. So it always starts out 'ATC clears,' and we write down the key words that follow: the call sign, the destination, the departure, altitudes, departure frequency, and squawk."

"Squawk?" Donna wrinkled her brow. Like most of the traveling public, the word was simply pilot gibberish to her.

"Yeah, that's a funny word for the four-digit code we put in the transponder, the device that displays a discrete code on the controller's radar scope."

"Right. Sorry I asked." She rolled her eyes and leaned back in the chair.

"Another example of the shorthand I was referring to." Marsha nodded.

"Anyway, we understand all of that because we know what to expect. They don't give us that information randomly. Just imagine how that would sound. 'Okay, I understand that you want us to go to Memphis at 35,000 feet, and the route is the one on the flight plan the company filed for us. We should set the transponder on seven-four-six-eight. We should fly that Dade departure procedure and do the Lake transition and talk to the departure controller on one-two-five-decimal-zero. Is that correct?' And the controller might say, 'Yeah, that's right, and also maintain 5,000 feet during the initial part of the departure, and you can expect the departure controller to clear you to 35,000 feet about ten minutes after you depart.' We'd go back and clarify again, duh da, duh da, duh da. And round and round it would go until we got it right.

"A lot of these guys have had the experience of trying to communicate with foreign controllers," George went on. "The only thing that makes that possible is that they use these well-established formats, and we can at least hear the key words. Then we read back what we hear, very deliberately, and by relying on the format, they can pick up any errors we may have made and correct them quite easily."

"So English is the universal language in aviation?" Donna asked.

"Technically, it is, but lots of times you can tell the controller isn't the least bit fluent. I don't know about everyone else, but I find it very fatiguing to have to listen to that carefully. Coming back across the pond, when we get closer to the U.S., it's always such a relief to hear the English-speaking controller say, 'Roger, radar contact,' when we check in for the first time. It's music to our ears."

"Okay, thanks, George," Jack responded. "There are a couple of key things in what you said. First, that idea of communication formats, or even the routines that we rely on. But how does that relate to yesterday?"

"Well, there wasn't a recognizable format to what was said—there never is with real life—so we couldn't easily play it back in our heads for verification. With radio transmissions, you can actually hear the pattern: one-two-five-decimal-six, not seven. When it's random conversation, especially when it's a surprise and it's full of emotion, then it's harder to play back. And of course, the observer's first thought is not *I have to remember this so I can repeat exactly what was said.*"

"Right, and that rolls back in to my second point: We are much more inclined to remember something that we *expect* to see or hear. In an ATC clearance, we expect to hear the destination, the departure procedure name, the altitude, the departure control frequency, and the squawk. Then we mentally fill in the blanks when they read those to us. It's no different from walking down the street, coming to the corner crosswalk, and *expecting* to see that truck that's coming through the intersection. And that expectation dictates how we behave. We aren't surprised when the truck rolls by just a few inches in front of our noses. We don't step off the curb until we have looked for the expected traffic.

"So yesterday, the little drama you witnessed wasn't anything you *expected* to see. It didn't fit. Lots of you implied that it was so out of character that it was difficult to remember what was said or what the sequence of events really was. In fact, for Andrea, Donna's actions were so out of character that she simply couldn't hear her swearing."

David Hennessey squirmed uncomfortably in his seat as he glanced at the clock. "Jack, if I may, and I know we're running right up on the lunch hour, but what you are saying about the importance of context is very true. It is also extremely important to understand that when we rely entirely on expectation and context as the prompts for various behaviors, we run the risk of acting purely by rote.

"Your example of traffic at the city intersection recently had a tragic outcome when a British tourist in New York looked down the street to the *right*, saw no approaching traffic, and stepped out in front of a cab speeding through the intersection from the *left*. Obviously, he expected to see traffic approaching from the right, as it does in his country, not the left.

"So what you're going to see as we develop this program is that there are numerous paradoxes in human behavior; that a predictable and useful tool can also prove to be a trap. Very likely, that is not what our left-brained constituents want to hear, but somehow we'll need to demonstrate that reality in a way that will make intuitive sense."

Jack nodded his fervent agreement as he also checked the time. "Right on, Professor. More grist for the mill. Thanks."

"If we break right now, you may be able to beat the unwashed masses to the feeding trough. Once again, I want to thank Donna and Allen for their assistance. And I'm back in your good graces, right, Allen?"

Allen grinned widely and shook hands with Jack. "Yessuh, boss, you duh best." He put a hand on Donna's shoulder, and they strode out of the room like newlyweds leaving a Las Vegas chapel.

Chapter 12

DEBRIEF

The mood was somber as the 848 crew gathered in the conference room for the official debrief. Andy Caldwell had chosen a site in the executive office complex, away from the scrutiny of curious peers. He greeted every crew member, thanked each one, and provided them all with name tags. ANDY was scrawled in big blue letters over his right shirt pocket, which set the tone of the informality they could all expect in the day's proceedings.

Captain Danny Purcell had the most at stake since a finding of fault on his part could lead to the loss of his license and an excruciating recertification process, not to mention the inevitable cloud that would follow him the remainder of his career. If found culpable, he would always be known as 'the guy who pranged the seven-three in Pasco.' To an outsider, that might seem illogical. After all, no one was hurt, and the aircraft would likely be returned to service. However, *bending metal* is something few pilots ever experience in a thirty-year career, so when it happens, regardless of the circumstance, it has an enormous impact on a guy's reputation . . . and on his ego.

Even so, Danny carried himself with great confidence, perfectly turned out in a dark blue suit, tightly knotted burgundy tie, and highly polished black oxfords. Andy noted the care and concern he showed toward his crew. Barbara Haskell, the flight attendant injured in the incident, hobbled uncomfortably into the room, and Danny immediately embraced her and found her a chair at the end of the long table before introducing her to Andy. The arrival of the two other flight attendants and Gradin completed the team. The conversation was warm and positive. They acted as though they had known one another a lifetime.

Gradin's calm demeanor belied his churning insides. Never in a million years could he have foreseen a time when *he* would be the subject of an accident investigation. Once he had been the investigator, and that had been traumatic enough, but now *he* was under the microscope. Despite Andy's determination to mitigate the threat, an indefinable sense of foreboding tugged at Gradin's gut.

"Good morning, everyone." Andy raised both arms like a priest blessing his flock. "I'd like to get started now, so please find your nameplate on the table and have a seat in that location," he said, pointing toward the tables arranged to form a U. In an effort to foster collegiality, he had dispersed the crew members among the investigators and ALPA representatives.

Andy took a seat at the center of the table, bridging the two others. Keith Abernathy, the Omega chief counsel, and Rachel Roper, the stenographer and record keeper for the investigation team, sat on either side. Everyone else settled in and engaged in brief introductions.

—··· — — —··· — — —··· — — —··· — — —··· — — —···

"Let me tell you how I expect the day to go," Andy began as the room quieted. "I figure that we can accomplish what we need to by about 4:00. By then, we should have a very clear picture of what happened Friday night, along with a plan of action we all feel comfortable with. You will notice that all of you have a copy of the written statements provided by the crew, and we will take time for each of you," he said with a nod toward the 848 crew members, "to review what you have noted there and expand on those recollections if you have any additional insights today.

"The purpose of today's meeting is to compile an official account of the events leading up to your unexpected sojourn in the Eastern Washington desert last week. Two things are extraordinarily important to remember. First, anything and everything said here today is totally confidential—essentially, you are sworn to secrecy. Agreed?" Andy looked from face to face as everyone nodded assent. "Okay, good.

"The second thing is that today's conversation is *not* intended to find fault with anyone's actions Friday night. It isn't about your overall ability or performance. Our sole purpose is to find out *what* happened to see if we can uncover *why* it happened. Everyone with me so far?" He smiled and surveyed the room again. Everyone nodded.

"This is probably a good time to introduce all of the players. In fact, let's do this. Let me begin by introducing Danny Purcell. I believe that all of you know that Danny was the 848 captain. Danny's been in the left seat of the seven-three for about three years. Before that, he spent six years in the right seat of the DC-10 in L.A., right, Danny? He is extraordinarily well qualified, having been the squadron commander of a KC-10 unit at Travis several years ago. Danny, why don't you go ahead and introduce the crew."

Danny responded by giving a brief glowing description of each crew member. He told how Barbara Haskell, the senior flight attendant, had calmly and assertively directed passengers out of the two forward exits. She then jumped out, broke a bone in her ankle, and continued to direct people away from the aircraft.

He introduced and described the other two flight attendants with equal admiration, then focused his attention on his copilot. Gradin Jones, he said, "is as good as they come. As a Navy P-3 instructor pilot, he is particularly comfortable in the right seat and capable of multitasking better than anyone I've ever seen. If you check the transcript for cockpit configuration, you will discover that every switch and lever was set exactly as the evacuation checklist prescribes. He did all of that in a heartbeat, then bolted back into the cabin and herded people out of the over-wing exits, and finally out the aft exits. He was the last person off the aircraft. He even reminded me to bring the logbook and ops manual before he left the cockpit.

"Folks, Gradin's performance was absolutely textbook perfect. We all should be grateful," Danny concluded. Several people murmured their assent, particularly the flight attendants.

A brief wave of nausea swept through Gradin. No one would ever know that he had missed the fuel control switches on the evacuation checklist. Purely by chance, he saw them just as he swung his leg over the console to exit the cockpit. In one quick motion, he slammed the switches down to the cutoff position, thus avoiding a couple of very muddy faces. He shut it out of his mind and returned his attention to the head table. Andy also expressed his appreciation, then proceeded to introduce the five members of the accident investigation team. He particularly focused on the ALPA reps and made the point that they were the de facto representatives of the flight attendants, too. Those familiar with the history of the Air Line Pilots Association knew that it was so much more than a labor organization; it carried the safety banner for the entire industry. The association was invaluable in scrutinizing the obscure relationship of cause and effect, and its findings often led to significant improvements and contributions to the bottom lines of their parent companies.

Finally, he came to his own table, where he introduced Rachel Roper and Keith Abernathy, who provided some comic relief with his breezy, erudite spin on the legalities involved in accident investigations. "Folks, there is nothing more fulfilling in my profession than taking on the feds. They seem to live on another planet. 'Pilot error' is their mantra; it is the only conclusion they can see when a maze of contradictory evidence either obscures the facts or points toward the sacred cow of FAA culpability. I'm proud to say that no other airline in the industry provides the kind of support to its pilots that Omega does. I am also proud of your professionalism. It is a real pleasure working with you and the association."

With that, the meeting settled into the laborious review of the evidence, beginning with the written statements of the crew. Despite their intention to avoid any presupposition about the rudder, the focus was clearly fixed in that direction. Danny was quizzed thoroughly about any abnormality he might have experienced during the rudder check as they taxied out. This was the type of maneuver that is done by rote, and then verified in the reading of the checklist, and

Danny didn't recall any abnormal feel as he exercised the rudder pedals full-throw in both directions. He did joke about the occasional slip of the hand on the nosewheel tiller during the rudder check and how that would cause a sudden swing of the tail in one direction or another. The flight attendants smiled knowingly; they were accustomed to those infrequent excursions and usually managed to support themselves with both hands on the seatbacks as they walked through the cabin. But Danny insisted that he had been on his best behavior that night, and the flight attendants adamantly agreed.

A curious look appeared on Andy's face, and he interrupted to ask which of the flight attendants had been nearest the back of the airplane as they left the gate. Carol Unger assumed that it was she, and Andy asked if she had heard anything unusual from the tail section during the taxi out. She insisted that everything was normal but also noted that they were rushed through their safety checks due to the short taxi time in Pasco.

"Rachel, make a note reminding me to arrange for some supervisory pilots and flight attendants to ride a few legs on the seven-three and notice the typical sounds coming from the tail section during the control check." The uncomfortable truth was that at this point, no one could predict a possible recurrence, one that could have disastrous effects. Maybe they should alert flight attendants to notify the cockpit if there were unusual sounds back there. *But then again*, he wondered, *how many unwarranted concerns and needless delays would that lead to?*

✈

Lunch was catered. What seemed like a benevolent gesture from management was, in fact, an effort to shield the crew from the crush of uncomfortable encounters that lay ahead. For now, they were essentially sequestered, and Andy was determined to keep the anxiety in check. A working lunch also served the dual purpose of maintaining focus and maximizing available time.

Bill Eckerd, the ALPA member of the investigation team, found a seat next to Danny and motioned for Gradin to join them. "Guys, we need to start preparing for the inevitable proficiency check the fuzz always requires in situations like this. It usually takes several weeks for them to lay that on us, so that gives us plenty of time to make sure that you walk on water. You both okay? Any bumps or bruises?"

Both professed their Superman status.

"Good. How long did Andy say that he wanted you down here this week?"

"Didn't say. We were scheduled for that same rotation on Wednesday. Obviously, that's out, so I'm available as much as they need us," Danny responded.

"Me, too," Gradin assented with a faint grimace.

"We'll have a ground school guy give you a day of systems review. Then the next day, we'll get you in the sim and crank around the pattern for a while, get your confidence back and give you some hands-on time that should feel real good. No syllabus stuff, just yankin' 'n' bankin'. That okay?"

Both nodded.

"And, by the way, there will be an ALPA guy with you for all of this. I'm not sure yet who it will be, but I want you to know that you aren't alone in any of this. Our safety guys really believe we have an inherent flaw in those rudder actuators, but if we raise a red flag too early, we might jeopardize an objective look at the engineering data. So, unfortunately, the focus is on you guys right now, and we want to make sure this doesn't turn into a witch hunt. We'll blow the whistle whenever it seems necessary. Fair enough?"

"Fine by me," Danny responded.

Gradin thrust his jaw out and nodded in mock defiance. "Put me in, coach," he asserted with a clenched fist.

"Okay, I'll try to set up the systems review for tomorrow and the sim for Thursday morning. That way, you can get out of here Thursday afternoon and be home in time for dinner. I'll let you know later this afternoon."

He gulped down the last of his sandwich, patted both guys on the back, and made his way over to Andy. They conferred quietly for a moment. Then Bill left the room to make the arrangements.

Keith Abernathy slipped into the vacant seat and shook hands with both pilots. "Some days you get the bear, some days the bear gets you, I guess," he said with a dismissive shrug. "I love the way you guys handled yourselves out there. You are the clients a lawyer loves to represent. Not that I believe this will ever reach that point, but I just wanted you to know that I'm spring-loaded to respond to any FAA antics. And it can't hurt for Boeing to know that Omega Legal is squarely behind the crew. They may have the most to lose in this deal, so it may be a challenge to count on their unencumbered cooperation. It'll be fun to hold their feet to the fire."

He reached into his shirt pocket for a packet of business cards and handed one to each of them. "Call me if anything comes up that you think I should know. Home phone is there, too, so don't hesitate to call." He glanced at his watch. "Gotta hit the head," he said with a note of urgency. "I'll be in touch." A moment of silence allowed Danny and Gradin the chance to complete their meals. They chewed quietly and considered the upcoming events. The remaining cold cuts and salad were replaced with coffee and cookies. Everyone settled back into their original seats as Andy proceeded with the tedious reconstruction of Friday's events.

Most of the discussion focused on minute details: number of passengers and their injuries, response time of the emergency equipment and the specific action responders took, company response, and even the names of the personnel involved. Occasionally the crew was asked to clarify a point. There were transcripts of eyewitness accounts and statements from several passengers. Passenger comments were also available, and there were glowing accounts of the crew's performance to be included in the final report. Myriad details were recounted and recorded.

Gradin observed Danny's stoic demeanor, knowing he was wrestling with the responsibilities he faced as captain. Despite assertions to the contrary, he knew that no one could attend to the crew's best interests the way the captain could. And his self-interest was completely entwined with the welfare of the crew. Full vindication would attest to the strength of his leadership, but along the way, it would also be necessary to demonstrate superb aviation skills. *Easy, just like a fifty-year-old pitcher throwing a shutout,* Gradin mused.

True to his word, after a long break at 2:15, Andy wrapped things up by 3:45. Coke cans, coffee cups, and dog-eared documents cluttered the tables, but his secretary Penny Ramsey was the picture of efficiency as she assembled a neat stack of notes, photos, memos, and written statements. "Well, this should do for now," Andy joked as he tapped the ten-inch-high mass of documents. "You all get an A+.

"Now, just a word about what to expect as we move forward. Bud Sanders and his investigating team will carry the load from here on out. He may be in touch with you crew members for any clarification needed. There likely will be official depositions for the FAA. We'll bring you in for that, and trip drops are a given. Don't worry about this eating up your days off. And Keith and his folks will walk you through the deposition routine. You will not be hung out to dry, I guarantee you that.

"So questions? Comments? Complaints?" Most people shrugged and looked at the others for comment. Danny made a point of catching the eye of each of his crew. No one seemed concerned.

"Well, Andy, I think I can speak for the whole crew when I say that we are extremely grateful for the support that you and ALPA and the entire company are providing us," Danny ventured as the crew nodded. "I have a friend who flies for Brand X. He had a runway excursion several years ago, and his company *did* hang that guy out to dry. There were even conflicting details in the official company pubs, but poor ol' Rob had to go it alone. Essentially, he had to fight both the FAA and the company. Of course, ALPA helped, and he won, but it was a real nightmare.

"I may only be speaking for myself here, but I feel a tremendous amount of support." He nodded once emphatically.

"I do, too."

"Me, too."

"Yup," echoed the others.

●●●··━━━●●●··━━━━━●●●··━━━━━━━━━●●●··━━━━━●●●··━━━━●●●··

"You're welcome, guys," Andy said as he stood and gathered up the docs. "Bill, were you able to arrange the systems review and sim for these guys?" He looked at the ALPA rep.

"Yeah, I was about to talk to them about that," ALPA rep Bill Eckerd responded. He motioned to Danny and Gradin to join him. "So here it is, guys: room 118 tomorrow at 9:00. Willie Ashford will give you the review."

"Fantastic!" Danny said. "He was my instructor when I first checked out at Omega. He's a great guy; knows the airplane like he built it. And funny as a crutch, too."

"Good," Bill continued. "Then, on Thursday, you'll be in Sim 203 with Jeff Andrews at 8:00. He's an old hand—been on the airplane his whole life, I think. No briefing required. Just show up in time to fly. And remember, this is just for fun, just to get you back in the air and feeling comfortable. No need for any manuals. Well, maybe a spiral notebook or something, but travel light and try to enjoy. Any questions?"

"Nope, sounds good," Danny said. "Thanks for setting that up, Bill. It will feel good to have time in the box without all of the syllabus stuff we always have."

"Should be fun as long as we don't get that uncommanded rudder on short final." Gradin grinned.

"No chance." Bill elbowed Gradin's ribs and headed for the door.

"Drinks are on me, girls," Danny offered as he walked toward the flight attendants gathering their things. "Wanna walk across the street to the Hilton? That's usually a quiet place to get away."

"Sure, we can pretend it's an uneventful layover in Pasco."

"Yeah, except, for a change, the *captain's* buying."

Barb struggled to her feet. "And the old gal is on crutches," she said, then winced at the unexpected stab of pain. "Just get me on that 7:00 rocket to L.A."

"Ah, only a little ski accident, wasn't it?" Gradin asked as he helped to steady her. "Just back from the World Cup in Austria, as I recall. Would have won it all if that spectator hadn't run onto the course right at the finish of the downhill. A small price to pay for sparing his life." He grinned.

"I actually think the real story has more punch. Think of all the lives I saved with my heroics. And what do they say? 'It isn't the fall that hurts; it's the sudden stop that does the damage.'" They all drifted toward the door in conversation.

In the hotel bar, they finally settled around a table in a dark corner. "Uh, barkeep, whiskey for my troops and water for the horses," Danny announced.

"Excuse me, Captain, which ones are we?" an artificially timid voice asked.

"Your choice."

"Okay, make it whiskey. No, no, on second thought, I'll have a white wine, please."

The exchange mimicked the typical post-flight banter heard in hundreds of bars around the world every night. This is how teams are built and maintained. Their guard was finally down, probably for the first time since Friday. Drinks arrived, and Danny toasted their good fortune and good health. Barb added words of appreciation for the pilots' professionalism.

And just before they broke into a round of "Kumbaya," one of the women chortled, "Did I tell all of you about that funny little man who was the last passenger off the airplane?" No one nodded. "Well, he was the cutest little guy you've ever seen; completely unfazed by the circumstance. He shuffled back to 2R with his old worn briefcase clutched to his chest. Then he handed it to me and turned toward the door like he was gonna *walk* down the slide. It took me forever to get him to sit, and of course, because we were so close to the ground, it was more sit 'n' squirm rather than sit 'n' slide. By then, there were lots of people standing alongside to help. It was sort of surreal having everyone so calm—not nearly as exciting as a recurrent-training exercise."

"Thank God for small favors."

"Amen."

Gradin's attention lapsed, though he kept a grin pasted on his face and continued to nod at appropriate times. The desire to support the team trumped the impulse to withdraw, so he skillfully encouraged the conversation to flow.

"You know, ladies," Carol finally said, tapping her watch, "unless we want another night here in Graceland, we'd better get our buns over to the terminal."

"What gate is our flight?" Barb asked. "Alpha something," Jennie replied.

"Yeah, A12," Carol confirmed with a wave of a boarding pass.

"The airport van leaves here, what, every fifteen minutes?"

"Right, and it'll take me a couple of minutes to get out there," Barb sighed, reaching for her crutches. "You guys stay put and have another one for us." As she struggled to stand and the other flight attendants rose, both pilots scrambled to their feet and engaged in a round of hugs and farewells with their recently formed family.

"It's been a slice of heaven, gentlemen. Let's do it again sometime—uh, the drinks, that is." Carol beamed over her shoulder as two ambled, and one hobbled toward the door.

"Another scotch?" Danny asked as they settled back in.

"Sure, and I think I may do a salad, too," Gradin said, feeling his remaining energy drain away. He made no effort to conceal his fatigue; he could see Danny also slip lower into the upholstered armchair. They sat in silence.

Sarah stood with several other employees and waited for the bus to emerge from the evening darkness. Butterflies fluttered inside as she anticipated the possibility of another encounter with Brad Morehouse. She was flying the same trip all month: Los Angeles-Seattle-Anchorage the first night, then Anchorage-Fairbanks-Juneau-Seattle-Los Angeles the next. *Would they be teamed up again out of Fairbanks?* She knew it would be better if she never saw him again, but the thought was titillating, nonetheless.

The bus crept around the corner of the hangar and stopped in the designated spot. Air swooshed from the brakes, and double doors opened at the front and middle of the vehicle. Tired crew and ground personnel tumbled out and greeted friends waiting to take their places. The banter was both familiar and banal. "Yeah, 405 from Chicago is two hours late . . . the layover in New York was hair-raising . . . ship 345 is down for a generator change . . . headed for Maui tomorrow for a week," and on it went.

The last person off was Barbara Haskell as she struggled

with the crutches on the narrow steps. "Barb, oh, my God! I heard it was just a *twisted* ankle. Here, let me help," Sarah wailed as she reached to support Barb's elbow. Once firmly planted, Barb embraced her warmly. The staccato conversation continued, and she pointed to the bus. "You need to get over there for sign-in?" she asked.

"No, I'm okay. I always give myself extra time for the traffic. It was clear tonight, so I've got a few minutes to spare. I'll catch the next bus. What the heck are you doing out traveling around?" Sarah demanded.

"Oh, we had a day of debriefing in Memphis. Mamma Omega jus' takin' care o' da' help," she said, wagging a finger. "Makin' sure we all on da' same page. Know what ah mean?"

Sarah laughed. "Yeah, as if anyone needs to take care of you. Ginny called me Friday night to say it was you on that flight. That's where I got the *twisted ankle* impression. She said you guys were still up in Pasco and that everyone was okay. God, Barb, I can't imagine. Were you scared?"

"Well, you know, that stuff you hear about things going in slow motion is actually true. We swerved really hard during the takeoff roll, and it was obvious that we were off the runway. But the reversers came on immediately, and I guess because it's so flat up there, it didn't even occur to me to be scared."

She hesitated with her hand over her mouth. "Oops, there I go doing just what they said not to do." She paused, then straightened. "They really don't know what happened or why." She was standing, facing the brightly lit hangar. The twin 737s sat there with techs poring over both tail sections. She pointed toward the airplanes. "But that may give you a clue," she said with raised eyebrows.

"Makes me want to stay off that airplane for a while. But

if you want to stay out west, there's hardly a way to avoid it."

Sarah frowned. "Unless you want these damned all-nighters to Anchorage."

"Yeah, the pain we endure for time off. Speaking of which, how are Rob and the kids?"

"Oh, the kids are fabulous, the light of my life. Leslie is in nursery school this year, quite the little student. JR just follows me around all day when I'm home, tugging his blanket and asking a million questions. What a love," she said, tapping the luggage tag with her kids' picture. Then solemnly, "Rob is Rob; the angry, closed-off guy he's been since he left here, still in love with his cars. He raced Sunday in Lancaster and did pretty well, I guess. I try to keep the kids away from that as much as I can. Our day in the park was perfect," she said, brightening.

The conversation continued for several more minutes until the next bus arrived. They embraced again and promised to get together soon. Sarah was warmed by the encounter. She and Barb had started at Pacific on the same day twelve years earlier. They had remained close but spent little time together since Sarah's wedding. Her smile faded when she got one last look at the suspect 737s as the bus departed the maintenance area for the terminal.

When Gradin finally returned to his hotel, he entered the building through the side door to avoid the rollicking pack of pilots who inevitably congregated in the lobby. His room was dark, and the flickering fluorescent lamp cast blue shadows off the austere furniture. He collapsed on the bed and stared at the random Rorschach shapes in the plastered ceiling. An elephant's trunk wrapped around a writhing mermaid, and a flat, misshapen lobster reached its only claw toward the extended leg of a skinny dinosaur. Numerous combinations faded in and out of his consciousness. Alternately his eyes brimmed with tears as his breath came in shallow bursts before the calm of a frothy cloud formation or beckoning angel settled his breathing. Within minutes, his eyes closed, and muddled dreams took over completely.

The safety chain rattled and slammed at full extension as the door threw a sliver of bright light on the entry wall. "Oops, I'm sorry," a female voice exclaimed as the door closed gently. Gradin vaguely registered the unintended intrusion as he realized that someone had been given the wrong key at the front desk. He was surprised to find himself fully clothed on the bed, and he checked his watch to determine that he had been asleep for three hours; it was 10:30.

In Spokane, Alice and the kids would have finished dinner by now and settled down for their bedtime stories. *Charlie and the Chocolate Factory* was the current standard, and he could see his own *oompa loompas* nestled on the couch with their mom.

His eyes watered again as the recurring cold nausea swept through his system. *What a mess I've made. Three months ago, I was on top of the world. Now, look at me.* He grimaced, planted his feet on the floor, and removed his tie. Alice had engaged the emotional autopilot and gone away. Now, when he needed her most, he had no right to ask. His tough day at the office couldn't compare to her ongoing pretense as a loving wife in a failing marriage.

And it wasn't that he had simply stumbled and regained his footing. He was crashing out of control down a ravine, drawn by a hormonal allure stronger than the need for normalcy. Peggy continued to fill his senses; her taste, smell, murmurs, and hard-pounding passion consumed him whenever he opened that window in his psyche. "God help me," he whispered and closed his eyes in prayer. "Strength, please give me strength."

Chapter 13

LOFT FROM HELL

"Marsha, why don't you get us going with a description of your 737 crew study?" It was 8:01 Wednesday morning in Memphis, and the committee was off and running. Jack was painfully efficient at orchestrating a meeting.

"Okay." Marsha scrambled to her feet and moved confidently toward her previously prepared flip chart. "This was a study we did at NASA in which we evaluated the performance of randomly selected 737 crews from Brand X, not any of your stellar peers here at Omega. Basically, what we were after, without going into the study design criteria and protocols, was to determine what observable crew behaviors correlated with objective performance outcomes—in short, what successful crews did that the also-rans failed to do.

"We observed thirty-five crews flying exactly the same profiles under precisely the same conditions. You may be familiar with the growing use of line-oriented flight training—LOFT—in which crews are placed in a circumstance that exactly replicates a flight segment flown in real life, in real time. We simply gave them a flight plan, weather conditions, and all of the appropriate documentation and turned them loose. There was no additional preparation or briefing from the research team. Then the team set out to observe and record *everything* they did and said. We even counted the number of utterances they made in various circumstances.

"The scenario was pretty straightforward." She pointed to the route depiction on the first page of the flip chart. "A forty-five-minute flight from Richmond to Roanoke. Weather en route included thunderstorms, heavy rain and turbulence. They were to be dispatched in an aircraft with an inoperative radar."

"So let me get this straight," Patrick Finch interrupted. "These crews had no advance knowledge of what was coming. They just showed up cold and flew your scenario?"

"Exactly. And I'm glad you asked that, Patrick, because I failed to mention that we worked very closely with the ALPA safety committee at Brand X. They were completely on board and very supportive of this study. Obviously, the crews were totally protected. We only knew them by the first names they provided us. There was no license check, employee numbers, or any other identifying data. For our records, they were only numbers."

"What about check pilots and management guys?" Patrick pressed.

"Nope, only your basic line guys. No superheroes. And, I should add, we did all that we could to maintain a proprietary grasp on the script of the scenario. The crews didn't interact with each other, and there was very little chance any of them would share info with any of their peers. And when you think of it, particularly when they all completed the sim with at least a little egg on their faces, there was no real incentive to make some other guys look good. This was a no-jeopardy event, an extra day's pay for an hour in the box." She smiled.

"Mercenaries to the end," Jack joked.

"So as you can imagine, we threw a few curves at these guys, but all the same curves. It was a level playing field. First, in the weather briefing, the data showed a crosswind component that was slightly out of limits. The arrival ATIS showed the same, and I'll talk about that in a minute. Second, every crew experienced a B-system hydraulic failure at precisely the same elapsed time point. And finally, the weather conditions at the filed alternate were deteriorating throughout the event.

"These may appear to be innocuous factors, but as you will see, the multiplier effect can have a profound influence on an outcome," she emphasized.

"Yeah, so how many failed to get it back on the ground in one piece?" Vinnie quipped.

"Well, surprisingly, only three crews ended up in the weeds someplace. That's fewer than ten percent. Not bad. However, there were some very hairy situations up there, some with creative and sound resolutions, others with a big, blind luck component."

"So what was the takeaway here, Marsha?" someone asked.

"Let me turn the tables," she responded. "What *one* critical trait do you imagine most of the successful crews exhibited? And remember, our definition of success would likely vary from what those of you in the instruction/evaluation business would apply. I'll talk more about that later as well."

"That's an easy one," Bobby retorted. "I'll bet a day's pay that the best performers were the guys who know their stuff, the ones who can recite chapter and verse of the manual. Damn it, I don't know where we're goin' with this touchy-feely shit, but there's no substitute for knowledge and skill and command presence. No substitute, Marsha," he bellowed in disgust. "Either you can cut it, or you can't."

"Point well taken, Bobby. We did see a great deal of technical expertise, and in many cases, that was the difference between a positive and a negative outcome. But what else?" she queried.

"Situational awareness," Brad submitted. "It is so important to keep that big picture all the time."

"Now, you're moving a little closer to our findings." Her eyes sparkled with wry humor. "Break that down a little further, Brad. What are the key components of good SA?"

"Just as Bobby said." He squirmed forward in his chair. "Knowledge and psychomotor skills are—"

"I didn't say any *psychobabble* nothin'. Stick and rudder skills, damn it! How hard is that to understand?"

"Right, right, Bobby. I meant that yankin' and bankin' stuff. Ya pull back ya go up, ya push forward ya go down. That stuff. Right?" Brad asked with appropriate deference.

"Riiiight," Bobby exhaled through his teeth. "Keep it simple here, folks. For Christ's sake." He leaned back in his chair disgustedly.

"Okay, back to Marsha's question," Jack intervened. Bobby slouched further.

"Well, I suppose that the appropriate division of labor and responsibilities is also key," Brad continued.

"Exactly," Marsha followed.

"And priority—priorizi—oh, you know what I mean," Chester stammered.

"Well spoken for a Zoomie," Vinnie panned.

"I think I got that," Marsha followed. "That would be pri-or-it-i-za-tion. Right, Lieutenant?"

"Uh, yes, ma'am." Chester grimaced with a twinkle in his eye. "Anything with more than three syllables is upper-level stuff for me."

"The truth is that the primary success factor was not what we anticipated. We did see a great display of the expected skills—that is, technical expertise, workload management—things like that. However, we didn't find much correlation between those skills and overall outcomes.

"No more suspense," she said, flipping to the back page of the chart, on which she had written in bold, block letters: PLANNING. "Simple, eh? The crews that landed safely at their alternate or a secondary alternate most often were the ones who did the best planning, plain and simple.

"That is not to say that those crews were the ones to make the fewest identifiable errors or who handled the aircraft or communication with the greatest polish. They were simply the ones with the best outcomes."

She paused for a response. The room was quiet for a moment while David Hennessey surveyed the group curiously. "Marsha, expand on how you observed planning in the actual scheme of things. What did you see?" Jack prodded. "What we saw in the 'planners' were very collegial, self-effacing captains who engaged the copilots in the management process from the get-go.

"As soon as we turned the crews loose, we saw a variety of behaviors, probably not unlike what we might see among line pilots preparing for a typical flight. Some made a coffee run or head call the top priority. Some captains hoarded the paperwork and sent the copilot to preflight the cockpit. Others gave the copilot a military-style briefing, establishing the balance of power and captain's expectations. None of these were bad traits, mind you.

"However, the most successful captains went right to work, creating a plan with the help of the copilot. They sat down with the copilots and scoured the paperwork together for pertinent information. For instance, many of them—captains and copilots—discovered that the forecast destination winds were out of limits. And they planned accordingly. It caused several crews to look more closely at the alternate airport weather, and at least one of them contacted the dispatcher to arrange for a more suitable alternate before they even left the briefing room.

"So in essence what we saw among the top performers was that they not only had plan A, they also created a plan B, and often plan C. Imagine how fun it was to see the crews that approached the destination, checked the ATIS, and verified the crosswind out of limits. They simply stayed at altitude, requested clearance to an alternate with suitable weather, and, when they experienced the hydraulic failure, they just went through the checklist, noted the corresponding landing restrictions, and proceeded without incident. Pass go, collect $200.

"That was distinctly different from the crews who failed to detect the crosswind restriction. Those guys proceeded with the approach, bounced around in the heavy winds and rain, failed to break out at minimums, and executed a go-around before experiencing the hydraulic failure in the midst of a very-high-workload maneuver. Most often, those vignettes got very ugly. Some never did land successfully.

"I found it particularly interesting to imagine how similar the successful crews were to a John Wooden basketball team on a good night. What is it about Los Angeles basketball teams?" Marsha was adept with the sports analogies, knowing that an audience of pilots relates to the similarities with ease. "At any rate, I seriously doubt that Wooden starts those games by emphasizing basic skills—ball-handling, dribbling, passing, etcetera. He may mention them, but it isn't the prime emphasis. Sure, they warm up by practicing those things because those are the foundational skills. And, along with physical conditioning, they work on those individual skills for hours and hours on non-game days. But their overall game success depends on a great *plan*. John doesn't go to the locker room and say, 'Okay, guys, same plan as last night.' Hell, no! They craft a plan specifically designed for the circumstance at hand: player match-ups, known injuries, recent performance strengths and weaknesses. And they certainly have plans B and C. Maybe even D, E, and F."

"Excuse me, Marsha; may I interrupt for a minute?" Pat Finch rose and moved toward the front.

"Be my guest," she responded as she slipped back into her chair.

"Hold it, folks. I see a few people squirming in their seats. We should take a break, but first, let me thank Marsha for that briefing. Great stuff! Obviously, she was only able to scratch the surface, but we will return to those findings time and again. And who woulda thunk it?" He raised an eyebrow. "The right stuff is PLANNING? Be back at 9:20, please."

Jack huddled with Pat Finch, and Bobby joined them. The three slipped out the door, still deep in conversation.

Brad found Marsha. "Treat's on me as long as you settle for the twenty-five-cent coffee mess."

"Can't be as bad as the camp coffee I cut my teeth on," she said with a grin.

"Hey, I enjoyed your presentation. It makes perfect sense, but I've never heard it expressed in those terms. In fact, even though I saw it practiced all the time in the military, it was never acknowledged as a key to success. I try not to trade on my time with the Blue Angels, but I think you would be particularly interested to know more about how the team *really* functions."

They strode into a glorified closet equipped with a small stainless steel sink and a half-full steaming Pyrex coffee pot. He dropped two coins in a coffee can, filled two Styrofoam cups, and motioned toward a basket with the small paper bags of sugar and creamer.

"No, thanks, black's good. It looks simply, uh, chewable."

"This is where they train the flight attendants to make coffee." His arm swept around the small room as he handed her a cup. "You put it on. Go read a magazine for two hours, and when you come back . . . voilà."

"But where are the dirty aluminum pots? Those burn it so much more efficiently."

"Enough, enough." He grimaced. "As I was saying, Professor, I have *lived* your premise, vivid and high-speed. And it worked very much as you described Wooden's Bruins." They slipped past the crowd, gathering in the room and headed down the hall. "The only difference was that *we* had a player-coach in the lead aircraft. Our leader—our John Wooden—we simply called 'Boss.' Just as you said, we spent hundreds of hours every year practicing those basic maneuvers, building that foundation. We flew twice a day seven days a week to perfect the basics, first as a single aircraft, then a two-plane group, then four, and finally six. But now that I think of it, the learning really occurred in the briefs and debriefs."

"How so?" Marsha asked.

"Obviously, we had video, and we had a whole team of qualified observers. As I said earlier, before and after every flight, we briefed in exquisite detail. Everyone on the team had input: what they saw, what they did, what they failed to do, what they expected to do better. And you really had to check your ego at the door because there was nothing more dangerous than a guy who denied an error or, worse, denied the possibility of making an error. Errors were expected, but by being as thorough as we were, we could keep the errors small and manageable."

"It's so hard to imagine, watching those shows, that there were any errors at all. It always looks so perfect."

"Well, trust me, there are. But the part you might find most interesting has to do with planning. Before every show— and we're talkin' nearly 100 each year—we started the whole process with a comprehensive brief. And as you suggested, the boss didn't ever say 'same ol' stuff, guys,' even if we were flying exactly the same show, at the same location, under the very same conditions. As I said before, the boss articulated every piece of that plan.

"He talked us through every maneuver, in real time, just as it would take place. And we all internalized those pictures and cadences."

"You're singing my song here, Brad," Marsha said. "I left off my description of 'the LOFT from hell' right at that point." They both leaned against the wall outside of the classroom and gingerly sipped the coffee. "What we concluded was that those good captains who did the effective planning—and Bobby will love this one—created what we called a *shared mental model*. Everyone ends up having the same picture in his or her head of how something is going to unfold."

"I'd love what, sweet pea?" redneck Bobby blustered as he rounded the corner and nearly ran them over.

"Oh, Captain Clark, we were just thinking of you," Marsha said calmly.

"Yeah, so I heard. What is it that I would *love* so much?" he demanded.

"Well, I was just explaining to Brad how, in our study, the good captains—the ones like you, I'm sure—were the ones who briefed their crews in a way that allowed them all to have the same picture of what was likely to take place throughout the flight."

"Yeah, I brief 'em all right. And when I'm done, there's no question of who is in charge."

"That makes sense, Bobby," she cooed. "You certainly don't want any misunderstanding about that."

Brad remained silent, knowing that any mention of the Blue Angels to Bobby would trigger a condescending diatribe. "Our observers refer to that initial action by the captain as 'setting the tone.'" She raised her eyebrows. "Much of the remaining interaction flows from that first impression. You know the old saying, Bobby."

"Yup, and there's no chance that they'll walk all over you when you spell it out to start with. I've never had a mutiny." Bobby nodded confidently.

It ain't over 'til the fat lady sings, big guy, Brad mused. *Someday that copilot you have so artfully engaged will intentionally let you land on the wrong runway. Just like the guy did in Mexico City when so many people died.*

"Yo, back on your heads, kids." Jack stuck his head out the door and waved a hand at the three.

"Bobby, this is a great start to the conversation about team building. You probably have more experience in that area than anyone in the room," Marsha gushed in an effort to defuse the growing tension.

Jack remained standing at the front of the room. "I've asked Pat to give us a very brief overview of some psychological distinctions that often escape our attention. But first, Pat, how many psychologists does it take to screw in a light bulb?"

"Two?" Pat shrugged.

"No, just one, but it really has to want to change." Everyone in the room groaned.

"And how many pilots does it take to screw in the light bulb?" Andrea chimed in.

"None," Vinnie fired back. "We're not afraid of the dark."

"Ha! 'None' is correct. But I heard that pilots are so damned smart they never screw in a light bulb—but they do screw in a hot tub."

"Ooohhh, and how many flight attendants does it take?" Vinnie persisted.

"What, to screw in a hot tub?" she responded.

"No, the light bulb, damn it. It takes ten. One to hold the bulb and nine to turn the ladder."

"Hey, hey, hey," Jack yelped. "I've completely lost control again. On with it, counselor."

"I may have misunderstood, Jack, but I didn't think that it was the social skills of our crews that you wanted me to address. I thought it was basic human brain function." Pat stood and moved to the front.

"But that 'human' qualifier eliminates most of our pilots, Professor," Andrea said sweetly.

"Miss Goebel, proceed to the corner and stand silently facing the wall until further notice," Jack said, motioning vigorously. "I'm certain that there will be no further interruptions. Go ahead, Pat."

Andrea grinned and slipped down in her chair.

"Okay, please keep in mind that I'm speaking in generalities. It's just the average, everyday brain that I'm talking about here. I make no judgment about the likelihood that any of us would appear in such a subset."

"Is a 'subset' anything like a cockpit, or is it more like a hot tub?" Bobby groused.

"Good question, Bobby. It could be either, I suppose," Pat continued. "Very simply, here's where I'm going with this. Our brains have two equally capable hemispheres, left and right. Generally speaking, both of those hemispheres have distinctly different functional processes for solving problems. Think of it this way," he said, tearing off a blank page from the flip chart. Beneath it was a page with two columns of characteristics.

LEFT BRAIN	RIGHT BRAIN
analytical	creative
logical	free-thinking
detail- and fact-oriented	able to see the big picture
numerical	intuitive
likely to think in words	likely to visualize more than think in words

"Now, don't get too hung up on each characteristic. These are generalities that describe the aggregate. We tend to have a dominant hemisphere that significantly influences the way we conduct ourselves. So again, in a general sense, each of us can be described as either left-brained or right-brained.

"For instance, we can safely say that scientists are left-brained and theologians right-brained. Though, now that I think of it, I knew a Methodist minister once who was a PhD biochemist for Chevron in his early life. You can only imagine how those science-based, left-brained sermons played out."

A few hands shot up, and little conversations broke out around the room. "So hey, before I field those questions and open it up to conversation, let's do this. Count off by threes." He pointed to Kent Harvey at the table to his left to start. They all complied.

"Now, ones assemble at this table," he said, again pointing at Kent's table. "Twos here at the center table, and threes, to my right." He waited for the tempest to subside.

"Oh, God, look at that," Andrea chortled. "Vinnie, Jack, Bobby, and Loren all at the same table. Shouldn't they be way over there to the left someplace—or out in left field, maybe?"

"Andrea! Can it!" Jack cautioned through eyes narrowed in mock anger.

...▪—▪—▪...▪—▪—▪—▪...▪—▪—▪—▪—▪...▪—▪—▪—▪—▪...▪—▪—▪...

Pat moved from table to table, distributing stacks of blank paper.

"Here's what we're going to do. Each team is going to make paper airplanes, as many paper airplanes as you can in a ten-minute time frame. Now listen carefully, because there are some important stipulations, and I'm only going to say them once.

"First, every airplane must have the same design.

"Second, every airplane must be able to fly from one side of the room to the other.

"And third, each team member must participate in the actual production process.

"The winning team will be the one that makes the most airplanes that can fly across the room and hit the opposite wall. Simple enough?"

There were no negative responses.

"Okay, you have five minutes for research and development, then I will let you know when the ten-minute production phase begins. Have at it."

"Ooohhh baby, we've got this one in the bag, boys. I have the design that'll knock 'em dead." Jack rubbed his hands together in delight. "Check it out." He proceeded with a series of intricate folds that resulted in a blunt-nosed origami masterpiece. However, at the same time, the other three were also deeply involved in reliving their own childhood paper airplane adventures.

They all completed similar-looking planes and set out to convince the others that theirs was best. "Look how this beauty flies," Jack demanded. He held it to his ear and threw it like a dart. His creation sailed wings level for several feet, then rose swiftly into a full loop, and slammed straight down into the floor, not halfway across the room. "Aaahhh, bummer!" The others hooted and tossed their own inventions with varying degrees of success. A heated debate over the merits of each ensued.

A similar competition played out at the next table, including the raucous catcalls and colorful banter. However, at the third table, the one including Dr. Marsha Ann Hilbert, the mood was calm and methodical.

She, along with Kent Harvey, George Moffett, and Andrea Goebel, had apparently settled on a design within minutes. Then they went on to master the production scheme that Kent demonstrated with slow and calculated precision. Marsha took notes and established a step-by-step method for duplicating their simple design.

"One minute 'til production starts," Patrick barked.

Jack and Vinnie continued to wrangle over the prototype choice. "That damned blunt-nosed thing is always going to loop, Jack. You need the longer nose for longitudinal stability."

"No, no, you just add a little droop to the trailing edge," Jack insisted as he made minor slits in the back of the wings and folded down a one-inch tab on each. Again he launched his craft, only to see it wobble awkwardly, roll to one side, and spiral into the floor.

"Time's up. Now you have ten minutes to produce as many of your designs as possible. You have to settle on one of those, you guys," he said, pointing to Jack and Vinnie.

Jack's shoulders slumped in defeat as Vinnie began directing the production of his longer, sleeker model. The others followed along, though Jack was a reluctant contributor. He shook his head gloomily. "If the board of directors could only see us now. This would give them so much confidence knowing how the $11 million they allocated for this project is being spent."

After ten minutes, the frenetic activity ceased, and a tally was taken. Each table had a pile of dubious-quality productions, but the bluster was unrelenting.

Fortunately, Pat had a firm grasp on the situation, and he herded the cats into three groups standing behind a masking tape stripe on the floor on one side of the room facing the opposite wall. "Okay, one at a time, the chief pilot from each squadron will step to the line and fly his or her team's craft across the room. Only those aircraft that strike the wall while airborne will be deemed acceptable. Team one," he said, pointing toward Jack and Vinnie's table.

"Who's our chief? Well, how about 'age before beauty'? Bobby, show 'em how it's done," Vinnie coaxed.

"Oh, sure," Bobby responded, raising both hands in surrender. "Make me the goat. Negative, dudes. One of you aerospace geniuses can do the honors. I'm only minimum-wage labor here."

"Do it, Vinnie. This is your baby," Jack prompted.

Vinnie stepped forward and fired the first of his creations across the room. It sped straight as an arrow, then abruptly rolled to the left and smacked into the floor.

"Easy, big guy," Loren cautioned. "Finesse it like a 727. Just float it out there, nose high, and let it glide on home."

"Float like a 727?" Chester guffawed. "That would be 'float like a toolbox,' you mean, don't you?" He reached playfully for their pile of planes, grabbed one, and wadded it into a ball. Then he threw it hard toward the wall. It spun and arced hard to the right, but still managed to hit the target. "There you go—a Gemini capsule on its reentry trajectory."

"Just what we planned," Loren responded, crunching another of their creations into a ball. Vinnie followed suit while Jack and Bobby looked on scornfully. Crumpled paper airplanes cascaded around the room, few hitting the opposite wall.

"DQ, DQ." Pat thrust a thumb over his right ear. "You're outta here. The aircraft must have wings. Captain, take your team and return to base."

In mock dejection, all four slunk toward the door and exited. "I'll buy," one of them chirped. Then, without acknowledging the rest of the group, they disappeared down the hall toward the coffee room.

Pat ignored the exodus and continued. "Okay, team two, show us what you have."

The second team had greater success than the first. More than half of its craft found the target. Then team three stepped up to the line.

"We call this 'The Gender Bender,'" Andrea proclaimed on cue, displaying one of their creations for all to see. "You take a flaccid male design and form it into a perfectly straight projectile," she said. Marsha bowed her head in embarrassment as the room erupted in derisive hoots and howls.

"Please demonstrate, Ms. Goebel," Patrick played along. She ran her thumb and fingers along the fuselage several times, held it up for inspection, then puckered her lips, and blew gently on the nose of the plane. Without acknowledging the hilarity, she turned toward the wall, stroked the craft one last time, and cast it gently across the room.

"Bull's-eye!" she shrieked. "It works every time." She hopped gleefully and sailed two more with equal success.

"Go ahead, Captain, you're on a roll," Pat coaxed. Andrea continued, hitting the target with all but two of the planes.

"Hold the phones, we have a winner, folks. The Gender Bender prevails. Dick Rutan would be proud.[29] Now, please pick up the mess while I go find the lost squadron. Be back at 10:30." He smiled and waved them away.

The mood shifted back to calm collegiality as the committee returned, and the conversation went on for more than an hour. Several discussed right-brain/left-brain contrasts and ways in which those factors affected the conduct of the exercise. Pat continued as moderator. "So what was that silly paper airplane thing all about?" he deadpanned.

"Ego," Andrea chirped with a disdainful look at Jack. "Moi?" he responded incredulously. "You mean my insistence that I had the perfect design had an effect on the outcome of our team effort?"

"Yeah, if you'd only listened to me in the first place, we woulda killed 'em," Vinnie insisted.

"Oh, bull! A little tweakin', and mine was perfect." Loren and Bobby smiled in silence.

"You obviously were too busy to notice, but our stellar female designer quietly suggested a simple and functional design. Kent broke it down into the basic ABCs, and we all pitched in. No ego, just teamwork."

"Hmm." Jack thoughtfully stroked his chin and slipped out of his Santini persona. "So you mean that four guys with clashing egos were no match for two women and two men working together, that your team had a common objective, a *plan*, and a willingness to put aside your own needs in favor of the common good?"

"Ask not what your country can do for you . . . " Chester intoned.

"Yeah, sounds like a classic Republican/Democrat philosophical split."

"No, no, no," Jack interceded. "Stay focused here, kids. Let's translate our little exercise into cockpit dynamics. When you have a captain, or any crew member for that matter, who insists that he knows the answer and that everyone else needs to just fall in line, then you end up having a crew of one. He loses at least half of the brain cells available."

"Right cells or left cells?"

"It depends on who you lose, I suppose. But one way or another, a good leader wants input from as many sources as possible. It's often a real challenge for captains to demonstrate that openness."

Vinnie smiled as he spoke. "You'd be amazed at how often a captain will say to a crew that he wants them to tell him if they see anything they don't like, then completely shuts them down or ignores them when they bring something to his attention. You can imagine how effective the team is after that."

"Yeah, you may remember that Pacific lost an airplane down in Mexico one night when the crew was known to be having serious conflict," George said. "Every indication was that the copilot let the captain land on the wrong runway, *a closed runway*, even when he knew it was the wrong one. Of course, what he didn't know was that there was a dump truck on that wrong runway. They hit it, tore off an engine, and careened across the entire airport before slamming into a hangar. Perfect example of being dead right," he lamented.

"I rest my case," Vinnie proclaimed.

Jack went on. "So I hadn't expected to play into Marsha's hand like that, but just by chance, she got to act out the favorable behavior she had described to us earlier. Very subtly, she became the de facto leader, engaged the whole team, made a plan, carried it out, and succeeded impressively. All the while, four of us yahoos were jousting with each other and failing miserably.

"Quite frankly, that little experiment worked much better than I had imagined it would. We may want to include it in the program because here's what I imagine happening in the classes we conduct for our pilots. There will be a great deal of resistance, and the worst thing we can do is preach to them, tell them that they are doing it all wrong and that we have all of the answers.

"So what we hope to do, or at least I hope to do, is two primary things: provide some experiential learning—paper airplanes, problem-solving, give and take—and allow them to hear their peers talk. That may sound easy but think of this for a second. How many times does a captain get to hear other captains talk about how they do things or, better yet, how they *feel* about the things they do?"

"Ahem." Bobby scowled but refused to take the bait. "This program will simply be a catalyst for change, not a recipe for perfect behavior.

"Okay, okay, enough already. Let's go eat. Back at 1:00," he said with a salute.

Sharply at 1:00, Jack began again. "In February of 1981, one of our L-1011 TriStars departed San Diego for the all-nighter to

Memphis. Right after takeoff, during the initial power reduction, it became apparent that the stabilizer was jammed.

"Picture this carefully. They were very nose-high and reduced the power. What happened?"

"What happened to cause it, or what happened as a result of the power reduction?" Loren wanted to know.

"Good, right. Yes, I meant, what happened as a result of the power reduction?"

"Deceleration," George responded. "Exactly. And what could you expect next?"

"Well, ultimately, they would decelerate into a stall. That can ruin your whole day."

"Right, and if that had happened, we'd still be trying to recover from the enormity of the loss. But they didn't stall. They didn't even make the headlines. Instead of allowing the deceleration to continue, the captain simply added power and resumed a steep climb.

"At first, the rest of the crew wasn't even aware of the circumstance. So he alerted them to what was happening, asked the first officer to declare an emergency, and requested clearance to proceed straight out without altitude restriction.

"So they stabilized the situation—bad pun, sorry—they flew the airplane and proceeded to solve the problem. They got out the after-takeoff checklist, then went right into the jammed-flight-control checklist. But when they completed the checklist, they were left with no answer to the problem. And by the way, George, as a result of the creative solution and a great outcome, the L-1011 checklist was revised."

"Yeah, I'm pretty familiar with that one; it's very innovative."

"It sure is. Put yourself in this situation. You've completed the checklist and haven't resolved the problem. You're nose-high and climbing. Well, it just so happened that this captain had a well-developed right brain.

"First, he kept the big picture in mind and requested a turn toward Los Angeles. He also had the senior flight attendant come up so they could include her in what was going on. Then, just on a hunch, the captain began reducing power on engines one and three, the wing-mounted engines. And what do you suppose happened?"

As though on cue, George responded, "The nose began to fall, and the rate of climb decreased."

"Precisely. No one had ever really thought of it before, but on the TriStar—and the DC-10, for that matter— asymmetrical thrust has a longitudinal component as well as a lateral component."

"Whoa, whoa, whoa," Andrea pleaded. "Human-speak, please."

"Sorry. Just think of the fact that the engines are always pushing at the point where they are attached to the aircraft. On two-and four-engine aircraft, we have always dealt with the fact that a loss of power on one engine will result in the engine on the opposite wing pushing that wing harder, and thus faster than the wing with the faulty engine. And that additional push—or thrust—will cause the aircraft to turn toward the bad engine. We call that asymmetrical thrust. Though we don't do it typically, you can actually turn an aircraft by using asymmetrical thrust. Does that make sense?"

"Yup." She nodded intently.

"The point is that we had never considered—or needed to consider—the complex aerodynamic shift that occurs when the wing-mounted and tail-mounted engines are producing different amounts of thrust. With all other systems functioning normally, you simply adjust the stabilizer trim and continue. Andrea, see me at the break, and I'll draw you a diagram."

"Okay."

"So our right-brained captain had intuitively discovered that by creating asymmetry between the wing-mounted and tail-mounted engines, he could induce enough change in nose attitude to control the climb and the descent of the aircraft.

"They spent nearly an hour off the coast, west of L.A., carefully experimenting with a variety of power settings and configurations. That also provided time for the flight attendants to prepare the passengers for, for—what shall we say?—the possibility of a less than perfect landing. Once they were satisfied that they could handle the aircraft with unique thrust combinations, they set up for an approach to the east and landed without incident."

"Did I miss anything, Captain Clark?" Jack looked at Bobby, who smiled impishly. "Sorry to blow your cover, pal." Now it was clear. Bobby Clark had been the captain of that ill-fated TriStar.

"No problem, my friend. I'm as tired of the ugly persona you laid on me as everybody else is. Let me comment on the jammed stabilizer. Then I'll address the redneck issue."

He sat forward in his chair as everyone smiled at the ruse. "Your characterization was unduly complimentary, Jack. That night we had the most effective team effort I have ever experienced. Most of you don't know this, but Loren Hughes was the copilot on that flight, and I am forever indebted to him for his superb performance. The thing he did best was to maintain the big picture. He worked with ATC in explaining the nature of our problem and in positioning us right off the end of the runway in L.A. while we played with the various configuration and thrust combinations. And though what he did was creative, it was also very methodical. No wonder he has that degree in systems management. We also had a great SO who took charge of the coordination with the flight attendants and the communication with the company. He was amazing."

Brad noticed the looks on people's faces, not believing that this was the same Bobby Clark, who had been pushing their buttons for the last two days. "And I really stand by some of my rednecked ranting," Bobby said with a grin. "We *did* rely very heavily on technical expertise. We did everything by the book—that is, as far as the book would take us. As Doctor Hilbert so eloquently noted, the technical expertise of our crew was foundational to our success. If we had fumbled with the checklist, bungled the communication, and failed to fly the aircraft competently, we could never have gotten to the creative stuff. In a sense, it was left-brained competence that allowed us to access the right-brained solutions."

"That's an interesting way to connect the dots, Bobby," Marsha followed up. "I think what I'm hearing you say is that by being technically competent and disciplined in your approach to the problem, you were able to carve out some time to explore various creative options and save 200 or so lives. Interestingly, another of the conclusions we arrived at in our study was that successful crews *create time* for problem-solving. You did that extraordinarily well," she said with a respectful nod.

"We did, and of course we were lucky, too. Unlike the United crew in Portland, we had more fuel than we knew what to do with. We could have stayed airborne for six hours. All that time, we spent planning and experimenting was to our bene-fit. We burned nearly 20,000 pounds of fuel. That allowed us to have a lower approach speed and a shorter landing roll.

"Now, let me address the issue of my abrasive personality. It was Jack's idea precisely because that ugly attitude is very prevalent among many of our old-school captains, even some of the copilots. We are going to encounter that in our classes, and we need to plan accordingly." Bobby paused and looked intently from face to face. Murmurs percolated as the group realized this thoughtful and charming pilot was the antithe-sis of the irascible provocateur he had portrayed until then.

Brad was particularly relieved to realize that the guy had been goading him intentionally. When they met during the break, Bobby expressed his sincere admiration for Brad's Blue Angels experience and the fact that he was recognized as a stellar performer. They exchanged stories, and several more layers of Bobby's disguise peeled away. It turned out that he was also a Navy pilot, a Vietnam (F-4) Phantom driver. Un-like Brad, he had stayed in the reserves and completed his twenty-year career as the commanding officer of a reserve squadron at Miramar.

Bobby's close friendship with Harley Hall gave him particular reverence for the Blue Angels. He and Harley had been squadron mates in VF-154 back in the mid-sixties when they had two combat cruises aboard the *Ranger*. Apparently, Hall was a bigger-than-life character who had an enormous influence on everyone he met. His inspiration prompted Bobby to remain in the reserves after he began his airline career at Omega.

Bobby went on to explain that Harley was known for two things in particular. In the early seventies, he had been the leader of the Blues. They were flying the Phantom during those years, and it was a window-shattering event when they streaked by in tight formation, only a few feet off the deck, with the lead aircraft—Harley's—in a rock-solid inverted position.

They both knew that the glamour had given way to the reality of the war when Harley returned to the fleet to become CO of VF-143 aboard the *Enterprise*. Naval aviators of that era will never forget that Harley Hall was the last of their brothers lost in Vietnam. He was shot down late in the afternoon on January 27, 1973, the official last day of hostilities.

"What an awful sight that must have been, a wounded Phantom limping toward the coast but rolling out of control just before they went feet-wet. Both he and his RIO[30] parachuted safely. They were even seen futilely racing around on the ground."

Bobby pulled up his right shirtsleeve a little to expose the POW/MIA bracelet he wore with "Captain Harley Hall" inscribed on it. "I've stayed in touch with his wife. She is an amazingly strong woman. The government hasn't been very helpful. First, they claimed he was killed on the day he was shot down, but then they changed the story and said he was being held captive. We know he wasn't released with the others in 1973, and none of the POWs had seen him or even heard anything about him.

"But Mary Lou hasn't given up, and I'm sure there is more to the story yet to come." They both nodded their heads sadly and were silent for a moment. Bobby put a finger on his lower lip and rolled his eyes up in thought. Then he looked directly at Brad. "You know, it is often that kind of loss that builds the most character in those of us still here. I know I wouldn't have gone on to achieve what I did in the reserves without Harley's influence."

He put a hand on Brad's shoulder. "I also know you experienced a big loss on the Blues, and I'm guessing you may be beating yourself up over that one. At some point, teams always fail, Brad. Bring the lessons you learned from that to this program. Share that stuff with us. Make your buddy's life and death count for something."

"Hmmmm." Matt's image played through Brad's head. "Yeah, I will, Bobby," he finally said resolutely.

After the break, Jack gave Bobby the reins, and the pilot happily trotted the group off in a new direction. "We can all learn so much from the Eastern disaster in the Everglades."

The older heads nodded in assent.

"Go ahead, Bobby. This is a good time. Give us the blow-by-blow on Eastern 401. Several of these folks don't know the story," Jack said.

Bobby stood and continued to talk. "Okay. This was back in December of 1972.[31] The Eastern TriStar was approaching Miami, and, just like United in Portland almost exactly six years later, they had an unsafe-nose-gear light. No, more accurately, they did not have a safe *down-and-locked* indication. They notified approach control and requested VFR holding west of the airport.

"So there they were, motoring around in the pitch black over the Everglades. The copilot was flying while the engineer and captain troubleshot the problem. They were off to a good start, but it went downhill—quite literally—from there.

Here, let me show you what we've worked up with the first of that $11 million we have to spend. Get those lights, will you please, Jack?" He motioned to the switch near the door.

The four-by-eight projection screen lit up with the video re-creation of the accident. Three pilots sat in a TriStar cockpit. Hoots and guffaws followed as everyone recognized that Bobby Clark was the actor in the captain's seat. A written synopsis of Eastern Flight 401 scrolled slowly up the screen, and the dialogue began with the captain talking on the radio and the copilot at the controls.

At 23:33:05, the captain spoke: "Well, ah, tower, this is Eastern, ah, 401. It looks like we're gonna have to circle, we don't have a light on our nose gear yet."

The tower responded. "Eastern 401 heavy, roger, pull up, climb straight ahead to 2,000, go back to approach control, one-twenty-eight-six."

Copilot: "Twenty-two degrees, twenty-two, gear up."

Captain: "Put power on it first, Bert. Thatta boy. Leave the damned gear down 'til we find out what we got."

Copilot: "All right."

Engineer: "You want me to test the lights or not?"

The light test failed to illuminate the suspect light. Bobby allowed the video to run as the three pilots bumbled around trying to remove the nose gear light from the socket. The captain seemed oblivious to the copilot asking him whether he, the copilot, should continue to handle the controls as he watched the engineer lean forward and wrestle with the light on the panel to the copilot's left. Yet a minute later, he instructed the copilot to connect the autopilot. The copilot complied by raising the autopilot engagement switch into the on position.

Then the captain asked the copilot to see if *he* could remove the nose gear light. Again the copilot leaned forward and began wiggling the light unsuccessfully. The copilot continued to struggle with the light as the captain sent the engineer down into the electronics bay to check the nose gear position visually through a viewing port in the nose of the aircraft.

By this point, the entire committee was squirming in their seats as they observed the crew in a muddle with no plan whatsoever. No one was really flying the airplane.

The crew asked random questions, made unconvincing assertions, and uttered one expletive after another.

"How much fuel we got?"

"Fifty-two-five."

And, "West heading you wanna go left or—naw, that's right, we're about to cross Krome Avenue right now."

Followed by: "I don't know what the fuck is holding that son of a bitch in!"

At about that moment, a pronounced click was heard coming from the instrument panel. People groaned, and Bobby paused the projector.

"Note the time," he said, pointing to the digits in the lower left of the screen. "That click occurred approximately seven minutes after their missed approach. It may not have been obvious to all of you, but the sound was the autopilot disengaging, probably as a result of the copilot leaning forward on the controls. But keep watching," he said as the video came back to life.

None of the Eastern 401 pilots had heard the click, nor did any of them seem to hear the altitude warning horn alerting them to an altitude deviation greater than 250 feet. There was no visible horizon, and all three sets of eyes were focused on the faulty light. The aircraft slowly drifted toward the swampy abyss.

The engineer made a second trip to the electronics bay but returned without successfully sighting the crosshatch on the top of the nose gear coupling.

"Now, pay close attention to this part," Bobby said. "They are trying to reassure each other."

Captain: "I'm sure it's down; there's no way it could help but be."

Copilot: "I'm sure it is." Captain: "It free-falls down."

Copilot: "The tests didn't show that the lights worked, anyway."

Captain: "That's right." Copilot: "It's a faulty light."

"But then the engineer kinda timidly says this." Bobby had timed his remark perfectly. The voice from the screen spoke. "I don't see it down there."

For the next thirty-five seconds, the captain and the flight engineer discuss how to illuminate and observe the nose assembly through the viewing port.

At 23:41:40, the approach controller said, "Eastern, ah, 401, how are things comin' along out there?"

To which the captain responded, "Okay, we'd like to turn around and come back in."

The controller issued a left-turn clearance at the moment the copilot looked down and said, "Hey, what happened to the altitude?"

Captain: "What?"

Copilot: "We're still at 2,000, right?" Captain: "Hey, what's happening here?"

Three seconds later, at 23:43:12, there was the sound of impact, and the video playback stopped.

The room remained dark and quiet.

"Amazing, huh?" Bobby switched the lights on and strolled back to center stage.

"Yeah, you sure got a sense that no one was in charge," Kent offered.

"Yes, and the fact that the captain really confused the situation by not establishing *who was to fly* and *who was to fix*, as they say. The copilot even asked if the captain wanted him to fly but got no response. And then the captain directly involved him in the troubleshooting process. There was no one minding the store."

"So was it poor leadership or poor followership, Bobby?" Andrea asked.

"Both, I suppose." He shrugged in resignation. "You might also say it was a matter of corporate culture. Things were pretty loosey-goosey on some of the Eastern flight decks back then. There wasn't the structure we're beginning to see so much of today in the airlines. But we have a long way to go at Omega, probably more than most other airlines. Doctor Hennessey reminded us that we're known as 'The Captains' Airline,' as though captains can do no wrong." His look of dismay said even more than his words had.

"Bobby, may I jump in here for a second?" Loren asked. "I told you about the little black books and all of the weird behaviors copilots had to keep track of ten years ago."

"Engineers, too," Chester insisted.

"Oh, absolutely, Chess. And you probably remember this. In 1986, NOVA ran a special program on the implementation of CRM in the airline industry. After United in Portland, the FAA strongly recommended that airlines adopt such training, and most did.

"Yeah, Omega's reluctance to get with the program must have pissed off the big guy, because it was only months before we had the awful summer of '87." Vinnie chuckled.

"You guys at Pacific had it right," Loren continued as he nodded at Brad and George.

"In many ways, we did." George squirmed a little uncomfortably in his chair. "But a lot of our peers seem to forget that we lost that airplane one night down in Mexico as a result of a terribly dysfunctional crew interaction. It was known that the crew had been feuding all month, and things apparently were so bad that when the captain set up to land on the wrong runway, the copilot let him do it.

"Obviously he hadn't given any thought to the reason the runway was closed. As I said earlier, just after touchdown, they hit a dump truck, tore off an engine, and the rest is history. The chief pilot told me that listening to the voice recording was one of the most horrifying experiences he ever had. It was forty-five seconds from the impact with the truck and their certain death. The verbal exchange was pretty awful.

George went on. "So yeah, generally speaking, at Pacific, we had a pretty collegial atmosphere in our cockpits, but we had our share of turkeys, too."

"We had an incident in Minneapolis that had a really big impact on how subordinate crew members were perceived at Pacific," Brad followed up. He went on to describe a Pacific 727 landing with one main gear retracted, how the copilot made the landing, and how, as a result, captains were forced to recognize the wealth of experience and competence the other two pilots on the flight deck had. "Gone are the days of pilot apprenticeship in an airline cockpit," Brad concluded.

"You know, it's that experiential learning that we're after here in the program," Jack said. "We have to give our guys an opportunity to see a better model of good crew work. They are going to be a captive audience for a couple of days, as I imagine it, and we don't want to waste a moment of that experience. "Thanks for all of your input today, folks," Jack said with a sigh. "My head is spinning. Take the rest of the day off, and I'll see you in the morning." He wiped his brow as his audience quietly dispersed.

Chapter 14

HOMECOMING

Brad dialed the hotel operator and listened to the recorded message. "Hi. Sorry to have missed you. We have dinner with the bigwigs tonight, and I didn't want to bother you late. I'm on the 4:30 to Seattle tomorrow afternoon. I hope they think the new wardrobe tips and talking points are worth the bundle they spent bringing us here."

The message continued rather hurriedly. "I have an office day, Friday. I'm not on the air, so I should be home for dinner. You're back Friday, right? Dinner at home sounds nice. Call me at the office on Friday, and we'll figure out what to do. Bye."

Audrey was so damned efficient. No rambling or *uhs* and *ahs*, just the essentials.

His gut churned as unsolicited images flashed through his head. Beautiful Audrey poised in front of the camera, or primping at her dressing table, or meticulously tending her roses. Then sassy Sarah Marconi out of uniform—jeans, maybe, or in a tiny bikini strolling with him on Kaanapali Beach, or the ultimate—standing in front of him wearing nothing but a smile.

He shook his head to regain composure, checked his address book, and dialed Mrs. Schroeder on the island. Mrs. Schroeder and Peppy, her wirehaired terrier, lived just across the fence and provided a home to Admiral when Brad and Audrey were both away.

"Hi, Brad. Oh, yes, your boy is doing just fine. He peeks through the fence from time to time just to make sure that he isn't missing anything over there. Takes Raggedy Andy whenever we go out in the car. Peppy keeps him busy—wears him out, I think. Are you still planning to be home Friday? Well, good, he misses you. Wanna say hi?"

"Admiral," Brad said coaxingly into the phone. "Admiral, come here, boy, your commander-and-chief is on the phone."

Brad waited for the sound of his clattering feet on the hardwood floor. "Go ahead, Brad," Mrs. Schroeder said.

"Hey, big guy," he bellowed. "Hey, Admiral, let's go for a run. Get your ball, boy. Let's go!" Brad listened to the jingling collar tags at the other end of the line, and to the fast, heavy breathing. He laughed.

Mrs. Schroeder got back on the line. "Ha, a little puzzled, as usual, but he definitely hears the voice he knows so well." Then in the background, as she turned from the phone, "Yes, Addie, that was your dad. He'll be home soon; now go get in your bed. Good boy."

The conversation went on for several more minutes. The weather, the Sonics, and the stock market were Mrs. Schroeder's primary interests, and they all were pretty unpredictable at that moment. Though Chambers, McDaniel, and

Ellis were on a romp, it was not like the glory days of the 1979 NBA championship.

✈

His phone rang almost as soon as he hung up. "Hello. Please state your name, address, and credit card number," he answered, then caught himself. Then at the sound of her voice, "Oh, Alice, I'm sorry. That's not what you wanted to hear, I'm sure."

He sat in the desk chair and grimaced. "How're you doin', girl? I know some of the story."

"Oh, Brad, I'm so hurt and confused. I don't know what to do," she said with a tremor. "What's happened to him? This whole thing reads like a cheap novel, certainly not the greatest love story Spokane has ever known. It's all gone now, Brad. It's all gone." Her voice trailed off painfully.

"Alice, I know it must feel like the end of the world. I really do understand that. But Gradin hasn't changed. Honestly, he hasn't. He's just come face to face with something he's never known about himself before."

"But why, Brad? Why?" she wailed.

"Alice, hold on, please. It's not about you, as strange as that may sound. This is about Gradin wrestling with his own deep-seated demons. I don't pretend to know what those are, but I do know that he's tormented right now, too. Mostly because he feels so bad about the pain he is causing you. You and the kids are his life, Alice. Really."

Brad said all of this without having given much thought to the dynamics involved. He loved the guy and admired how utterly devoted he was to his family. Gradin went to extraordinary lengths to keep them comfortable in their hometown, near two sets of grandparents and generations of old friends. Rather than pull up stakes and move to an Omega crew base, he put up with a killer commute to Los Angeles three or four times a month. Then he spent another four days in the reserves at Whidbey.

"Alice, listen, we have to get something straight right up front. I love you both. I want to support you both, and I refuse to say anything to one of you that I couldn't say to the other. And the truth is, I don't have any secret information. I didn't know about this until two days ago. With all of the 848 stuff going on, Gradin broke down and told me—just that it happened, no details.

"He is really feeling defeated right now, as hard as that may be to grasp. Not just one but two awful things he never imagined are happening to him both at once. Talk about the world collapsing around your ears."

"Oh, God, I know, Brad. It kills me that I can't be more empathetic. Am I being selfish?"

"Of course not. You need to circle the wagons and just keep the home fires burning. Give him a chance to get a grip. As much as he would like it otherwise, putting the accident behind him successfully is his first priority. He has to focus. His sense of self-worth wouldn't survive the title 'ex-pilot.'"

"Okay, okay. I'm so glad to hear your voice and to hear that Gradin is still the guy you've known and loved all these years. I'm also very grateful that you are there for him, quite literally. Why *are* you there, anyway? Gradin didn't tell me."

"Oh, that's a story for another time. But one last thing and this is something I would—will—tell both of you. Contrary to my steely, derring-do demeanor, I am a great believer in psychotherapy. My college professor dad has had a ton of it, and to me, he has the healthiest perspective of anyone I know. It didn't come easy, but he has really worked on getting to know himself. Socrates would be proud. You may want to give it a try."

"Yeah, our minister is telling me the same thing. It's just such a foreign concept to me. It seems like admitting failure," she said with a moan.

"So, what's wrong with failure?"

"What do you mean?"

"That's how we learn, Alice."

"Oh, fine. So what was Gradin supposed to learn by humping some damned flight attendant?"

"Whoa, whoa. I'm not talking about him, I'm talking about you. Don't try taking the speck out of *his* eye—you know the bible story. But hold it. I've said way more than I wanted to. Please trust that I won't take sides here. The best I can do is to be a sounding board."

"I know. You've already helped me despite my little tirade. Thanks."

"You're welcome. I love you guys."

"Okay, pat him on the butt for me, or whatever you macho guys do to show affection."

"No, that's your private domain. I'll just tell him we talked."

Brad breathed a long sigh as he replaced the receiver. He envied Gradin, the family man. But then again, there was a price to pay for all that perfection. The tightly packed persona was bound to burst at some point.

Smoke roiled behind the bar and across the mirror silhouetted by whiskey bottles. You had to figure that the smokers were either old captains or non-pilots. Brad gravitated toward the relatively smoke-free zone at the far end and elbowed Bronco off his stool.

"Hey, blue balls, how're they hangin'?" Bronco exhorted. "That seat will cost you a beer." He elbowed Brad back.

"Consider it done." Brad waved two fingers toward the bartender. "Learnin' anything?"

"Not much, but I can tell you that those ground school guys are really tipped over about the Pasco thing. Our instructor, Wally Andrews, is a retired Boeing guy. He was there when they were designing the airplane. Says they really rushed to get it into production to compete with the DC-9. He thinks it's a design flaw."

"Yeah, I'm thinkin' the same thing. A guy on the CRM committee is chairman of ALPA safety. He says there have been indications of a problem since the airplane was first introduced. I think it was Frontier that had an airplane—the same airplane on two different days—that fell out of the sky twice. They tried to say that it was a yaw damper problem. The more they sell of 'em, the more reluctant Boeing is to admit to any flaw."

"Well, hell yes! Can you imagine the liability they would have if it were proven that there was a defect? Particularly since they have denied that possibility since the airplane started flying in the sixties. Jesus, it would be billions."

"Shows how impotent the FAA and NTSB are. I'm sure they know that something's wrong, but there are a lot of jobs and a lot of tax revenues up there in Seattle."

－－－･･･－－－－－－･･･－－－－－－･･･－－－･･･－－－－－－･･･－－－－－－･･･

"Sounds like spurious emissions to me." Brad grinned as he clinked his glass with Bronco's.

"The really sad part is that Boeing has solved the problem on the latest-generation airplanes. The seven-five and the seven-six[32] have redundant actuator systems and load limiters that prevent rudder deflection beyond a few degrees. Works great, lasts a long time. But I guess the retrofit for the seven-threes would be prohibitively expensive. Money is doin' all the talkin' on this one," Bronco concluded.

"Yes, and our good mutual friend has his ticket on the line right now because of it. The FAA will give him a special check sometime next month. And you know how they could eat your lunch if that was the objective."

"Sounds like a fun day to me. So when do I get to know who this mutual friend really is? And why do you know when the rest of the world doesn't?"

"Purely by chance." Brad took a long drink and exhaled. "He called me right after it happened—just two hours after, actually."

"Ohhhh, okay, now I can imagine who it might be." "You probably can, but I'd really appreciate you keeping a lid on it."

"No problem, no problem. Wow, that really is close to home. How's he doing?"

"Ah, stiff upper lip and all that. He was with a great captain, I guess, so that takes a lot of the pressure off."

"Speaking of the seven-three, when do you start flying it?" Bronco changed course.

"Next month. Only one more trip on the Studebaker. I'm hoping I get to stay in Seattle. It's such a small category up there, and half of those copilots could be a flyin' captain someplace else in the system."

"Yeah, you'd be middle of the pack down in Dallas; probably the same here."

"I can't stand the idea of commuting. I'd much rather sit home on reserve and not have as many guaranteed days off."

The conversation continued through another beer and a burger, then they called it a night.

Pilots have recurrent dreams. Brad drifted off to sleep into the scene with his friend Navy Lieutenant Junior Grade Jennifer Timerro squirming uncomfortably in the jump seat of the National Airlines 727 several years earlier, certain that her sparkling white uniform was being soiled by the grungy lap and shoulder harness, nostrils flaring at the stench in the workaday cockpit.

Her shiny gold aviator wings and matching golden locks had prompted the captain to insist that she join them in the cockpit for the short, late-night flight from Mobile to Pensacola.[33]

> "Pensacola approach, National one-niner-three, 7,000."
>
> "One-niner-three, roger. Expect ASR approach runway 25, fly heading zero-seven-zero, descend, and maintain 1,700. Over."
>
> "Roger, present heading down to seventeen," the old, gray copilot responded with false bravado as they descended eastbound into the night sky over Escambia Bay.

"Uh, National 193, be advised that an Eastern 727 just missed approach. Currently, we're reporting 400 overcast, wind one-niner-zero and seven, over."

"One-ninety-three copies," old gray replied. Then, looking over his shoulder at Jennifer, he said, "Some guys just can't cut it, I guess. No guts, no glory."

She was looking skeptically around for the checklist. "Not this much fun in a helicopter, huh, Jen?"

"Uh, yeah, this is fun, all right," she stammered nervously. "We always go through the checklist before we start the approach."

"National 193, left to three-four-zero, descend to 1,500, over."

The crew worked feverishly as they scrambled to descend, configure for approach, stumble through a checklist from memory, and comply with the controller's instructions: "Fly heading two-five-zero and commence descent to minimum descent altitude."

"Okay, take 'er on down, boss. MDA is four-eighty."

"Roger," the captain said. He reduced power and wobbled the wings as he reached over to ensure the landing gear handle was down. "Goin' down," he announced. "Jesus, these guys are as fucked up as Hogan's goat," Jennifer whispered to herself. Knowing that she shouldn't even be in the airline cockpit observing such gross incompetence,

······ ·— —·· ··· ·— — —··· ·— — ·—· ···· ·— — —··· ·— — —··· ·— — —····

she wished she had never gotten on the plane.

"WHOOP, WHOOP, PULL UP," the automated warning voice bellowed. "WHOOP, WHOOP, PULL UP."

"Come on, guys, do something," she whispered through clenched teeth.

"WHOOP, WHOOP—" and the voice stopped as the copilot spun a knob next to the altimeter.

"Shouldn't you . . . ?" she pointed toward the flashing red light, then froze as she saw the altimeter. Ten feet? At that instant, a deafening roar reverberated from mid-cabin, and they all lurched violently against their shoulder harnesses. BOOM! The fuselage slammed into Pensacola Bay as bags, manuals, soda cans, and coffee cups hurtled through the air. The cockpit went dark, and seawater rushed up through the floor panels.

We're alive! she thought, then frantically released her harness and reached toward the overhead escape hatch.

The dream suddenly and inexplicably coalesced with images of Matt's death. *Why didn't I speak up? Why didn't I say something sooner?* Brad shuddered at the splashing images of the National Airlines 727 and Matt's Blue Angels Skyhawk. *Speaking up—challenging the leader—isn't part of our aviation culture yet. That has to change.* Returning to sleep, he rolled over and clutched the extra pillow.

✈

"So, let's look back and see what we've learned so far." Jack began at 8:00 on Friday morning. It would be a short meeting. "Crew performance has numerous identifiable components, so how we want to describe it is sort of arbitrary. But thus far, here's what you've told me." He created a bullet list on a new page of the flip chart:

- **Technical competence is not only essential, it is a given.**

"No one ends up in the cockpit of a commercial airliner without proving his technical and psychomotor abilities."

"Or *her* abilities," Andrea corrected with a raised eyebrow. "Right."

- **Communication drives effective interaction.**

"This will be a fun one to play with because it works both ways. We should be able to provide all kinds of models for effective *and* ineffective communication."

"Amen," Bobby whispered.

- **Planning fosters favorable outcomes.**

"Or, from the old heads, 'planning prevents piss-poor performance. The five Ps,'" Vinnie suggested.

Marsha smiled. "Yes, your technical description corroborates our findings."

They exchanged winks.

- **Situational awareness results from the appropriate application of all skills.**

"Oooh, that's a biggie," David Hennessey cautioned. "We'll need to home in on that one a bit."

"Okay. Let's leave it that way for now, and maybe you can take the lead on a better description of SA, David."

"Sure, I'm happy to do that," he responded.

"Then I think we can round it out with these three:"

- **Workload management**
- **Crew coordination**
- **Team building**

"Jack, what's the big picture here? How do you imagine imparting these great truths to our pilots?"

"Yeah, good question, George. Andy has already gotten a letter from a Miami captain accusing him of embracing a communist plot by even considering a CRM program for Omega pilots. 'It undermines captains' authority,' he said. 'It would make us weak and soft.'"

"Are you serious?" Andrea almost choked.

"God's honor." Jack raised his right hand in a pledge. "We have some real wackos out there. Very few, I'm glad to say, but it's something we need to be sensitive to. We need to be prepared for those attitudes in the program we create. It's going to require us to engage those folks in a way that they get to hear themselves talk and hear how out of sync they are with their more enlightened peers.

"And it will have to be a soft sell. Fortunately, when we talk about actual incidents and accidents, we will be talking about 'all those other guys,'" he emphasized with two-fingered quotation marks. "People love to see how other people screw up, and quite frankly, I'm imagining a number of exercises that don't have any apparent relationship to flying at all. In this organization, maybe most organizations—I don't know—there is an underlying belief that the older or more senior you are, the more capable you are."

"Ha! It's only the older and more senior guys who believe that," Chester insisted.

"True, Chess, there is significant prejudice on both sides. We want to move toward an appreciation for how good teams function, not who's smartest, meanest, or even most knowledgeable."

"Yeah, we had a pretty interesting example of good leadership in Seattle a few years ago when Lenny Wilkens was the player-coach of the Sonics. He certainly wasn't the greatest player in the lineup, but he was an effective leader nonetheless."

"Good example, Brad. We have the opportunity to slip facts like that into our patter without having to be too direct. Most of all, we want our pilots to experience, or at least observe, how teams can function most effectively when the interaction draws on the skills of every member of the team. Creating that, I think, is our main challenge."

"Amen," David Hennessey intoned sonorously. "We aren't going to see massive change take place overnight. The most we can hope for is a gradual shift toward a more inclusive style of leadership among the captains and a more participatory type of followership from the subordinates. It's going to take time, folks. It will happen grain of sand upon grain of sand."

"Lest you believe this process has no scientific basis, we are going to provide you with a ream of data to drive the development of follow-on training," David continued. "Almost the first thing the pilots will do in our—that is, *your*—program will be to complete a written survey. We've used this with other airlines, and it gives a valid baseline of leadership/followership characteristics and attitudes among the group.

"We will also collect data from actual observations of flight crews in action. Typically, the company gives us the authority to ride jump seat on a no-jeopardy basis. In a month's time, we can usually observe 100 crews. We only look at the interactive side of the equation. My team is made up of former airline guys who also have an academic background in human factors.

"The thing I think you will find most interesting is not necessarily the initial picture we get, but rather the change in the picture over time. Now a lot of that depends on the quality of training you provide them, but I must say that I am very impressed with what I have seen here so far. You have assembled a great team, Jack. Andy Caldwell and the board of directors are obviously 100 percent behind the project, and by and large, you have an extraordinarily talented pilot group.

"One anecdote and I'll shut up. We also work with teams in the medical field, and not long ago, we had a young emergency room doc from Switzerland with us during a training of pilot observers from ol' Brand X airlines. This doctor made the point that in his business, they bury their mistakes," David said with a wry snicker. "He said that if hospitals in this country were measured by the standards airlines are, they would be known for crashing a 747 every day of the year."

He paused and slowly gazed from person to person. "This is an extraordinarily *safe* industry, folks. It's very important to understand that." David's passion was palpable. "The problem we face is that with the anticipated growth in air travel over the next several decades, the minor number of accidents we incur each year now would translate into a very substantial aggregate loss in the future. The traveling public would be both frightened and outraged. We simply can't afford to let that happen," he concluded with a brows-raised grimace.

Jack allowed the point to penetrate for a moment, then said, "So here's what I want to do. We'll meet again as an entire committee on April 25th. In the meantime, I want you to work as small teams of two or three to research and design group exercises to provide that experiential learning we've been discussing. We've drawn up a list of guidelines and resources, so you won't be entirely in the dark. I've even gone so far as to match up the people who either have the greatest access to each other or particular skills and background that will be valuable."

He proceeded to distribute packets of information to the teams he had selected. Brad was glad to discover that he was paired with Marsha Hilbert. They were asked to "develop the tenet of PLANNING into a palpable behavioral outcome." *Yeah, first it needs to be defined in terms that pilots can get their brains around,* he thought. *Something like PLANNING WORKS or ALWAYS USE THE FIVE Ps.* He knew Marsha would agree.

George, Chester, and Andrea were asked to focus on team-building skills.

Everyone's satisfaction with their assignments was evident in the buzz of conversation that followed. "Hey, Jack." George waved a hand. "Can I piggyback for a moment on what David said?"

"Sure, go ahead."

"I'm very excited to be working on the team-building concept. I think we do that very well in the C-5 community, and we may be able to incorporate some of those things here. But there are also some great examples of Omega teams working really well out there on the line.

"Several months ago, we had a TriStar taxiing out in L.A. when the senior flight attendant called the cockpit and said that there was an unusual sound coming from the number two—the tail-mounted engine. Now, the term 'unusual sound' isn't very specific and wouldn't ordinarily raise any red flags. But this particular captain took the comment seriously and sent the second officer back to investigate.

"When the second officer returned to the cockpit, he said that he couldn't really tell . . . that he simply wasn't familiar with the sound of an idling L-1011 engine in the back of the airplane. Well, the captain felt sure that these flight attendants knew that sound well. They were a senior crew who always flew Honolulu on the TriStar. Plus, he also understood how important it was to listen to the input from the entire crew.

"Consequently, he chose to return to the gate and have the mechanics check it out. And sure enough, there was a problem—the engine-drive hydraulic pump had a bad drive bearing and could have failed once they had full power on the engine, like maybe right after liftoff, or halfway through the takeoff roll. Neither is a good time for that pump to disintegrate.

"So good stuff happens, too, guys," he concluded enthusiastically.

"With that, I pronounce this meeting adjourned," Jack said with an expansive gesture as jovial banter filled the room.

Brad was on the noon non-stop to Seattle.

Chapter 15

REVERBERATION

The clatter of her heels reverberated off the concrete walls of the stairwell as the steel security door thumped closed above her. No one would imagine the butterflies fluttering through her as she navigated the steep stairs leading to the pilot lounge. BAM! The release mechanism sprung free with a solid push, and Brad stepped through the door below. He paused and looked up the stairs, then broke into a wide smile as he recognized Sarah staring down at him. "Ah-ha, Florence Nightingale," he said.

"Nurse Ratched, maybe. Never a nightingale." She quickly regained her composure and continued rather brusquely, "I was just coming to leave you a note. Thought maybe you could tell me more about what happened during that flight we shared. The governor really was pretty upset, you know."

"Before I explain all of that, congratulations. You were magnificent. You saved that guy's life."

She blushed. "A past life kicked in. Before this glamour job, I really was a nurse."

"Ahhhh, that makes sense. You deal with authority figures with such cultivated disdain."

"Yeah, doctors can outdo you guys for big egos any day."

"Speaking of big egos, you're right about the governor being upset. He went right to the board of directors with his concerns."

"So, what really happened?"

"Well, ya know, I was just the third in command up there. Very little decision making falls on me."

"Oh, sure, the Blue Angel just sits on his hands and takes orders?" She feigned exasperation.

"Yeah, that's *former* Blue Angel," he emphasized, leaning against the stair railing. "Now, I'm just Joe Shit the Ragman, number 7,967 on the Omega seniority list—only 7,966 seats behind the top dog."

"Hmm. So something really did go wrong?" She narrowed her brilliant blue eyes quizzically.

"All I can say is that I wasn't particularly proud of our performance. Most of the time, all I can do is be master of ceremonies; keep the show moving and the conversation cooking. Truth is, a lot more conversation would have been helpful. Maybe that's where I failed," he said with regret.

"Well, just so you know, the governor and his aide—that slimy little creep—were very impressed with your appearance. You talking to them did calm the waters a bit. But I think what you are telling me is that you can't shed any more light on what was going on. Right?"

"Correct. Hey, this is a lovely conversation we're having, but a hot cup of coffee might warm things up a little. You have time?" Brad asked.

"Uh, well, sure," she stammered, patting her short red hair. "We don't push until 6:00. I should be at the gate by 5:00."

"Lead the way," he said, pointing toward the upper door.

Sarah turned and strutted provocatively up the steps, her perfectly fitted skirt accentuating the sensuous curves and certain delights within. Brad turned his head and shook it in chagrin. *I've just been away from home too long,* he assured himself. Eyes down, he ascended the stairs into the concourse.

"Oops, look who's coming." Sarah poked Brad's ribs. "His ears must be burning."

Bags in tow, a bedraggled Dick Hamlin was schlepping toward them. He smiled wanly at seeing Brad, then more broadly when he recognized Sarah. "Well, well, if it isn't Hotshot and the EMT," he sniped, ignoring the true significance of Sarah's heroics.

"Why, Captain Hamlin, what a pleasant surprise," Sarah cooed.

"Hey, Dick," Brad said. "Late getting in from Juneau again?"

"Yeah, why is that damned trip such a jinx for me? This time we had no trouble getting in there, but we couldn't get out. Sat on the deck for nearly five hours. At least we didn't have the governor to contend with this time. I hope that he finally got there last week. Did you hear anything?"

"Yeah, not surprisingly, he called my father-in-law, who, of course, called me that same night. He wasn't a happy camper. I was able to convince him that whatever happened on the flight was strictly a crew issue, and there wasn't any reason for concern," Brad said with false bravado.

"Well, speaking of concern, I think all three of us should file a NASA report just in case. In fact, what I'll do is write mine and leave copies for you and Alex in your mail folders. You don't have to parrot what I say, but at least we can have all of the times, altitudes, and that stuff all the same. Tell it like it is. Fear not." He gestured meekly, tipped his hat to Sarah, and shuffled toward the stairwell.

"So there really was something, wasn't there? What is a NASA report?" Now she showed genuine concern.

Brad took Sarah's elbow and ushered her through the crowd toward the cafeteria while he reflected on the conversation. "I think Dick just gave me permission to include you in this little drama. And, as I think about it, that makes perfect sense. You *were* there, and you—those of you in back—were the recipients of our little faux pas."

He led the way to the coffee bar, paid, and found an isolated table in the far corner overlooking the Omega gates. "This way, we can keep an eye on your airplane. You in the Studebaker down there at B5?" Brad asked.

"Studebaker?"

"Well, 727 if you prefer. Everything has an acronym or code name, you know that."

"Yes, I know. You guys have some, we girls have some. It's only fair."

"Oh, ho. And what is your favorite, you little minx?" he snickered.

"Can't tell, I hardly know you," she teased. Then, changing tone, "Now, what the hell is a NASA report?"

"You want the short version or the $1.98 full-blown text?"

"I have more than an hour, so let's have all the gory details." She pushed her chair back and folded her arms.

"Okay, you asked for it." Brad leaned forward and thought for a moment.

"In 1974—December 1, 1974, to be exact—a TWA 727 was headed for Dulles late at night. They were coming in from the west." Brad placed the pepper shaker on the table to his left to represent TWA. Across and slightly right, he set the salt cellar. "This is Dulles airport." On a straight line between the salt and the pepper, his coffee cup was a significant obstacle, in this case, a 2,000-foot hill along the approach path, he explained. "Oh, and here," he said, placing a sugar packet on the table, "was the final approach fix, just six miles from the end of runway one-two.

"When the aircraft was forty-four miles out—way out here," he jiggled the pepper shaker, "the air traffic controller cleared them to intercept the final approach course and continue inbound." He moved the pepper slightly in the direction of the salt.

"So at this point, they were at 7,000 feet descending to an assigned altitude of 6,000. Seconds later, the controller cleared TWA 514 for a VOR approach to runway one-two."

"How do they decide what numbers to call the runways?"

"Oh, those two digits always correspond to a magnetic heading. So runway one-two is oriented on a one-two-zero heading. That make sense?"

"Yup."

"The technicalities here are a little complicated—even for pilots, I should add. Shall I go technical or skip over that stuff?" he asked earnestly.

"Technical. I'll tell you when I'm lost." She settled deeper into her chair.

... — — —... — — —... — — —... — — —... — — —...

"Okay, well, I have to back up and talk about the air traffic control system for a sec. The entire U.S. is divided into sixteen or eighteen different sectors, or centers, as they're called, like Los Angeles Center, Oakland Center, Seattle Center, etcetera. You've probably heard that on the radio when you're in the cockpit. Right?"

"Uh-huh."

"So when we are en route, we are talking to controllers in one of the *centers*. Then, when we get close to a major airport, we talk to a controller who is responsible for all of the air traffic approaching and departing the area, usually within about a twenty-five-mile radius. And within five miles of the airport, we talk to the tower, controllers who are actually out there in the tower looking at the runways, taxiways, and surrounding airspace. Good so far?"

She nodded.

"Back to TWA. At forty miles out, they were still talking to Washington Center. An unusual thing happened in that the center controller cleared TWA for approach way out there. Typically it is the approach controller who does that when the airplane is much closer to the airport. But it was late at night, there wasn't much traffic, and there was no reason not to.

"A niggling little problem came up for the crew, and that was, what altitude were they cleared to descend to? Under normal circumstances, the approach controller gets the aircraft established on the final approach course, *then* clears them for approach. At that point, the pilots can consult the approach plate—that little diagram you may have seen clipped to the control column."

Again, Sarah nodded.

"But since these guys were forty miles out and the only altitude restriction depicted on the final approach course was an 1,800-foot crossing altitude at the final approach fix," Brad pointed to the sugar packet on the table, "these guys began descending to 1,800 feet. The problem was that this hill out here," Brad said, jiggling the coffee cup, "is 2,000 feet high," he emphasized with a grimace.

"So they hit the hill," he said as the pepper shaker collided gently with the cup, "and all ninety-two people on board were killed.[34] That's bad enough, but the real tragedy was that another crew from another airline had had the same experience several weeks earlier. They did not hit the hill, but they realized how close they had come and had the courage and foresight to share their concern with airline management. Management even went to the FAA, but it didn't spread the word to other airlines, or even to the air traffic controllers involved."

"That is sad."

"Yes, but the entire episode spawned the birth of the NASA reporting system I was referring to. The clear thinkers—and there are surprisingly few of them out there— realized that there was a glaring need for a system that would encourage pilots and air traffic controllers to openly report their own errors and inadequacies."

"Uh-huh."

"It probably sounds simple, but there is so much potential liability involved that it took a long time to work out all of the details, particularly to provide immunity to those who make the reports. No one is gonna come forward if they risk being punished. So they had to get the controllers union, the Air Line Pilots Association, airline management, *and* the FAA all singing from the same sheet of music.

"Now what we have is a program where we all can submit a NASA report when we experience a problem that might ordinarily result in some kind of punishment and be immune from that punishment. Probably the most significant aspect of the program is that it sheds light on situations that would never be known about otherwise. The truth is that pilots and controllers make errors of some sort every day."

"Like what?" As with most airline people, she was genuinely interested in knowing what really went on behind that cockpit door.

"Well, like the TWA crew or the other crew that had a similar experience. Both of those crews failed to read the small print, quite literally. If they had looked *very* carefully, they would have seen that there was a minimum altitude depicted for the airspace sector they were in as they came up on that final approach fix." Again he motioned to the sugar packet.

"But wasn't it their responsibility to have seen that, small print or not?" Sarah was a bit incredulous.

"Yes and no," Brad responded. "There was tremendous ambiguity about who was responsible in this particular instance. This gets complicated. You wanna hear it?"

"Try me."

"Okay. When we are flying what is known as a depicted route, one of those airways that appear on the charts between two navigation fixes, there are published minimum altitudes. In the same way, when you are established on a published approach, there are minimum, or sometimes mandatory, altitudes depicted along the approach path.

"These guys weren't in either of those circumstances. They had been taken off the depicted route and assigned both a heading and an altitude to fly. When the controller—

and remember, this was the en-route controller, not the approach controller—gave them clearance to intercept the final approach course and cleared them to fly the approach, he did not assign an altitude for them to maintain. His manual—the regulations as he understood them—did not require him to do that. By the same token, the pilots believed that in not assigning an altitude, the controller meant for them to descend to the altitude depicted at the next fix on the approach profile.

"Sadly, the FAA had known about this potential confusion for a couple of years without taking any action to clarify things for everyone involved. The NTSB investigation mildly chastised the FAA for its inaction, and ultimately it was the recommendation of the NTSB that led to the establishment of these reports—administered by a neutral party, NASA."

"I get it." Sarah sighed. "You really did have a problem on that flight last week. There was some sort of violation or potential violation, right?"

"Right, and I consider you part of the crew and therefore sworn to secrecy. Okay?"

"Oh, Brad, I'm sorry. Of course! I didn't mean to sound flip about this. My big mouth is my worst enemy sometimes. Forgive me. I won't say a word, I promise," she insisted.

"I know you won't. It's just better not to involve anyone who wasn't an actual player."

"So can you say what it was, or am I left with just the knowledge that *something* went wrong up there? And by the way, I really was a player. You should have seen me scrambling around in back there, soothing all those frayed nerves and cleaning up the mess."

"Yeah, I hadn't thought of it that way. You're absolutely right—you were directly involved—and now I apologize for not being more sensitive." Brad laughed as he realized how they were each trying to placate the other. He went on. "Well, the problem was really simple. Alex climbed through our assigned level-off altitude. Purely by coincidence, we hit that turbulence at exactly the same time that I noticed we were 400 feet above the assigned altitude. I yelped, and Alex pushed the nose over pretty abruptly. So what you experienced in the back was a combination of the turbulence and the correction that Alex made."

"So why was it *your* responsibility to see that Alex level off at the right time?" she quizzed.

"Technically, it isn't, but probably the greatest advantage in having three of us up there is that we can back each other up. In reality, it was more Dick's responsibility than mine, but he was in the midst of changing radio frequencies, and his head was down looking at the center console. It's just a matter of good teamwork, and we weren't a very good team at that moment."

"That was it? There wasn't anything that went wrong in Juneau or when we went around down there by Seattle."

"No, nothing at all wrong in Juneau. That all played out just as it is scripted. The problem at Paine Field—compounded by your nearly dead passenger—was that we had run out of options. Dick hadn't thought through the possibility that we might not make it in to Paine. We didn't really have enough fuel to go over to Spokane, which was our actual alternate. Dick was flying by then, and just by chance, both Alex and I saw the departure end of the runway as we turned out of the missed approach. We were up a creek without the proverbial paddle."

Sarah shivered, recognizing how her personal radar had told her as much. They really had been in peril. "How often does something like that happen, Brad?" She winced.

"Too often, actually," he responded. "Especially here at Omega. You've heard of our awful summer of '87, right after the merger. Our guys have been making an inordinate number of mistakes since then. In fact, that's why I'm here right now. I just got back from Memphis, where we spent a week planning the first phase of CRM training for our pilots."

"CRM?"

"Crew resource management. It's the touchy-feely side of the equation."

"Is this something *you* thought up?"

"No, no. CRM has become part of the training regimen at most of the other airlines. The Omega Board of Directors is so concerned about our performance that they have mandated that we develop such a program—they allocated $11 million for it, so we know they're serious. Andy Caldwell, the VP of flight ops, asked me to be on the committee. It's pretty interesting stuff."

"I can see that it pays to have a father-in-law on the board," she said with a wry smile.

"Yeah, nepotism is alive and well at Omega. But hey, enough about me, let's talk about airplanes." He winked.

"Oh, fun," she said, throwing the packet of sugar at him. "How about favorite funerals instead?"

"*Touché.* You know, you have an unfair advantage over me. My conversation with the governor, which you listened in on," he wagged a finger at her, "provided a mini-biography of me. What about you? Any interesting skeletal remains?"

"No, my greatest assets are very much alive: a towheaded girl and a little red-haired male munchkin." The pride washed over her face. "Which, by the way, I need to check on," she said, looking at her watch. "Will you excuse me for a minute, Brad? I have to call home. Be right back."

"Sure." He watched admiringly as she glided around the mass of tables on her too-tall heels. His head filled with prurient images, and he struggled to regain the picture of her as a wife and mother—*another man's wife*, he reminded himself. He clenched his teeth and looked at his watch—4:15, still enough time for a more lighthearted conversation.

A pink glow filled her cheeks when she returned ten minutes later. "Thank God for grandparents. A stroll in the park, pizza, and a *Muppets* movie with dinner. Can't beat that."

Brad jumped to his feet and held her chair.

"Ah, yes, a chivalrous Blue Angel," she teased. "Thank you, sir."

"How old are these lucky little munchkins?" His smile was warm.

"Two and four." She beamed and extracted pictures from her wallet. "Leslie is four, goes to nursery school three days a week. And JR, God help me, is a future drag racer like his dad." The two-year-old sat reclining on his plastic go-cart, arms folded and confident. *Must have a powerful role model*, Brad realized.

"Beautiful kids. And a drag racer, too?" He raised his eyebrows.

"Oh, yeah. Well, he's a mechanic by training; used to work for Pacific when we were first married. In fact, it was his idea that I become a flight attendant. And to think, I gave up such a promising career in medicine," she said with obvious self-deprecation.

"I'll bet you were good."

"I loved it, but Rob was having a meltdown on the job, and we were hooked on the travel privileges. It seemed like a good idea for me to fly so he could quit and buy an auto parts store in Camarillo. And I guess the allure of all the time off was just too much for me." She rolled her eyes.

As their stories continued to unfold, they unconsciously leaned closer and alternately fiddled with the salt, pepper, cups, and saucers. "Gotcha, the classic queen's gambit." She bumped the salt shaker away with the pepper.

"He counters with the rabid rook rebuke." Brad retorted as the ensuing clatter drew stares from the road-weary passengers. A comfortable calm settled over them, and their propinquity was both entrancing and frightening as legs occasionally touched for more than a moment.

Sarah's head popped up. "Oops, time to run." She tapped her watch. He pushed back his chair and stretched. "Yeah, it's like one frog said to the other frog." He paused.

"And that was?" she prompted, slinging her purse over one shoulder.

"Time sure is fun when you're havin' flies."

"Pilots." She huffed and pranced toward the exit in mock disgust. "Looks like we're on time, and the natives are already restless," she said, gazing at the passengers milling around and noting that every seat at the gate was filled. Then she turned and smiled up at him. "Don't know how many flies I had, but it was fun. Let's do it again sometime."

"You on that Fairbanks-Juneau thing next Friday?"

"Well, not right now, but maybe I could be," she responded coyly.

He reached into his shirt pocket and extracted a folded white paper. "Here's a copy of my next trip. It goes out Tues-day, back on Friday. Maybe we'll bump into each other out there." His effort at nonchalance collapsed into a sheepish smile.

"It could happen." She snatched the paper, twirled, and headed for the jetway door, so her broad smile wouldn't show.

Chapter 16

BAINBRIDGE ISLAND

The rain fell as it can only in Seattle. His late departure from the airport put him deep in the pack of Friday-evening commuters. *Oh, for one of those portable phones I've been reading about.*

Lost in the hormonal fog, he had forgotten to call Audrey as he had intended to when he got off the plane. It was going to be a long time before he got to the ferry. He struggled with the question of whether to get off I-5 to make the call or to wait.

He opted for the latter and slipped back into the reverie of the day's events. As pleasant as they had been, he was also aware of the queasiness in his stomach. It was all a part of the universal paradox he discovered in college philosophy. Every bright object has a dark side. Every good person has negative traits. Every happy emotion has corrosive potential. It goes on and on. He knew that. Every randy thought has . . .

He refused to speculate as he squinted at the blaze of lights magnified in the sheet of rain on the windshield. *How can it be that it is bumper-to-bumper going both ways?* he puzzled. *Maybe everyone should just trade houses.*

The relatively short drive from SeaTac to the Pier 52 ferry landing took Brad more than an hour. When he arrived, the line of blinking red brake lights extended back for two blocks. The next ferry was in twenty minutes, but judging from the length of the line, there was no chance of making that one. It was another forty-five minutes before the 7:30 opportunity. Better make that call.

He set the brake, left the engine idling, and grabbed the umbrella from the back seat. The bank of phone booths was less than a block away, but he had to wait—three other guys were making similar calls. Finally, he had his chance. He swallowed hard before saying, "Hi, honey, I'm really sorry. I'm at Pier 52, but the traffic is backed up a mile. Should be on the 7:30. I apologize for being so late."

"Damn it, Brad, why didn't you call sooner? I've been saving dinner."

"I know, I know. We were late getting in. I got tied up at the airport and forgot to call. I'm sorry."

"Whatever." She yawned distantly. "Yeah, well, I think I'll go to bed. My body is still on east-coast time."

"Get some rest. I'll be there when I get there. Love you," he said feebly as he pushed the rickety aluminum door open for the next poor soul.

He returned to the Land Rover, dug out his winter parka, and settled in for the hour-long wait. A background of classical music and pelting rain helped ease the coursing adrenaline from his system. He closed his eyes, took a deep breath, and fixed his focus on the strong, transcending cadence he often experienced when powering his kayak through the dark Puget Sound water.

At precisely that moment, 2,300 miles east in North Carolina, the right wing of a Metroliner sliced into the water, immediately submerged and ripped away at the engine mount. At 150 miles an hour, the aircraft careened end over end across the reservoir and smashed into the trees beyond. Less than one minute after lifting off on the final leg of a Friday evening commute, all twelve occupants lay dead in a thicket west of Raleigh-Durham International Airport.

Brad would never consciously correlate the contrasts of that moment—the titillating torment he sought and the torturous anguish thrust upon the friends and families of the twelve. In aviation, everyone relies so trustingly on superior engineering, complex systems, finely honed skills, protective regulations, and faultless judgment to survive. In every category, there was human failure at play that night—faulty engineering, a failed system, known lack of skill, inadequate regulation, and extremely poor judgment.

At some level, it was always a human factor that undermined the baseless tranquility of the moment.

A faint ringing punctuated Audrey's Sunday morning meditation. She rushed to the phone and answered it with an expectant, "Good morning, this is Audrey."

"Oh, Audrey, hi," an unfamiliar female voice responded. "This is Doctor Marsha Hilbert. Brad probably hasn't mentioned me, but he and I are working on a project together for

Omega Air Lines. We're on the CRM committee that met last week in Memphis."

"No, he hasn't mentioned you, Doctor Hilbert, but we haven't discussed last week at all yet." Audrey's voice matched that of a beautiful and powerful news anchor.

"Call me Marsha, please." Her voice was ingratiating. "I'm really sorry to interrupt your weekend, but there was an accident in North Carolina Friday night. I have some very unusual information about it that I wanted to share with Brad. Is he available?"

"It wasn't an Omega airplane, was it?" Audrey asked with concern.

"Oh, no, no. I'm sorry; didn't mean to give that impression. No, this was a local commuter, a Metroliner. It went down right after takeoff, and all twelve people on board died."

"Wow, I'll have to dig a little deeper in the paper. I didn't see anything about it. Oh, and to answer your question, no, Brad isn't here right now. He's out with the dog and the kayak."

"Ah ha, I should have known. He told me about you and the kayak, but not the dog, now that I think of it."

"That's a surprise. He loves us all in the reverse order: the dog, the kayak, then me. Admiral is a big ol' Saint Bernard. When Brad is around, they are inseparable. He actually has two kayaks. One is a two-seater, not for me but for the admiral. So no doubt they're out there having an adventure someplace. It's a beautiful morning, so I don't expect them home for another two hours or so. Can I have Brad call you when he gets back?"

"Well, yes, if it doesn't interfere with your day's plans. If that doesn't work, tell Brad he can reach me in the office almost any time tomorrow. He has my card but let me give you the numbe anyway."

········ — — —···· — — — —···· — — —···· — — —···· — — —···

✈

Two hours later, as Audrey napped, Brad dialed the number. He got right to the point. "Marsha, this is Brad. What's up?"

"Oh, Brad, thanks for getting back to me so soon. This isn't interrupting anything for you and Audrey, is it? It really can wait 'til Monday."

"Nope. Both she and the dog are napping. I've got nothing but time."

"Well, good. Sad as it is, this is an amazing windfall that landed in my lap. It happened just this morning. From talking to Audrey, I gather that you didn't know about the accident Friday night in Raleigh-Durham."

"You're right, we hadn't heard anything about it."

"It was in the *Globe* this morning, page thirteen. The truth is I hadn't seen it either 'til I got a call from one of my former students who is doing her doctoral thesis down at North Carolina State. It just so happens that she has a ton of inside information about this airline, even specific stuff about the crew."

"Whoa, you don't ordinarily get details about an accident until months later. Lay it on me," he said.

"Well, this little commuter operates under the American Eagle banner, but it is really Air Virginia," she scoffed. "They have been through the wringer recently, and my unnamed source—let's call her Natasha—has been following every move. In fact, she has direct contact with your ALPA national folks in D.C. As you know, they are really pushing the 'One Level of Safety' agenda."

"Yeah, Loren and I talked about that last week in Memphis."

...▪ ▬ ▬ ▬▪•• ▬ ▬ ▬ ▬▪•• ▬ ▬ ▬▪•• ▬ ▬ ▬▪•• ▬ ▬ ▬▪•• ▬ ▬ ▬▪••

"Sadly, Air Virginia was a disaster just waiting to happen. On December 17, only three months ago, they had a Metro go down on approach to Dulles. Obviously, the results of the investigation aren't out yet, but Natasha assures me that it was pilot error—they had forgotten the engine anti-ice, and those cold carburetors froze up in the warmer, moist air.

"Of course the captain was fired, but Natasha has seen an initial draft of the accident report, and in it, the NTSB will cite both the FAA and the company for inadequate oversight of its check airmen, inadequate training of the captain, and, get this, ' . . . the pilot in command's improper in-flight *planning* and *decision making.*'"

"Incredible!" Brad exclaimed.

"Hang on, this gets even more twisted. On January 15, AVAir filed Chapter Eleven and shut down, completely shut down. Then on February 3, they started up again. That's not even three weeks ago, so you can imagine how sharp the pilots were.

"Friday night it was the copilot making the takeoff in rain and low visibility. She had only been back at work for two or three days, and Natasha has seen her training record. It was abysmal. To make matters worse, the copilot's mother died in November. So, not surprisingly, she was really struggling. Sometime before the bankruptcy, a check pilot had even recommended her termination. She couldn't seem to stay ahead of the airplane, but there is no record of either company management or the FAA taking any further action."

Marsha continued her diatribe. "To compound all of this, the captain Friday night had attempted to call in sick, then apparently thought better of it and showed up anyway. They have a very restrictive sick leave policy that might have cost him money—tough to handle at those wages, particularly after a month-long furlough.

"There may also have been a problem with the stall warning system right after liftoff. They were given an immediate right turn to accommodate departing jet traffic behind them. If a warning light had illuminated at that moment, it's easy to imagine how the copilot could have lost her scan and just flown into the ground—well, the water in this case. Everything—absolutely everything—was stacked against them."[35]

Brad released a deep breath. "Amazing story and really astounding that you got all this info so quickly. Whew."

"Yeah, my guess is that Natasha will be muzzled as soon as the investigators know how much *she* knows. This is very sensitive stuff. They always keep a lid on the details until the report is published. And the truth is I would be crazy to go public with any of this. My reputation would be zilch."

You mean there really is something that trumps self-promotion? he thought to himself.

"You know, Brad, there is another aspect to this that intrigues me, too. Remember when Jack was making the list of CRM characteristics?"

"Yeah, the situational awareness, communications— that stuff?"

"Uh-huh. For some reason, I was a little uncomfortable with planning as one of those characteristics. Now I understand why. Now I see that planning is a subcategory of preparation."

"Hmm. And the other subcategories?"

"I'm not perfectly certain but see what you think. I imagine a total of three: planning, training, and organizational support. When you consider the Raleigh accident in terms of

264 WE'RE GOING DOWN

those factors, you see that all three played an enormous role in the outcome."

She ticked off her points:

"First, they were inadequately trained.

"Second, they were very poorly supported by the organization—the company, the aircraft manufacturer, the FAA overseers, even ATC if they gave them an immediate turn right after liftoff at night in the weather.

"Finally, you have planning, poor planning. For instance, why did the *plan* include a very demanding takeoff by a very marginal copilot?"

"ALPA will love you for this, Marsha. In many ways, what you're saying takes the monkey off the pilots' backs. You know how often accident investigations go right for pilot error and overlook all of the mitigating factors.

"In fact, we had a situation just last winter where a crew landed in Kalispell in a snowstorm while trucks were out plowing the runway. That airport doesn't have a tower. So when that's the case, all pilots are responsible for communicating with other aircraft—and occasionally ground personnel and equipment—on a common published frequency called UNICOM.

"So these guys did that—made the call in the blind on the published frequency, didn't get a response from anyone, and assumed they were the only game in town. Imagine those surprised snowplow drivers when a fifty-ton 737 zinged by in a swirling cloud of snow. It was pure luck that no one was injured."

"I'm lost. How does this relate to preparation?"

"In two ways, really. First, if the crew had *planned perfectly*," he emphasized, "they would have found a note buried in the flight plan that said, 'snow removal in progress' and that told them the trucks were monitoring one-twenty-six-five or something, rather than the standard UNICOM freq.

"So the pilots failed in their planning. But the organization also failed by not ensuring that such vital information was highlighted or set apart from all that other meaningless gobbledygook in the flight plan." Brad's voice rang with emotion. "Okay, I get it now, and you are exactly right. I think you said it when we were talking in Memphis. You pointed out how the Blue Angel team was a lot more than six airplanes and six pilots. There is an extended team out there that we want the pilots to consider."

"Yeah, like that TriStar captain in L.A.—the one who went back to the gate when the flight attendants heard an engine that simply 'didn't sound right.' The flight attendants turned out to be a crucial safety component in preventing something big."

"Exactly! You build your team with as many key players as possible. You *extend* it."

Brad couldn't see Audrey listening surreptitiously from the bedroom as the conversation continued for another ten minutes. He and Marsha agreed on a time to meet in Boston for a couple of days of development. Seeing Harvard and working in such a prominent scholarly atmosphere was as close as he'd ever get to any gold-plated post-grad education.

The conversation reached an amicable conclusion as Brad looked ahead to his final trip as a 727 engineer.

Chapter 17

EROS

By late February, the wet weather dragged on even the rustiest, mossiest Northwest natives. The hot, dry Phoenix air that greeted the crew was a welcome respite, and by 2:30 Brad had settled into a poolside chaise with his 737 study notes. It was his last trip as engineer on the 727, and he needed to refamiliarize himself with the new airplane by the following week.

Occasionally his mind filled with an image of Sarah Marconi, but he found that the accompanying picture of her embracing a victorious, macho drag racer with two kids at her side did a lot to cool his jets.

The Mexican food in Phoenix was the best, and the whole crew gathered at 5:00 for happy hour and dinner. At 6:00 the next morning they blasted off from Phoenix, then hit L.A. and Seattle. By noon they terminated in Portland, back in the rain.

The Benson Hotel downtown was a sumptuous experience. Brad pushed himself hard in the workout room. With warm weather on the way, he was focused on building his upper-body strength to get the most from his kayak.

The message light in his room blinked. "You have one message," the recorded message responded to his inquiry. "Hey, sailor, buy a girl a drink? Lobby lounge at 4:00?" Click.

The shiver he felt might have been from the wet, sweaty T-shirt cooling on his body, but he knew better. By now, the timbre of Sarah's sexy, low-pitched voice was etched in his brain.

He collapsed into the overstuffed chair and toweled his face. *How to play this one? It's not the ol' Navy bachelor days,* he reminded himself. And Sarah's intentions weren't entirely clear. She was probably as confounded as he was. *Stay cool,* he told himself. *If there is anything you excel in, it's staying cool.*

So there he sat at 3:55, idly thumbing through his study notes, sipping a glass of water. At 3:58, Sarah peeked around a column on the mezzanine level, spotted him, then descended the back stairs and exited a side door onto Oak Street. Five minutes later, she bustled through the revolving front door in her trench coat, carrying a Nordstrom bag and her oversized purse. She headed directly for the elevators without glancing at the bar.

Hmm, very cool as well, Brad acknowledged. "Oh, nurse," he called as she passed. "Can you take a look at my chart and tell me how I'm doing?"

She stopped and looked his way. "Why, Brad Morehouse." She raised a hand demurely to her mouth. "Whatever are you doing here?"

"Oh, just enjoying the scenery. Join me?"

"Well, yes, thank you. I might as well enjoy the scenery, too." She circled back to the bar and stood by the table.

"I hope you won't mind, my sister may be joining us. She left me a message asking me to buy her a drink here in the bar at 4:00."

"It will be very nice to meet your sister; I look forward to it. She lives nearby?" Sarah played along as she flopped her bag and purse in a chair and unbuttoned the trench coat.

Brad stood and helped with her coat, 'til the sight of her perfectly contoured cashmere sweater elicited a stammer. "Well, no, uh, Albuquerque really—must be up here on business." He coughed self-consciously and sat back down.

"What an amazing coincidence this is seeing you here in Portland. Who would have imagined?" She smiled, now quite endearingly.

He returned the smile as he reached out to touch her hand. "Nice to see you so soon."

She squeezed his hand for a moment, then released it, sat back and exhaled. "Nice to see you, too, Bradley Blue." She winked. "Buy me a drink, Lieutenant?"

"Name your poison."

"Ahh." She breathed comfortably. "White wine would be lovely."

"Hey, before we do this, let me offer an alternative."

"Okay," she said curiously.

"Have you ever been to Powell's bookstore? It isn't far from here." He turned to look outside. The sun was poking through mostly cloudy skies. "It looks like the weather has broken a little. We could walk up to Powell's, poke around for a while, then I'll buy you dinner *and* that glass of wine."

"Ooooh, this is no ordinary sailor. The guy must be a captain, maybe even an admiral."

"No, Admiral's the dog," he said with a grin.

"The dog?"

"Yeah, my Saint Bernard. He runs a tight ship, has me well trained."

"I should say so—very high marks on manners, quick wit, and even elocution. And yes," she said, nodding emphatically, "a stroll up to Powell's and a little bite to eat sounds divine."

"Great. I need to drop these notes off in my room and grab my coat."

"Good, that will give me time to take my booty up to my room, too. Nordy's half-yearly sale." She reached in the bag and extracted a small Dodgers baseball jersey, size 3T. "Birthday coming up next week."

"Very cool. He's a lucky kid." Brad stood and instinctively reached for her chair.

Ten minutes later, he requisitioned a big striped golf umbrella from the bellman, and they set out up Oak Street toward Burnside. Conversation was effortless. In the book-store, bursts of laughter and moments of languor mixed perfectly.

"Remember this one?" He held up Khalil Gibran's *The Prophet*.

"Oh, gosh, way back in a poetry class someplace," she fudged.

"It's a must-have," he said, tucking it under his arm and continuing to peruse the poetry section. Sarah disappeared for fifteen minutes before returning with her find.

"You know *this one*?" Her eyes twinkled.

He looked quizzically at the weathered volume. "Nope."

"My dad is a World War II aviation buff. Saint-Exupéry is his favorite. There are passages in this that he recited like the bible. I'll read some to you at dinner."

"Mmmm, speaking of which, I'm famished." He checked his watch. "You ready?"

"I am, and it looks like you're runnin' on empty there. We need to feed this man." She patted his flat tummy and slinked away through the musty stacks.

Glad to know she notices such things, he thought, knuckling his abs.

Jake's Famous Crawfish, a Portland standard for nearly 100 years, was perfectly unpretentious yet succulent. At 5:30, it was elbow to elbow at the bar but early for the dinner crowd. Seating was plentiful. "View of the ocean if you could, please," Brad said as he followed Sarah and the hostess to a window table. He held out a chair for Sarah. "This will have to do," he said as he motioned toward the sidewalk under the green awning. "Must be low tide."

Sarah kept pace. "Yeah, the crustaceans are restless tonight," she said, referring to the sea of umbrellas dancing every which way in the rain that had started up again.

"Something to drink?" the hostess inquired as she seated them.

"Oh, yes, please. White wine for me. Maybe a local Chardonnay?"

"The Sokol Blosser is my favorite."

"A glass of that then." Sarah looked up pleasantly. "Olympia dark draft for me, please."

"Of course. Alex will be your server. He'll be right over." The hostess turned and disappeared.

"No hurry." Brad basked in the moment. Then he retrieved their books and calmly thumbed through *The Prophet.* She watched expectantly as he stopped to read, then searched further. He would have enjoyed knowing that his lean, muscular physique was a taunting distraction.

Finally, a big smile filled his face. "Here, this is one of my favorites." He cleared his throat and spoke in low, resonant tones.

And a youth said, "Speak to us of Friendship." Brad took a long, deep breath, then proceeded, emphasizing the parts he obviously liked most. *Your friend is your needs answered . . . you come to him with your hunger . . . you seek him for peace . . .* He paused, and Sarah bowed her head in concentration. *And let your best be for your friend.*

His voice trailed off, and he waited through her long silence.

"Umm, beautiful," she finally ventured. "I especially like the emphasis on bringing one's best to a friendship. I hope that I always do that with you." Her intense blue eyes held his.

"I'm sure that you will. Me, too. I don't want you to ever think that I'm primarily motivated by selfish impulses."

"Oh, and what might those impulses be, Bradley Blue?"

"Well, you know, uh, like the impulse to kill time or the impulse to stroke my ego with a beautiful woman on my arm, or the impulse to have someone tell me how wonderful I am . . . that kinda stuff."

Alex interrupted. "If I may, Chardonnay for the lady, and Oly dark for the gentleman." He placed a glass and small carafe in front of Sarah, then ceremoniously poured an ounce or two and waited for her to taste.

"Very nice," she responded, and he filled her glass.

"Have you two lovely people decided on something to eat?" His affectation was distinctly effeminate.

Brad responded cordially, "We're gonna need a little time, Alex. Check back with us in fifteen minutes or so."

"Yes, sir. Anything else I can get you right now?"

"Nope, we're good. Thanks."

"Thanks, Alex," Sarah added with an engaging smile.

Brad raised his glass. "To a deep and abiding friendship."

Blushing, she raised her glass in a toast. "To a very deep and abiding friendship." Her eyes sparkled.

"Okay, now it's my turn," she said, grabbing the Saint-Exupéry book, *Night Flight*. "Listen to this. André Gide wrote the preface. This is you, Brad. I want you to savor every word for yourself but let me read you his description of the world seen through the eyes of an aviator." She opened to the front and virtually whispered the opening stanza.

> *Already, beneath him, through the golden evening,*
> *the shadowed hills had dug their furrows, and the*
> *plains grew luminous with long-enduring light.*
> *For in these lands, the ground gives off this golden*
> *glow persistently, just as, even when winter goes,*
> *the whiteness of the snow persists.*

"For you, my gentle friend." She handed him the book as her eyes brimmed with tears. "Read it to me sometime." She tousled her own hair to regain her composure.

"And for you, you friendly little minx. Read it to me sometime, too." He smiled broadly as he handed her *The Prophet*.

They knew the relationship had changed. Colors were more intense, flavors more complex, jokes funnier, silence sweeter, and this moment, all-consuming. Anyone watching would have envied their marital bliss—wedding bands say so much.

✈

The light rain beckoned them closer under the umbrella. Sarah clung to his arm as Brad took the long way home. They wound through the darkened landscape along Park Avenue, then back to the north along brightly lit Broadway.

Warmth and familiarity greeted them in the lobby of the Benson. Brad returned the umbrella, shook the rain from his jacket, and looked at his watch. "Well, my fine-feathered friend, we blow outta here at zero-dark-thirty. I should call it a day, one of the happiest days I can *ever* remember," he added. "Walk you to your room?"

"Why yes, thank you." He couldn't know how her heart was pounding as she turned toward the elevator, removed her coat, shook it, and draped it across her arm. "I'm in 316."

They were silent in the elevator, and as they walked slowly down the hallway. Sarah turned to him and leaned against her door in a tantalizing pose. "Brad, I had the best time a girl can have." She stuffed her hands in her jeans pockets, fidgeted uncomfortably, then looked up. "I'm not accustomed to such lavish attention."

"I'm sorry to hear that. You deserve the best." He looked down at her seriously, and again they were silent. Finally, Sarah summoned her courage, placed her hands on Brad's cheeks, and gently drew him toward her. Her ample breasts compressed warmly against his chest as her moist lips touched his. The kiss was long and sweet, and they both moaned faintly. Coats and books tumbled to the floor. "That is quite a bedside manner you have, Ms. Nightingale," he stammered awkwardly and then kissed her again deeply. She responded with equal ardor, keenly aware of how aroused they both were. With both hands on his chest, she looked at him earnestly. "Brad, I'm in heaven. These are the most powerful feelings I can remember ever having. I need to think. You need to think." She tapped a finger on his nose. "We could be diving into something that would drown us both. If we sleep together now, it will totally change everything we've experienced tonight." She shook her head and bit her lip. "Does that make sense?" She wrinkled her brow in question.

"Of course it does, love." He thrust his hands in his pockets, rocked on his heels, and beamed at her. "You are a treasure." He paused and sighed. "I want to honor the memory of the evening just as it is. And, as I said earlier, I don't want to be a slave to impulse."

He looked at her somberly. They breathed slowly and rhythmically as their eyes bore into each other's. He bent to retrieve the coats and books and rested his head for a moment against her hip. When he stood, their parting kiss was exquisitely warm and gentle. His fingers gently stroked her cheek. Then he turned and walked away down the hall.

Chapter 18

SPOKANE

Gradin tiptoed out of the room, eased the door closed and latched it silently. The floor creaked as he padded down the hall past the kids' rooms and into the kitchen. As always, the coffee was ready to brew, and he pushed the button. The digital clock read 5:30. It was 7:30 in Memphis, he realized. The coffee maker gurgled, and he poured a bowl of cereal, then retrieved his flight bag from the garage.

As the refrigerator swung shut, a crumpled crayon drawing of an Omega airplane on the door caught his eye. A snowman perched awkwardly on the wing and standing near the nose of the plane, a stick figure with an oversized hat and yellow stripes on the sleeve stood smiling broadly. Big block letters across the top read DADDY IS GOOD.

Yeah, right, what a good little boy I am. Is that anything like GOD IS GOOD? Gradin winced. With self-disdain, he shuffled a little jig as he dumped milk in the bowl of cereal. A final hiss of steam signaled the end of the brew cycle, and the welcome aroma of coffee filled the room. *What could be better than this?* he wondered with a gnawing emptiness in his gut.

He spread out an array of manuals and propped the large rigid photo of the cockpit overhead panel on a chair in front of his Barcalounger. The FAA check ride was scheduled for March 4, not quite three weeks away.

Preparation was everything at this point. This wasn't just the run-of-the-mill check ride he and Danny were preparing for. These were two careers on the line. Typically the examiner comes in with at least neutral expectations. For Danny and Gradin, there would be a life-sized image of the precariously perched 737 superimposed over the entire process. Any lack of knowledge or procedural misstep would spell professional disaster.

He extended a small telescoping pointer, leaned back in the chair, and slowly began touching every switch and dial on the overhead panel photo. As he did, he recited a list of minutiae to himself: the component affected; the electrical power source; any hydraulic, pneumatic, communication, or navigation system affected; the method of actuation; and the circumstances and limitations for its use.

The oral exam invariably took this tack, and the rule of thumb was to offer no more information than necessary. If the examiner wanted to know more, he would ask. More than one guy had dug his own grave by confidently rambling way beyond the basics. *Just stay with facts,* he reminded himself.

As he studied, Gradin occasionally paused to consult a manual, then backed up and delivered the spiel to himself correctly. The process was very similar to the method he had coached five-year-old Melinda to use in her piano practice. When you make a mistake, repeat the entire phrase—sometimes the entire page—without an error before you go on. Five years old or thirty-five years old, he knew it worked equally well. Three cups of coffee and two hours later, he was beginning to stow his gear when a thundering little herd rounded the corner and leaped into his lap. "Daddy, Daddy, you're home," Melinda yelped as she planted a dozen rapid-fire kisses all over his face, then firmly nestled her head against his neck. Bucky immediately jumped down and tugged at his hand.

"Dad, come see the new sled Grandpa Buck brought us. It is so cool," he insisted.

"Whoa, whoa. Let me get this stuff put away." He set Melinda back on her feet, then folded the charts and replaced the books in his bag.

"Dad, can we go sled in the park after breakfast? I wanna watch *Sesame Street*."

"That's already over, Buck," his big sister chided.

Mornin', kids. Nice to have your daddy home, huh?"

Alice stood in the doorway, forcing a smile.

Gradin rose, stepped toward her, and kissed her cheek. Her shudder was palpable as she turned and bolted into the kitchen. "Dad bought the kids a new sled?" He followed, maintaining an up tempo.

"Not exactly. Go look." She pointed toward the door to the garage as she poured the last of the coffee.

Bucky led the way. "Look, look. Isn't it cool, Dad?"

"That's my old Frequent Flyer—or Stanley Steamer—or what did they call these things, Alice?" he shouted back through the door. "Fearsome Flyer? What was it?" he asked as he admired the tall, old sled with shiny runners and faded oak planks.

"Flexible Flyer," Alice finally responded vacantly.

"That's right, the old Flexible Flyer. What great times I had on this thing. It never was mine, you know." He returned to the kitchen and closed the door. "Dad always claimed it as his, and we had to take care of it as such. Think how big and sturdy that thing is. He used to ride it, too, when I was a kid. He would pull it with a rope behind the truck with Aunt Trudy, Uncle Will, and me all riding." Turning to the kids, he added, "Wow, are you guys ever lucky."

"Hey, I was thinking I'd fix the breakfast. French toast, anybody?" He rubbed his hands enthusiastically and opened the refrigerator.

"Me, me!" Melinda and Bucky both shouted.

"Dad, can I have mine with jam this time?" Bucky asked with a scowl.

"Sure, big guy."

"Yuck. Not me. I want Grandma's maple syrup," Melinda insisted.

A tear trickled down Alice's cheek as she sipped her coffee and quietly escaped without the kids noticing. Gradin kept pace with Melinda and Bucky despite the pique of shame. As he stirred the milk and egg, he issued directions on the fly.

"Mel, set the table for three, please. I think your mom has gone back to bed for a while."

"Buckmeister, pour some orange juice for us, please," he said, quickly plunking three glasses on the table. The milk-soaked whole-wheat bread sizzled in the pan until the flurry of activity subsided, and all three murmured satisfied *mmms* and *ahs* as they ate.

With military precision, breakfast was completed, and the kitchen cleaned within minutes.

"It's a beautiful day in the neighborhood, a beautiful day in the neighborhood . . . " lilted from the TV as Melinda nestled down with her dad on the sofa. Mr. Rogers' soothing blather calmed them all. Even hyperactive Bucky tranquilly assembled a Lego tower as he listened.

Alice appeared and startled them with the announcement that she and Barb were going shopping. "Presidents Day sales, you know," she asserted with false enthusiasm. Leaning back into the room, she said, "Don't forget the party at the Hanford's tonight. Heavy hors d'oeuvres. Starts at 6:30. I think it is mostly the PTA crowd."

"Mom, what about us?" Melinda demanded.

"Sally's coming at 6:00. She'll give you your baths. Oh, and we're doing church and dinner with Mom and Dad tomorrow, just so you know." She stared directly into Gradin's eyes, then was gone.

He consciously kept the momentum up throughout the day. His need for physical exertion matched the kids' need for his attention. So the trip to the sledding hill was especially vigorous as they alternated between the plastic platter and the Flexible Flyer. Their favorite was the three-pack with the kids seated in front and Gradin on the back, steering with his feet. They found their own little trail through the trees in Comstock Park, their red Christmas scarves, plaid jackets, and wool mittens contributing to the Currier & Ives appearance of their frolic. They repeated the run nearly a dozen times.

Completely exhausted, they returned to the house for grilled cheese and tomato soup at a little past 1:00. The welcome chatter was incessant. "Billy this" and "Billy that" and "Susie's picture wasn't as good as mine" and "Mrs. Nelson let me be the line monitor twice last week." On it went.

A Saturday afternoon nap was often a problem. Not on this day. All three nestled on the bed while Gradin read from their favorite book, *Charlie and the Chocolate Factory*. They drifted off in two or three minutes, and Gradin finally escaped to his own anxious slumber.

That evening, he and Alice walked the three blocks to the Hanfords' house in silence. It was a brightly lit Cape Cod with frilly curtains that framed the happy faces of their friends and neighbors.

"Gradin, buddy." Bill Hanford greeted Gradin with a bear hug. "How the hell are you doin' after all that Pasco stuff last week? Get your ass in here." He stepped back, then graciously leaned to peck Alice on the cheek and help her with her coat. Several others crowded around, allowing her to slip inside unnoticed.

Not that he asked for it, but Gradin was the center of attention, and after quickly dispatching a second scotch, he managed to hold court with ease. He recounted the specifics and told how they lurched off the runway and ended up smashed against the berm. "Guys, I need you to understand that it wasn't that big a deal. The best part was that the whole crew worked so well together. They're all really special people. Omega had us all in Memphis this week to debrief. It was almost fun.

"I wish you could all meet the captain—name's Danny Purcell, one of those *bon vivant* bachelor pilots you'd read about in *Playboy*. Lives on a boat in Marina del Rey. Takes it up to the San Juans in the summer. Grown kids, thirty-year-old hard-body girlfriend, and a Porsche Carrera convertible. Right off the set of *Miami Vice*."

"So what happens now?" Roger Stanislaw, the straight-laced accountant, asked disdainfully. "Do you go right back to flying?"

"Oh, noooo. Not until the FAA gets a big chunk of our asses. They work on the 'guilty 'til proven innocent theory.' We'll get a full-blown oral and a sim check, and of course, they hold all the cards. Fortunately, the company really stands behind us, so we're not out there flappin' in the breeze. In fact, the company attorneys love to do battle with the feds. And to top it all off, the Air Line Pilots Association also provides us top-notch legal counsel. It will be a cast of thousands with Danny and me at the tip of the spear."

It all sounded rather gallant, and Gradin's demeanor certainly betrayed no lack of confidence. The Cutty Sark assuaged his concern, and he reveled in the opportunity to let it all out.

Gradin could see that Alice wasn't at all amused. She probably thought he should be hanging his head in shame, not basking in adulation. She retched and escaped to the powder room in tears. Despite the remorse that shot through him, he persevered.

"Yeah, remember Korean Air 007?" he responded when questioned about his Navy Reserve flying. "We were over there just six months after that happened, actually flying a patrol not far from where they went down. All of a sudden, our radar operator reports two bogeys airborne from the island where they launched on that 747. They were about 200 miles away, doin' warp nine right for us."

... ▬ ▬ ▬...▬ ▬ ▬...▬ ▬ ▬...▬ ▬ ▬▬...▬ ▬ ▬...▬ ▬ ▬...

"Oh, fun, what does a big airplane like that do to avoid being hit? Do you have chaff and all that ECM[36] stuff?" one of the guys asked.

"Nope, ain't nothin' to do but wait," Gradin said with a shrug.

"What about that big stinger of the tail, is that a cannon or something?"

"No, no." Gradin was clearly enjoying this as he took another sip of scotch. "That thing is called a MAD boom— not like *boom* from a cannon." He chuckled at the irony. A couple of other guys smiled with the same realization. "MAD is an acronym for magnetic anomaly detector. It can sense an anomaly in the magnetic field. More specifically, it can detect a large object several hundred feet under the ocean surface.

"You have to be right on top of whatever it is—I mean *right on top*, 200 or 300 feet over the water."

"That's how you find submarines out there in that huge ocean?" Roger was incredulous.

"Not really. It's only how we *confirm* what we already know. If we were actually in a hot conflict, a MAD contact would quite literally trigger a torpedo launch. The sensor operator would call 'MAD MAD MAD,' and we'd pickle the torp." He made an exaggerated motion with his thumb, similar to the one required to release a torpedo.

"But it sounds like you'd be flying away. Don't you have to be aiming at the target?"

"Nope, it's a homing torpedo; finds 'em by itself."

"Hey, what about those two bogeys comin' at you at warp nine?"

"Not much of a story. The best we could do was to look non-threatening, and unlike 007, we had not penetrated Soviet airspace. At about the time the radar operator was spotting them coming, our radio lit up with coded warnings from U.S. ground radar sites. I don't know how it works, but we have over-the-horizon radar capability and those guys at a U.S. military site in Japan could see the same thing happening. You gotta realize that at any one time, there are probably half a dozen different reconnaissance airplanes airborne along the Soviet periphery over there. We all monitor the same HF radio frequencies."

"HF?"

"High frequency. Depending on the atmospherics, HF has a very long-range capability—thousands of miles sometimes. Those are the frequencies we use during ocean transits. Everybody does, in fact, the airlines as well as the military.

"Anyway, on the frequencies we monitor, there are periodic transmissions of coded messages. You would probably laugh to hear it because they say things like, 'Sky King, Sky King, do not answer, do not answer,' followed by a long string of alphabet quads: Charlie-Hotel-Mike-Juliet, Romeo-Zulu-Hotel-Kilo, whatever. Every tactical military flight has a cipher to break the codes.

"Ninety percent of the transmissions are bogus, but once in a while, you get a valid match for an actual message. And sure enough, right after we saw the bogeys, we got a Sky King message confirming that there were enemy aircraft headed our way.

"I guess the irony for me was that we were just a bunch of rummy civilians motoring around over there in an old unarmed P-3. What kind of threat could that be? Obviously, they were pretty sensitive about something to have gone after that 747."

"Yeah, what the hell was that about?"

"Well, apparently, KAL had programmed their inertial nav systems wrong, and they were significantly off course, like a 180 miles or so."

"And they didn't know that?"

"Nope. They were so reliant on their inertial nav system that they weren't even monitoring anything else. I know it sounds nuts, but we had a TriStar do the same thing over the Atlantic just last summer. Nearly hit another U.S. airliner."

"Jesus! How can that be?"

"Complacency." Gradin's nonchalance made the point. "It just gets built into the culture. It's just another day at the office out there. You have these very sophisticated computer systems, and everyone assumes that they will outperform human intelligence. The problem—and, of course, the beauty—is that they will only do what they are programmed to do. The fact was that they were flying exactly where they had programmed the airplane to fly.

"You can bet that at Korean Air the procedures for programming the inertial nav systems have changed since then. Most of our mechanical systems have multiple redundancies. Our human systems need to have the same."

"How does that work?" Roger continued to probe.

"Well, I know for a fact that the procedures at Omega are very specific and very redundant now. I rode the jump seat of an MD-11 from Tokyo to L.A. recently. It was really interesting to watch how they handled the nav. One guy programmed both inertials separately—they can be set up to simply copy one program directly to the other system. After the route was entered and verified, the other pilot went back and confirmed that each waypoint had been entered exactly as depicted on the flight plan.

"Then, en route, they used every available navigation aid to continue to confirm that the airplane was flying the designated route. For instance, the ground-based nav aids are good for a couple of hundred miles off the coast, so you can verify your track the good old-fashioned way for the first thirty minutes or so. And this MD-11 crew created a handwritten howgozit[37] right on the margin of the flight plan. So, at every fix they recorded all of the correlating data they had available to them. Now they compare their actual progress with the planned performance—I'm talking about location within a mile or so, and time within a few seconds. If the figures don't match, that's a red flag, and they dig in to figure out why.

"If KAL had done that, they would have discovered right away that they were veering off course—even before they left Alaska, they were diverging. The air traffic controllers share some of the blame here, too, because they saw the error and didn't call them on it."

"Wow, a whole combination of things."

"Yeah, it's always, always, always that way." Gradin was emphatic.

"So what about your rudder problem? Was that a whole combination of things?" one of the men asked.

"Almost certainly yes. When it's all said and done, there will be a chain of circumstances that triggered that whole thing. Boeing claims that it isn't the airplane, but they have a helluva lot to lose if it is."

He raised his hands in protest. "Enough of this, guys. How 'bout them Redskins? It looked like Elway was gonna do it, but that second quarter for the Skins—thirty-five points, wasn't it?" He referred to Washington's recent rout of Denver in the Super Bowl.

"Yeah, it was amazing. Four TDs by Doug Williams. MVP, wasn't he? Guess we'll be hearing a lot about that guy in the future," someone commented.

Gradin had succeeded in shifting the conversation away from flying, and he was grateful for the break. After football, kids became their focus, and gradually the wives integrated the huddle, and mixed groups broke off in their own discussions.

Alice was the exception. She sequestered herself in the breakfast nook with her two closest friends and confidantes. *Are they getting an earful of my guilt and betrayal?* he wondered. *Guess it goes with the territory, but this is ominously unfamiliar territory for me.* His shoulders sagged for an instant in despair. A single comment penetrated the arctic chill on the trek home. "You were quite the hero tonight," Alice sniped. He knew she was itching for a showdown, but he gritted his teeth and doggedly rejected the bait. *Gotta get through that sim first.*

At 10:57 Sunday morning, Gradin bent down to adjust the tie and smooth the white collar under Bucky's jacket. He looked up to see Ken and Marjorie waiting at the top of the steps of the entrance to Spokane's First Methodist Church, both smiling. Melinda scampered up into the welcoming arms of her grandparents. Alice followed and accepted their warm embrace somberly. Gradin and Bucky followed, shook hands with Ken, and pecked Marjorie's cheek. All three genera-

tions smiled at the contrived formality and Bucky doubled over giggling at the fake jab to the stomach thrown by Grandpa Ken.

"You okay, kid?" Ken whispered to Gradin as they turned and stepped through the heavy oak doors.

"Hangin' in there, Ken, thanks," he nodded.

A jolting *BONG* reverberated from the bell tower. Melinda clung to her grandmother's hand as the entire family jumped in surprise and scurried into the sanctuary. The church bell sounded again, then echoed away as they slipped into the center pew near the back. Gradin inhaled deeply as the comforting aroma of church coffee, and lilacs filled his senses. With his exhalation and the ensuing quiet, an emotional calm replaced the incessant chatter in his head.

Padraig MacDonald, their Scottish pastor, smiled down from the pulpit. Holding his hands outstretched, he spoke the familiar call to worship. "The Lord is in his holy temple; let all the earth keep silence before him." The choir followed with a lyrical introit, and the soft cadence of the liturgy comforted the flock. Fifty-five minutes later, Paddy concluded his message of hope and reconciliation with the simple and direct admonition from the Book of Micah:

He has showed you, O man, what is good; and what does the
Lord require of you but to do justice, and to love kindness,
Then slowly and emphatically:
and to walk humbly with your God.

He closed his bible, beamed benevolently at the congregation, then sat down as the choir murmured an extended, cascading choral *Amen.*

Tears streamed down Alice's cheeks. Marjorie handed her a handkerchief and patted her arm, acknowledging how stressful Gradin's accident had been for her stoic daughter. "He's right here beside you, sweetheart. All is well." She smiled, lovingly stroking Alice's back. Alice only cried harder.

Chapter 19

HARVARD

The cross-country trip was uneventful, filled with ruminations but absent conclusions. By 10:30, he was ensconced in the hotel, and by 8:30 the next morning, he wound down the hall of the old office complex and knocked on the door of Marsha's office.

"Hey, the blue boy arriveth." Jack's jocular voice welcomed him as Marsha opened the door. She greeted him with a warm and genuine, broad smile, a handshake, and a sisterly hug.

He turned to Jack and snapped a salute. "Ensign Morehouse, reporting for duty, sir."

"At ease, GI. Stand easy and speak," Jack commanded.

"Uh, well, I'm speechless, really. How does a kid from Bellingham, Washington find himself in the hallowed halls of Harvard? I must have taken a wrong turn back there someplace." He jokingly turned to leave.

"No, no, as long as you're here, we may as well pick that unfettered brain of yours. Have a seat. And always remember Yogi's advice, young man."

Marsha took the bait. "And that is?"

"'When you come to the fork in the road, take it.'"

"Yeah, cuz 'if you don't know where you're going, you'll wind up somewhere else.'" Brad nodded matter-of-factly.

"Hmm, I never thought of it that way." Jack scratched his chin quizzically.

"Pilots! Damned pilots," Marsha blurted. "It's never, 'Hello. How are you? Nice to see you.' It's always some spontaneous Abbott and Costello routine. Where the hell does that come from?"

"Uh, basic insecurity, I guess, Doc." Jack was only half-joking.

"Marsha. It is nice to see you. How's everything?" Brad patted her knee and looked attentive.

"Enough, you two!"

"Oh, how was my weekend?" Jack continued. "Thanks for asking. It was ducky, really."

The humorous facade gave way to an earnest description of events that had occurred with an Omega crew at JFK on Saturday. First, Jack described how crew schedulers scrambled to find a crew for the New York to Orlando flight, how the inbound crew had diverted for weather, and there were no domestic reserve crews in position to cover the flight.

"So this brilliant crew scheduler said to himself, *Hey, self, aren't those international 767 crews qualified on the 757? Yes, I believe they are, and it happens that we have a ton of those guys available.*

"Now understand, this has never been done before," Jack continued. "But technically the 757 and 767 are interchangeable, and there is nothing in the contract that says you can't use an international crew on a domestic route.

"So imagine how surprised old Captain Numb Nuts was when they called him out to fly the New York-Orlando shuttle. Then he about dropped his teeth when he got there and discovered that he was on a 757 rather than a 767."

"Hmm, I smell trouble brewing here."

"Oh, you have no idea, girl." Jack smiled ruefully. "Picture this. The full airplane has been sitting at the gate for an hour and a half, waiting for some lazy old pilots who probably forgot to come to work. There was no explanation from anyone about the absence of a crew. Everyone was in the dark.

"The pilots arrived, threw their bags in the cockpit, and realized that they didn't have any domestic charts. So the captain sent the copilot down to the lounge to find some charts while he began the preflight. And while he was fumbling around, the senior flight attendant came up and engaged the captain in a little small talk. She was appalled to hear him say, 'We aren't even qualified on this damned airplane. I haven't flown a 757 in five years.'

"Not surprisingly, she slunk away and shared her concern with the other flight attendants standing around in the front galley. She wasn't very discreet, and some passengers in first class overheard bits and pieces of the conversation—things like, 'They aren't even qualified on this airplane' and 'They don't have charts for the route.'"

"Oh, no! Can you imagine hearing something like that?" Marsha was rattled.

"It gets better—remain seated, remain seated," he joked, holding up both hands. "So as they went through the checklist and came to the RAT switches—that's the ram air turbine that drops down to provide hydraulics to the flight controls when there is a dual-engine failure—"

"Comforting." Marsha squirmed.

"Anyway, they couldn't find the RAT switches. They just weren't there. So intrepid aviators that they are, they called maintenance to come and solve the problem. And the time is grinding on and grinding on.

"The mechanic came up, and the captain jumped all over him. 'Hey, this damned airplane doesn't have a RAT. How the hell can we take an airplane up without a RAT?'

"'Uh, Captain, the RAT switches are right back here,' the mechanic said, pointing to the aft circuit-breaker panel. 'This is one of those airplanes we got from the Saudis. It's a hybrid,' he said very deferentially.

"The captain continued his tirade and pissed off the mechanic, who walked out of the cockpit muttering, 'Those guys have no idea what they're doing up there.'"

"Jesus Christ!" Brad had finally been brought to a boil.

Jack pressed on. "Yeah, you can imagine the mood in back by then. The flight attendants turned white, passengers in the front got up to leave the airplane, and when word spread to the back, there was a near riot as people jostled to get the hell off the airplane."

"Holy shit, what happened then?"

"They canceled the flight and rebooked everyone on other flights, hopefully on other airlines, too." Jack breathed a conclusive sigh.

"And you were that captain, right?" Brad cracked.

"No, but I did get to spend some time with him. Andy called me at home and had me go down and meet with the entire crew that evening. Consider this the first of our official

CRM events. It looks like they will use us to intervene with crews when shit hits the fan."

"Hmm, not a bad idea," Marsha said.

"Well, we'll have to develop a protocol, and we'll need buy-in from ALPA, but there may be some upside here. I can imagine some cases in which this kind of intervention can occur in lieu of certificate action. That would be a major break-through."

"Ahem," Marsha exclaimed. "You are probably wondering why I called you here this morning."

Jack bowed his head in embarrassment. "Sorry."

"Brad, I told Jack the story about the American Eagle down in Raleigh, and how that has caused me to rethink the concept of planning."

"Yeah, I like that broader perspective encompassed in Preparation," Jack responded earnestly.

"That's good because I've stumbled onto some more gems that help underscore the critical importance of each one of those components, sub-categories of planning, training and organizational support. A little background first. You both remember the Northwest Mad Dog[38] in Detroit last summer, and the Continental DC-9 in Denver just a few months ago."

"Yup." They both nodded.

"Neither of the official NTSB reports is out yet, but I do have copies of their preliminary findings."

"How the hell did you do that?"

"Reliability. My contact knows that I will never use what she gives me for anything but research. And that's exactly what we're doing right now."

Three manila folders were stacked on Marsha's desk. She selected two of them and opened the first. "This is that

Metro-liner, AVAir 3378, that went down in Raleigh. It's a treasure trove of evidence that the FAA—part of the *organization*—had an enormous role in this tragic accident. Brad, you probably remember much of what I was fuming about when I first got this info."

Marsha went on to describe how the FAA had failed to oversee this small carrier as it navigated through Chapter Eleven reorganization and a one-month shutdown. She explained how rules that apply to major carriers do not extend to the regionals, and that a large company with financial stress is accorded special scrutiny while small carriers are not.

"In fact, the disregard of the FAA borders on gross negligence." Marsha's temperature was rising. "From everything my source, Natasha, can find, there is no record that the POI[39] ever rode with a crew, attended a training session, or even visited the company headquarters. Jesus, can you imagine? Here is a company teetering on extinction, and this guy had completely checked out. He was politicking for a new job in Europe someplace."

"Our tax dollars at work." Jack shook his head.

Brad followed with, "Well, Congress wanted a deregulated industry. I guess that's what they got. No oversight whatsoever."

"Yeah. Survival of the fittest. But you've got to be pretty damned fit to survive a 150-mile-an-hour plunge into a reservoir." Marsha rolled her eyes.

"There is more to this organization piece." She went on. "Consider the manufacturer's part. This particular airplane has a—let me see here." She thumbed through the pages. "Yeah, here it is. It has a stall-avoidance system that will literally push the control column forward when it senses an impending stall. "Sounds like a good concept, but imagine what happens when there is an *uncommanded* activation. You're flyin' along, fat, dumb, and happy, and all of a sudden, you have forty pounds of pressure pushing nose-down. And from what I understand, this system is known to give false activation warnings. There is speculation that 3378 had a false warning shortly after liftoff."

"How could they possibly know that?" Jack questioned. "That airplane doesn't have either a voice recorder or flight data recorder."

"You're right, but those NTSB guys know exactly what to look for. As I understand it, the light filaments in the warning system were broken. Similar filaments in lights that were not illuminated didn't break. So the theory is that they got this light, and it became a distraction. Rather than maintaining a shallow bank turn, they allowed the aircraft to roll into a steep bank and dive into the water. The captain could easily have been distracted by his effort to deactivate the system.

"In fact, they did some calculations to determine the likely point of impact under those circumstances, and the calculations corresponded exactly with the actual splash point."

"Sounds sad but true."

"And do we know why this very inexperienced copilot was making the takeoff that night?" Brad inquired.

"That's another interesting piece of the puzzle. The fact is that under Part 135 of the Federal Aviation Regulations, the copilot is *not allowed* to make the takeoff when the weather is below standard takeoff criteria. The inexperienced flight management team had misinterpreted that regulation.

"But here's the kicker. Last fall, AVAir discovered their error in interpretation and reported it to the FAA. However, they did not implement a change in operating procedures. They just kept blundering along, and the damned POI was AWOL, so the FAA didn't insist on a change."

"Yeah, they didn't even get the ol' 'Hi, I'm from the FAA, and I'm here to help,'" Jack exclaimed.

"Not even." Marsha continued, "Can you imagine United or American discovering a gross violation of FARs in their op specs and essentially saying, 'Oh, well, we'll get to that when we revise the manuals next time'?"

"Somehow, I don't think so."

"And, of course, I haven't said anything yet about the abysmal performance of the first officer. They were just carrying this gal and look what it led to. On the other hand, the captain was no Buck Rogers, either. His training record is littered with examples of poor performance."

"Great combination on a cold and rainy night."

"Yeah, you get what you pay for. What do those guys earn? A buck-ninety an hour?" Brad asked rhetorically.

Marsha grabbed the second folder and pressed on. "Which leads nicely to the Continental crash in Denver. There are lots of mitigating factors here, but the one that jumps out at me is the history of poor performance by the copilot. He had been fired for failing a check ride at another carrier, and there is evidence that Continental did not know that."

"Marsha, let me interrupt here for a moment because I can sense where you are going, and there may be some stuff here that isn't fully obvious to you." Jack sat forward with a worried look.

"Have at it," she encouraged.

"Well, first, what does the name Frank Lorenzo mean to you?"

"Uh, CEO of that conglomerate of airlines, and I guess that includes Continental, right?"

"Anything else?"

"Nothing that I'm aware of." She was puzzled.

Jack was agitated. "That fucking son of a bitch is the most evil person the industry has ever known. Please excuse the profanity."

"That's okay. Don't sugarcoat it," Marsha responded. "Tell us what you *really* think, Jack."

"He has single-handedly destroyed one of the great airlines. In 1981, he won a long-running battle for control of Continental. And lest anyone believe that this was a genteel discussion among like-minded entrepreneurs, it's important to remember that the CEO of Continental, Al Feldman, committed suicide in the process.

"Then the prick filed Chapter Eleven and busted all of the unions. The unions actually fought it in court and won—it was determined that you can't unilaterally revoke union contracts simply because you are in Chapter Eleven. But their win was after the fact, so in effect, Lorenzo won, and he hasn't stopped since.

"At this very moment, he is in the process of dismantling Eastern. He is selling off their assets and buying the plums for Continental at pennies on the dollar."

"But how does any of this relate to the accident?" Marsha inquired earnestly.

Jack took a deep breath to calm himself. "Well, it will be interesting to see the final report on this. I'm wondering if the NTSB will tackle the issue of the duress that Lorenzo's shenanigans have caused at Continental. Damn it, they used

... ▄ ▄ ▄... ▄ ▄ ▄... ▄ ▄ ▄... ▄ ▄ ▄... ▄ ▄ ▄...

to be 'The Proud Bird with the Golden Tail.' They were a class act. Now look at 'em; they're a hodge-podge of losers.

"Last year, he combined Frontier, New York Air, and People Express." He ticked them off with his fingers. "All under the Continental umbrella. He had effectively locked out the good pilots from ALPA. He hired a bunch of scabs to replace them, and off they went. Shit!" Jack sat back and folded his arms in disgust.

"Okay, I get it now." Marsha's voice was soothing. "You're suggesting that the pilots in the accident may not have been the sharpest blades in the drawer."

"Exactly."

Brad jumped in. "Marsha, there is an unspoken pecking order in this industry. We literally never talk about it, but it is known, nonetheless. It's like the rankings in college football. You've got USC, Ohio State, and Michigan—that would be Omega, American, and United. Then you have everyone else. Pilots all know that if you can't play for the big guys, you hope to wind up on a smaller team that has a great program, like Alaska or PSA.

"Lorenzo has combined a bunch of losing programs in an attempt to put together a winner, and from what you are telling us about the accident in November, those passengers paid the ultimate price for low-quality labor. Ten years ago, that copilot would never have been playing in the big leagues, I guarantee you that."

"Wow, you've really nailed this one," Marsha confessed. "The data indicates that the copilot over-rotated on the take-off—six degrees per second rather than the standard three—so he essentially pulled the aircraft into a stall before they were even airborne."

"Right, and where was the captain? It's his job to monitor and counteract stuff like that," Jack offered calmly.

"Yeah, they had paired two rookies on this trip, though there is no indication that either knew that about the other," Marsha concluded. "There is indication that the first officer actually lost complete control of the aircraft, actually flipped it on its back, during an engine-out maneuver in the sim."[40]

"See, you're singing our song. In all my years in the airlines, I have never heard of a guy doing that. Lorenzo must love the concept that if they don't meet your standards, you simply lower the standards. End of problem." Jack shrugged.

"So, what's the bottom line here, Marsha?" Brad asked. "Is there a piece in this that applies to our program?"

"Indirectly, yes. It has to do with organizational support. It may turn out to be your most important task, convincing everyone in the organization that the work they do directly impacts flight safety. Obviously, it's up to Jack, but there may be value in working up a presentation that can be made to departments throughout the company, probably beginning with the board of directors."

"Hmm, good idea."

"And let me go out on a limb here," she went on cautiously. "It strikes me that the training atmosphere at Omega is pretty adversarial, or, at the very least, competitive. It seems that your pilots are sort of on trial when they show up down there for training. I know that isn't always the case, but I have seen it more often than not."

"Yeah, I notice that, too," Jack conceded. "We're like a bunch of alpha dogs sniffing each other out, seein' who has the biggest balls."

"Don't forget that I'm a ranch girl from Montana. I know the game. But don't you think something can be done to change that? Isn't there a way to get all of the training guys to see themselves as coaches rather than referees? That would certainly contribute to our concept of organizational support." Jack was scribbling a note to himself. "I'll arrange a meeting with Hank Maxwell, our training director. It'd be good if we could all be there. Should be able to do it during the April meeting." Then, without missing a beat, he said, "And speaking of April, I'm famished."

"Good point. You are obviously feeling a lot more like you do right now than you did this time yesterday." Brad was quick to follow.

"There you go again. Damned pilots." Marsha rolled her eyes, closed the folder, and motioned toward the door. "Be my guest."

The walk across campus was textbook Ivy League. As they walked, Marsha raised another question. "What do you think the ramifications of the PSA suicide are for us?" They were all aware that in December, a recently terminated employee boarded a PSA flight with false credentials. Once airborne he shot his former supervisor and both pilots, which led to the death of all forty-three souls on board.[41]

"Hmm." Jack paused to think. "My guess is that it was a unique incident. It probably won't ever happen again. Obviously, a bulletproof cockpit door would solve that kind of problem, but all the evidence points to the benefit of cooperating with a hijacker rather than resisting.

"In the broader scheme of things, there needs to be a process for identifying people who are likely to snap like that. It was about two years ago that that postal worker in Oklahoma killed a bunch of people in a post office there."

"I always worry about the copy-cat effect," Marsha said. "Just last month, a former employee of one of those high-tech firms in the Bay Area shot seven people in the workplace. That was only two months after PSA went down not too far from there. Scary," she concluded with a shiver.

Lunch conversation veered from the weather to the Red Sox to Dukakis and the presidential race, then to Ollie North and Iran-Contra, and finally back to aviation.

"Did you hear about the seven-three that lost an engine on the early departure from Dallas last year?" Brad asked no one in particular as he picked at his salad. "So the guys were workin' away, getting set up for an emergency landing on the departure runway, when one of the flight attendants came up and said, 'Hey, did you know that we just lost an engine?' And they replied, 'Yeah, we know, we're headed back for an emergency landing right now.' She persisted, 'No, I mean we really lost an engine. It fell off the airplane.' Up to that time, they thought it was merely an engine failure." They all laughed and continued eating.

As Jack consumed the last morsel of his sandwich, he appeared lost in thought. Finally, he said, "Marsha, you're causing me to realize that our responsibility in developing this program goes way beyond pilot training. It's really about reshaping the entire culture—the company, the FAA, even ALPA. Everyone has to see his or her role as a critical element in the flight safety equation.

"I'm going down to Memphis tomorrow. Now that we have the big picture, I think it's time to brief Andy. In reality, we need his blessing to take this thing to the next level. And ultimately, the board has to sign-off on it before we create the finished product."

Brad fidgeted and struggled to remain focused as their work began again.

"Okay, my dear Captain Mumford, you've got the airplane." Marsha mimicked the cockpit transfer of authority. "This one is right up your alley."

"Yes, and a lovely one it is indeed," he responded, opening the folder. "Just a quick synopsis. Northwest 255 departed Detroit[42] —or, more accurately, *attempted* to depart Detroit— on the evening of August sixteenth last summer. The airplane was full, and they were headed for Phoenix, to continue on to Santa Ana. It was the Friday night special to Disneyland."

"So far, this sounds familiar," Brad responded with a grim smirk.

"Yes, and I'm sure you will remember the rest. They forgot the flaps, rotated into a stall, and everyone on board except one small child was killed.

"Marsha gave me this one because it will likely be a big piece of my thesis next year. In the eyes of a researcher, it is a treasure trove of flawed human performance. For a pilot, it is a nauseating reminder of how critical the mundane is to our survival.

"And I guess that I haven't said this before, but I am totally with you on the morphing of the *preparation* category, Marsha. This damned thing was the perfect example of how important the multiple aspects of effective preparation really are. Most frightening to me is the similarity between the performance of this crew and what I see among Omega crews."

"How so?" Marsha prodded.

Jack scratched his head and thought for a moment. "Well, it's a little difficult to untangle the interrelationship of factors, so let me hit them one at a time before I try to relate them.

"First, the Northwest crew had no checklist discipline whatsoever. On thirty minutes of tape from the cockpit voice recorder, not once did the captain call for and respond to a checklist. There should have been four of them: the be-fore-start, the after-start, the taxi, and the before-takeoff.

"While they were at the gate, the transcript shows that the copilot attempted to initiate the before-start checklist by simply reciting the first item, 'brakes.' A few seconds later, the captain did say, 'Let's do the checklist.' A few seconds after that, the copilot responded, 'Checklist complete.' He did the challenge-and-response items silently, entirely by himself, which is absolutely contrary to the whole point of having a checklist."

"So was this consistent with the company culture, or do you think it was unique to this crew?" Marsha asked.

"My guess is that it was a cultural norm. It certainly is at Omega. But the investigators are pretty careful not to draw that kind of conclusion. More baffling, though, is the fact that the before-start checklist was the last checklist mentioned on the tape. So they not only failed to call for checklists, they literally failed to do them." Brad shook his head glumly.

"Correct. Their protocols are much like ours. As soon as they are waved away, it is standard procedure for the copi-lot to extend the flaps. And for some reason, the transcript shows that instead of doing that, he switched frequencies and got the latest ATIS immediately following the wave-off.

"Let me digress here for a moment. I commute to Mem-phis on ol' Brand X about half the time, so I have dozens if not hundreds of trips in their jump seats. Those guys are perfectly standardized and disciplined. I've never seen it change."

"Why the difference at Northwest?" Marsha was now the devil's advocate.

"Expectation!" Jack responded emphatically. "It doesn't matter what the book says if the leaders don't require that everyone adhere to the standards. I think they even say that in the NTSB report." He rifled through the pages.

"Yeah, right here." He paraphrased. "The NASA psychologist testified that evidence suggested that the way the checklists were used was directly related to the number of errors made by the pilots. The flight crews that performed their checklist duties 'by the book—with challenge [and] response methodology—tend to perform more effectively.'"

Jack looked ahead to the testimony of a psychologist. "He testified that he was not familiar with any body of research relating to the construction and presentation of checklists, but it was his opinion that 'there are probably many ways to do a checklist correctly. What's important is that everyone agrees on how it should be done, and it's done the same way every time by all the people who are concerned.'"

Brad picked up the conversation immediately. "You left out the mitigating factor of the takeoff warning horn."

"Oh, absolutely. Had that system not failed, this never would have happened. I simply wanted to focus on the human factors piece."

"I think that I'm with you guys here," Marsha interrupted. "You're saying that the takeoff warning system ordinarily monitors key components critical to a normal takeoff."

"Right, a horn should have sounded when they added power with the flaps up."

"Jack, we're headed for the same problem here at Omega, I guarantee it." Brad sat forward on the edge of his chair. "When the merger occurred, Pacific had a procedure that required the crew to check the takeoff warning system prior to every takeoff. As you know, Omega doesn't do that. It's gonna bite us one of these days."

Jack was equally adamant. "Not if I can help it. This damned company is going to become the model of cockpit discipline and standardization. I'll rattle every cage in the chain of command, I promise you."

The clipped conversation continued incessantly, and Brad was relieved to note the growing synergy between Jack and Marsha. She, Jack's thesis advisor, was now his subordinate on the steering committee, and the role reversal had an energizing effect on them both. Brad kept pace as necessary, but the other two were stoking each other's fire, and he was certain they would welcome his absence from dinner that night. He headed for home instead.

Chapter 20

FIREWORKS

The seat belt sign extinguished, and Brad grabbed a blanket and two pillows from the overhead bin, then stretched out in the empty middle row of the 767 bound for Seattle just as the man across the aisle spoke.

"Miss, excuse me," he said, then pointed anxiously out the window into the dark sky. Carol McCarthy smiled placidly and leaned over to see what he might be seeing. "Look at that. Look." He was quite concerned.

"Uh, sir, I'm not sure what it is you are looking at."

"Those sparks. See those sparks coming out of the engine?" the passenger insisted.

She shifted her gaze farther back and shielded her eyes. *Uh-oh, this could be a problem,* she muttered to herself. "Thank you, sir, I'll let the captain know." Then she hustled up the aisle toward the cockpit.

Brad bolted upright, stepped back a row, and looked out toward the right engine.

Damn!

"Ring me up, Robert," Carol requested urgently. "We have a possible emergency back there!" She stepped toward the cockpit door as her fellow flight attendant pressed the cockpit-call button. The door unlatched, and she stepped in.

"Hey, George, a passenger just pointed out some sparks coming from the right engine. Is that normal?"

"Hmmm, shouldn't be. Right engine, you say?" He leaned forward and scrutinized the engine instruments. After a moment. he leaned back and said, "Looks normal, but why don't you go back and take a look, Scott?"

"Will do," the copilot said as he unbuckled his seat belt, hooked his headset over the window crank handle, and ran his seatback. Before he could move, the red light and fire bell answered their question.

"Okay, delay that, Scott." George held out his hand to motion him back into his seat. "Silence the horn, and let's run the engine-fire checklist."

Carol stood in awe as the two pilots calmly commenced the checklist. She hadn't noticed, but George immediately disconnected the autopilot and gripped the yoke with both hands. From memory, Scott deliberately reached over and tapped the right power lever. "Right side?" he asked, just as he'd practiced so many times in the simulator.

George also reached over to confirm the right lever. "Close," Scott said as he pulled the power lever back to

the closed position, while George pushed the left lever forward to compensate for the power loss on the right.

Then Scott opened the abnormal-procedures booklet and read aloud from the checklist. "Condition: Fire is detected in the affected engine or airframe, etcetera.

"AUTO-THROTTLE SWITCH, OFF." George disengaged the switch.

"THRUST LEVER, CLOSE." He pulled the thrust lever all the way back. Scott continued to read.

"FUEL CONTROL SWITCH, CUT OFF.

"If engine fire warning light remains illuminated:

"ENGINE FIRE SWITCH, PULL.

"Rotate to the stop and hold for one second. If, after thirty seconds," Scott read as he reached up and started the clock, "engine fire warning light remains illuminated—"

They both counted silently. Scott started to reach for the engine fire switch a second time.

"Wait," George's hand shot out to prevent Scott from reaching the switch. They waited anxiously as more than thirty seconds elapsed.

"Ah, good show." George breathed with relief as the light extinguished. "Okay, finish the checklist, Scott, and I'll get us clearance back to Salt Lake.

"Carol, let everyone know that all is well, and we are returning to SLC. Should be arriving in about fifteen minutes. Why don't you leave that cockpit door open so you guys can come up as needed? And Carol, thanks for the heads-up. Ya done good." He gave her a thumbs-up, smiled, and turned back to the instruments.

"Thanks, George. And I know you're busy, but when you can, will one of you please make a PA and tell the folks what we're up to?"

"Yup, we'll get to that as soon as we can."

Brad felt the sweat on his palms as he watched the flight attendants huddle in the forward galley and discuss the situation. With their plan in mind, they all moved through the cabin, confidently explaining to passengers what was happening.

It was eerily calm. Two sleeping kids hadn't stirred since the aircraft had taxied away from the gate.

The air traffic controllers provided the crew carte blanche as they returned to Salt Lake City. The descent was smooth and gradual. Within fifteen minutes, the aircraft rolled slightly right and intercepted the final approach course to runway 16L.

"Omega 665, Salt Lake tower, cleared to land one-six-left, wind one-three-zero at five."

"Cleared to land, one-six-left," Scott replied routinely. The passenger who had reported the fire, Nick Elmer, squirmed uncomfortably as he saw the glow of flames silhouetting the right engine just prior to touchdown. Brad also saw the fire return, and his stomach churned.

"Omega 665, Salt Lake tower, your right engine is still on fire. I say again, your right engine is still on fire."

George maneuvered the lumbering aircraft down the runway and applied reverse thrust to the left engine. They ignored the tower's call while the aircraft slowed. Finally, Scott said, "You want that high-speed there?" He pointed to the taxiway coming up at an angle on the right.

"Yeah."

"Omega 665 will take hotel three and hold there. Please send the equipment," Scott told the tower calmly. Then, looking at the captain, he asked, "Evacuate?"

"No. Hang tight. I don't want to dump a planeload of passengers out there for the fire trucks to run over." George set the brake and raised both hands as if to say *I'm not touching a thing.*

"Folks, this is the captain speaking. Please remain seated. I repeat, remain seated." Scott spoke with his most authoritative voice on the PA.

A cross-current of headlights and red flashing beacons flickered over the tarmac, and the momentary radio silence was broken. "Omega 665, this is the fire marshal, Red Dog 1. How copy?"

"Red Dog 1, 665, read you loud and clear."

"Okay, 665, we're just gonna douche ya down here. Confirm that the right engine is shut down, sir."

The sticky fire-retardant spray pelted and coated the right side of the aircraft, obscuring any view of the fire from the cabin.

"Affirmative, the right engine is shut down; has been for fifteen minutes."

"And, the fuel is shut off?"

"Affirmative."

"George, are we going to evacuate?" Carol stood with hands on her hips.

George continued talking to the fire marshal before addressing Carol. "Yes, sir, the fuel valve to that engine is closed."

Then, "Uh, no, Carol. We need to let these fire guys have time to get the fire out. What you can do is get people focused toward the left side of the airplane. Just calmly move them over to that side, and whatever you do, don't use the word 'evacuate.'"

Brad couldn't suppress a smile as the flight attendants moved confidently through the cabin, reassuring people and coaxing them toward the left-side emergency exits. *This was a script written in CRM heaven,* he marveled.

His call to Marsha Hilbert the following morning brimmed with enthusiasm: "You should have seen that crew! It was textbook. They provided us a perfect in-house case of CRM at its best. We can create a video. It would be so powerful to show our crews that some of their peers already have this stuff figured out."

He went on excitedly for several minutes before hanging up. Then on cue, Audrey stepped into the room and stretched languidly. "Nice relationship you have there."

"Very smart woman," he replied guardedly.

"I know. She and I talked for a few minutes several weeks ago. She has the inside scoop on a lot of good stuff."

"Wow, your ears really perk up to that." He stared at her disdainfully. "You know, we never have discussed your using the privileged information about the Pasco accident. That really torques my jaw."

"Clever way to put it," she fired back with a sneer. "In my profession, nothing is off-limits, not even your jaw."

"Ooooh, harsh."

"You think that's harsh," Audrey said defiantly. "Sounds like a storm brewing here."

She walked toward the window, nervously raked her long fingers through thick brown tresses, then turned to face him, hands on her hips. "Well, how about this?" She paused for effect and stared. "You get your college-professor girlfriend, and I get my corporate-news-mogul boyfriend."

"Your wh—?" Like a sucker punch thrown before the opening bell, Audrey's stinging blow caught Brad flat-foot-ed. He stood slack-jawed, then shook his head to clear the cobwebs. All the possible rejoinders stuck in his throat as he struggled to focus. An argument was illogical, an accusation unnecessary, a threat childish. Good thing, because no words came to him.

"Listen, Brad. You were pretty sexy back when you had that blue rocket strapped between your legs. You were definitely in the fast lane, really going places. But the stupid kayak, big dog, and hourly-wage job leave me cold. You're not the same person I met five years ago.

"Frankly, this whole small-town scene is a drag. I really get off playing with the big kids in New York. In fact, they've offered me a job, and I'm taking it."

Audrey stood there, staring with an insolent air.

Brad called for Admiral and left the house in a daze. He had always doubted himself, wondering whether marriage would eliminate his attraction to other women. *Well, no, but wouldn't the commitment render that point moot?* 'Til now the answer had always been yes, but several days prior in Portland the entire landscape had changed. *So why am I feeling so hurt and angry? It's my ego. I know it and reject it all at once.*

For several hours, he walked with Admiral before stumbling up to a phone booth and dropping several coins into the box. "Dad? Brad," was the best he could do.

"Bradley, my favorite son. How are you, m'lad?"

"I've had better days, Dad. You gonna be home for a while?"

"Nothin' on my dance card for several weeks. What's up?" His dad's cheeriness was a welcome counterpoint.

... — — —... — — —... — — —... — — —... — — —...

"I'm going to load up Admiral and the kayak and come up—if that's okay."

"I'd be honored. You be here in time for dinner? I just bought a case of a magnificent Zinfandel. You can help me with that."

Brad looked at his watch. 3:30. "We should be there by 7:00, maybe sooner. Thanks, Dad. See you soon." He hung up and turned toward the house.

There was a note on the kitchen table. *Brad, I am so sorry. Please don't hate me. A.* Her suitcase was gone.

Within minutes he had thrown his own things in a duffel and dumped Ad's food into a plastic bag. The gentle giant pranced around in excitement, sensing a new adventure taking shape.

With the kayak strapped tightly to the top and the dog bed scrunched comfortably in back, the Land Rover rumbled onto the 4:30 ferry to Seattle. By 5:15, they had taken their place in the flow of northbound traffic toward Bellingham. Brad was numb.

His father's hard-won serenity was a soothing testament to years of searching and self-reflection. When Brad's mother died on the operating table on Brad's tenth birthday, his world began revolving in dizzying circuits that never stopped. Though he and his sister, Elizabeth, regained their footing and appeared to prosper, the trust was gone. The assurance that adults could always make things turn out right shattered.

Even so, twenty years later, no place on earth could provide more comfort than the Morehouse family home on the hill overlooking Puget Sound. Admiral curled by the fire as Brad swirled the ruby-red nectar in a crystal goblet, then tasted. "Mmm, good stuff, Dad."

"Glad you like it."

Walt savored the rich, hearty varietal in silence, and several minutes passed before Brad finally said, "Audrey's been doing some other guy."

"Oh?"

"Yeah, dumped it on me this afternoon. Right out of the blue."

"Hmm." More silence followed. Then Walt asked, "How are you handling it?"

"I'm not sure that I am. I just left."

"Not a bad idea, for starters."

"How so?"

"Well, it seems to me that everything depends on what you do next. You have a lot of choices to make. Remember Rumi?"

"Which part?"

"'Don't grieve. Anything you lose comes round in another form.'"

A reluctant grin covered Brad's face. "Yeah, she may already have come around."

"Hmm, not surprising. What does that tell you?"

Brad was immersed in thought. Finally, he looked up and frowned. "Well, it certainly seems to suggest that we were headed this way all along."

"Probably not *all along*, but quite possibly from the time Audrey decided not to have a family. Brad, despite all of our cultural mythology, marriage is an arrangement that best provides for the nurturing of children. Our society depends on it for that reason primarily. On the flip side, it may have been Margaret Mead who said it best. 'We have got to face the fact that marriage is a terminable institution.'" He tossed off the quote with an ironic smile.

"Hmm. Yeah, maybe."

"Who's the lucky girl?" Walt asked after another thoughtful break in the conversation.

"Well, she is anything but lucky. She's in an unhappy marriage and likely to remain there—has two kids and a lifestyle that works well for raising a family. I know that I can't have a clandestine relationship, especially after experiencing the business end of the cudgel." He grimaced.

"Ah, I see."

"Hey, where's that dinner you promised me?" Brad changed the tone as he jumped up and headed for the kitchen. They ate ravenously, and he filled his father in on the events of the past two months. The principles of CRM were music to the ears of an anthropologist, and with the help of a second bottle of wine, they swapped tales of human behavior for several hours.

"Dad, you remember that airplane that hit the Fourteenth Street bridge in D.C. a few years ago? This is right up your alley."

"Hmm. It sounds familiar, but I don't really remember anything about it."

"Well, the more I think of it, the more it seems like an aviation culture phenomenon. Ready for this?"

Walt filled their glasses. "Let's go over by the fire," he said with a wave of the hand.

They settled into the overstuffed chairs and savored the warmth and wine for an extended pause. Admiral snored contentedly.

"Okay, let me try to abbreviate this horror story. It was a cold and windy day in the capital." He smiled. "Actually, it really was the worst snowstorm in Washington that winter."

"When was this?"

"January of 1982. It involved an Air Florida 737 headed back down to Florida on a Friday afternoon milk run. Now, just as background—a little *contextual* piece of this whole thing—Air Florida was in financial difficulty at the time, so it's impossible to believe that the crew didn't feel pressed to keep the airplane in its expected rotation. Deliberate caution wasn't an option. The captain was an F-16 guy accustomed to flying around in a warm climate. I don't know the background of the copilot."

"I'm with you so far," Walt said with a proud twinkle. "Now, it was snowing really hard, so even before they left the gate, they had the airplane deiced. Then, in all of his wisdom, when they were cleared to push back ten minutes later, the captain chose to power out of the gate—that is, to use reverse thrust to move the aircraft backward. And the only thing they accomplished was to stir up the air, suck snow into the engines, and blow it all over the wings again. No movement of the plane. They finally had to use a tug with chains to get underway. More expense for the company," he emphasized with raised eyebrows.

"Uh, earth to cockpit?" Brad's dad played along.

"Yeah, exactly. So there they were in the conga line moving slowly toward the runway when our boy genius chose to pull in close behind a DC-9—you know, with those two tail-mounted engines—and use that exhaust from them to melt the snow that had accumulated on his wings. Of course, what it really did was to melt the snow and blow the water out toward the wingtips, where it froze solid.

"What they really should have done was to go back to the gate and be deiced again, but they didn't seem to have even a basic understanding of the ramifications of ice on the wings.

... — — —... — — —... — — —... — — —... — — —...

"The voice recorder picked up the copilot saying, 'It's a losing battle trying to de-ice these things. It gives you a false feeling of security, that's all it does.' And the captain blithely responded, 'Well, it satisfies the feds.'"[43]

"Not good." Walt shook his head.

"Correct. Then, amazingly, as they proceeded through the takeoff checklist and came to the engine anti-ice step, the captain responded, 'off.' Here again, it's the cultural piece—they don't typically fly in areas where icing is a factor. Ninety-nine times out of a hundred, they will respond 'off' to the engine-anti-ice question on the checklist. It was the normal, comforting flow of business as usual. The accident investigators were so incredulous that they sent the tape to an FBI forensics lab just to confirm that the captain had actually said *off*. It was confirmed."

Brad went on. "So when they were finally cleared for takeoff, they compounded the problem by not recognizing that they had much lower than normal power being produced by the engines. It was an understandable mistake because almost everyone using those engines sets power with reference to the EPR gauges—that's engine pressure ratio. They saw what appeared to be normal EPR indication—pressure-inlet probes in the engine intake were partially frozen over and produced a faulty reading—but the corresponding indications of engine output were low. Engine rpm was about seventy percent of normal."

"And they could get airborne with that?" Walt was incredulous now.

"Well, yeah. It was a much longer takeoff roll, but they did get airborne. The copilot recognized that something wasn't right, and he sort of stated it, but not in a way that would grab anybody's attention. 'God, look at that thing. That don't seem right, does it? Uh, that's not right.' He was stammering something like that.

"But the captain just let 'er keep rollin', and responded, 'Yes it is, there's eighty,' indicating that the airspeed had reached eighty knots.

"The copilot kept whining, 'Naw, I don't think that's right. Ah, maybe it is.' Then, just before liftoff, he worriedly said, 'I don't know.'"

"So all of that doubt but no definitive statement from the copilot and no decisive action on the part of the captain?" Walt summarized.

"Exactly, and what's worse is that even once they were airborne and wallowing along in a stall, they never did add that additional thirty percent of power that was available. Fucked up as they were, they almost certainly would have flown out of their predicament if they had just slammed the power levers to the firewall." Brad fumed and took a long, calming sip of wine as Admiral stirred and moved to curl at his feet.

"And that last piece may have been a cultural thing, too, Dad. I have no way of knowing, but it seems logical that company managers had cautioned the pilots to take real good care of those engines, and in the back of his mind, the captain was afraid of the repercussions from over-boosting the jets."

"Isn't that a valid concern?"

"Hell, no, it isn't, especially when you're going down like that. Excuse my frustration here, Dad," he apologized. "As much as I chafe under a lot of the Mother Omega bullshit, I must say that it's great to be working for a company that is financially sound. The explicit instructions we have—and this is built around the likelihood of wind shear more than anything else—is that when you need more power, use all you've got; we'll worry about the integrity of the engines later."

"Ahhh, there's your anger. I wondered when that would show through. You are never angry for the reason you think my son." Walt smiled paternally. "But back to Air Florida." He straightened himself in the chair. "Even without the loss of life, just think how much less it would have cost them if the crew had either gone back to the gate or added that extra power. Are they still around?"

"Nope, went out of business in the summer of 1984."

"Not surprising, I guess."

"Yeah, it would be nearly impossible for a small company to survive that kind of disaster."

Only the sounds of the crackling fire and Admiral's solid breathing disturbed the silence. Finally, Brad concluded his longer-than-expected diatribe. "The thing that bothers me most is how poor the communication was. It's an industry-wide cultural thing—it's like you're showing your vulnerable underbelly if you communicate thoroughly and aggressively. Like that's not what real men do. But being a 'real man' is not what flying commercial airplanes is about."

They remained silent for several minutes.

"That is exactly what happened in the operating room when your mother died, you know," his father said quietly. "No one could face up to the surgeon. Even when they saw him misplace a clamp, they kept quiet." Walt exhaled deeply.

Brad was stunned. It had never been acknowledged that a medical error by a great surgeon had killed his mother. That had always seemed so implausible. Brad sat silently for a while, absorbing the painful truth, then got up and stood by his father's chair. "We've paid a big price—the world pays a big price for bullheaded behavior. We're going to beat that at Omega, Dad. I promise you."

Exhausted, he stumbled to his room sometime after midnight.

Chapter 21

CHECK RIDE

The day would be arduous, Gradin was certain of that. Their licenses were, after all, on the line. Any screw up would be significantly magnified by the circumstance. He also knew that in addition to showing his own best stuff, Danny would attempt to shield Gradin from any unreasonable attention. To do all that, it would be necessary to keep the mood positive and genial. Leadership 101.

ALPA sent Bob McKnight as the pilots' advocate. Ideally, he would be a speck on the wall, but if required, he could bring the full weight of the association to bear on the proceedings.

The company had provided Mike Eversley, one of the most qualified and best-liked 737 instructors on the property; he was also known as a pilot advocate.

John Cunningham was the FAA examiner, and his reputation had no rival. Gradin knew the guy was a grade-A, super-prime, gold-plated, jaded, inflated asshole. He girded himself.

Introductions were short and sweet—no trivial niceties or game plan from this guy. Mike and Bob settled in at the back of the small, claustrophobic briefing room. The suspect pilots took center stage at the single table in the room, while Mr. FAA swaggered to the front of the room and began.

"Mr. Jones, tell me about the 737 hydraulic system." Game on. Gradin began speaking as though he had written the entire 1,500-page manual.

"Sir, the 737 has three hydraulic systems: A, B, and standby. The hydraulic systems power the following aircraft systems: flight controls, leading-edge flaps, trailing-edge flaps, landing gear, wheel brakes, nosewheel steering, thrust reversers, and autopilot."

"And Mr. Jones, what capabilities are lost when the A hydraulic system fails?"

Gradin responded flawlessly.

"The manual expresses a caution about ground operation of the electric pumps. Do you recall what it is?"

"Minimum fuel for operation of the electric pumps is 1,676 pounds," Gradin said with authority.

"And why is that?" Cunningham persisted.

"The heat exchangers for systems A and B are in tanks 1 and 2, respectively. Fuel quantity below 1,676 would uncover the heat exchangers and cause overheating of the system."

"Which system?"

"Either system, sir."

On and on, they droned as Danny fidgeted in his seat. "What is accomplished by placing the engine hydraulic pump switch on?"

"The blocking valve in the pump allows pump pressure to enter the system."

"And why do we leave the switches in the on position at shutdown?"

"To prolong solenoid life," Gradin continued in measured tones.

"Stop!" Danny raised both hands and jumped out of his chair. "We need a break here. Gradin, you're doing great, man," he said as he patted Gradin on the back. "Why don't you go with Mike and Bob. I need some one-on-one with Mr. Cunningham."

"Just a minute here," Cunningham objected. "I'm conducting this examination."

Danny ignored him. "Gentlemen, if you will excuse us, please." Danny abruptly opened the door and ushered the three baffled pilots out of the room. Then he closed the door quietly and turned to the FAA examiner.

"Your little oral quiz has become an inquisition, John. You've gone over the top, and we're simply not going to put up with it. Don't you get it? We're the good guys, for Christ's sake! We had an airplane go nuts on us, and now we're the culprits? Get a grip, God damn it!"

"Captain, you're out of line here. The conduct of the evaluation is my responsibility and mine alone."

"Too bad you didn't think about that before you started. What you need to see is that we are a competent crew, not that we can design and construct a 737 from scratch. Your questions for Gradin were off the chart!" Danny's eyes were blazing. "The actual temperature of hydraulic fluid required to illuminate the over-temp light? Give me a fucking break! What in the hell does that have to do with flying and managing the airplane?"

Danny grabbed the 737 systems manual and pounded it on the table in front of Cunningham. "Show me where you find that in the manual," he demanded.

"Ahem," the examiner coughed nervously. "To my knowledge, that number isn't in the manual. But it's my job to test for depth of knowledge."

"No! No! No!" Danny was livid. "Don't you get it, John? The more useless trivia you demand that we cram into our heads, the less likely it is that we will respond correctly to an actual system malfunction. It shouldn't be our memory we rely on to solve systems problems—memories are flawed, especially when we're under pressure. That's why we have the friggin' checklist!

"What you want to know is what a pilot will do when that damned light *does* come on. Well, first of all, you want to know that he distinguishes a *red light* from an *amber light*. The last thing you want is for a crew to get all tangled up in solving a problem that doesn't deserve their attention during a more critical maneuver. That's why I say, in my takeoff briefing, that if we have an *amber light* after eighty knots, we will continue the takeoff and solve the problem once we are safely airborne. "You see it all the time, I know you do," Danny pressed on. "Guys go heads-down to solve a minor problem and completely forget to fly the airplane." His voice softened perceptibly now that he had John's complete attention. "Are you familiar with that incident we had in Los Angeles when the captain shut down both engines just after takeoff?"

"Uh, no, I don't think I am."

"Well, this was a classic case of a guy knowing too much—or rather, thinking he knew what was going on. So there they were, just after liftoff, crossing over the coastline, climbing through 1,500 feet, when they got an electronic engine-control light—an *amber* light, I might add. It didn't require any immediate response.

"So the captain, clever fellow that he was, said to himself, *Oh, I know what that is, and I know what you do about it.* After all, he had just been through recurrent training—probably a check ride just like this one—where they ask all of the in-depth questions about systems and procedures that have no relevance to operating the aircraft.

"So again, the captain, without consulting a checklist, reached down and shut off the EEC switch. When that didn't extinguish the light, he shut off the other EEC switch. Problem was, he had shut off both fuel control switches, not both EECs!"

"Oh, God," John whispered.

"And down they went. I guess it got pretty quiet in the back, and the flight attendants knew that they were going in the drink. To their great credit, they were able to get people into their life vests in a matter of seconds. Fortunately, both engines relit when they put the fuel control switches back in the on position.

"There's more to the story, but my point is that memorizing systems minutiae can be a trap rather than a benefit. I'm sure you agree with me that what we want to see is crews who have the discipline to fly the airplane first, and *then* use the appropriate checklist to work through a solution to whatever problem they are faced with."

John Cunningham reluctantly nodded his assent.

"And there are some other things you may lose sight of, too, John." Danny was on a roll. "These copilots and engineers of ours are the best pilots in the industry. They are not apprentice pilots. And damn it, you know that. Weren't you with Braniff in your previous life?"

"Yeah, I was," he replied sheepishly.

"So Gradin Jones, in his other life, is an aircraft commander—a patrol plane commander, they call it—on the P-3 up at Whidbey Island. He is an instructor pilot on one of the most complex airplanes in the world. He manages a crew of twelve warfare systems specialists. He probably has 4,000 hours of flight time, and he can fly circles around me.

"My point is that you have a seasoned, proven crew here. You've seen our training records. There isn't a glitch in either of them. So your job is simply to watch us, maybe ask a few basic questions, but mostly just observe how we function as a crew. Maybe you'll see something that deserves attention. Maybe you'll even discover that there is a procedure, policy, or protocol that is flawed. If you happen to do that, then we all benefit; the entire industry might benefit."

"Okay, okay. You make your point. I have my marching orders, you know that," John responded plaintively.

"I'll bet you do," Danny hissed.

"It isn't that they want to bust you guys, but you know how Boeing is paranoid about this rudder control problem. There are billions of dollars at stake here, and you know as well as I do that one of the FAA mandates is to 'promote aviation interests' in the United States."

Now on the defensive, John picked up the line of reasoning. "So if there is any indication that pilot proficiency is a factor, that will deflect attention from the rudder problem."

"Yeah, and you'd get a big ol' pat on the back for rooting out incompetent pilots at Omega. Everyone knows what a bunch of ne'er-do-wells we are."

"Well, it hasn't come to that yet, but there is concern," John replied with growing confidence.

"That's a subject for another day. What I want to ensure is that we get a fair shake, John. No more nitnoy minutiae. Agreed?"

"Yeah, I can agree to that."

"And if there is a difficult question that comes up legitimately, ask *me*. I'm the guy in charge."

"Okay."

"So when we come back in, let's go right to limitations, then jump in the box," Danny concluded. "I'll go find those guys, and we'll be back in about ten minutes. That work?"

John Cunningham nodded reluctantly as Danny Purcell disappeared.

"So what I'll do is alternate questions between the two of you," John said glumly when they were all resettled in the briefing room. "These are the limitations right from the book." He opened the 737 operations manual to the LIMITATIONS section. "We'll just go back and forth." He pointed from one to the other.

"Okay," they both responded in unison. "Runway slope?"

"Plus or minus two degrees."

"Maximum takeoff and landing tailwind component?"

"Ten knots," the other said.

"Turbulent air penetration speed?"

"Two-hundred-eighty, or point-seven-three Mach." John completed the questioning within ten minutes.

"Gentlemen, that concludes the oral portion of this exercise. Why don't you take a break, and I'll meet you in the box in fifteen minutes."

"We can do that," Danny responded confidently and cuffed Gradin's neck as he headed for the door. "Come on, I'll buy the coffee."

The unwritten protocol for every simulator session at Omega was that the crew would enter the box, as they called it, first, and the instructor or evaluator would arrive at a designated time later. That way, the pilots had time to get settled in their seats, perform their numerous preflight responsibilities, and discuss all of the last-minute, pertinent crew stuff.

Twelve minutes later, Gradin followed Danny into the darkened cockpit. This time the fuzz was already seated. The examination was underway. Danny dropped his flight bag to the left of the captain's seat and turned to conduct a simulated briefing with the senior flight attendant. Gradin carefully checked the panels behind both seats for any tripped circuit breakers.

Not surprisingly, the rudder control circuit breaker was open. Gradin smiled as he reset it and searched for any additional Easter eggs John might have hidden away for them. Then he proceeded through several checks that he would ordinarily accomplish before going outside for the exterior walk-around. He scrutinized the aircraft logbook for noteworthy discrepancies and, satisfied with his progress thus far, he said to Danny, "I'm headed outside to look around."

"Consider it done," John interjected tersely.

In response, both pilots settled into their seats and began building their nests—the very personalized arrangement of all their charts, manuals, pens, pencils, sunglasses, coffee mugs, and even family photos that all pilots make prior to departure. The following ten minutes were filled with a quiet routine that they exercised to the letter. All the items to be accomplished prior to engine start, all twenty-eight pages of them, were conducted entirely from memory. Both the captain and copilot performed different checks, equipment set-up, and overall preparation. Navigation charts were arranged and folded just as they liked them, the flight plan was meticulously reviewed and highlighted with yellow marker, and the copilot called for and copied the clearance from ATC, along with the latest weather information for the departure airport, which he provided to the captain. Finally, satisfied that they both were ready, the captain said, "Before-start checklist."

Gradin positioned one last switch, picked up the checklist, adjusted the microphone on his headset, and began to read.

"Exterior and interior preflight?"

"Complete," Danny responded, as they both looked one last time to verify the position of every switch.

"Logbook?"

"Checked."

And on it went, both playing their roles flawlessly. Any neutral observer would have marveled at the quiet, collegial efficiency of the team. This could easily have qualified as a training demonstration for new pilots. Danny was clearly in charge, while Gradin was confident, thorough, and deferential. The conversation flowed easily, and humor punctuated the mundane give-and-take.

"Down to the final items," Gradin said as he clipped the tattered page to the control column as a reminder. The final items were derived from the paperwork delivered by the gate agent just before pushback.

Danny reached up and depressed a call button in the overhead panel. "This is Dorothy," an effeminate male voice responded.

"Dorothy, it looks like we are about five minutes from push-back. Anything we can do to help back there?"

"Why no, Captain. Thank you so much for asking. We're ready as soon as we have the final paperwork." The instructor overplayed his role.

"Very good, just checking." Danny grinned at Gradin. "Hey, was there anything in the logbook that might indicate a problem with the rudder control system?" he asked. "I hear that guys have been having problems with that. We sure as hell don't want to end up out in the weeds someplace."

"No, sir, the book's clean. I think that problem must be someone's imagination." They both laughed nervously. Gradin was certain that John was not amused.

"Okay, gentlemen, final numbers." The instructor, now playing the role of gate agent, handed Danny a computer printout several pages long. As the instructor stood watching, Danny scrutinized the pages carefully, first ensuring that the date and flight number were correct. More than one crew had actually gone flying with incorrect data. Satisfied that there was no mischief involved, he handed Mike the signed copy of the flight release, which acknowledged the captain's assumption of control and responsibility for all aspects of the flight.

"Have a safe trip, gentlemen." Mike turned and resituated himself at the simulator control panel behind Danny's seat. Danny and Gradin consulted the documents, agreed on the appropriate numbers, and applied the final settings to the airspeed indicators and elevator trim device. Then Mike said, "Captain, this is Dorothy. Cabin safety checks are complete; we're ready for push-back."

"Thanks, Dorothy," Danny responded as Mike simulated the sound of a slamming door. "Give 'em a call, Gradin."

Gradin requested clearance to back out of the gate from company ramp control personnel responsible for movement in the terminal area. "Ramp, Omega 800 to push from gate five-zero."

"Omega 800, ramp, cleared to push," Mike responded.

Danny casually reached up and positioned the red blinking anti-collision light switch to on. Then he forcefully depressed the tops of both rudder pedals to release the parking brakes and triggered the intercom switch on the control column. "Ground, cockpit. Brakes released, cleared to push," he said, just as he would to an actual tug driver.

"Motion coming on, guys," Mike said. Then, as the tug driver, "Roger, brakes released, here we go."

The windshield panels lit up with the perfectly animated nighttime image of gate fifty in Los Angeles. A small jolt signaled the commencement of motion. The cockpit teetered gently while the fluorescent number 50 grew smaller, and taxiway lights came into view as the aircraft turned in reverse away from the gate.

Once aligned in the alleyway, facing south between terminals five and six, the voice of the tug driver said, "Captain, set your brakes, please."

"Brakes are set; you're cleared to disconnect," Danny responded.

"Cleared to start engines. Stand by for wave-off," the driver concluded.

"Roger. Let's start 'em both, Gradin."

"Two and then One?" Gradin asked. "Yes, please."

"Roger." Gradin reached overhead and positioned several switches to remove air pressure from the air-conditioning system and direct it to the engine starters. Once the air pressure registered approximately thirty-five PSI, he said, "Air is up, turning Two," and reached for the number two engine start switch in the overhead panel. "Taking air," he noted as air pressure dropped on the gauge.

Then both pilots directed their attention to the engine instrument panel, a vertical array of gauges centered between the captain's and copilot's instrument panels. They observed the engine rpm increase gradually and stabilize in the required range.

"Fuel," Danny said as he raised the fuel-control lever to the on position. Simultaneously, Gradin reached forward and started the sweep-hand timer on the clock.

They both fixated on the EGT (exhaust gas temperature) gauge, which indicates a rapid rise when fuel ignites in the engine. Nothing happened as they continued to watch. After fifteen seconds, Gradin calmly said, "No light-off."

"Roger, continue to turn," Danny responded as he abruptly slammed the engine start lever to the cut-off position. Gradin eyed the clock as he held the spring-loaded start switch in the on position. The air-driven starter continued to spin the engine turbine and purge fuel from the combustion chambers. At sixty seconds' elapsed time, Gradin said, "Air is off," as he moved the engine start switch to off.

"Roger. Aborted-engine-start checklist," Danny commanded.

Gradin methodically reached for the checklist and confirmed that the appropriate steps had been completed. "Checklist complete," he concluded.

"Roger. Good job, Gradin. Why don't you give ramp a call and tell them to pull us back to the gate?"

"Very well done, gents," Mike stood and intervened. "Let's consider that problem resolved, and I'll give you both engines." He reached forward between them and placed both fuel control switches in the on position. The engine instruments all sprang to life. "After-start checklist is complete, Danny," Mike concluded and sat down again.

"Okay. Give 'em a call, Gradin."

"Ramp, 800 taxi," Gradin responded with a radio call. "Omega 800, ramp, taxi straight ahead, hold short of Charlie and contact ground on one-two-one-decimal-niner."

"Roger, hold short of Charlie, and ground on one-twenty-one-niner," Gradin responded.

Danny pretended to look out the left side window. He issued a salute to the imaginary member of the push-back crew. "We're waved away and cleared left."

Gradin looked to his right and responded, "Cleared right." Then he grabbed the flap handle and clicked it through several notches to the fifteen-degree detent.

Danny pushed the power levers up slightly until motion became apparent, then he reduced power to idle and said, "After-start checklist." He stopped the aircraft perpendicular to the string of blue lights denoting taxiway Charlie and waited for Gradin to complete the checklist.

"You ready?" he asked, and Danny nodded his assent. Gradin dialed 121.9 into the radio and spoke with accustomed ease and authority.

"Ground, Omega 800 at Charlie eight, taxi on the Loop."[44]

"Omega 800, ground, taxi two-five-right, Charlie, Charlie four, Bravo. Monitor tower on one-two-zero-niner-five crossing Foxtrot."

"Roger, Omega 800, two-five-right, Charlie, Charlie four, Bravo. We'll go to tower crossing Fox."

"Eight hundred, roger," Mike responded as the ground controller.

Danny added power and turned the aircraft left to join taxiway Charlie, distinctly outlined in the dark by blue lights. Once established, he called, "taxi check," and Gradin began to read and either position or verify the position of critical switches and levers.

At "flight controls," both pilots maneuvered the three sets of control levers. Gradin pulled the control column as far back as it would go, then pushed it full forward. In the actual aircraft, the horizontal elevator panels in the tail section would rotate downward and upward, corresponding to the movement in the cockpit. Similarly, he rolled the steering column full right and full left, pretending to observe deployment of the spoiler panels on top of the right wing. Danny also looked toward the left wing at the appropriate moment, then gripped the tiller (the small nose wheel steering device located left forward of the captain's seat) and pushed the rudder pedals full right and left, very consciously noting any unusual feel in the system.

"Tops," Gradin said in reference to his check of the elevator and ailerons.

Ordinarily, the captain responds, "Bottoms," and the copilot continues the checklist. However, today Danny said, "Gradin, give the rudders a check for me. Something doesn't feel right."

"Charlie four is coming up here, boss." He pointed out at the cross taxiway to their right.

"Thanks. Hang on a second for that check." He maneuvered the aircraft ninety degrees right and almost immediately ninety degrees back to the left onto Bravo taxiway. "Okay, give it a try."

Gradin slowly and deliberately depressed each rudder pedal full throw.

"Whattaya think?" Danny asked.

"It seems to bind up at the full-throw position on the left. Let me try it again." He maneuvered the rudders. "Yup, there's definitely a lot more friction on the left side."

"Well, I sure wish we'd had that indication up in Pasco. We wouldn't be going through *this* ordeal if we had." Danny smiled and looked over his shoulder at Mike.

"Good job again, guys," Mike responded. "That feel actually simulates a frayed cable in the pulley mechanism. Presumably, that is exactly what you would feel. End of problem. Flight controls check okay," he concluded.

The simulated aircraft continued eastbound on the taxiway. To the left, the skyline along Century Boulevard appeared, and one could imagine people at the airport Hilton looking out at the crawl of airplanes around the south complex at LAX.

Crossing the taxiway marked F, Gradin reached down and selected 120.95 in the radio control panel. "We're up on tower,"[45] he commented to Danny.

"Thanks."

"You guys ready?" Mike asked softly.

"Yup. Let's rock 'n' roll," Danny responded confidently. "Omega 800, Los Angeles tower, taxi into position and hold, two-five-right."

"Position and hold two-five-right," Gradin said. "Takeoff check," Danny requested.

"Roger." Gradin positioned several switches, looked sideways, and reported, "Clear right." Then he grabbed the checklist and read the final items aloud.

"Transponder/TCAS/radar."

"Set."

"Exterior lights."

"On."

Danny muttered his personal inventory as he ensured the final critical items were in place. "Switches, bitches, sparks, and lights."

"Checklist complete." Gradin smiled at Danny's irreverent flair.

The aircraft swung into position on the centerline of runway 25R in Los Angeles. Rows of white lights outlined the runway, and a dim line of lights depicted the runway centerline. It was a bright, clear night with stars and the blinking red lights of other aircraft in sight.

"I'm gonna give you a little weather here, guys," Mike said as fog enveloped most of the runway. "RVRs are six, six, and six, and I will assume that you have checked the book to confirm that you have takeoff minimums."

"You're all heart," Danny mumbled.

"Omega 800, fly heading two-three-five, maintain 3,500, cleared for takeoff."

"Head 235, cleared to go," Gradin responded.

"You ready?" Danny took a final look at Gradin, who nodded. "Let's go fly." He pushed the power levers forward, hit the auto-throttle switch, and fixed his gaze down the runway. The feeling of acceleration was quite real as the simulator sat back on its long, spidery hydraulic legs, forcing the occupants back in their seats. Runway lights flashed by at an increasing rate, and Gradin announced, "Eighty knots, engine instruments checked."

Nose wheel bumps and oscillations were very similar to those felt in the actual aircraft, and Danny focused exclusively on the runway centerline lights as the speed increased.

"V1, V—POWER LOSS," Gradin blurted.

Danny responded to counter the swerve from the loss of power by immediately applying heavy foot pressure to the opposite rudder pedal and pushing the power levers forward to the stops. "Max power," he commanded. The nose drifted several feet to the left, but within a second more right rudder pressure brought it back to centerline.

Gradin kept the cadence. "V2, VR," he said as they exceeded the required takeoff speed.

Danny raised the nose to the specified twelve-degree-up attitude. Next came the most difficult part of the engine-failure maneuver, climbing straight ahead through the imaginary goalposts off the end of the runway. The computerized monster both displayed and graphed the flight path for the evaluator to see. The pilots had only their compass for guidance, and with power on just one engine, the nose pulled fiercely toward the dead engine. It took most of Danny's leg strength to apply the necessary rudder pressure.

"Gear up. Declare an emergency and request a straight-out departure."

"Roger, gear up," Gradin said, quickly slamming the gear handle up. "Tower, Omega 800 with an engine failure. We're declaring an emergency. Request straight-out departure, over."

"Omega 800, roger; understand you have an engine failure. Depart straight out and maintain 3,000."

"Roger, we'll climb straight out, maintain three, and we'll get back to you with our intentions in a moment."

"Roger, 800."

Climbing with the power from only one engine was a tedious, slow-motion maneuver. "Drifting slightly left, Danny," Gradin cautioned as they climbed through 500 feet. Danny rolled the control wheel to the right and put more pressure on the right rudder with his tired, shaking leg. Again they tracked back to the 249-degree heading of the runway. Danny reached to the center console with his right hand and spun the rudder-trim wheel multiple turns to the right. Backpressure from the rudder pedal diminished as Danny breathed deeply for the first time since liftoff. He focused to maintain airspeed and heading precisely.

"Approaching 1,000." Gradin continued to recite his lines in a crisp staccato. An orange bug marked the 1,126-foot level-off altitude. As the altimeter crept toward that marker, Danny reduced power imperceptibly, eased pressure on the right rudder, and gritted his teeth in concentration as the altimeter needle stabilized on the bug. "Autopilot on," he commanded as he adjusted the rudder trim knob. "After-takeoff checklist and engine-failure checklist. We'll maintain flaps fifteen."

They had nailed it. No one could have flown the maneuver more precisely. Despite the asymmetrical thrust, their flight path was straight out the extended runway centerline at exactly the prescribed airspeed. It spoke volumes about the power of the subconscious mind learning from vividly imagined experience. Danny had practiced this maneuver dozens of times in his head, and this had simply been another in a string of flawless executions.

Gradin recited and performed the items on the two checklists as the theatrics continued. They climbed to 3,500 feet and followed the guidance of the approach controller directing the crippled jet back to LAX for landing. The hand-flown engine-out approach was equally tedious and demanding.

"Set me up for the ILS twenty-five-right approach, Gradin. Familiarize yourself with the approach. Tune and identify the radios. Set the speeds and altitudes. Check the NO-TAMs and weather, and let me know when you're ready," Danny instructed.

Every detail was critically important; Gradin was thorough and deliberate as he attended to each one of them. "Inbound course is 249, Danny." The captain dialed the numbers in the course window. "MDA is three-oh-two." They both made that adjustment to the altitude cursor. "Flap-fifteen approach gives us a double white bug at 137." Both set that on the airspeed indicators. "I'm ready, boss."

"Okay, Gradin, if you'll take the aircraft, I'll brief the approach. We're heading zero-seven-zero, 150 knots at 3,500 feet."

"Roger, I have the aircraft," Gradin said as he gently placed both hands on the control column and fixed his gaze on the flight instruments.

Then Danny reached into his flight bag, extracted several pages, and arranged and clipped them to the control column. Next, he reviewed each detail and touched the gauges with a finger as he verified the appropriate settings. He consulted the flight plan for any Notice to Airmen (NOTAM) trivia that might apply, things such as inoperative approach lighting or runway constraints from construction.

Following his thorough review, he said, "Okay, Gradin, if you're ready, I'll brief the approach."

"I'm ready."

"We're going to fly the ILS two-five-right approach to Los Angeles. The plate is eleven-dash-eight, November 6, 1986."

Gradin followed along on his plate as he continued to monitor the performance of the airplane. "Inbound course is two-four-nine."

Danny went on to articulate every important detail of the approach. He covered every critical item, down to the wind direction and velocity, the procedures for a possible missed approach, and his intentions after coming to a stop on the runway. "Any questions?" he concluded.

"No, except you failed to mention what a stellar job you intend to do and that nothing can go wrong, go wrong, go wrong." Gradin smiled.

"Yeah, you wish." He raised his eyebrows and assumed control. "Okay, I have the aircraft again. Let's do the descent and approach checklists."

"You have the aircraft; checklists coming up," Gradin responded. Once again, they ground through the meticulous detail. As they did, the approach controller issued a three-four-zero heading. Gradin advised make-believe passengers and flight attendants of their progress and expectations. Critical switch positions were verified for the third time, and finally, he concluded, "Descent and approach checklists complete."

Mike leaned in. "Danny, if you would, please, click off the autopilot now," he requested. The cockpit lurched slightly, and Danny toggled the elevator trim switch on the control column as he readjusted to the feel of the single-engine 737. "Omega 800, fly heading three-zero-zero. Cleared for approach, ILS runway two-five-right. Contact Los Angeles tower on one-two-zero-nine-five at Shell, over."

"Roger, cleared approach two-five-right, tower at Shell," Gradin replied crisply. Then, seconds later, he said, "Localizer alive," as the narrow, white indicator on the compass—the course deviation indicator (CDI)—began to move from the far right toward the center of the gauge. Danny initiated a gentle left turn and toggled the elevator trim up farther. He worked hard to maintain altitude and airspeed; the evaluation criteria required that he be within a couple of digits on either side of the prescribed figures. Hypothetical wind was blowing from the left, and he found it was necessary to hold a two-four-*two* heading in order to track the two-four-*nine* inbound course.

Gradin monitored the progress intently. "Coming up on Shell at twelve-point-six DME, Danny." He reached down and set 120.95 in the radio control head. "Los Angeles tower, Omega 800, Shell," he stated succinctly.

"Omega 800, Los Angeles tower, cleared to land runway two-five-right. Wind two-one-zero at one-zero, RVRs 600, 600, 600, over."

"Roger, Omega 800, cleared to land."

"RVRs are good, and there's SHELL, cleared down to 3,200, Danny."

"Roger, landing gear down," Danny said as he reduced power on the remaining engine and allowed the aircraft to descend the scant 300 feet. "Landing checklist."

"Roger, landing checklist. Speed brake, armed. Landing gear, down/three green," Gradin said, alluding to the landing gear indicator lights. "Flaps, fifteen/fifteen. Checklist complete, cleared to land two-five-right. You have a left-quartering headwind about ten knots." Then, noting a slight move-

··· ━ ━ ━···━ ━ ━···━ ━ ━···━ ━ ━ ━···━ ━ ━···━ ━ ━···

ment of the white horizontal glide slope, Gradin added, "Glideslope alive."

"Roger," came the quick response as Danny labored to hold altitude and airspeed until the glideslope indicator was horizontally centered on the gauge. Very carefully, he reduced the power, adjusted for the expected yaw to the right, and allowed the nose to drop a degree or so as they sped across the ground at nearly 200 mph.

Finally, the glideslope and centerline indicators were both perfectly crossed as the simulated aircraft proceeded down the approach path toward the runway. The VSI (vertical speed indicator) showed a descent rate of 600 feet per minute, just what he wanted. With each passing mile—one every twenty seconds—the parameters for success became more and more exact. Danny's corrections were infinitesimal.

"Two hundred above," Gradin said firmly.

Danny's eyes left the gauges for a split second to check for external cues. "Nothing in sight," he responded, quickly shifting his gaze back to the gauges to maintain the narrowing course and glide path.

"One hundred" was the next call, followed by a flurry of rapid-fire comments and actions.

Danny: "Nothing in sight."

Gradin: "I've got the rabbits. *Minimums!*"

Danny: "Runway in sight."

Gradin: "Sink's seven."

The jet pounded the runway forcefully as Danny dropped the nose and applied right rudder to track the centerline. Simultaneously he slammed the power lever to idle, lifted it over the mechanical stop, and applied maximum reverse thrust on the right engine. The nose lurched to the right, and he struggled to keep it aligned with the runway center-line by applying more left rudder pressure.

White centerline lights blurred beneath them as they decelerated down the fog-shrouded runway. "Eighty knots," Gradin called, a signal for Danny to reduce reverse thrust and steer with the tiller of the nose wheel.

"Remain seated! Remain seated!" Gradin simulated a command to the passengers as they came to a stop on the runway. The flight attendant call chime sounded. Gradin grabbed the black handset. "Speak," he said tersely.

Mike's voice imitated the urgent call from a flight attendant. "Captain, there is fire coming from the left engine."

"Roger, stand by to evacuate. Wait for our call. We'll go out the right side," Gradin exclaimed with a sense of déjà vu.

Even in the pressure of the moment, Danny smiled. "Emergency-shutdown and evacuation checklists," he requested calmly.

"Roger." Gradin grabbed the checklists and completed them.

"Checklists complete." Then he picked up the handset and spoke to the passengers with perfect clarity, assuming the authority of the captain. "Folks, this is the captain speaking. Look to the right side of the aircraft—the *right* side—the copilot side. Follow the instructions of your flight attendants. We are going to evacuate on the right side of the aircraft. EVACUATE, EVACUATE, EVACUATE!"

He reached overhead, switched the battery to off, grabbed his flashlight and ops manual, and bounded out of his seat. "Don't forget the logbook, Danny," he said.

"Whew." Mike breathed loudly. "Set the brakes there, Danny." Then, emphatically, "Great job, guys! You nailed that from engine start to shut down. Beautifully done, gentlemen." His enthusiasm reflected the relief *he* felt at the successful scenario. FAA examiner John Cunningham could not be immune to his glowing assessment. No egg on any faces, at least not yet. "Let's take a break. I'll put things back in order here. Get some coffee, and when you come back, all we have left are a couple of trips around the pattern for you, Gradin."

Bob McKnight opened the door in the back of the simulator, which triggered a loud buzz and flashing red light signaling an unsafe condition as the bridge swung down into place over the concrete chasm. The simulator was perched on multiple long hydraulic actuators, looking much like a giant praying mantis in a cavern. John immediately disappeared across the bridge toward the break room.

His victims followed nonchalantly behind. "You were absolutely stellar, dude." Danny shook Gradin by the neck and smiled. "There wasn't one flaw in that script. You made every call and kept an eye on me the whole way. You deserve a field promotion, Commander. Another coffee?"

"Sure." Gradin was less sanguine, knowing that his turn in the barrel was about to begin. Bob caught up and added his official ALPA endorsement. "Perfect, guys. Thirty minutes to go, and you're home free. John seems a little thunderstruck; nothing to complain about," he said with a smile.

"Omega 800, cleared for takeoff," Mike said as he resumed the multiple roles of instructor, air traffic controller, and the other bit players.

"Roger, 800 cleared for takeoff," Danny responded as he followed up on the power setting commanded by the auto throttles.

Gradin guided the jet down the darkened runway with the rudder pedals and eased back on the control column at the appropriate time. "Positive rate, gear up," he called when they were safely airborne.

"Gear up."

Danny responded by reaching across the center console, raising the gear handle with gusto.

"What the fuck?" Gradin exclaimed as the visual display abruptly canted to the left. The flight controls froze in place as the aircraft pitched nose-down and slammed into the ground. BAM! The cockpit jolted violently down to the right, lights went out, and a body flew forward between them. This was no longer a simulation; the simulator had fallen off its hydraulic struts.

"Jesus Christ!" John Cunningham shrieked from where he was awkwardly pinned between the captain's control column and glare shield. "Oh, my fucking knee! Get me outta here!"

Bob McKnight braced himself with one arm and extended the other down for John to grab. Danny struggled to release his harness, pushing vainly against the controls wedged in his lap. Mike grabbed the intercom. "Control room, cockpit. We have an emergency up here. The sim crashed, and we have an FAA examiner injured. Execute rescue procedures, over."

"Hang on, John, we'll get you outta there in just a second." He spoke as calmly as possible while he unfastened his seat belt and struggled to stand on a floor pitched crazily down to the right. To brace himself and still have leverage, he had to kneel behind the console. From that position, he was able to reach both arms forward and support John as he squirmed out from under the glare shield. "Son of a bitch! It's my right knee, guys." He exhaled painfully.

"Okay, easy now," Bob coached. "Get your left foot down behind Gradin's seat, and we'll pull you up. Will that work?"

"Yeah, I can get it down there. Just a sec."

John squirmed farther to his left and found that the copilot control column was locked in place. "Here, let me pull myself with my left." John squirmed. "Give me a boost, Mike." He rose to a crouch with his right leg rigidly extended in front of him.

"Let's get you turned around, John, and you can lie down back here." Mike crawled back and swept away the books, coats, and papers strewn on the floor. Even instructors and examiners often failed to properly stow their gear, and now the cockpit was an utter mess.

Bob held John's left arm as he swung awkwardly down and pushed himself into a sitting position in the open space on the floor.

"How long does it take to evacuate this damned thing?"

Danny and Gradin sat mute, knowing that John's injury superseded the discomfort of being pinned in their seats by the control columns. Gradin's mind raced. *Was that something I did?* he wondered. *The damned thing all of a sudden just froze up and crashed. And even if it wasn't my fault, would John Cunningham know that? Thank God for ALPA.*

"Hey, buddy, you okay?" Gradin looked over and appreciated Danny's concern.

"Yeah." He managed a feeble smile.

"No, no! You were perfect. This damned sim has a history of goin' tits-up. I know that it's happened before. It won't look good for the company, but as far as I'm concerned, we're done. We did everything possible to show that we know our stuff. The company and the fuzz'll have to work it out from here," Danny concluded angrily.

If only it were that simple, Gradin mused. The FAA holds all the cards, he knew that.

Chapter 22

PAINFUL ENCOUNTER

Two hours later, Gradin ambled down the concourse toward gate A12, the connecting flight he would take through Salt Lake City to Spokane. John Cunningham's injury and the broken sim had consumed everyone's attention. Bob McKnight rather audaciously had assumed responsibility for Danny and Gradin—ALPA would fight the remainder of this battle, he asserted defiantly—and sent them home. What he knew, which apparently no one else had seen or articulated, was that Cunningham's injury resulted not from a simulator gone wild but from his unfastened seat belt, a clear violation of his own FAA regulations. "The guy doesn't have a leg to stand on," Bob concluded with a grin.

As much as Gradin longed for complete vindication, the image of the airplane rolling hard to the right and slamming into the ground was the enduring, nauseating memory of the entire episode.

✈

"Oh. My. *God!*" the woman coming toward him exclaimed as she dropped her bags and held a hand to her mouth. "Where have you been?" Tears filled her eyes as she walked slowly toward him and threw herself into his arms. "I've been so damned worried. Gradin, what happened? Why haven't I heard from you, baby?" She clung to him.

"Ahhhh." He embraced her fully. The comfort was undeniable, and they both absorbed the warmth of the moment.

"God, Peg, you feel so damned good," he said as he righted himself and looked intently at her tear-streaked face. "Where are you headed? Do we have time to talk?"

"I'm working the 3:05 to Salt Lake." She wiped her cheeks with the back of her hand. "I was just going for coffee."

"Here." He handed her a handkerchief. "That's my flight home. It's at A12, right?"

"Yes. Thank God, I'll get to see you. I need to be there in five minutes to board. Give me the lowdown on what's going on." She braced herself.

He grabbed her arm, helped gather her bags, and moved out of the concourse to an empty boarding area. They sat with their backs to the moving crowd.

"Alice found a note."

Peggy gasped and lowered her head into her hands. "Oh, no," she whispered through her tears. "Gradin, I'm so sorry. God, she must be devastated. I can't imagine." The contradiction was so glaring, the desire to possess an unavailable man and the simultaneous sympathy for the wife.

"Well, and that isn't all. You probably haven't heard this, but I was the copilot on 848 in Pasco."

"Holy shit!"

"Yeah, I haven't flown since then. Just two hours ago, the captain and I had a check ride with the FAA. And it ended in disaster."

"Whattaya mean?"

He explained. "God, I can't imagine what you've been going through." Then a fearful look crossed her face. "Gradin, Alice won't tell, will she? She won't call my husband or something, will she?" Peggy's face scrunched up in anguish. "He couldn't take it. You know about his bad heart."

"No, no. That's not her style. She'll suffer through this in silence. We haven't even talked about it yet. We've had sort of a tacit agreement to wait until I was finished with this check ride. My whole job—my *whole life*—depends on getting back in the cockpit. And right now, I'm not feeling all that confident."

"Jesus Christ," she whispered, then looked at her watch. "Damn, I have to get to the gate. Let's walk." She stood, swung her purse over her shoulder, and grabbed her new roller bag.

"What a way to end the day. A seat up front." Gradin dropped his newspaper in seat 2D, on the aisle, and handed his blazer to a waiting flight attendant. The first scotch and soda arrived within seconds and quickly disappeared along with a portion of the day's stress. Number two went down more slowly, and he relinquished a half-full glass to the smiling flight attendant just before takeoff.

He slept for more than an hour before the aroma of steak and potatoes triggered a salivary response. He opened his eyes. "I am told by a reliable source that you prefer the steak and red wine, is that correct?" the same smiling face asked with a twinkle.

"Uh, well, sure." He gathered himself and returned the smile. "Thanks."

It was the first real food of the day, and he was ravenous. It disappeared indelicately along with two glasses of Cabernet. Two hours into the flight, the unsolicited coffee and Kahlua arrived along with a note. "See you in the aft galley at 5:15." Good sense and restraint were drowned in alcohol as he wobbled down the aisle, past the sentry, who looked up conspiratorially over her glasses and winked. The galley was partially darkened and smelled predominantly of Peggy's perfume. "Come here, you, we have ten minutes," she whispered.

There was no holding back now as he moved forward and embraced her fiercely, her body strong and compact under his hands. She cradled his face and kissed him deeply, then breathlessly said, "I don't have any underwear on."

He reached to confirm, and the fabric of her uniform slid silkily over her naked hips. She wrestled him into the corner, reached into his pants, and swung a leg up around his thighs.

"Peggy, stop," he groaned quietly. "We can't. Look at us. We're just *one glimpse* away from being fired." He was amazed at how sobering another threat to his career could be. Gradin pivoted her nakedness away from the flimsy curtain as she dropped to her knees. "Oh, God, stop. It's over, Peg—it's over." With an impatient tug, he lifted her into his arms and embraced her sympathetically.

"Don't leave me, Gradin. Please don't leave me," she murmured against his neck.

✈

The 11:00 p.m. drive from the airport to the house was a blur, with fire in his gut and topsy-turvy images of 737 schematics, the spiraling simulator, a sexy but sad flight attendant, and now, Alice.

She greeted him somberly, then immediately turned away from the mixed aroma of booze, coffee, and perfume. "You seem to have survived the day with gusto," she challenged, hands on hips.

He dropped his bags and stumbled into his chair. "You have no idea." He heaved a deep sigh.

"Hmph! Story of my life, I guess. I never have any idea. The cheap perfume is a nice touch." Now her look was defiant. "Oh, God. Yeah, I ran into her in the terminal in Memphis; she hugged me full-on, nothing more. It's over with her," he stammered. "I love you, Alice. This is the only place I want to be."

"Yeah, right. You'll have a hard time convincing a jury of that."

His blood ran cold. *No, God, don't let it come to that,* his mind pleaded silently.

"You'd better get some sleep. The kids both have soccer in the morning." She retrieved a quilt and a pillow, threw them on the sofa, and disappeared.

His dreams were chaotic—ringing ears, smashing metal, grinning faces, a dark, dense forest, and a burning heart. At first light, he untangled himself from the sweat-drenched quilt, teetered toward the bathroom, and sat dizzily on the toilet. The excrement flowed like a black ribbon into the bowl. Then he toppled to the floor, unconscious.

"Mom! Mom!" Melinda shrieked and shook her mom's shoulder. "Daddy's hurt, Mom! Hurry."

Guilt instantly gripped Alice's heart as she bolted out of the room. Bucky stood transfixed at the door to the bathroom as Gradin rose to his elbows. "Hi, Buck," he said absently.

"Gradin, what—?" Her eyes saw the purple streak of slime down the side of the toilet. "Oh, God, honey, that's blood. Melinda, get the quilt and pillow off the couch," she commanded. "Honey, does it hurt? Are you in pain?"

"Pain? Noooo." He elongated the word with a puzzled look. "What happened?"

She forced the pillow under his head. "Here, put your head down," she said as she flung the damp quilt over his shivering body. "It looks like you passed a lot of blood, but you say there's no pain, right?"

"Right," he responded slowly.

"Okay, stay right there, I'm going to call an ambulance."

Ambulance? he thought. *I'm just lying here on the floor. Nothing's wrong.*

"Mr. Jones, Mr. Jones, can you hear me?" A blurry face leaned in over him.

He blinked and shook his head. "Uh, yeah, I can." Then, struggling to comprehend, he asked, "Who are you?"

"I'm Doctor Alexander, Mr. Jones. You are in the emergency room of Sacred Heart Hospital. It appears that you have some internal bleeding, and we're trying to determine where it is coming from."

"Huh. Was I in an accident?"

"No, no. You lost consciousness at home and were transported here by ambulance."

"Oh." Then, confused, he looked to the other side. "Oh, Alice, hi. Am I okay?"

"Gradin, we don't know. They're going to run some tests. In the meantime, they're giving you blood, and everything seems to be stable. Your heart rate was about 130 when they brought you in."

"Yeah, your heart was working pretty hard to circulate the smaller amount of blood you had left."

"Oh."

"Mr. Jones, are you experiencing any pain? Any discomfort in your midsection?" the doctor continued, placing a hand gently on his chest.

"Uh, no, everything feels normal." He shook his head. "Well, wait. Maybe a little acid stomach, like after too many cups of coffee some mornings."

"Okay, that's good information," the doctor responded and turned away to confer with his colleagues. Then, turning back to Gradin, he said, "We're going to set up to perform an endoscopy. We'll insert a small tube with a miniature camera into your esophagus and take a look. The nurses are going to apply Benzedrine to anesthetize your throat, to cut down on the gag response. It'll take fifteen minutes or so for that to take effect."

Half an hour later, he felt his eyes bulging as the device burned its way into his chest. "There you go," Dr. Alexander pointed to the undulating landscape of pink flesh on the monitor. "No problem there. And—" the focus shifted to another area—"good there."

Within ten minutes, the thorough exam was complete, with no definitive outcome. The rigor of the procedure, combined with the anesthetic, induced a sleepy calm as Gradin was wheeled to his room. Alice gathered his things, arranged them in the small closet, kissed his sweaty brow, and slipped away.

"This is the observation phase," she was told. "We need to monitor the hematocrit to determine whether or not the bleeding has stopped. Since we don't know the source, it may be necessary to go in and take a look. We won't make that decision until tomorrow. Looks like he'll be spending the night."

The phone was ringing as she climbed out of the car in the garage. When she picked up, a man's voice asked for Gradin. "I'm sorry, he isn't available right now. Is there a message?"

"Is this Alice?" She confirmed that it was. "Alice, this is Danny Purcell, Gradin's partner in the Memphis fiasco yesterday."

"Oh, yes, Captain Purcell. Gradin has spoken so highly of you."

"Well, thanks, but he is the guy who really shines. And call me *Danny*, please. Hey, I'm just calling with some mixed news."

"Oh, God, we could really use some good news right now."

"I know this has been a real ordeal, but the worst part is finally over. I just got a call from Andy Caldwell—you know, our VP of flight ops in Memphis."

"Uh-huh," she said.

"It seems that, despite that major crash of the sim, the FAA has chosen not to require a re-fly."

"The sim crashed?"

"Oh, yeah, didn't he tell you?" Danny sensed a problem. "Well, as a matter of fact, *no*. It was nearly midnight when Gradin rolled in. The smell of whiskey and perfume was so strong that we didn't get around to a recap of the day's events." Alice couldn't keep the bitterness from her voice.

"Oh, God, Alice, I'm sorry. I know exactly how that goes. You see an old friend in the terminal, she gives you an innocent hug, and you're dead—you smell like her for the rest of the day. I've spent more time explaining that one than I care to count."

"Uh, Danny, stop. There is a bigger problem here. Gradin is in the hospital with internal bleeding. They don't know where it is coming from."

"Damn!" his voice came through the phone loud with shock. "Alice, how bad is it? When did it start? Is he in stable condition?"

"Yeah, he's stable. He was sound asleep when I left the hospital a few minutes ago. I don't know when it started, but it showed up early this morning when he sat on the toilet, passed a lot of blood, and fainted on the floor."

"Jesus Christ."

"They're giving him blood, and they say they may need to do surgery to determine the source but won't make that decision until tomorrow morning."

"Oh, wow." He looked at his watch. "I'm coming up. I think I can make the connection and be there by tonight."

"Danny, that isn't necessary. He's going to be just fine."

"I know he will, but we've been through a lot together the last few weeks. Gradin is family," he insisted.

"What hospital?"

"Sacred Heart. It's on Eighth and McClellan."

"Okay. Tell him I'm coming. And before I go, is there anything I can do for you, Alice? You've been through the wringer, too, I know that."

"Thanks, Danny. I'm fine. My parents live nearby, so they have the kids. Gradin's family is close, too, and we have a great support network. However, I know that he will feel honored that you are coming up. That is above and beyond the call."

"Not at all," he insisted. "You take care, and I'll see you tomorrow."

Alice collapsed on the sofa in tears. Buffeted by the bewildering mix of emotion and practicality, she finally fell asleep.

Chapter 23

HOSPITAL

Danny and his girlfriend, Cynthia, rode with the crew to the hotel where they had booked a room for the night. Cynthia had rearranged her weekend to accompany Danny and comfort this young dynamo she'd heard so much about. At 10 a.m., they stood expectantly in the doorway to Gradin's room.

He knocked lightly. "Hey, tiger."

Gradin's pale face responded with a broad smile. He feigned an effort to get out of bed. "Am I late? Just a minute, I'll be right there, oh exalted one. Where's my uniform?"

"Down, boy, down. Better take this first." He placed three bottles of Pepto-Bismol on the tray in front of Gradin.

"Ah, my favorite." He scrutinized the label. "1988. A very good year."

"It is now—a good *day*, that is. I hope Alice told you about the call from Andy yesterday."

"She did, indeed. I can't tell if it's good news or bad news." Then, smiling at Cynthia, he said, "Danny, you didn't tell me your daughter was so beautiful."

"Daughter? You wish. Eat your heart out, kid. Cynthia Gardner, meet my former good friend Gradin Jones."

"I wish the circumstances were different, but it is a great pleasure to meet you, Gradin."

"My pleasure." He extended his hand.

Danny kept the chatter moving. "Well, talk about bustin' a gut. What's the prognosis here, Commander?"

"Don't know yet. They say they'll make a decision by noon."

"Knock, knock."

Alice stuck her head into the room. "Some very special visitors for Dad." She ushered the kids through the door.

"Daddy, Daddy, Mommy says we can have a puppy!" Melinda ran to the bed without noticing Danny and Cynthia. Bucky dawdled past them with an uncertain stare.

"This must be the famous Captain Purcell." Alice extended a hand and smiled.

"Uh, yes, ma'am. I confess, I'm the one who planted that 737 in the weeds despite your husband's gallant efforts to the contrary." They both laughed and embraced gently. "And may I present Cynthia Gardner. Alice Jones."

"Hi, Cynthia. So sorry that you guys are spending your weekend up here in the far north. It must be lovely in L.A. right now."

"Nah, nothin' but sunshine and ocean breezes. We needed to get out of the heat." Then, turning toward the bed, Danny asked, "Hey, who are these little movie stars?"

"I'm not a movie star, I'm Bucky Jones!"

···— — —···— — —···— — — —···— — —···— — —···— — —···

"Ah-ha. I should have known. You look an awful lot like that pale-face in the bed."

"He's not a pale-face; he's my dad. And that's my sister, Melinda." He pointed proudly across the bed.

Danny continued the lively exchange as Cynthia whispered to Alice, "The kids are gorgeous. You must be so proud."

"No time for that—they keep me going dawn to dusk." The phone rang, and Alice moved quickly to answer it.

"Gradin Jones' room," she said with an official tone, then perked up. "Brad. How are you? Thanks for calling back." She paused and listened. "Well, I just got here, and we haven't even had a chance to talk yet." Leaning over the bed, she peered at Gradin. "He *looks* pretty good. Wanna talk to him?" She passed the phone off.

"M'main man Bradley Blue, how ya be?" When Brad commented on the animated conversation he could hear in the background, Gradin said, "Well, we've got a little Grand Central Station action goin' on here."

The phone conversation continued as Alice explained who was on the other end. When she got to the part about the CRM training development, Danny's eyes lit up. "Andy Caldwell mentioned that yesterday. He wants Gradin and me to be instructors in the program. Nothing like crashing an airplane to make us experts in the accident-prevention business."

"Oh, that's really wonderful. Gradin is a teacher at heart.

He has been an instructor pilot almost his entire career. Have you told him yet?"

"No, we just arrived a couple of minutes before you did."

As quickly as the mayhem had begun, it was over. Alice and the kids headed for church, Cynthia and Danny went out to explore Spokane, and Gradin slipped back into a fitful sleep. At precisely 11:15, new warmth pulsed through his body. It felt good as he awoke. He read a couple of get-well cards, glanced at the Sunday paper, and greeted the nurse with a warm smile.

"Why, Mr. Jones, I do believe that you are looking better—finally, a little color in those cheeks." She reached down for a pulse in his wrist and appeared to listen intently. "Hmm, very good. Sixty-five. We'll get one more sample here." She extracted a vial of blood from the needle embedded in his forearm. "The doctor will be in to see you at about noon." She gave his hand a motherly pat and disappeared.

So Andy wants our expert perspectives in the CRM program, eh? I'm assuming that Brad will also be one of the instructors; that could be fun, he imagined. *But odd, Brad didn't sound like himself on the phone this morning ,said he was calling from Bellingham. Hmm.* His mind ricocheted through the events of the past week.

"Good news, Mr. Jones." Dr. Alexander strode briskly into the room. "The hematocrit is up; looks like the bleeding has finally stopped. Let's hold off on the surgery and see if this is a consistent trend. My guess is that we're out of the woods." Holding the chart behind folded arms on his chest, he asked, "How do you feel? Noticing any difference?"

"Uh, yeah. I began feeling the strength coming back just after 11:00. It was really noticeable."

"Well, that isn't surprising. Up to that point, you were losing blood at about the same rate you were assimilating it. The hematocrit was thirty-nine percent when Jan took the last sample. That's up from the twenty-seven percent we were seeing yesterday.

"Now that your brain is functioning again, it's time for a little math." He smiled jovially. "A typical male your age

will have approximately 3,800 *meters* of red-blood-cell surface area; that's 2,000 times the amount of skin surface we
have. Just think of a ballpark thirty-five trillion red blood cells.
You're probably up a couple of trillion since 11:00. Not bad."

"Well, hey, no wonder I feel better. I was imagining only a
couple hundred million."

"Smart-ass." The doc winked and turned to leave. "We're
gonna have to throw you out of this place. I'll check back at
about 3:00."

Alone again in his room, a sublime realization engulfed
him. What he had felt at 11:15 had been the wound healing.
He knew from long experience that at 11:15, every Sunday,
Paddy MacDonald raised his voice in prayer to what Gradin
perceived as the universal presence that exceeds all understanding. *Thank you, Lord,* he whispered to himself.

"Whattaya mean she left?" Gradin was stunned as he listened
to Brad on the other end of the line. "Where did she go?"

"I have no idea. She dropped it on me last weekend; wanted to believe that I have something going with that Harvard
doc on the steering committee. It was a tit-for-tat opportunity. Says she is going to take a job in New York."

"Oh, man." Gradin thrust his head back into the pillow.
"What the hell is wrong with us? First, I tip over, and now Aud
goes bonkers on us."

"Well." Brad paused as he formed the thought. "I'm not
exactly Mr. Clean here, either. Technically I haven't fallen off
the fidelity wagon, but if I did, I certainly know where I'd like
to land."

"That's appropriately obscure." Gradin shook his head and smiled. "Is there more to the story, or do you want to just leave me dangling?"

"You're sort of a captive audience. Here's the fifty-cent version." Brad relished the opportunity to get it all out, and as he recounted the events, he experienced an unwelcome rush of emotion. He ended with, "Just a little kissing, and that was it."

A flushed red face popped around the doorjamb. Seeing Gradin on the phone, Paddy simply waved a big paw and stepped back into the hall.

"Well, pal, you may be tiptoeing through a minefield for a while. I'm glad you're up in Bellingham; your dad is a good sounding board. And speaking of spiritual counselors," he said in an exaggerated, loud voice, "mine has just arrived. Oh, and the doc has threatened to throw me outta here, so I may get to go home tomorrow. What's the number up there? I'll give you a call." He scribbled a note and signed off.

"Reverend MacDonald, please come in," Gradin beckoned with mock formality.

Paddy's eyes sparkled as he entered the room and stood smiling down at Gradin. "Ah, you're lookin' better than I expected, laddy," he emphasized with a concocted brogue.

"What time was your community prayer this morning, Paddy?" Gradin looked at him earnestly.

"Oh, fifteen past the hour, I suppose, same as always. Why do you ask?"

"Did you mention me?"

"Well, of course, I did, lad, along with all the sick old ladies and starving Armenians."

"Ha, good company, indeed." Gradin smiled wanly. "That's when the bleeding stopped, Paddy. At exactly the time that you and the congregation were offering that prayer, I felt a surge of warmth. I figure it was the wound healing over because I had a very noticeable increase in energy. How do I express my gratitude for that? Why me and not the thousands of people who are more deserving, Pad?"

"It's all part of God's plan, son, a wisdom far beyond anything we mortals can comprehend."

"I don't deserve it."

"None of us do. That's the point, Gradin. The grace of God defies all understanding, and you, maybe more than many others, need to understand that right now. You are literally tearing yourself up inside, you know that?" Paddy put both hands on one of Gradin's and looked deeply into his eyes.

"Alice talked to you?"

"Yes."

"So, you know what I've done?"

"I know what *she thinks* you've done."

Gradin looked away as tears filled his eyes. "It's true, Pad. I had an affair. I've defiled my marriage."

"Damaged? Yes. Defiled? I don't think so. Paul said it best in Romans 7:19: 'For the good that I would I do not: but the evil which I would not, that I do.' It's part of the human condition, lad. Sounds to me like you're in pretty good company."

"He was talking about adultery?"

"That, among other things."

"Things that *he* did?"

"Sounds like it to me."

They were silent as Gradin regained his composure. "Pad, I very honestly cannot explain why. It was a hunger unlike anything I've ever experienced before."

"Makes sense to me." Paddy nodded his affirmation.

"Why?" Gradin demanded angrily.

"Well, it's pretty complex, and I may be wrong here, but as I see it, you've been on the straight and narrow your entire life. Am I right?"

"Yeah, I suppose so."

"And you've done everything other people expected of you, right?"

"Uh-huh."

"Finally, you did something exclusively for *yourself*. Now don't get me wrong—I'm not condoning what you did. That desire for independent expression came out sideways, and there are consequences that are hurtful and need to be cleaned up. But it *was* an act of self-expression, something new in your life worth exploring—*other* forms of self-expression, that is." Paddy winked compassionately.

Gradin exhaled deeply. "Okay, so what now?"

"Well, obviously, the first priority has to be regaining your health. With any luck, this internal upheaval you've experienced will be the only warning you'll need. What's your status at Omega?"

"They don't know about the bleeding thing, and it isn't something I necessarily need to tell them. However, I will have to tell my FAA doc, and I suppose they will have some say over when I can go back to flying. The good news is that we got through the FAA check ride on Friday, but we don't know if we've been cleared of all culpability yet."

"Yes, Alice told me. Of course, it's also part of what tore you up inside, you know. You lived up to the most exacting expectations a person could face."

"Yeah, I suppose."

"Anyway, while you're recuperating, let me bring you a couple of books. When you're better, come spend some time with me. There's another world out there that you need to see."

Chapter 24

REDEMPTION

A shadow silently drifted across the lawn, then froze around Gradin's kneeling form. He winced protectively and rolled back into the sun as a tattered manuscript slapped on the ground next to his head.

"Top o' the mornin, lad." Paddy MacDonald's smiling face beamed down at his young friend and parishioner. "Some light reading for your leisure time—an advance copy from a friend of a friend."

"Ah, me friend, Paddy, what a relief." Gradin rose, pulled off his dirty gardening glove, and extended his hand. "For a moment, I was sure the angel of death had come for my rotting corpse."

Paddy furrowed his brow in disapproval. "Just as I suspected, lost in a fog of self-flagellation."

"Self-adulation, you say?"

"Funny." Paddy flashed a crooked smile, then bent down and retrieved the manuscript.

"Time to get started on your reeducation, my son. One of my favorite thinkers is Carl Jung, and this guy Thomas Moore works wonders with Jung's mumbo-jumbo." He thumped a finger on the title, *Care of the Soul*.

"The question might be, can he work wonders on *my* mumbo-jumbo?" Gradin took the manuscript and stared at it blankly.

Paddy smiled compassionately and remained silent. Finally, he put a hand on Gradin's shoulder and motioned toward the concrete steps to the porch. "Come on, let's go sit.

"You remind me of the young golfer a friend told me about," Paddy said. "Seems that this young guy was going through a rough patch, maybe something like you. He was paired up with this weathered old friend of mine, and the youngster was having a really horrible round. Worst of all, he was beating himself up mercilessly. Swearin' and carryin' on about every mistake he made.

"The old guy remained quiet and focused for the first eight or nine holes. Finally, after the youngster shanked one into the pond and blew his stack, the old codger said very calmly, "Sonny, ya oughtn't to get so upset. You're not that good a golfer."

Gradin laughed and hung his head in anticipation of the obvious.

"Sonny, ya oughtn't to be so upset; you're not that good a person," Paddy whispered as he patted his friend's knee.

"Amen," Gradin said with a solemn breath.

"God gave us the freedom to become what we will, in all of our breadth and depth. Every one of us bumbles and stumbles along—every one of us." He allowed the thought to percolate.

"Jung makes a great deal about the significance of shadow. Everything has a shadow." He held the manuscript into the sun and cast a shadow on Gradin's face. "See, you're on the dark side now. You can't have a light side without there being an equally significant dark side. That's true of our personalities as well. The brighter and shinier they are, the more likely it is that something equally dark and mysterious resides on the other side of the illumination."

"Hmm."

"Just look at the current news. Jim and Tammy Bakker, the best-known evangelists in the country. They raise a million dollars a week for their 'church.'" Paddy emphasized "church" ironically with two fingers. "Now their whole empire and their collective personae are unraveling. Lots of darkness there."

"Yeah, darkness is a good descriptor. I have felt that a lot, like skulking around in the underworld," Gradin responded through clenched teeth, his chin in his palms, elbows on his knees.

"Funny you should mention the underworld." Paddy continued, "Moore really revels in the mythology that shapes the soul. What may seem like a calamity to us can also be seen as the painful sculpting of the soul. It has a great deal to do with the entire family. Let me read you just a bit of this. That okay?"

"Sure, go for it."

Paddy flipped directly to a dog-eared page and began. *Today professionals are preoccupied with the " dysfunctional family." But to some extent, all families are dysfunctional. No family is perfect, and most have serious problems. A family is a microcosm, reflecting the nature of the world, which runs on both virtue and evil.*

He looked ahead and found a concluding passage: *Care of the soul doesn't require fixing the family or becoming free of it or interpreting its pathology. We may need simply to recover soul* by *reflecting deeply on the soul events that have taken place in the crucible of the family.*

"In other words, *shit happens.*" Paddy relished the profanity. "It sure does," Gradin said with an exhale.

"Yes, I can imagine that your over-riding perspective is that it's all heaped on your head right now. Alice is hurt and confused, but don't forget that she has her own shadow at work in this whole process. I have no idea where she may be in her personal growth. However, I do know that this time is a unique opportunity for you both. Clearly, things will never be the same." He paused and placed a hand on Gradin's knee. "Not the picture-perfect image you have both nurtured for so long, but very likely a deeper, soulful, tangled expression of who your family really is."

The door swung open, and Alice stepped onto the porch, a steaming mug of coffee in her hand. "Padraig MacDonald," she exclaimed in surprise. "How nice to see you. Coffee?" She offered the cup to him.

"Only if you'll join us," he insisted as he took the cup. "Well, okay, if I'm not interrupting."

"Not at all. We've just commenced the reeducation of Gradin Jones. I'll probably need your help."

She rolled her eyes and faked a smile. "Back in a second. Anything in your coffee, Paddy?" she asked over her shoulder. "No, black is fine." Turning to Gradin, he said, "Lots of goodwill remaining there. You're a lucky man."

"I know."

✈

"Uncle Brad, tell Paddy about the time you punched out," Bucky prodded.

Lively and comforting dinner conversation filled the room, and Gradin knew it was the first breath of normalcy Alice had experienced in weeks. Paddy and Gloria MacDonald had joined them, and Brad Morehouse was there as he and Gradin prepared for a Utah mountain biking adventure. It was old home week, and everyone was enjoying the familiarity.

"No, no, no! A guy never wants to admit that he hasn't made as many landings as he has takeoffs."

The joke was lost on Bucky, who persisted, "But that was so cool! You were just flyin' through the air like a rocket."

"Sounds like there's something about being a Blue Angel that is more literal than I imagined," Paddy exclaimed with raised eyebrows.

"Well, this was long, long, ago and far, far away, pre-Blue Angel."

"Tell him, Uncle Brad, tell him."

"No, why don't you tell him, Buck? You know the story."

"Oh, yeah, I do." Bucky squirmed forward in his chair, balancing so he could use his hands. "Well, see, Uncle Brad was flyin' around one day with this other guy, and they were tryin' to land, and the engine quit, and the other guy pulled the ejection handle, and they went sailing through the air." Bucky stood and assumed a flying-Superman pose. "He landed in the grass and was all bloody, and then he was a Blue Angel."

"Not bad there, Superman." Brad nodded.

"Wow, is that the selection criteria?" Paddy smiled. "Hardly—to the contrary. If I'd been the guy who pulled the ejection handle, I never would have made the team. I was a student then, and the instructor made a snap decision. I had no choice in the matter."

"Tell 'em about the blood . . . tell 'em about the blood," Bucky persisted.

"No, no. There's always blood in a thing like that." Brad attempted to minimize the gravity of the event.

"But you were really gushin'. Blood all over the place."

"Time out." Gradin raised both hands and formed the letter T. "That is enough, Buck," he said firmly. "This is dinner conversation, and it isn't polite to talk about gory things while people are eating. And the truth is that we are all thankful that Brad is okay and that he is here at dinner with us."

"Amen."

"I'll drink to that and to the fact that Gradin walked away from the plane in Pasco." Paddy raised his glass, and eyes glistened gratefully.

"Wonderful casserole, Alice," Gloria said as she passed a bowl to her left.

"Thank you. I had lots of help from my little sous-chef." Alice tousled Melinda's hair affectionately. "Plus, this little Wonder Woman has a starring role in the dance recital tomorrow night. Right, munchkin?"

"Yes, and Jill and Rachel are dwarfs."

"Her chums," Alice explained with a wink.

"Mommy, is Uncle Brad going to come to the recital?"

"Why don't you ask him, sweetheart?"

Melinda waited impatiently for Brad to finish his conversation with Paddy then seized her opportunity. "Uncle Brad, Uncle Brad, are you coming to the recital tomorrow night? I'm Snow White."

"Only if I can be Dopey," he responded with a silly face. "Noooooo," she giggled.

The conversation meandered from the recital to mountain bikes to gardening to Scripture.

"And you know why God created Eve," Alice said with a rare twinkle.

"So, there'd be someone to remind Adam to take out the trash?"

"Well, that and a million other things." Alice glanced at Gloria. "But the truth is that when God completed Adam, he stood back and looked him over, scratched his beard, and thought for a moment. Then he said, 'Nah, I can do better than that.'"

"Oh, ouch," Paddy protested.

"Mommy, is that true?" Melinda was confused by the joke.

"Of course it is, sweetheart. Look how wonderfully we women turned out." She pushed her chair back and began clearing the table. "Now, help me with these dishes, munchkin. You too, Buckmeister."

Chapter 25

CANYONLANDS

"Hello, Brad." A plaintive female voice interrupted Brad and Gradin's march through the Salt Lake City terminal. They both stopped and looked toward the gate where anxious passengers clustered around the boarding podium. Gradin knew who he was seeing. A pert, shapely little redhead, blue eyes blazing.

"Uh, Sarah." Brad was befuddled. "How are you?" He stepped toward her and extended a hand.

"I'm fine. Long time no see," she said flatly and shook his hand.

"Well, yeah, a lot has happened since—"

"No need to explain," she interrupted, glancing away. "Hey, I'd like you to meet Gradin Jones. Gradin, this is Sarah Marconi."

Sensing an opportunity to help, Gradin enthusiastically said, "Of course. You match the description perfectly, Sarah. Brad has told me all about you."

She flushed with a flicker of hope. "Oh, has he now?" She searched Brad's face as he failed to conceal a broad grin. "And just exactly what did he tell you?"

"Oh, you know. Typical boy-meets-girl stuff—Benson Hotel, Powell's bookstore, Jake's for dinner, a lazy stroll down Broadway. It's a little hazy after that." He winked.

"Yeah, it is for me, too. I can't remember what happened after that." She stared earnestly at Brad. Then, catching herself, she said, "But anyway, your name is familiar too, Gradin. Weren't you on the Pasco 737?"

"Nice to be so well known—sort of like ol' Joe, the bridge builder." They all smiled at the worn joke.

"Hero is more like it," Sarah persisted. "I was supposed to have been on that trip, but I found one that fit my kid plans better." She glanced at Brad, knowing that she wouldn't have met him otherwise. "But my close friend Barbara Haskell was working that trip instead."

"Oh, wow! She was magnificent," Gradin said.

"She says the same of you and the captain. What's his name?"

"Danny Purcell. Great guy. Have you seen Barb recently? How's her ankle?"

"She actually called me a week or so ago. Says Omega is giving her as much time as she needs. As you can imagine, she isn't rushing to get back."

"Good for her. I hope she really comes back strong. Hey, Brad, why don't I go get our gear and line up the rental car? You two need some time. I'll meet you down at the Avis counter in fifteen or twenty minutes." Then, to Sarah, "Now I understand why ol'—what's his name? Oh, yeah, 'Hotshot'—

why ol' Hotshot's heart is all aflutter. Happy to meet you, Sarah. Treat him right," he quipped, then disappeared into the crowd.

Sarah blushed again and looked at her feet. It was an awkward moment for them both. Finally, she summoned her courage and looked into his eyes. "I've missed you, Brad."

"Mmm, nice to hear that. A lot has happened since Portland. You have a minute?"

Brad couldn't know that his words had set off a mild panic in her. "Yeah, we just came in from L.A. Sit for two hours, then go to Dallas. What are you and Gradin up to?"

"Oh, a little male bonding, mountain biking, and camping down in Moab. Great time of year for that. I have two weeks of vacation. Then back down to Memphis to pull that CRM program together. Let's go over there." Brad pointed to the empty boarding area across the concourse.

"Okay."

They wandered over and sat facing each other. "So, like I said, a lot has happened."

She braced for the worst. "Audrey left me."

The words stung and resounded confusingly through her head. It was not at all what she had expected. They were silent. "Brad, I'm sorry," was all she could muster.

"Yeah, a real kick in the pants. But then look where I was headed."

"Where were you headed?" She searched his eyes. "Well, you really rocked my world last month."

"But that was last month, you're telling me?"

"No, it's the same this month, but now I'm faced with the reality of wanting another man's wife."

She thought for a moment. "Different if only one of us is unfaithful, I guess." She looked at the ceiling to stave off the tears. "Lots of eligible women out there, Brad."

"I'm not interested."

"I can imagine how hurt you must be. I really can."

"Hmm, yes and no. Audrey and I were never a perfect match. For thirty years, I pushed hard and competed like a demon, then decided to get off that track and enjoy a simpler life. Audrey is just getting a taste of her own power, I think. She fell for one of the corporate media moguls in New York. She's going back there to be a local news anchor and rising star. She admits that it's a power trip."

"You never wanted kids?"

"I'd love to, but I can't—took a direct blow in the nether region when I was in the Navy. I wanted to adopt, but Audrey wouldn't go for it. So I get my kid fix from Gradin's. I'm an honorary uncle." He smiled. "Gradin's going through something similar to this right now, but he has a great wife and a beautiful family. I think they'll survive."

"What do you mean, 'something similar'?"

"Oh, he's way tipped over with a flight attendant. His wife found out, and he literally busted a gut."

"What?"

"Yeah, he's been under a whole lot of pressure—commuting to L.A., Navy Reserves up at Whidbey. Then the Pasco accident. Way too much."

"And the busted gut?"

"Ruptured ulcer, I think." Brad paused. "Good time for both of us to get away to the most peaceful place on earth. You ever been down to Moab?"

"No, but I've seen it from the air. That's near the big red earthen arch, isn't it?"

"Yeah, Arches National Monument. We're going to camp just south of there in Canyonlands. Amazing red vistas. It feels like you can see a million miles. Perfect time of year, too. The desert wildflowers are just coming into bloom."

"Mmm, sounds wonderful."

Brad quelled his yearning. "I'd better get down there and meet Gradin. We have a four-hour drive to make, and we wanna be able to get a camp set up before dark."

"I wrote you a note. I was going to drop it in your box when we go through Seattle." She fumbled through her big tote and extracted a long envelope. "You may as well have it now. Good for some laughs or something." She handed it to him and stood to leave.

"Sarah, I—I want you to be happy. I want you to be in a place to enjoy your kids and your home and the rest of your family. You deserve that."

"Okay, well, uh," she stammered. "I hope to see you again, Brad. You rocked my world, too, you know."

He placed his hands on her shoulders and kissed her forehead.

"Be well," she whispered, resting her head on his jacket long enough to dab the tears now running down her cheek. Then she turned and strode purposefully down the concourse.

"You know, a woman could never understand this."

"Whattaya mean?" Gradin responded as he maneuvered the Chevy Blazer up the freshly paved road into Canyonlands.

... — — —... — — —... — — —... — — —... — — —...

"We've driven for four hours, hardly said a word, and we're both comfortable and happy with that."

"Yeah, I like it. And you've been pretty lost in whatever Sarah gave you, too."

"Ah, man, I'm really a basket case." Brad disconsolately buried his face in his hands.

"Why? She put a big guilt trip on you?"

"No. Very much the opposite—a wrenching expression of possibility. Good bedtime reading." He tossed the pages toward Gradin and gazed out at the stunning scenery. "I think I really blew it."

The road split the high mesa in half, with the jagged red canyon cut deep on either side. "That's where we'll camp." Gradin motioned to a lightly worn trail to the west. "But you gotta see the Shafer Trail in this light." He continued south toward the overlook.

Moments later, they both inched forward on their bellies and peered into the incredibly deep variegated canyon.

"God, how ridiculous is this? Two pilots scared shitless of the height. Wouldn't want any of our Air Force buddies to see this."

They gazed contentedly at the vast chasm etched in the red rock below. A shoe-sized fragment broke loose from the edge and disappeared silently down the face of the cliff. Eventually, the sound of its impact reverberated faintly in the distance.

Brad pointed to their right at the ribbon of sand winding perilously back and forth up the rock face. "That the Shafer Trail over there?"

"Yup, fun ride down but gonzo abusive comin' up. We might wanna save that one for the end of the week."

"Yeah, or maybe next year sometime," Brad said with a grin.

"We'd better go get the tent set up before it gets dark."

Both squirmed back from the edge before standing.

They were quietly efficient, arranging the camp perched on the step of a west-facing arroyo. A deep orange tint lit the horizon, and their small fire cast shadows on the craggy junipers. A lone coyote wailed nearby, and the pack responded with incessant yips and yowls.

"I've heard some interesting stories about the mountain lions down here," Brad mentioned as they anchored the corners of the tent with aluminum stakes. "A guy told me about being out there east of Slickrock with his dog a few years ago. All of a sudden, he found himself lying in the trail, his dog dead at his side, and a cougar starin' him down just a few yards away."

"Holy shit," Gradin said with a final whack on the tent stake.

"Fortunately, the guy had a walkie-talkie and called his brother, who was nearby. The brother fired a rifle a few times and scared the cat away. The guy had a broken shoulder—he thinks he must have shrugged instinctively when the cat jumped him from an overhang. Obviously, the dog got involved and saved his life."

"Whoa. Well, how does the old saying go? There may be cougars, but at least there are snakes?"

"Comforting." They both moved closer to the fire and warmed their hands.

Hot dogs and beers capped the day as the overwhelming quiet of the desert surrounded them, each sound magnified by the stillness. Finally, Gradin went to the truck and retrieved Sarah's note to Brad. He angled his back toward the fire, and the flickering light illuminated the page.

"I gave her a copy of *The Prophet*," Brad said. "She's referring to the piece on friendship that I read to her that night at Jake's." Gradin read aloud.

> *Gibran beseeches us to laugh, my friend; to meet our hunger fearlessly, without regret for the grief to come.*
>
> *You enliven me with fiery heart, my friend; I long for peace in your absence, emboldened by the ebbing tide that foretells the impending flood.*
>
> *You refresh me with sweetness in your eyes, my friend; all hopes, thoughts, and desires made possible in the dew of our awakening passion and the unclaimed joy of feverish coupling.*

"Wow, she composed that?" Gradin asked. "Cool."

"Yup. Then she goes on to quote Gibran." Brad stood and stretched. "I've gotta go to sleep. Enjoy." Brad patted Gradin's back, shuffled toward the tent, and fell quickly to sleep while Gradin sat by the dying fire quietly, absorbing a few painful truths. His steamy relationship with Peggy didn't begin to meet the standard set by Brad and Sarah's connection. What he had with Peg was pure excitement—total ego. He accepted that now. But even imagining her in this context raised his temperature.

Jesus, what's wrong with me? He breathed deeply. *Maybe Paddy's concern is worth pursuing. I obviously get a real jolt when I cross the line that way.* "Brain chemistry," Paddy said, "possibly even mild depression." *Me?*

Tears filled his eyes as he doused the fire and mouthed a silent prayer. *God help me.*

✈

The following days provided nonstop adrenaline. The headlong plunge down the unforgiving bike trails at Slickrock resulted in both an incredible rush and painfully tangled mishaps. Brad was the first to launch over the handlebars—the biker's infamous *endo*—when he mistakenly squeezed the front brake and catapulted himself into a heap at the bottom of the steep rock face.

They wore bruises and scrapes like war paint on the long day's ride to Grand View Point Overlook. No amount of water quenched their thirst, and a shady overhang provided cover for an extended break before the return ride to camp.

Gemini Bridges was a ballbuster, a gentle descending trail to a magnificent tabletop overlook. Shade, a nap, lunch, water, and trail mix delayed the killer trip back up the rutted jeep path.

Endorphin-driven fatigue brought more peace, masculine silence, and occasional thoughtful musings each ensuing day. Brad talked at length about his father's successful coping with depression, causing Gradin to wonder more about his own father's dour demeanor. They speculated together, and Brad encouraged Gradin to check it out.

There were funny recollections of peewee football, Cub Scouts, frogs in beds, Halloween firecrackers, the first car, summer jobs, and fraternity pranks, but never women. Somehow the topic was soothingly off-limits.

As promised, the final morning found them bounding down the treacherous Shafer Trail, then basking in the sun. The view from the canyon floor was like looking from base camp to the summit of Everest, and they watched with interest as a bedraggled group of bikers crept by, heads bowed fearfully in anticipation of the painful ascent. Within minutes most were off their bikes, pushing. Others zigzagged to ease the demand, and some gratefully boarded the support van for a ride to the top. It was easy to laugh as they reclined in the shade.

The word *pain* was laughably inadequate. It might have compared to cross-country runs in OCS, daily doubles in high school, or never-ending wind sprints in college, but the hour-long climb exceeded them all combined.

For the first couple of minutes, they cajoled each other and playfully jockeyed for position. Glee quickly gave way to focus and finesse—up out of the saddle most of the way, but too far forward, and they lost traction; too far back, there was no leverage. Their heart rates climbed and plateaued. Thighs burned and screamed for relief. An occasional swerve toward the edge sent the endorphins surging over the lactic-acid burn, while sweat blurred sunglasses, stung the eyes, and soaked their T-shirts.

A threesome careened past in the opposite direction. "See what we have to look forward to?" one blithely re-marked to the others.

They ground on, cranking the lowest granny gear for inch-by-inch progress up the torturous incline. Fifty-five minutes and thirty seconds from the start, side by side, they crested the ridge, dismounted and tumbled into the shade, exhausted.

Chapter 26

ALOHA

"Mom, look. Is that a hole in the roof of this airplane?" Twelve-year-old Kim pointed toward the ceiling of the 737. An eerie whistling sound crescendoed into a deafening shriek as miscellaneous objects pelted toward the expanding tear in the fuselage. Kim's head snapped back, and her sunglasses ricocheted down the aisle as a torrent of frigid air blasted into the cabin.

The standing flight attendant was suddenly gone, and sunlight poured through the jagged fissure. "Mom? Mom! What's happening?" Kim shouted over the roar. Connie cradled her daughter's head and yelled, "It's all right, it's all right, it's all right," knowing they would be dead in an instant.

She held Kim fiercely, covered her eyes with one hand, and fought to make sense of the chaos. Terrified passengers were buffeted mercilessly by the air and debris blasting through the cabin at hundreds of miles an hour.

Floor panels bent, the cockpit dropped, and the aircraft pitched into a rapid nosedive. Not knowing the fate of the cockpit crew, flight attendant Michelle Honda crawled through the hurricane conditions screaming for anyone who could fly an airplane. No one responded as they hurtled toward the sea.

At the same moment, as the air in the cockpit cleared of fog and flying objects, Captain Robert Schornstheimer and First Officer Mimi Tompkins donned their oxygen masks and initiated an emergency descent.

The deafening roar from the sky-filled chasm drowned every attempt at communication. Air traffic controllers could only watch in horror as the radar blip that was Flight 243 plunged toward the sea. At 14,000 feet, Tompkins switched their radio to the tower frequency in Kahului, Maui. The controller was startled to hear an unknown aircraft declaring an emergency in an excited and garbled transmission.

Schornstheimer wrestled the crippled jet as Tompkins explained in broken phrases to the tower that they had experienced an explosive decompression and would require medical assistance for an unknown number of passengers and crew on arrival. "We'll need all the equipment you've got!" she shouted into the radio.

Maneuvering the aircraft was a delicate task. The fuselage twisted and groaned with every steering input. Flap extension below the five-degree position made it feel uncontrollable, so Schornstheimer elected to maintain the five-degree setting and attempt to land forty knots faster than normal. The challenge intensified when the left engine failed, and he was forced to compensate with substantially more power from the right engine. The damaged aircraft structure twisted toward the breaking point.

Seconds before certain disaster, the airborne wreckage touched down and rolled to a stop on runway 2 in Maui. As the remaining engine was shut down, the deafening roar was supplanted by the moans and desperate cries for help from the battered passengers.

Miraculously, only one person perished. Eight were seriously injured, fifty-seven slightly injured, and twenty-nine remained unharmed.[46]

Andy Caldwell was accustomed to evening phone calls at home, so it was no surprise to hear the voice of Dick Hoxsworth, the Los Angeles chief pilot, as he answered the phone. "Andy, sorry to bother you." Dick seemed out of breath. "I just got a call from my wife in Maui. Have you heard about this yet?"

"No, what're you talking about?" Andy asked.

"This will be big news, really big. Connie and our daughter, Kim, were flying from Hilo back to Honolulu this afternoon on Aloha. They had just leveled off when all hell broke loose. There was a major explosive decompression—a huge section of the upper fuselage tore away, and a flight attendant was sucked right out of the airplane!"

"Holy shit!" Andy responded as he collapsed into a chair. "Are Connie and Kim okay?"

"Yeah, they were way in back, and she says it looked like it was about the first five rows or so where the roof blew off. It was absolute mayhem—everything was torn to shreds, and she was absolutely certain they were going to die. Fortunately, she was so focused on comforting Kim—she's twelve—that she didn't have time to be scared. Said the aft fuselage was twisting and creaking like it would break away at any moment. All they could do was keep their heads down and pray."

"God, I'm glad they are both okay, Dick. Will they be able to get home all right?"

"Oh, sure, Connie is a real trouper. She lived through my two WestPac[47] tours, so she figures it was her turn for some excitement."

"Well, listen." Andy regained his composure. "This will very likely be watershed for our CRM steering committee. In fact, they may want to talk to Connie sometime if that would be okay."

"Oh, I'm sure she would be happy to cooperate," Dick said. "We have an inside line to NTSB investigations, so we may be able to incorporate their official perspective when we launch our program in July. There must have been some amazing crew performance out there.

"Dick, thanks for the call. Give Connie my best," Andy concluded. Then he immediately dialed the Holiday Inn and asked for Jack Mumford, the CRM committee chair.

Ten hours later, the steering committee members clustered around a table, inspecting several black-and-white photos of the Aloha 737 faxed to them from the newspaper in Maui.

"That airplane could not possibly have flown," someone insisted.

"It is completely torn to shreds," George whispered incredulously.

"Okay, gang, let's get on with it," Jack said. "Take your seats and brainstorm with me about how to incorporate this event into our program."

"Jack, this is the perfect scenario for the application of our six primary CRM skills. This could really be the focal point of our entire program," Vinnie said as he jumped up and scribbled the six skills on a whiteboard:

- Planning
- Team Building
- Workload Management
- Decision Making
- Situational Awareness
- Communication

"They did all of this stuff really well."

"Whoa, whoa," Andrea interrupted. "Why did this happen in the first place? Where was the breakdown?"

"Well, we won't know why that section of the fuselage broke away until the investigation is complete." Jack raised a hand and pointed to the board. "Marsha has modified the concept of planning. The change will almost certainly encompass the problem with the Aloha flight. Marsha, tell us about the evolution of your thinking concerning planning."

"Sure. You want the long or short version?"

"Give us the whole nine yards."

Marsha proceeded to describe the American Eagle accident in Raleigh-Durham and how that had prompted her to settle on preparation as a key skill, with planning, training, and organizational support as subcategories. She made a persuasive argument that the cause of the accident could easily be traced to deficiencies in each of the subcategories. And knowing where Jack was going in the discussion of Aloha, she made a particular point that the success of every flight is directly related to the level of organizational support provided the crew. She concluded that without yet knowing the reason that the skin peeled away from that 737, one could surmise that the accident would not have happened had they been flying a perfectly maintained aircraft.

"Yeah, and doesn't that same concept apply to the Northwest and Continental accidents?" Jack prompted her.

"Absolutely. Do you want me to go over those, too?"

"Please."

She explained in great detail how both accidents could be tied to a breakdown in organizational support. For Northwest, the failure of the takeoff warning system had allowed the crew to commence the takeoff without the flaps extended. In a different vein, Continental—the organization itself, in this case—allowed two low-time pilots to be paired together in very challenging weather conditions.

"Aren't we opening a can of worms here by making aircraft warning systems the culprit in these things?" David Hennessey queried.

"Marsha, if I may?" Loren Hughes raised a hand and spoke emphatically. "David, what this does is create a balance of responsibility between the pilots and the organization. We can't train pilots to use a particular warning system, require them to respond to and even depend on those warnings, and then hold them solely responsible for providing the backup that a malfunctioning warning system fails to provide."

"You lost me, Loren." David furrowed his brow.

"Well, we are talking about a passive failure or at least an unknown failure of a warning system. In most cases, we are allowed to go flying without such a system if it is known in advance so the crew can take additional precautions. It is reasonable to assume that the Northwest crew would have been particularly aware of the flap position if they had been dispatched with an inoperative takeoff warning system."

David nodded. "Okay, I get it."

Loren continued. "My guess is that every one of the pilots in this room has applied power for takeoff and gotten a takeoff warning horn. Most of those times, it is simply a matter of the elevator trim being a degree or two out of limits. We make the adjustment and off we go, no harm, no foul. The same would be true if the flaps weren't properly set, a fatal error in most instances."

Pat Finch cut in. "David, historically, accident investigations tend to conclude that pilot error is the primary cause. It's almost a knee-jerk reaction. And there is no denying that pilots do make errors that often lead to catastrophe. But for the most part, these are seasoned professionals. Just look at that KLM captain on Tenerife. He was their most esteemed pilot. The PR department tried to reach him immediately after the accident to be their authoritative spokesman. Imagine the shock when they discovered his role in the disaster."

"But wasn't that pilot error plain and simple?" David pressed.

"Yes and no. It is vitally important to dig deep enough to uncover the mitigating factors. Rather than affixing blame, it is more important to learn what other crews can do differently. There was a similar dynamic in Portland, and it was determined that specific training in problem-solving and effective crew interaction was needed for United pilots. And here *we* are in the same boat."

The conversation dragged on, and Brad was able to add a persuasive description of the well-oiled Blue Angels organization and the fact that their airborne success could easily be traced to the performance of every team member on the ground, and how crucial it is to create a culture that capitalizes on input from everyone on the team.

By day's end, they all had their marching orders. Not surprisingly, Marsha and Jack were to focus on the Aloha accident. Brad was to collaborate with a presentations specialist in Seattle. The others had similar assignments; the team would reconvene June 1 to tie it all together.

Before any of that, Andy had a special assignment for Brad alone.

Chapter 27

INTERVENTION

Let the fun begin. Brad strode confidently across the corridor and extended his hand. "Good morning, Captain, I'm Brad Morehouse. I'll be your jump-seat rider today."

The small, Napoleon-like Captain Melvin Sprague grunted, shook hands firmly, and muttered, "Better'n a stick in the eye, I guess. More like four days, isn't it?" He turned and keyed in the combination to the jetway door. "Give us a few minutes to get set up down there, will ya?" The door slammed behind him.

Brad shrugged, moved over, and stood patiently at the boarding desk as the agent hammered the keyboard for what seemed like five minutes. Brad could easily have been one of Ross Perot's new recruits, or maybe even a stealthy young FBI agent in gray slacks, blue blazer, white shirt with a loosely knotted tie, and the shiniest black loafers to ever grace the Dallas airport. Finally, without a word, the agent handed him a boarding pass. Instead of a seat number, it read JSR—jump-seat rider.

"Go ahead and board whenever you like," she finally said with a smile.

"Thanks." He saluted with the ticket, stepped away from the desk, and blended in with the 6:00 a.m. business crowd.

Always a grumpy lot, most were sipping coffee and poring over the morning paper. An elderly couple leaned into each other and dozed.

This was a new chapter for both Brad and Omega. A week earlier, this crew he was about to meet had cheated death when they landed in Dallas, turned off the runway at midfield, and proceeded directly across the active, parallel runway without clearance from the tower—a significant FAA violation. Brad would have four days to observe them, give them some CRM pointers, and report back to Andy Caldwell. This was in lieu of an FAA penalty—not a bad deal for a crew that had narrowly avoided disaster.

Boarding was called. Brad waited several minutes before slipping into line and ambling down the jetway. The key was to be a fly on the wall—not an operations guru, just a quiet observer. "Good morning, guys," he said as he stepped into the 727 cockpit and was struck by the familiar foul smell. Omega cockpits were filthy, an issue that failed to register on management's radar.

The eager new engineer looked up and smiled nervously. "Brad Morehouse." He smiled and extended his hand. "I'm Evan Crosby, Brad." The engineer was obviously intimidated.

"Roger Samuels." The copilot waved over his shoulder. "Just call me Sam."

........— — —...... — — —...... — — —................... — — —......— — —...

"Roger, Roger." Brad couldn't resist. Then he felt stupid. "Sorry, Sam. You probably don't get that more than four or five times a day, right?"

"Usually not more than that," he said with a smile. "Captain, okay if I stow my bag back here?" Brad kept the chatter going in an effort to set a relaxed tone.

"Yeah, but don't call me Captain. I'm Mel."

"Thanks, Mel. Hey, can I get you guys anything from the back?"

"Nope."

"No, thanks."

"I'm okay."

They're all reading from the same script so far. Brad smiled to himself as he stepped out of the cockpit and peeked into the galley.

"Can I help you, sir?" An annoyed flight attendant looked up from the limes she was slicing for the morning Bloody Marys. Her grandmotherly appearance and sour demeanor made him feel like a ten-year-old again.

"Oops, sorry." He pointed to the ID badge hanging around his neck. "Forgot that I'm not in my monkey suit. I'm Brad, your jump-seat rider. Just wanted to introduce myself and let you know that I'm available to help if anything comes up."

"Well, good. Just put on that other smock and start delivering these drinks," she shot back with a nod toward the apron hanging on the oven door.

"Uh, you know, I tried that once. Made such a mess that I'm banned from the galley for life. I stick to stuff like resetting flush-motor circuit breakers and replacing nasty seat belts."

"Wonderful, I'll let you know if we need you."

... ▬ ▬ ▬... ▬ ▬ ▬... ▬ ▬ ▬... ▬ ▬ ▬... ▬ ▬ ▬... ▬ ▬ ▬...

He returned to the cockpit without the coffee he was craving, settled into the rear jump seat, and sat quietly. *Like watchin' paint dry,* he acknowledged to himself. All on their best behavior, the crew plowed through the before-start checklist without missing a beat. The engineer even turned and briefed Brad on the use of the oxygen mask dangling by the window, pointing out the dangerous possibility of grabbing the captain's mask by mistake. It was one of the stories emblazoned in the minds of all new engineers, the time the captain donned the wrong mask and couldn't communicate throughout an entire emergency. *You get a gold star, Evan.*

The setup time requested by Mel had obviously given them a chance to work out their game plan—likely Mel had admonished them, "Do not, *do not,* DO NOT screw up a taxi clearance." As the aircraft crept along the taxiway, they were the slowest moving object in Dallas. Typically, the flow of activities and the movement of aircraft were smooth, effortless, and rather brisk. *These guys are like three old grannies in a borrowed Cadillac—dangerously slow.*

Brad watched the crew dynamic with keen interest. Mel dominated the show. For every decision, Evan and Sam looked to him like a basketball team, always checking with the point guard before taking the shot. *Painfully inefficient, even dangerous,* Brad concluded.

Nine hours and four legs later, the 727 rolled to a stop at the gate in Miami, and one last time the rote behaviors played out flawlessly: brakes set, fuel chopped, rotating beacon off, seatbelt sign off, pitot heat off, etc. Mel checked in with the ground handler and received clearance to release the brakes, while Sam held the checklist and scanned the overhead for appropriate switch positions. Evan flipped a series of switches, scanned the gauges, then grabbed the logbook and entered fuel remaining and oil quantities in designated blocks.

The pace subsided as Brad peeled himself out of the jump seat and stretched lazily. "Nice job, guys. Just another day at the office, huh?" Mel refused to respond, and the others were all business. "I'll buy the beer," Brad said as he grabbed his jacket. "See you out front."

"I guess the joke about mandatory happy hour didn't register with the boss, huh?" Brad looked around the bar area for Mel, then eased himself into a chair at the table with the two other pilots.

"How much trouble do ya think we're in here, Brad?" Evan asked as he took a long sip of beer. "Is this just the precursor to the FAA getting all over our case?"

"No, this should be it. I watch, we all talk, and the FAA and Andy Caldwell are happy," Brad responded.

"This stuff go in our training record?" Roger asked.

"Nope, it all stays under the radar. And speaking of radar—anyone get a fix on the flight leader?" Brad continued to scan the room, looking for Mel.

"Nah, he pretty much stays to himself. He's probably up in his room mapping out the next big road trip on his Harley. That is all the guy thinks about. The trip last week started just like today. But by some time the second day he was off in never-never land. He just can't stay focused."

"And that's what happened with the runway crossing in Dallas?"

"Yeah, he hardly briefed at all. Didn't say which high-speed (taxiway) he intended to take and then went roaring right across the parallel runway before I could even open my mouth. I assumed—"

"Ah, yes, the ol' ass-you-n-me blunder."

"Exactly. But this guy is so damned hard to work with, Brad. He just can't listen. He knows it all and is offended by any input. I'm just there to jerk the gear and keep my mouth shut," the copilot said as he continued to fume.

"I know. We see a lot of that in this fine old captains' airline. And it's gotta change, or we're all history." Brad's tone was solemn. "The company can't possibly survive another accident. Of course, the real irony, in this case, is that in his written statement, Mel says that it was 'the failure of the co-pilot to notify him' that led to the excursion."

Sam choked on his beer, and it spewed all over the table and out his nose. When he could finally speak, he said, "Jesus Christ! Are you fucking kidding me? What a flaming asshole." He angrily wiped up the mess he'd made.

"Easy there, Tonto. You gotta live to ride again," Brad said, smiling again.

Evan sat mute as the easy banter swirled around him. Unlike most of his peers, he wasn't cut from military fabric. He was one of those hardworking civilians who had beaten all the odds and landed a job at Omega at age twenty-five. He'd simply lived in airplanes from the time he was sixteen. Five thousand hours for someone his age was unheard of. And now his treasured airline career hung by a thread. First-year pilots were on probation. Any whiff of a problem could result in uncontested termination, and Evan was scared.

Brad sensed his anguish and adopted a more collegial tone. "Guys, let me share an idea with you that came from one of the good old check pilots back at Pacific. He said to the copilot and me, 'Gentlemen, your job is to make the captain look good.' Sounds simple but think about it."

"Make this flamer look good?" Sam was incredulous.

"You're damned right!" Brad shot back.

"How? And, for that matter, why?"

"Sam, we aren't talkin' about who is right or wrong up there. It isn't a contest! We're talking about getting the job done safely. You gotta check your ego at the door and be the best-damned follower in the world. And that doesn't mean you have to be a pansy. You simply have to be very competent and provide the captain all the information and assistance you imagine a good leader would ask for, even before he asks for it. It's more of a dance than a military parade. Don't confuse submissiveness with followership, if there is such a word. My guess is that every great leader almost certainly was a great follower at some point. That make sense?"

"Hmm, let me chew on it for a while." Sam sipped his beer, stared at the ceiling, and allowed his agitation to subside.

Brad shifted his gaze. "And Evan, the same goes for you too, my man." He clinked Evan's glass and smiled broadly. "It seems to me that we get very confused in this business. Because aviation requires so much technological expertise, we automatically assume that technology, or those very objective left-brained skills, will provide the answers to all of our problems up there. That is seldom the case. Remember Apollo 13?"

Both Evan and Sam looked puzzled. "Yeahhhh . . . " one of them said tentatively.

"How'd it begin? 'Okay, Houston, we've had a problem here'?"

"Oh, okay. Yeah, yeah. I remember now," Evan said.

"So sure enough, they had a problem. A big one. And it took the whole damned team in Houston and around the world to come up with a solution. There is no organization on the planet with more checklists and left-brain thinkers, but there was no book answer to that one.

"I think the best part was when they threw those engineers into the classroom and had 'em build a CO_2 filter out of the junk they knew the guys had up there. It ended up being made with duct tape, a sock, and a checklist cover. The crew would have died without that contraption."

"Thought you said there was no checklist for that one." Evan smiled.

He's finally listening, Brad realized as he ordered another round.

Sam picked up the story. "I remember now. It was Ken Mattingly, the original mission commander—a guy who got dumped because he was exposed to measles—who figured it out. It took Mattingly getting in the sim and working for hours to create a new set of procedures to maneuver the module precisely into position for reentry without depleting the batteries in the lunar lander. Damn! Talk about teamwork."

"Now you're getting the picture, guys. You don't have to be perched on a fat wallet in the left seat of an airliner to be a key player. Because when you make that guy look good, you're gonna develop some trust, and when you have that trust, he's more likely to involve you in the decision-making process. It feeds on itself. And voilà! You build a team."

"I'll drink to that."

"Back in the saddle again, out where a friend is a friend," Sam warbled as he flipped switches and built his nest in the cockpit.

"You gonna be okay there, cowboy?" Evan joked.

"Yup. Got 'er under control here, pardner." Then, looking to his left, he said, "Ready for the checklist when you are, boss."

"I'll let you know," Mel groused.

Sam glanced back at Brad, then plunged ahead. "Roger that." He held up a note with the ATIS information. "They're departing eight-right. Oh-two on the altimeter." He pointed at Mel's gauge and waited for him to make the adjustment. "Clearance on two when you're ready."

"Jesus! Calm down. I've got stuff to do over here." Mel pretended to scrutinize every item on the flight plan, high-lighting key pieces with a yellow marker. He extracted maps and charts from his flight bag and arranged them for easy access, then worked from the top left of the overhead panel all the way to the engine gauges upfront, touching and confirming the required settings and limits. Finally satisfied, he grumbled, "Okay, give 'em a call."

The captain's domination was unrelenting, and Brad squirmed with discomfort, occasionally catching the eye of Sam or Evan. The two gamely attempted to provide Mel seamless assistance, acts that were largely ignored. A *Napoleon complex extraordinaire*, Brad concluded as the day wore on.

On the final landing of the day, Mel slammed the throttles closed, raised the thrust reversers, and applied the brakes.

The 727 pitched forward and slowed abruptly. He stowed the reversers, popped the speed-brake handle down, and nosed the jet toward the edge of the runway as he moved the number three fuel-control lever to off.

"Omega 198, right turn there at Bravo. Contact ground twenty-one-nine," the tower advised.

"Right on Bravo, ground point nine," Sam responded as he ratcheted the flap handle up, reached overhead to turn off the pitot heat, and adjusted the radio to ground control frequency. "Ground, Omega 198; clear at Bravo, to gate ten." The transmission ended with a squeal as Mel steered the aircraft across the parallel runway toward the terminal.

The jet bumped to a stop at the gate, and Brad stared fiercely at the back of Mel's head. He knew the guy was jerking his chain. Activity subsided as he stood and spoke with newfound resolve. "Sam, Evan, why don't you both go out and do the walk-around? I need a minute with Mel."

The two junior pilots grabbed hats and scrambled for the exit. Mel glanced over his shoulder with a slight smirk. "What's up?" he asked.

The long pause was deafening. Brad closed the cockpit door, leaned against the back of the copilot seat, purposefully crossed his arms, and stared down at Mel. He took a deep breath and waited even longer, just for effect. "Captain, in my previous life, every member of the team, starting with the leader, debriefed each flight by fessing up to the mistakes we all made. Most of them were indiscernible, but we all knew when we screwed up. Will you please tell me about the mistakes you made? Just from touchdown to the gate will do for now."

"Uh, whattaya mean?"

"You know what I mean. In the time it took us to roll down the runway and taxi to the gate, I counted at least six FAR violations, including the fact that you never had clearance to taxi to the gate."

There was a knock at the door. "Captain, excuse me." The gate agent stuck his head into the cockpit. "The tower would like you to call them on this number, sir." He laid a slip of paper on the flight engineer table and closed the door hurriedly.

"What? We didn't get clearance to the gate?" Mel was incredulous.

"No, damn it! Sam called, but he talked right over another transmission. Didn't you hear the squeal?"

"Jesus Christ! That incompetent SOB!"

"Hold it, hold it, hold it! You are the guy in charge here, Mel!" Brad pointed defiantly at the captain. "If there is any incompetence, it exists because you set the tone of incompetence or, at the very best, nonchalance. You not only fail to hold those guys to a high standard, you don't even hold yourself to a high standard.

"The first day, you started out like gangbusters. Now you've let your guard down. You act like you're drivin' a milk truck around rural Alabama. This is not your grandfather's 727, for Christ's sake. This is serious business, and you, Captain Sprague, are expected to behave like the consummate professional you're paid to be."

Mel's head bobbed like a floating apple. Then he slid his seat back, stood, and grabbed his hat. "Better go give the man a call."

Brad exhaled deeply and shook his head in disgust. Yet he was aware that he had spoken more forcefully than ever before. The ride to the hotel was quiet. *No beer and nachos tonight.*

The next day would provide a new opportunity and possibly the crew's last chance to show they could do the job correctly.

"Okay, guys, new game plan." Brad pulled the door closed and addressed the hapless crew. "I don't have to tell you that things are not going real well. So here are my expectations. Do it by the book! And for God's sake, slow down, just like you did on the first day. This isn't a race—you get paid by the minute. Does anyone here realize that on rollout here yesterday, you all were in violation of FARs? Every one of you got busy reconfiguring the airplane too soon. You are not supposed to touch one damned switch or lever until you are safely clear of the runway. You know that! So get it right, guys."

Brad smoothed the hair on the back of his head and thought for a moment. "What I most want to see is that you're working together as a team. Back each other up. Confirm any time you aren't absolutely certain of anything. Even when you are certain, repeat back a clearance."

Looking at the copilot, he said, "Sam, when ground didn't come back to you with a taxi clearance yesterday, you should have held up your hand and said, 'Hold on a second, Mel. We don't have clearance in.' I know this is a Podunk airport, but you have to behave like it's DFW.

"And Mel, you should have verified with Sam that there was a clearance, that there actually was a response from ground. It sounds so damned simple, and we've come to expect it to flow like clockwork, but communication doesn't occur when we say something; it only happens when we get feedback that what we've said was heard and understood.

Communication 101, guys." He noted the mask of chagrin on their tense faces.

"My apologies, gentlemen." With his job on the line, Mel had obviously given the issue some thought. He turned in his seat to address his two subordinates. "I was sure that incident we had last week in Dallas was a fluke. But judging from what we did here yesterday, there is an obvious trend. We have been dangerous, and my goal is to turn that trend around. I need your help."

Mel's comments were right out of a textbook, and the other two pilots nodded their assent.

"The first thing I'm going to do is listen more." Mel sat silently and looked at his two young charges.

"Uh, yeah, that would help, Mel, and I'll try to give you the best info at the right time," Sam insisted.

"Me, too," Evan added.

"And Brad, you're on the team, too, you know. Please speak up if you see something that isn't right. That work?" he asked earnestly.

"You got it, boss." Brad was relieved.

Thirty-six hours and nine legs later, he dragged himself into Andy Caldwell's office in Memphis. "Brad Morehouse to see Captain Caldwell," he announced to the secretary.

"Oh, hello, Brad. Please have a seat. I'll let Andy know you're here." She glanced to see that the phone was not in use, then knocked on the door and stuck her head in. "Brad More-house to see you."

"Excellent!" Andy's voice boomed. "Get in here, counselor. I can't wait to hear the verdict."

"Mission accomplished, sir." Brad extended a hand and smiled broadly as he stepped into the spacious office.

"No kidding? You really got through to that yahoo?"

"Well, he had his ups and downs."

"Funny. About sixteen, I would guess. Here, have a seat." He motioned to the upholstered chair next to his desk.

Brad settled in and recounted the entire four-day spectacle, including the dramatic turnaround that occurred on the third day. "It wasn't until I went one-on-one with Mel that the light seemed to come on. It was almost fortunate that the crew had that taxi-clearance screwup. That was a degree of incompetence they couldn't rationalize. From that point on, he got the bit about leadership by example—he became a model citizen."

Andy smiled faintly and gazed into the distance. "So, this CRM stuff works, huh?"

"Could be. It really could be."

A grim-faced John Haddington stuck his head into the office. "Sorry to interrupt, Andy, but something important has come up." His flashy silk tie contrasted with the grave look on his face.

"Oh, hi, boss. Come on in," Andy replied with a concerned look. He stood and waved John toward the sofa. "Have you met Brad Morehouse? He just got back from our first CRM intervention. Says it went really well."

"Good job, Brad. Keep up the great work," John commented absently.

An important signal had been sent, and Brad scrambled up to leave. "I'll have the written report to you by tomorrow afternoon, Andy. Happy to meet you, sir," he said hurriedly and exited.

Haddington paced and rubbed the back of his neck as Andy closed the door and returned to his desk. "The damned insurance underwriters have us by the short hairs. The not-so-subtle message is that if we have one more serious pilot screw up, we are toast. Rates would go so high it would drive us under. Worse than that, they have sided with the FAA on the rudder question. No one can prove it, but there is a consensus that the Pasco thing was pilot induced."

"Oh, bullshit!" Andy blurted.

"Of course, Boeing loves that perspective, too," John continued.

"Yeah—surprise, surprise."

Haddington finally collapsed on the sofa. "The worst part may be that even if we could trace the problem to a design flaw, our voice would be drowned out by that triumvirate. They all have a dog in the fight, and we're the juicy bait."

They both sat staring blankly out the window.

Chapter 28

FIRST CRM CLASS

"Elmer Busby, you old horned toad . . . " Raucous conversation wafted from the spacious classroom as thirty pilots milled around five circular tables in Omega's new training complex. "This is my kinda trainin'. No tests, no sim checks, all the doughnuts you can eat, and a bunch of happy talk about how *not* to crash airplanes. How hard can that be?" Jay Snyder joked as he elbowed his way into the continental-breakfast line behind his old pal.

"Damned communist plot is what it is," Elmer growled. "They wanna take away all the captain's authority. Give the copilot and engineer veto power or somethin'. You watch, this is gonna be a goddamned disaster." He squeezed a second sticky bun onto his plate next to a token piece of melon. "I'll go find us a table."

"Hey, Jay, what're you up to?" another voice asked.

"Oh, 'bout five-ten. Used to be six foot 'til they jammed me into that damned Mad Dog. Can hardly breathe in that little cockpit compared to the TriStar."

"Oh, yeah, the price you pay for all that glory. Now you get to make all the decisions." Willy Hillman pretended to stroke the new captain.

"Ha! Once we get this CRM shit goin', it's gonna be nothin', but a group grope up there. Nobody'll be in charge."

Guys jostled one another playfully, maneuvering to fill small paper plates and find a seat. Herman Miller's finest reclining armchairs graced every table, each arrayed with a container of pencils and colored markers, with a bright-red pendant on a twelve-inch stick. Each red flag had bold white lettering that read *Bullshit*. It was meant to be waved in challenge to something strongly disagreeable said in class.

A large backlit screen displayed a colorful slide: "Welcome to Omega CRM. We Love to Fly, and It Shows." At precisely 8:00, just as Brad and Loren Hughes stepped into the room, a pilot jumped up and began waving the red flag and shouting, "Bullshit! Bullshit!" before a single word was uttered. A wave of laughter swept through the room and quickly subsided. Without comment, Brad dimmed the lights and rolled the video. A hush fell over the room as one of Omega's first DC-3s lumbered across the screen to strains of Beethoven's Ninth and the familiar voice of the company's first chief pilot began recounting the growth and progression of his beloved airline.

"In the early days, we'd finish our day at some little town like Monroe, Louisiana, and the captain and copilot would walk into town. The captain got a sleazy motel room. The copilot usually slept in some farmer's barn," he emphasized with a twang.

‥— —‥‥— — —‥‥— — —‥‥— — —‥‥— — —‥‥

He described the newer and bigger jets as they streamed across the screen, all with the distinctive and evolving Omega livery. After several minutes, the warmth and nostalgia gave way to a disturbing montage of airplanes flying into the ground, exploding in flight, or hurtling off the runway into the trees. The eerie music faded, and the screen filled with the words, "We don't come to work expecting to crash an airplane." The familiar face of Captain Jerry Gibbons filled the screen. "I certainly had no intention of crashing my airplane. Quite the opposite, as you can imagine. But notice how things played out for me on that cold and rainy night back in December."

Forty mesmerized faces stared intently at the re-enactment on the screen. Unseen in the back of the room, Jerry watched with the steering committee as his unmistakable image appeared on the screen.

"Omega 435 heavy, right to zero-five-zero and call Atlanta on one-two-two-decimal-six."

"Roger, head zero-five-zero, and Atlanta twenty-two-six, 435 heavy," Jerry responded from the left seat of the giant MD-11.

The copilot dialed the new heading into the flight control panel, and the camera panned to the attitude indicator, showing a slight right turn, as a chime sounded from the overhead. "I'm off," Jerry said to the copilot. "You've got the radios."

"Rog, I got 'em," Bill Sorensen responded. He spun the dial once, then was distracted and obviously failed to complete the frequency change.

Jerry grabbed the interphone handset. "This is Jerry. What's up?"

"Jerry, this is Maureen. Hey, we're smellin' smoke here in the front lav. It seems like I can almost see it seeping out of the wall between the lav and the cockpit."

"Not good," Jerry responded. "Hang on, I'll send Monty back."

"Monty, step back there and see what you think. Maureen says there's smoke in the front lav."

"I'm gone." Monty Wilson, the relief pilot, bolted out of the jump seat and into the cabin.

"Bill, I've got the airplane." Jerry put both hands on the yoke and nodded to the copilot. "You keep the radios."

Bill raised both hands and said, "Roger, you've got the aircraft Jerry, and I've got the radios."

"Hey, take a look there," Jerry said, pointing at the screen of the flight management system (FMS). "If we have to do a high-dive, what looks like the best place to go?"

"Uh, let me see, we're about fifty short of Richmond."
"Good, let's count on that. I've been in there dozens of times."

Ding, ding. Bill quickly punched the button to unlock the cockpit door.

Monty rushed into the cockpit and leaned on the back of the captain's seat. "Jerry, she's right. There's smoke in there, and the wall is hot. This is the real deal!"

"Shit! Okay, guys, let's do this. Monty, you jump in there," he said, pointing at the copilot seat, "and Bill, you work with Maureen to fight the fire if it really erupts."

"All right." Bill looked skeptical as he triggered the motor to drive the seatback. "You've got the radios." He motioned to Jerry as he attempted to remove his headset, which became tangled in his flight bag. He wrestled with it for a moment, then leaned forward to release the pressure on the cord and flipped it off his head to the right. He unbuckled and jumped out of the seat.

In the classroom, Elmer Busby squirmed in his seat. All eyes were riveted on the screen as several pilots gnawed on a knuckle, all-knowing they were watching a disaster in the making.

"Atlanta, Omega 435," Jerry spoke calmly into his lip mike. There was no response.

"Atlanta, Omega 435, over." Still nothing.

"God damn it, did we miss that frequency change?"

"Shit, my fault, boss." Bill slapped his head and leaned over the control panel to dial in the frequency.

"What was it again?"

"Damned if I know—the interphone rang just as we shoulda switched."

"Shit!"

"Give me a second here, boss." Monty struggled to free his feet from the headset cord.

"Guys, we've gotta go down," Jerry said urgently. "Put 7700 in the transponder, Monty. We can't wait to get clearance."

The discomfort in the classroom mounted. Elmer rolled his eyes and looked at the ceiling. They had all been there at one time or another, struggling for an answer and knowing that the wrong move could spell disaster. Now they watched as the number one guy in the MD-11 fleet fumbled and bumbled into a nightmare.

On the screen, Jerry frantically keyed data into the FMS while Monty dialed 7700 into the transponder. The 7700 code would cause an emergency blip to appear on the air traffic controller's radar panel. *There'd be no goin' back now.*

The following ten minutes seemed like an hour, with every miscue caught in the probing eye of the camera. Lightning flashed, and the cockpit rocked with turbulence as the hapless trio plunged resolutely toward a landing in Richmond.

Every observer knew the mayhem caused by a NORDO (no radio) aircraft descending through the busy north-south corridor along the Atlantic coast. And those same observers cringed at the confused and inept performance of this crew. A collective chill and reluctant knowledge swept through the room. *Ah, there but for the grace of God—*

At length, a semblance of order returned as radio contact was restored, and Jerry maneuvered to intercept the final approach course for runway 34 in Richmond. All three pilots had donned smoke masks and goggles. Conversation was clipped and muffled as they completed checklists and prepared to land their jumbo jet on the relatively short, dark, and rain-soaked runway.

"Omega 435 heavy, Richmond tower. Cleared to land runway three-four. Wind two-seven-zero at one-five, gusting two-zero. The equipment is standing by, gentlemen. Say your intentions."

Monty looked at Jerry.

"We'll evacuate." Jerry's speech was nearly unintelligible in the smoke-mask interphone.

The observers all knew the drill. In the sim, you let the aircraft impact the runway. No style points awarded for a smooth touchdown, and with a heavy airplane and relatively short runway, it was essential to get it on the ground and get the reversers in. There was a significant jolt, the nose came down hard, and Jerry's right hand ripped at the reverser levers. The cockpit pitched forward, and the aircraft slowed rapidly.

"Eighty knots," Monty said as he pulled the mask away from his face. "Sixty, forty, thirty, twenty," he said as they shuddered to a stop.

Jerry reached forward and set the brake, then picked up the microphone. "Evacuate, evacuate, evacuate! I say again, evacuate, evacuate, evacuate." The screen went dark as the class released a collective sigh. Several wiped sweat from their brows, but most stared solemnly at nothing in particular.

The lights finally flickered on. The "Welcome" message returned to the screen as Loren Hughes—without his signature cowboy boots—stepped to the front of the class. "Yes, welcome to Omega CRM, gentlemen. My name is Loren Hughes. Joining me is Brad Morehouse." He pointed to Brad, who smiled and saluted casually. "For the next day and a half, we're going to take you through a series of exercises and discussions intended to both alter attitudes and create some new skill sets necessary to function more effectively in our complex working environment." He paused thoughtfully, right hand on his chin.

"We are *teams* out there, guys, and there is ample evidence that many of our teams—maybe even people you know—are not performing at the highest level."

"Yeah, 'we're *learning* to fly—and it shows.'" A burst of laughter erupted in the classroom as the perpetrator slid down in his chair.

Loren shook his head ruefully. "Maybe we should change the slide." He nodded at the screen behind him. Then, to Brad, he said, "Make a note of that, *garçon*."

The tittering continued. Loren smiled and pressed on. "Ordinarily, at this point, we will be asking each table to compile a list of the crew errors you saw in the video, but today we'll get it right from the horse's mouth." He motioned to the back of the room. "Jerry?"

Heads swiveled abruptly as Jerry Gibbons stood and worked his way toward the front, shaking a few hands and slapping some backs. The most senior check pilot in the entire company had lost some of his Lee Marvin swagger. There was a stoop in his shoulders, and a weary-executive look replaced the sky-god glimmer.

"You got the wrong end of the horse there, Loren." He smiled and shook Loren's hand, then turned toward the class. "How does the old saying go? If it looks like shit and smells like shit, you can be pretty sure . . . " He nodded and grimaced simultaneously.

"I guess the first point I want to make, guys, is that this *can* happen to any of us, and at this famous—now infamous—captains' airline, we have neglected the basics of good teamwork for way too long. It takes more than Larry, Curly, and Moe—though we did a pretty good imitation, you have to admit. Anyway, it takes a better team than the Three Stooges to operate one of our aircraft in the safest and most efficient way possible, and like it or not, ladies and gentlemen," he paused and gently wagged a finger, "we are talking about great management skills. Boring stuff. Not the old stick-and-rudder heroics. We have to leave the derring-do and white silk scarf to Snoopy and his Sopwith Camel and get serious about managing our way to safety."

Heads bobbed. God had spoken, and it registered on the pilots' somber faces. Jerry went on to tick off the errors. "I flew solo up there. Why I chose to have Bill and Monty swap seats, I will never understand. In reality, Bill was probably the most competent guy in the cockpit because he had just come out of training, and he'd been a 767ER copilot before that. The swap cost us valuable time and shattered our continuity."

Jerry's painful enumeration was punctuated with vexing questions and penetrating insights. Finally, in closing, he delivered the *coup de grâce*. "Here is the worst part, folks." He held up a hand while the chatter subsided. "This didn't make the news, but you're hearing it right from the horse's . . . whatever. When the passengers went down those slides, they went sprawling all over the tarmac. We were still dumping fuel, and it was a slippery, stinky, sickening, dangerous mess out there. My fault."

His audience sat silently. Thirty seconds elapsed. "And with that, my dear friends," he said with a sigh, "I implore each and every one of you, regardless of your aircraft type or seat position, to put your hearts and souls into this program."

He stared at the floor for a moment, then looked up.

"Folks, you must know this, but I'll say it one more time since I seem to have your attention. The very fate of our airline depends on a much higher standard of performance than we've been delivering out there. We don't get any more chances. The FAA, the media, insurance underwriters, and, most of all, the traveling public are expecting much more from us. And I, for one, intend to deliver." He shook Loren's hand, nodded to Brad, and walked out of the room to thunderous applause.

"No commies so far," Elmer whispered to himself.

Chapter 29

CALAMITY

Brad chuckled to himself at the *Live Nude Buns* marquee over the porno shop on Century Boulevard as the Hilton van backtracked to the hotel entrance. It was June 20, he was on his third trip of the month, and he had finally reached his comfort zone in the 737. But it had taken a while. Like an all-star baseball player changing positions from first baseman to catcher, his job required a whole new perspective. The game was the same, but his view of things was much more comprehensive.

The long layover in L.A. was a welcome respite from early departures the past two days. Three crews, a Texas oil executive, an IBM suit, and four Japanese tourists tumbled off the bus and ambled through the spacious lobby. "Well, you're on your own tonight, Brad," the captain commented as they waited in line at the crew sign-in desk. "My parents live down in Laguna. I'm gonna rent a car and get outta here before the traffic piles up on the 405."

"No problem, boss. I'm gonna hit the gym and take in the scenery out at the pool."

Ten minutes later, there was a knock at the door as he pulled on his shorts and tucked in a gray Seahawks T-shirt. "Room service," a strong, familiar voice beckoned from the hallway.

She stood there, almost defiantly, a roller bag, hanger bag and big tote arranged neatly at her feet. "I was just in the neighborhood; thought I'd stop by."

He was stunned. "Uh, buh, uh ... come in, Sarah, please." He regained his composure and reached to help with her luggage. "What are you doing here? Are you headed out on a trip?"

"Yeah, I leave at 11:40 tomorrow morning: Phoenix-L.A.-Seattle. I was hoping I could ride to the airport with you."

"You're on my trip? You're working that trip?" Brad's heart thumped frantically against his ribcage. He dropped the bags in the closet alcove and turned to face her. She stood staring earnestly at him, a red-checkered blouse tied neatly across her midriff, white shorts, and platform sandals accentuating her magnificent legs.

"I'm running away from home. Thought maybe I'd go with you as far as Seattle and see what comes up." She stepped into the spacious room and ran her fingers across the bedspread. "Two beds, two people, plenty of space to hang out here 'til morning." She continued her penetrating stare.

"Wait, what? Whattaya mean you left home? Where are the kids? What about your husband?"

"I took the kids to my parents' in Woodland Hills. Left Rob a note saying that I wasn't coming home."

"What?"

"Brad, don't worry." She held up a hand. "This has been brewing for a long time now. Rob is a very angry and unhappy man. I can't deny it any longer. It isn't good for the kids, and it certainly isn't good for me. You aren't responsible for making me do something stupid. Honestly."

"Well, I—" nothing else came out as he wrestled to comprehend. Finally, Brad breathed deeply, and a broad smile spread across his face. "Welcome my, lady. I am truly honored." He bowed and swept an arm toward the table by the window. "Please join me."

"I come prepared, m'lord." She grabbed her tote and tiptoed across the room. "For our reading enjoyment." She retrieved her copy of *The Prophet*. "And for medicinal purposes." She extracted a bottle of Sokol Blosser Chardonnay and two delicate glasses. "Should your hunger persist." She displayed a cellophane bag of gourmet mixed nuts. "And finally, if for some reason the electricity fails us." She produced three small scented candles.

"Prepared indeed." Brad motioned for her to sit as Sarah looked deeply into his eyes, then settled elegantly into the chair. "May I?" He held the wine for her approval.

"Please," she responded and rummaged in her bag for the corkscrew.

The bottle was perfectly chilled, and the cork emitted a pleasant *pop*. He poured ceremoniously. "Welcome to your new life." He toasted and looked down at her expectantly.

"Maybe *our* new life," she countered with a twinkle Brad couldn't miss.

They savored the oaky nectar in silence, gazing out as one silent jet after another drifted toward the unseen Los Angeles runway. Then, without a word, she rose and slipped into his lap. "May I?" She touched a finger to his lips.

"Please," he said and embraced her hungrily.

Tangled together in the morning light, they lay spent in each other's arms.

"Breakfast?" he finally inquired.

"Yes, I'm ravenous."

"I noticed."

A pillow muffled his protest as she lunged full length across his head. His hand between her legs elicited a squeal and frantic squirm followed by an explosion of unrestrained laughter. "Yes . . . breakfast. You want me to call?" she asked, exhaling gleefully.

"Yeah. A Denver omelet, orange juice, and coffee."

She made the call, and they nibbled at each other as they waited. They ate contentedly when the food arrived.

"Can we be serious for a minute?" He dabbed marmalade on his toast and held her gaze.

"Sure."

"So what happens now that Rob has found your note?"

"Well, first of all, he may not have found the note yet.

This is a race day for him, and he wasn't planning to come home last night. He knows the kids are with my parents during my trip. And second, I don't think he cares. He doesn't like me very much anymore. We don't really fight; we simply have different interests and priorities—different friends, even. The fact is, I don't know Rob at all."

"Hmm." He rubbed his chin thoughtfully, then gave in to an irrepressible smile. "Lucky me."

Suspended in a euphoric haze, Brad maneuvered the jet over San Diego along the Ocean-One Arrival to Los Angeles. A local weather system had developed during the night, with gusty winds and driving rain from the east toward the coast.

In the back, Sarah nimbly steadied herself as she moved down the aisle of the buffeting 737. Brad would be pleased to know that she, too, was giddy with the fervor of their new love. "Alan, why don't you go ahead and set us up for the ILS to seven-right?" Brad asked.

"Will do." Alan Conrad, the captain, consulted his approach plate and made the necessary adjustments to the flight management system and mode control panel. "Okay, Brad, you're set. You want me to take the aircraft?"

"Yes, please." Brad provided the required description of the present flight regime. "We are tracking into Oceanside, descending out of two-three for seventeen, 300 knots. You've got the airplane." He motioned with both hands toward the captain.

"I have the airplane," Alan confirmed with both hands on the yoke.

Brad busied himself confirming the computer inputs and manual setup, then completed the detailed brief that enumerated all of the critical procedures, checkpoints, and expectations.

"It looks like they want us to use Bakersfield as an alternate; the weather in Palmdale looks okay, too. So why don't I take the airplane back, and we do the descent checklist?"

The formal exchange occurred once again, and the checklist was completed as they leveled at 17,000 feet.

"Omega 425, descend to one-zero-thousand and contact approach on one-two-eight-decimal-five."

"Descending to ten, and approach on twenty-eight-five, Omega 425. Good day," Alan responded as he spun the dials on the second radio head and flipped the switch.

The clipped conversation continued rapid-fire, as they completed the descent and approach checklists. The auto throttles cycled constantly to maintain airspeed in the gusty conditions. Brad monitored a dozen key factors simultaneously, noting they were descending just north of Catalina Island, still in the clouds.

"Omega 425, descend to 3,000, turn right zero-two-zero, cleared ILS seven-right, and tower one-three-three-niner at FUMBL."

"Jesus, three items is my max," Alan complained in jest to Brad. Then, on the radio, "Okay, let me see if I got all that. Omega 425 is descending to 3,000, turning right to zero-two-zero." He pointed to both the altitude window where Brad had set the descent altitude and the heading window showing zero-two-zero. "Cleared for approach seven-right, tower at FUMBL, Omega 425."

"All correct, 425. You guys have a great day," the controller responded with a chuckle.

"They're givin' us a really short turn-in. You're gonna need the boards to get down."

"Yeah, I can see that," Brad responded as he clicked off the auto-throttles, reduced the power to idle, and reached for the speed-brake handle. "Goin' down and slowin' down at the same time defies logic." They both smirked as the rumble from the speed brakes began.

"Looks like you are about three miles from the intercept and six miles from TIMSE. I don't know why they always give us such a short final when they're landing to the east. Damn it!" Alan said.

"Good practice, boss. They don't even run it this tight in the sim." Brad scrambled to simultaneously accomplish everything—slowing down, leveling off, intercepting the final approach course, and configuring the aircraft for approach.

"CDI is alive."

Brad turned farther to the right and waited for the auto-pilot to capture the inbound course.

"Here comes TIMSE," Alan reported.

"Roger. Gear down, flaps twenty-five. Give me flaps thirty. Before-landing checklist," Brad requested.

"Okay, glide slope's alive, glideslope capture. Technically, you are only cleared down to 1,800 until FUMBL, so I'll put that in the window. You'll need to reengage the approach mode at FUMBL. Here comes the landing checklist."

"Holy shit!" Brad bellowed as the airplane snapped into a seventy-degree bank turn to the right. Wailing from the auto-pilot-disconnect warning system split their ears as Brad struggled to regain control. "It's that goddamned hard-over rudder, Alan. I've gotta reduce power on the left!" He pulled the left power lever toward idle and slammed the speed-brake handle down.

··· — — —···— — —···— — —···— — —···— — —···— — —···

"Get max power on that right side, Brad, we're going down!" Alan bellowed.

Brad ran the power up on the right engine, but the aircraft continued rolling to the right. "Flaps fifteen, gear up! We've gotta go on over, Alan," he barked as he snapped the right power lever to idle. "Flaps five."

"Jesus, Brad, you're gonna kill us!"

"No, no, hang on, boss. It's the only way to get back to level." They were ninety degrees of bank, one wing pointing straight down and the other straight up. They were about to roll over in the most perilous maneuver an airline crew had ever attempted. Gradin, Pasco, and the photo of the twisted 737 flashed through Brad's mind. *Fall out of the sky or make lemonade* were the only options available.

"Oh, fuck," Alan whispered as he pressed back in his seat and stared through the eyebrow window in the overhead panel. Debris from the floor ricocheted all over the cockpit as the aircraft rolled hard to the right.

"Call my speed and altitude!" Brad shouted.

"Omega 425, approach. Say your intentions," the frantic controller called.

"Uh," Alan looked back at the instrument panel. "One-eighty and increasing rapidly. Two thousand. Jesus God!"

The roll rate increased as the nose fell below the horizon. Brad felt for the optimum control input as he stared at the artificial horizon while the world spun crazily around them. *Too much backpressure and the wings will come off,* he thought.

The few unbuckled passengers tumbled, and people screamed as the aircraft continued its corkscrew revolution in the sky. An infant dangled by one leg clenched fiercely in her mother's left hand as someone cushioned her head from slamming on the sidewall.

"Two-twenty, 1,200—you're seventy degrees left bank now."

The windshield filled with the angry dark ocean as the roll toward level slowed, and Brad eased power back up on the right engine.

"Two-fifty, 800 feet"—above the fiercely churning sea. "Okay, we're back to level." Brad panted as he steadied the yoke full-throw to the left.

"You want the flaps up?" Alan deferred to Brad completely now. The copilot was the leader in this instance—the situational leader—just as they'd emphasized in class.

"No, we may have damaged those actuators. Let's just leave 'em at five and live with it. I think we can maintain wings level at 240. You'd better get back to approach and declare an emergency."

"Oh, yeah, okay." Alan was nearly incapacitated with fear as he fumbled for the dangling microphone. "Uh, approach, Omega 425. Uh, we just experienced an upset. We're declaring an emergency, over."

"Omega 425, approach. Roger, we observed that. Say your intentions, please."

"Stand by." The captain sat bewildered.

"Alan, it looks like we can climb very gradually if I trade a little airspeed for nose attitude." Brad manipulated the yoke ever so slightly to achieve a gradual climb. "Damn. As the airspeed bleeds off, I lose aileron authority." The right wing dipped slightly but stabilized. "If we can just hold this bank angle, we can get some altitude back."

"Yeah, but then what? We have no chance of getting this sucker on the ground, at least not on the runway." Alan threw up his hands in despair.

"American 99, SoCal approach. Make an immediate left turn heading two-seven-zero, climb, and maintain one-zero thousand, over." The routine radio transmissions continued.

"Roger, American 99 turning two-seven-zero, climbing to ten."

Brad strained to hold the control column fully deflected to the left. He could see that, with full deflection, at precisely 180 knots, he could achieve a 300-foot-per-minute climb. *Jesus, ten minutes to climb just 3,000 feet,* he realized. At the moment, they were below a thousand feet, in heavy rain showers, and the strain of holding the yoke was beginning to show.

"Start workin' toward 2,000 feet, Brad. I've got to get you some help up here."

"What?"

Alan released his grip on the yoke long enough to toggle the radio select switch to the interphone position, and hit the flight attendant call button.

"This is Kathy in the back," a terrified voice answered. "Kathy, this is Alan. We're going to be okay, so I need you to reassure the passengers. But right now, get Mario to come up here immediately. The door will be unlocked."

"Okay."

He resumed a two-handed grip on the yoke and strained for greater throw to the left. "Let me hold this a minute, Brad. Take a quick break." Alan had regained his composure.

Reluctantly, Brad released pressure and shook his arms to restore circulation. "You want me to tell approach what's goin' on?"

"Hang on a second; we need to get Mario involved here. Keep an eye on the VSI for me."

With two knocks, the door opened, and a muscular young flight attendant burst into the cockpit. "How can I help, Captain?" Mario was wiping his bloody hands on his pants, his eyes as big as silver dollars.

"Goddamn. Are you okay?"

"Yeah, yeah, I'm fine. It's Sarah. She got launched into a galley door when we snapped to the right. Hit her head. She's bleeding pretty bad. I think she's unconscious." He glanced sympathetically at Brad.

"Shit!" Alan spat.

Brad clenched his jaw, stared back at the instrument panel, and seized the yoke with a death grip. "I'm back on here, Alan." The image of Sarah fueled his blazing resolve.

"Okay, Mario, look. Our rudder just slammed all the way to the right. It won't move. If we get full aileron throw to the left along with full power on the right engine"—he pointed at the right power lever in the full-forward position and the flight controls deflected all the way to the left—"we can hold this shallow bank and climb very slowly." He motioned toward the needle of the VSI showing a 300-foot-per-minute climb. "It's an absolute bitch to hold that much aileron, and I need you to help. Get yourself situated so that you can hold the yoke. It doesn't matter if you sit on that center console; you won't hurt anything. Lean over here and get hold of this right side of the yoke." Alan pointed to the control wheel in front of the captain's seat.

Mario leaned forward, rested his right elbow on the left-forward edge of the center console, and grabbed the yoke.

●●● ━ ━ ●━●●● ━ ━ ━ ●●● ━ ━ ━ ●●● ━ ━ ━ ●●━●●● ━ ━ ━ ●●● ━ ━ ━ ●●●

"Whoa!" Alan gripped the yoke fiercely as the plane wobbled. "This is going to be real tricky because you can't apply any pressure either forward or backward on the yoke. You've got to follow along with Brad and at the same time, give us max throw to the left."

"Okay." Mario pushed the yoke to the left and looked at Brad for feedback.

"Good, that's it," Brad responded with a nod.

"Now guys, here's what I think we need to do. First, keep climbin' this sucker as high as we can get. Correct me if I'm wrong, Brad, but it seems to me that once we have some altitude, we can reduce power on that right engine and establish a higher than normal speed, gradual descent straight ahead. Am I thinkin' about that, right?"

"I think you're right. Get up here a little higher, and we can try it out."

"All right, so that's step one. There is no chance of landing in L.A. without goin' off the end of the runway into rush-hour traffic on the 405 or slammin' into the terminal. Same at Long Beach or Ontario. The weather in Palmdale is good. We need to get over there and make a space shuttle approach to a million miles of runway at Edwards."

"Good call, boss. I've been in there, and there's nothin' to hit for miles around," Brad confirmed.

"Mario?" Alan inquired.

"Uh, well, yeah. I'm just along for the ride here, guys," Mario responded through clenched teeth.

"How's your arm?"

"I'm only good for three more hours." He grimaced. "Okay, here we go.

"Approach, Omega 425 is declaring an emergency with a hard-over rudder. We can only turn right, and we are limited to a 300-foot-per-minute climb, over."

"Omega 425, roger. Understand you are declaring an emergency. Say your intentions," the controller replied.

"Approach, 425, we'll need to climb in our present position, then we're requesting clearance direct to Edwards Air Force Base. Our only chance is a long straight-in to a *very* long runway," Alan said emphatically.

"Roger, 425. Say souls on board and fuel remaining, please."

Alan shuffled through the paperwork. "Eighty-six souls and, let's see here, one-point-eight hours of fuel, over."

"Approach, 425, stand by, please. I'll be back with you in a couple of minutes." Alan reached down and selected PA on the radio panel. "Kathy to the cockpit, please," he said in his most soothing voice. "Brad, let me take it for a minute. Catch your breath. But hey, monitor the climb, too, will ya?"

"Yup."

"I'm here, Alan." Kathy squeezed into the cockpit. "What can I do?"

"How's everybody in back? What about Sarah?"

"There's a doctor tending to her right now. I really don't know anything. The passengers are doing pretty well, though they are certainly aware that we have a big problem with the cockpit door open like that."

"Oh, God, I didn't think about that. Well, here's the deal. We have a hard-over rudder, which means that we can't do anything but make continuous right-hand turns. We're out over the ocean west of LAX. We are climbing very slowly, and when we get enough altitude, we can descend slowly and fly straight ahead. We're gonna go over to Edwards Air Force Base in the desert. The weather is clear there."

"Alan, we are at 2,000 now," Brad said.

"Good, keep climbing. So, Kathy, Edwards has an extremely long runway—that's where they land the space shuttle sometimes—so we can land fast and roll forever without hitting anything. You're gonna have to do everything in back by yourself. That okay?"

"Sure. Everyone is already buckled in, ready for impact." She smiled faintly.

"Well, use your best bedside manner. Let 'em know that this is all gonna work out fine. And hey, why don't you close that door when you go? We'll leave it unlocked."

"Okay, give me as much warning as you can for landing."

"Will do; thanks. Mario, how ya doin'?"

"No problem, Alan."

"Here, let me give you a little break." Alan grabbed the controls tightly.

"Thanks." Mario stood, shook his hands, and arched his back. "You okay, Brad?" he inquired with a hand on his shoulder.

"Yeah, buddy. Good job!" Brad remained focused. "Approaching 3,000, Alan."

"Good. Let's go on up to six. That'll take another ten minutes. Then we can take our first vector toward Edwards."

The wrestling match with the stricken airplane continued as Omega 425 limped through the pelting rain and wind off the coast of Santa Monica. At length, they reached 6,000 feet, and Alan spoke to the controller. "Approach, Omega 425 requesting a vector for Edwards and descent to 3,000, over."

···—— ——···—— ——— ···—— ——— ···—— ——— ···—— ——— ···—— ——···

"Omega 425, approach, roger. Fly heading zero-one-zero, descend and maintain 3,000, over."

"Roger, 425 heading zero-one-zero, descending to 3,000."

"Okay, Brad, you ready for this? Keep that turn in, and as you pass north, I'll begin reducing power. Let's keep the flaps at five and do all of this at 180. That way we won't have to deal with any new variables."

"Wait, Alan, I've got an idea," Brad responded breathlessly.

"Okay, what?"

"Let's get established on that vector, then I'll tell you."

"Right. I have zero-one-zero dialed into our CDI. Here comes three-five-zero, there's north, reducing power. How's that?"

"Yeah, I can hold wings level, but look at this," he said as he released some back pressure on the yoke and allowed the airspeed to increase to 190. "The faster we go, the less aileron it takes."

"Wow, you're right," Alan agreed. "So okay, let it accelerate to two-ten, and we'll stay with flaps five. Does that sound good?"

"Yeah."

"At this rate, we'll cover about eighteen miles before we need to climb again, right?"

"Yeah, but check this," Brad ventured as he eased back on the yoke imperceptibly and added a little power on the right side. "We can maintain altitude, maybe even climb a little."

"Oh, baby, you done broke da' code. Hot damn!" Alan exclaimed.

"Hey, Mario, reach over here and hold this position. Can you do that?"

"No problem." Mario repositioned himself over the center console and gripped the yoke again.

Brad threw his head back and shook his arms vigorously. "Goddamn," was all he could muster as he wiped the sweat from his forehead.

"Good job, Mario," Alan said, following along on the controls as his new second mate stared at the attitude indicator and made small adjustments.

"Approach, Omega 425, over." Alan spoke with renewed confidence.

"Omega 425, go ahead, sir."

"Approach, 425, requesting a climb to one-zero-thousand."

"Sure. Uh, Omega 425, climb and maintain one-zero-thousand, present heading, direct Edwards. You got things under control up there?" The controller was baffled.

"Yes, sir, enough that we can maintain heading and climb very slowly. D'you have the current Edwards weather, over?"

"Roger, 425. Edwards weather: clear, temperature seven-five, wind zero-seven-zero at one-five, altimeter two-niner-niner-eight."

"Thanks. Have you notified them of our intentions?"

"Affirmative, 425. I'll plan to turn you over to Edwards at the top of your climb. They'll have the equipment standing by. Over."

"Roger."

"Alaska six-oh-one, Coast approach on one-two-eight-decimal-five."

"Roger, Alaska six-oh-one, one-two-eight-five, good day."

Brad was vaguely aware of the normalcy around them as the controller maintained the constant chatter with other aircraft while providing emergency assistance to them. There was a big picture to maintain, and he could see Alan shift his attention to the remaining details of their flight.

"Brad, Mario, how're your arms? You both okay?"

"Yeah, yeah, good," they responded.

"Okay, hang in there while I get caught up here. And by the way, you're passing five for one-zero thousand."

He grabbed the folded card and ran through the after-take-off and climb checklists. When he got to fuel, he paused for a moment. "Whattaya think? We're at about twelve on the fuel. Leave more in the left side to help counter the yaw?"

"Yeah, good idea," Brad responded.

"Okay, I'm gonna turn on this altitude alert light to remind us."

"Rog."

"I'd better talk to the folks. Can you handle the radios, Brad?"

"Yeah, sure."

Alan toggled the PA switch, caught his breath, and spoke with all the calm and authority he could muster. "Ladies and gentlemen, this is Captain Conrad speaking. As you are undoubtedly aware, we have experienced some difficulty with our flight controls. We are currently climbing on a northeasterly heading toward Palmdale, where the weather is clear.

"The flight control problem we have will require that we land with a higher than normal airspeed, and for that reason, our intention is to proceed to Edwards Air Force Base, where they have an exceptionally long runway complex.

"We expect to arrive at Edwards in approximately fifteen minutes. Please give your full and undivided attention to Kathy as she prepares the cabin for landing."

"Short and sweet," Alan commented to the other two as he clicked off the PA mike.

"Yeah, but you forgot the part about 'Thanks for flying Omega.'"

"Ha! We're out of seven climbing to ten."

The airplane lurched, and Brad struggled to right it. "Oops, sorry, guys. My hand is so sweaty I can hardly hang on," Mario apologized, quickly wiped his hand, then gripped the yoke firmly again.

"Let me take it a minute; you need a break." Alan anchored himself in position and also grabbed the yoke. "I've got it."

"Whew. Ahhhh." Brad slipped down in the seat, and alternately rubbed each arm. "I think we are high enough now, Alan. We're only thirty miles south of Edwards. We should be able to start a gradual descent and get lined up on the lake bed while we're still a long way out. Whattaya think?"

"Good idea. Will you coordinate with ATC? I'll hang on here for a while so you can be fresh for landing."

"Fresh, my ass." He scrunched his face in pain. "But yeah, I'll give 'em a call. Approach, Omega 425, we'd like to stop our climb here at seven and switch to Edwards to set up for landing."

"Roger, 425. Contact Edwards approach on one-two-five-decimal-one. They know you're coming."

"Okay, Edwards, on one-twenty-five-one. Thanks for your help today."

"You're welcome, 425. Nice job, and good luck, guys."

Brad spun the knobs on the radio control panel and spoke. "Hello, Edwards approach, Omega 425, twenty-five-south for emergency landing on the lake bed, over."

"Hello 425, we've been expecting you. Squawk two-three-seven-six, turn right zero-four-zero, and descend at your discretion, over."

"There you go." Brad dialed in the new transponder code.

"Radar contact 425," the controller responded.

"Roger." Then, "Alan, you want some power off?"

"Yeah, try it about halfway back."

Brad pulled smoothly on the power lever. "You guys doing okay? How're your arms?"

"No problem. I'm good," Mario insisted.

"I'm okay 'til you wanna take over, Brad," Alan said. Then, looking up, he added, "Nice to be outta the clouds. I've got Edwards in sight up there to the left."

"In sight," Brad responded.

"Omega 425, Edwards, can you tell me a little more about the nature of your problem? Over."

"Roger, our rudder is jammed full right. We are compensating with as much left aileron as possible, along with differential power and increased airspeed. We plan to touch down above 180 knots, and as we slow, we'll likely drift to the right. But don't count on an air show."

"Okay, 425, in that case, we'll line you up to land north. You'll have several miles of lake bed out in front and off to the right. Do you anticipate evacuating the aircraft, sir?"

"Not unless there's a chance of fire," Brad responded as Alan nodded his concurrence.

"Understand, sir, thank you," the controller said.

"Alan, I can see the outline of the lake-bed runway."

"Yup, I see it."

"Approach, 425. What do you show as our distance from the touchdown zone?" Brad asked.

▪▪▪ ▬ ▬ ▪▪▪▪ ▬ ▬ ▬ ▪▪▪▪ ▬ ▬ ▬ ▪▪▪ ▬ ▬ ▬ ▪▪▪ ▬ ▬ ▬ ▬ ▬ ▪▪▪

"Two zero miles, sir. We show you out of 6,300. Edwards' field elevation is 2,300. Current wind is three-five-zero at two-zero, and Omega 425, you are cleared to land; the equipment is standing by."

"Roger, cleared to land, 425," Brad responded tersely. "You want me to take it now, Alan?"

"Yeah, let's do that. Let me get Mario off the controls first. Mario, you can let go; I have a good grip."

Mario exhaled deeply and drooped forward.

"Great job." Brad patted his back. "How does it feel, Alan?"

"Not bad. In this configuration, I think we're okay. Let's count on the gear at a thousand feet. I'll give you some extra power at that point. You ready?"

"Yeah," Brad said as he squirmed into an upright position and gripped the yoke. "I've got the airplane, boss; let's run the checklists."

"You've got it." Then, "Mario, head back there and tell Kathy we have about three minutes to touchdown. Make sure she is in the back, and you are upfront here. I'll give a 'brace' command a few seconds prior to touchdown, and if evacuation is necessary, I will command it. Any questions?"

"No, I'm on my way. Great job, you guys!"

"Okay, checklists." Alan meticulously covered every item. "Winds again, please," he transmitted to the controller.

"Three-five-zero at two-two," came the terse reply.

"Okay, that's good," he said to Brad. "A left crosswind will help us on rollout. And by the way—you're probably way ahead of me on this—the power equation will reverse on touchdown. Once you have the nosewheel down, get the reversers in, but only use the left one. *Left* reverser, got it?" Then, "No, on second thought, you've got to hold that aileron in. I'll get the reverser deployed, then you can have 'em as we slow. That work?"

"Yup."

"Approaching a thousand. Ready for the gear?"

"Gear down," Brad commanded calmly.

"Roger, gear comin' down, and here comes some more power on the right. Oops, watch your sink. Shoot for about 190 knots."

Brad adjusted the nose attitude minutely and maintained a speed fifty knots faster than normal.

"Lookin' good. Checklist complete; cleared to land."

"Roger, cleared to land," Brad responded out of habit.

"Two hundred." Several seconds elapsed. "One hundred, steady as she goes. Touchdown. One-ninety, one-eighty, one-sixty—here come the reversers—one-forty, beautiful."

"Okay, we're driftin' right; here comes the left reverse," Brad said calmly.

"One hundred, eighty, sixty, forty. Okay, I've got it, Brad. Take the rest of the day off."

"Hmph," Brad responded as his thoughts returned to Sarah. "Five, four, three, two, one," and the aircraft came to a stop.

"The APU is up. Shut 'em down."

Brad pushed the fuel control levers down and began unbuckling.

"Remain seated, remain seated, this is the captain speaking, remain seated." Alan spoke calmly on the PA. Then, to Brad, "Go check on Sarah. I'll get the checklist."

Brad rushed out of the cockpit and was greeted with loud applause and cheering. Sarah was stretched out on the floor of the front galley, her head in the lap of a distinguished-looking woman. "I'm Doctor Syrenap. She'll be fine."

"Thank you, Doctor." He knelt beside her, and Sarah's eyes blinked as she attempted to focus. They fixed on his face in recognition. "Brad? What happened?"

"You fell and bumped your head, silly. You're going to be fine." He squeezed her hand gratefully, and she smiled.

Chapter 30

EXONERATION

"Ground, Omega 425, request." Alan's voice broke the radio silence. "Ground, 425, we're gonna need your help with several injured passengers and with the transport of all passengers to a comfortable holding area, over."

"Uh, 425, roger. I'll notify the command post of your request."

Brad stepped back into the cockpit. "Sarah's okay. Good doc attending her. The other flight attendants have things under control in the cabin. Amazingly, we only seem to have four or five minor injuries. Just bumps and bruises. I told them to keep everybody seated until we get some buses out here."

"Good job." Alan held up a hand. "Ground, 425 again."

"Go ahead, 425," the controller responded.

Alan requested that a mobile stair unit be brought to the aircraft. Then, to Brad, he said, "Give me another second."

Brad nodded as Alan spoke into the public address microphone. "Ladies and gentlemen, this is the captain. I want to both congratulate you and apologize to you." He paused. "Congratulations on being among the first passengers to ever complete an aerobatic roll in a transport aircraft. You may be gratified to know that the pilot at the controls, my copilot Brad Morehouse, is a former Navy Blue Angel. I have no doubt that the safe outcome of our E-ticket ride was a result of Brad's extraordinary skill"—he paused and looked Brad in the eye—"and leadership.

"For the record, we experienced an uncommanded full deflection of the rudder, which caused that initial abrupt roll to the right. Brad immediately recognized that the only way to regain stable flight was to continue the roll, as we did. With increased airspeed, we were able to keep the wings level and land here at Edwards, where the runway is miles long. That allowed us to land very fast without the likelihood of exiting the runway."

Alan shifted in his seat and thought for a moment. "I appreciate your calm and cooperative response. The flight attendants are here to assist you in any way they can, and it is my understanding that we have at least one medical doctor on board who may also be of assistance. Transportation to the military terminal will be provided, and Omega will arrange for your transport back to Los Angeles just as soon as possible. "Folks, thank you again for your patience. I will provide you all the information I have as it becomes available." He turned to Brad. "Whew. What did I forget?"

"That should cover it, boss. If you don't need me for anything else, I think I should get my tail to a telephone and let Andy Caldwell know what is going on. The media is gonna have a field day with this one, and we need a preemptive strike. Okay with you?" Brad asked.

"Yup, I'll attend to it. Here comes the truck with the air stairs. Why don't you ride back to ops with them and give Memphis a call? And my suggestion is that they get the L.A. chief pilot over here to take charge," Alan concluded.

"Caldwell here." The voice seemed tense, and Brad understood why. "Andy, Brad Morehouse calling from Edwards Air Force Base."

"Brad? That was *you* on 425? Hang on, I'm putting you on speaker." He pushed the button, and a hush settled over the room of chattering operations managers and FAA officials. "Go ahead, Brad," Andy said excitedly into the speakerphone. "Yes, sir, it was me, and I can assure you this was not a damned yaw damper problem. We got full uncommanded deflection of the rudder just as we were turning on approach to L.A. We rolled seventy degrees right and had no chance of rolling it back to the left. I had to continue the roll and hope that we wouldn't either fly into the water or pull the wings off the plane." Brad paused to acknowledge his memory of Matt's plane hitting the water. *Hey, Matt, I pulled us out of this one,* he thought. He closed his eyes for a moment and continued. "We made a good one-g roll and recovered at about 800 feet."

Andy allowed the unsolicited testimony to continue despite the possible liability. While he listened, he scribbled a note and passed it out to his secretary. *Get Gradin Jones out of classroom 242 and bring him here ASAP.*

Andy knew that Brad was one of the best, and his performance spoke volumes for the CRM program. From what Brad described, the team had performed flawlessly. Brad went on with considerable detail, then concluded, "Alan is handling things out at the aircraft, and we don't seem to have any serious injuries. The Air Force will provide buses to get the passengers into the terminal. Can we get the L.A. chief pilot over here ASAP?" Andy nodded and scribbled another note for his secretary.

Gradin knocked and entered the office just as Andy was saying, "Good job, Brad. I have an office full of doubters here, and there is more than a little egg on some faces. This clearly vindicates the Pasco crew. Oh, and by the way, Gradin Jones just walked in." One of the operations managers filled him in on the event.

Brad smiled to himself at Gradin's vindication as he continued. "Andy, for the record, we do have one injured flight attendant, and she'll need medical attention. It happens to be the same gal who did such a stellar job with the heart attack up at Paine. The others are okay, and I think they can be used for crowd control until the L.A. chief takes over. Anything else you want me to attend to here?"

"Yeah, one more thing. When you left the aircraft, were the rudder pedals and rudder still deflected?"

"Yes, they were, and Alan was attempting to borrow a camera from someone to make sure we have a record of that."

"Good, don't touch a thing in that cockpit. And one last thing, Brad. Find a good ARINC frequency and keep an open line to Omega ops. We'll communicate with you that way about the L.A. chief and transportation for the passengers."

Gradin waved a hand to speak. "Hang on, Brad," Andy said as he acknowledged Gradin.

"Boss, we need to make absolutely certain that no unauthorized personnel get close to that airplane. It seems clear to me that someone got to the Pasco bird before the NTSB did."

"Good point, Gradin. Brad, get the MPs to quarantine that airplane."

"Will do," Brad responded.

Andy punched a button to end the call, then stared solemnly at the assembled leaders. Finally, he spoke. "Gentlemen, as of this moment, Omega Airlines will officially oppose the commonly held perspective that the 737 rudder control incidents the industry has experienced are a result of simple yaw damper malfunctions. We have every reason to believe that there is a design flaw in the power control unit." Andy's face was flush with excitement as he addressed the group. "Omega came very close to losing it all today, and it is time for the whole industry to look this one squarely in the eye before people are killed. We are not going to allow that to happen."

Back at Edwards, Brad stepped out of the truck at the aircraft just as an official sedan screeched to a halt behind him. A portly, puffy-faced suit lurched out and headed for the stairs.

"Excuse me, sir, you can't go up there," Brad said as he held up a hand.

"Of course I can. We built the rudder system in that airplane," the man said, flashing a corporate badge. "I'm here to figure out what you incompetent pilots did to the damned thing." The man was adamant.

Brad stepped between the man and the air stairs, folded his arms, and motioned to the MP standing nearby. "Sergeant, please explain to this gentleman that there is a federal quarantine on the aircraft. Only the NTSB can authorize access." He stared disdainfully at the corporate fat cat, who had no choice but to get back in his car and drive away.

The hospital information clerk told Gradin that Sarah was in room 401. The door was ajar. He reached around and thrust the bright-yellow helmet into view in the room. *Blue Angel Eight* was crudely scrawled on the oversized football helmet. Sarah giggled, and Brad bellowed in his best drill-instructor voice, "Enter. Stand easy and speak."

Gradin pushed through the door and stood smiling at his friends. Handing Sarah the helmet, he said, "I hope you have learned never to go flying with this guy without the appropriate equipment."

Despite the nasty wound and full head bandage, she sat up in the bed, donned the helmet, and grinned back at him. "You're a day late and a dollar short, Commander," she teased. "But they'll have to make these standard-issue for all flight attendants who fly with Brad from now on."

"Oh, give me a break, you two. I saved a hundred lives and the very existence of Omega Air Lines, and this is the thanks I get?" Brad spat in mock disgust.

"Speaking of our employer, check this." Gradin unfolded the *Los Angeles Times* and held it for both to see the headline: "OMEGA VINDICATED; TRAINING PROGRAM DEEMED BEST IN INDUSTRY. He read aloud.

In a Washington news conference late yesterday, FAA administrator Edward G. Cohen stated emphatically that Thursday's incident in the skies over Los Angeles resulted from a fault in the 737 rudder control system, not from pilot error.

"To the contrary, the crew performance exceeded every expectation we can justifiably have for pilots in this industry. They were faced with an untenable dilemma, nothing one would ever anticipate. Nevertheless, through a combination of great teamwork and extraordinary piloting skill, they devised a solution that saved the aircraft and the lives of all those on board.

"It is no secret that Omega has been under extreme scrutiny during the last several months. However, I am pleased to report that the company has made marked progress in addressing all of the relevant training and operational issues.

"Omega Air Lines now has the premier pilot training program, known as crew resource management. As a result, I have no doubt that the flight crews at Omega will soon set the gold standard for effective crew interaction in the industry.

"The FAA investigation into and evaluation of the incident has been completed. No further action is required."

The last of Brad's demons shriveled and died as he gratefully embraced Sarah and laughed.

"Wow, and to think that just because you happened to remember that a barrel roll is a one-g maneuver, we all look like Greek gods now." Gradin paused and looked earnestly at Brad. "Our friend Matt would be proud. You really stepped up to the plate out there, Hotshot." Then, with an awkward bump that served as a hug, he added, "Case closed, amigo.

Epilogue

THIRTY YEARS LATER IN LOS ANGELES

Ethiopian Airlines flight crashes just after takeoff,
killing all 157 aboard.
Los Angeles Times, March 10, 2019.[50]

Omega CEO Marcus Stonebridge folded the LA *Times* and pushed it across his desk toward the VP of operations. "Brad, we have to get out ahead of this MAX thing," he said. "As you well know, a big part of next year's marketing plan depends on us having thirty of those airplanes in our fleet. Boeing is doing it again: Just like with the rudder control system twenty-five years ago, they're sending up a smoke screen to obscure their culpability."

Memories from those years flooded Brad's mind. The incident he had experienced in 1989 when the 737 rudder slammed full throw to the right was just one in a series of events that had resulted in two fatal accidents. Boeing fought their obvious culpability with a vengeance.[51]

Brad looked up and chose his words carefully. "This time, in the 737 MAX, they developed a solution to a problem that didn't really exist. Any competent pilot would not be taken down by the change in handling created by those new CFM engines," he asserted firmly. "Even though those engines make it a bit more likely that the nose will pitch up and lead toward a stall, that is exactly why we have well-trained and competent pilots in both seats. Since the first airplane took off, there has always been the possibility of stall. That isn't new, but every pilot is trained to avoid exactly that. We aren't talking generalities here. When we refer to maintaining the appropriate nose attitude, we often specify it to the nth degree—as in fifteen degrees versus sixteen degrees, for example. Our pilots are trained and then evaluated on their ability to do that," Brad emphasized as he went on. "So the MCAS was conceived and designed to intervene when the pilots failed to maintain the prescribed nose attitude because the engineers assumed that, unlike pilots from major U.S. carriers, these 'novice' airline pilots would not have that same skill," he spewed in a single sentence. "As you know, for a long time there has been an effort from both Boeing and Airbus to create a 'third-world airplane,' one that even the least capable pilot can fly."

Stonebridge squinted. "Tell me more about that," he said.

Before Brad could respond, a light tapping on the door announced the entrance of Ellen Cathgart, Stonebridge's administrative assistant. She walked briskly across the room and whispered in his ear while handing him a note. He thought for a moment, looked at his watch, and then said, "Okay, set that up for 8:00 AM tomorrow in the conference room."

"Sorry. The board of directors is getting nervous about this. Go ahead, Brad."

"Well, in the U.S., at least 'til now, we've had the luxury of hiring only highly qualified pilots. And to ensure that happens going forward, the new FAA regs require a person to have at least 1,500 hours in order to just sit in the copilot seat at a major carrier. It ordinarily takes years to accumulate that much flight time, which generally equates to valuable experience as well as basic yankin'-n-bankin' skills, as we say. In emerging nations, it simply isn't possible to find people with those quals. They are starting from where we were nearly a hundred years ago, when a copilot was an apprentice and the captain was his instructor. If I have my facts right, the Ethiopian copilot had just 200 hours. That isn't enough experience to even taxi a big rig like that, let alone fly it and manage a significant malfunction simultaneously."

"Okay, I get it," the CEO countered. "Keep talking."

"So the first bad on Boeing was their effort to slip that MCAS—Maneuvering Characteristics Augmentation System—past everyone with a dog in the fight. The FAA and foreign regulators, the airlines themselves, and even the pilots and their unions were kept in the dark. They wanted the MAX to be just another variation of the 737s currently flying. One not requiring the additional—as in 'expensive'—flight crew training and certification process," he emphasized with a raised eyebrow. "Inexplicably, even many of the Boeing test pilots weren't apprised of this system, and the minor changes to the 'non-normal' operating procedures were never specifically referenced. They simply added new verbiage to the manuals and hoped no one would notice."

Seething at this point, Brad pressed on. "Here's the kicker: For as long as there have been 737s, there has been a switch on the center console near the copilot's left leg called the stab trim cutout switch. It was there in 1967 with the introduction of the 737 into service and it is on every one of those MAX aircraft sitting on the ramp up in Renton right now. Unchanged in all these years! Activate that switch and you remove all electrical input to the stabilizer trim motor, the component that was driving the nose down on those two doomed airplanes."

He took a breath. "In other words, it would take one or two seconds for a competent, well-trained, and aware pilot to reach down and trigger that switch in the midst of any uncommanded movement of the stabilizer. That's all they had to do.

"Incidentally, in both accidents the MCAS that precipitated those events was activated by faulty indications from one of many sensors—a possibility Boeing apparently failed to account for in their design specifications. In other words, the pilots got *erroneous* indications of an impending stall. A seasoned pilot would immediately have recognized the indications as false because the airspeed and nose attitude were normal."

"Ouch. I see how the MCAS is flawed, but what happens after the pilots disable the trim motor? Can they still fly the airplane?" Stonebridge asked quizzically.

"There are two matching wheels about the size of a dinner plate on either side of the center console." Brad sat forward and motioned with his hands. "Rolling those wheels forward or aft allows the pilots to manually position the stabilizer to any position they want, preferably one that will contribute to straight and level flight." He smiled. "At that point it would be the captain's call whether to continue on, proceed to a more suitable airport, or return. Apparently, those two crews eventually did activate the stab trim cutout switches, but when the nose-down pressure remained they failed to manually trim the nose up and instead repositioned the switch from *cutout* to *normal*. That amplified the problem when the MCAS pushed the nose down again. Oh, and to add injury to insult, simply engaging the autopilot also takes the MCAS out of the loop. Obviously those poor pilots didn't do that and weren't ever trained to do it. Too expensive to require that additional training, I guess," Brad said, shrugging helplessly.

"Oh, Lord." Marcus shook his head in disgust. "What a goat rope!" Following a deep sigh and a long silence, he raised his voice adamantly and wagged a finger at Brad. "Okay, here's what I want you to do: Bring Gradin Jones in as the project officer on this; he's a really capable thinker. We need our own action plan," he spat furiously. "Omega can't go *down* with the MAX."

AUTHOR'S NOTE

Enjoy the ride? I hope you can get back on an airplane with complete confidence that you will arrive safely, at least when you ride on a major U.S. carrier. You are safer in one of those seats than nearly anyplace else on Earth.

But don't believe for a moment that automated aircraft systems are responsible for making air travel safer. Look carefully and you'll find the secret—that the best *trained* pilots produce the best results. As I write this in January 2020, the Blue Angels are in El Centro, California, training the team for the upcoming show season. They will fly two or three times every day for three months. And even with all this training in the air, before and after *every single flight,* they review safety and operating procedures in minute detail. You get the drift. They call it the 5Ps—Planning Prevents Piss Poor Performance.

So Brad Morehouse is a fictionalized version of the real deal, and I chose to have such a character because he represents the power and importance of training. Gradin Jones represents the other side of the equation—the deliberative, collaborative style needed for effective team performance. And finally, Sarah Marconi shows up as one of my actual aviation heroes—a Salt Lake City flight attendant and grandmother who did exactly what Sarah is purported to have done in saving a man's life. She continued providing CPR when the doctors looking over her shoulder said there was no use. The man survived. Unrelenting tenacity is the third key ingredient in the success formula.

My characters live on. You heard Brad discussing the 737 MAX with the Omega CEO. Thirty years after wrestling a crippled 737 through an impossible maneuver and saving the lives of everyone on board, he continues to ensure that rigorous training undergirds all that happens operationally at Omega. Along the way he got lucky when Sarah agreed to marry him and then headed off to medical school. Now she is a teaching physician in emergency medicine at UCLA, where she brings CRM principles to bear in the medical community. You will be hearing much more from them all in the future.

With that as background for the sequel, I'm going to conclude with one last shot at the 737 MAX issue. I can't contain my passion about this, because the crux of this debacle lies in training—or, more specifically, the absence of it.

In 2021 the Blue Angels will debut a new jet, the biggest and baddest model ever made of their aircraft—the F-18 Super Hornet. In essence, the plane is an F-18 MAX, which in a perfect ironic twist is provided by Boeing. In order to accommodate this upgraded version of earlier F-18s, the Navy is leaving nothing to chance. Currently, the Super Hornet is being evaluated being evaluated for the Blue Angles by Navy pilots, some of them former Blues, in order to provide all the data and information about the differing performance characteristics the team will need to accommodate. The 2020 show season will be cut one month short at the end and the 2021 season one month short at the beginning to create the additional time necessary to train. They can't afford not to get it right.

Apply just an ounce of that logic to the introduction of the 737 MAX. Just a smidge of that caution and the traveling public would never have heard of the MAX. No one would have died and billions of dollars would have been saved. Despite the new system's technological flaw, human factors brought those planes down because the pilots hadn't been trained to deal with that eventuality. Now that I'm sitting tall on my high horse, I'm yelling loudly: *When you (engineers and manufacturers) attempt to automate pilots out of the equation, you will inevitably end up killing people! You have extremely skilled and competent human operators who need appropriate training. It is absolute folly to imagine otherwise.*

Oddly, the earliest example of this overreliance on automation occurred in 1988 at the Habsheim Air Show in France. An Airbus—an A320 flown by the chief training captain at Air France—was to perform a low pass over the runway followed by a steep climb away from the airport. However, he flew lower than anticipated and in so doing the aircraft automation "thought" it was time to land and would not respond to the captain's attempt to add power for the climb. Riveting video shows the aircraft smashing into the trees at the end of the runway and exploding into a cloud of dark gray smoke.[52]

My assertion about the key human ingredient might ring hollow except for the stark contrast in performance between major U.S. carriers and all others. You, the traveler, deserve stellar crew performance. My wish for you is exemplified in the parting admonition often heard from my peers: "Fly safe." And the only way that can happen is to have superbly trained flight crews, regardless of the expense.

ART SAMSON

Author Art Samson grew up in Eastern Oregon alongside an older naval aviator brother, an idealized mentor who coached the youngster in the power and purpose of effective team behavior. Under his tutelage, Art emerged as a trusted leader among his peers. The list of accomplishments is typical of kids in small-town America during those years: class president, football team captain, national honor society member, thespian, singer, and all-around good guy. Those accomplishments earned him a leadership scholarship to Lewis and Clark College in Portland where he captained the swimming team and won every event he swam in championship competition. He graduated in 1968 with a degree in English.

Thus the stage was set for Art to follow his revered brother into the Navy where he earned his wings of gold in 1970 as the Vietnam War raged on. As an instructor and commander of a multi-engine anti-submarine-warfare aircraft, he developed a critical sense of coordinated teamwork within his 12-member crews. On more than one occasion, he found himself nose-to-nose with a Soviet submarine lurking just beneath the ocean surface. Pity those submariners had there been an actual conflict.

Art's leadership and team-building skills served him well during 27 years of airline flying.

In 1989 – the year during which *We're Going Down* takes place – his airline launched a full-throated training regimen known as crew resource management (CRM) for its pilots, all ten thousand of them. The challenge was to shift the collective focus from a top-down management style to a cooperative, problem-solving protocol orchestrated by enlightened leaders. Not a small task. Samson was one of the first pilots selected to deliver this training, and the attitudinal shift among flight crews was profound.

At the airline, he also served as an FAA-designated 737 check pilot and crew conflict mediator. He directed the company's pilot instructor school and taught an aviation human factors curriculum that he created to college students at Westminster College in Salt Lake City where he completed a Master of Professional Communications degree.

He currently resides on the water in Coronado, California, the home of naval aviation.

ENDNOTES

1. V speeds are scientific notation for critical airspeeds.
2. Horizontal Situation Indicator.
3. Aeronautical Radio Incorporated, a company that provides aviation radio links throughout the world.
4. The word Zulu refers to Greenwich Mean Time.
5. Federal Aviation Administration.
6. NTSB/AAR-75-13.
7. A selective-calling radio system that can alert an aircraft's crew that a ground radio station wishes to communicate with the aircraft.
8. WOXOF is pronounced "walks off" and stands for weather-obscured ceiling zero in fog.
9. Expected further clearance time.
10. NTSB/AAR-79/05.
11. Seven-three is slang for a 737 aircraft.
12. FO = first officer.
13. SO = second officer.
14. CAG = carrier airgroup commander.
15. Studebaker = 727 aircraft.
16. The FAA will require a thorough evaluation in the 737 flight simulator.
17. NTSB/AAR-84-09.
18. MDs = McDonnell Douglas aircraft.
19. Diesel eight = DC-8 aircraft.
20. NTSB/AAR-79-07.
21. Three-nine-oh = 39,000 feet.
22. Seven-two = 727 aircraft.

... ━ ━ ━... ━ ━ ━... ━ ━ ━... ━ ━ ━... ━ ━ ━...

23. LEDs = leading edge devices.
24. Split-S = flew in an arch similar to the upper half of the letter S.
25. IP = instructor pilot.
26. NORAT = the North Atlantic region.
27. Inertial navigation system.
28. PC = proficiency check.
29. Dick Rutan and Jeana Yeager were aviation pioneers who flew nonstop around the world in nine days, completing the trip on December 23, 1986.
30. RIO = radar intercept officer.
31. NTSB/AAR-73-14.
32. Seven-five and seven-six = 757 and 767 aircraft, respectively.
33. NTSB/AAR-78-13.
34. NTSB/AAR-75-16.
35. 35 NTSB/AAR-88-10.
36. ECM = electronic counter measures.
37. Howgozit = how goes it.
38. Mad Dog = McDonnell Douglas MD-80 series aircraft.
39. POI = the FAA principal operations inspector.
40. NTSB/AAR-88-09.
41. Wikipedia: PSA flight 1771.
42. NTSB/AAR-88-05.
43. NTSB/AAR-82-08.
44. The Loop was the name of the assigned departure route and was a required part of the request for taxi clearance in Los Angeles.
45. He has switched the radio to the tower frequency.
46. NTSB/AAR-89-03.
47. A military reference to the Western Pacific.

48. The Seattle Times, October 27, 1996.
49. Ibid.
50. http://jama.ama-assn.org/content/286/4/415.full.
51 Los Angeles Times, March 10, 2019
52 The Seattle Times, October 27, 1996.